"Francis, an ex-jockey, has a sense of pace that would be the envy of most of his former colleagues."

People

"Dick Francis is a skilled hand."

The Houston Post

"Mr. Francis writes intensely satisfying thrillers...vivid, fastmoving!"

Newsday

"A new Dick Francis mystery is always a treat."

The Cincinnati Post

"You can always count on Dick Francis for a good read."

Memphis Commercial Appeal

"Each of his novels is an unaccustomed delight."

Cosmopolitan

Also by Dick Francis

NERVE*
FOR KICKS*
ODDS AGAINST*
FLYING FINISH*
BLOOD SPORT*
DEAD CERT*
ENQUIRY*
FORFEIT*
SLAYRIDE*
THE SPORT OF QUEENS
TRIAL RUN*
WHIP HAND*
HIGH STAKES
REFLEX*
TWICE SHY*
BANKER*
BONECRACK
KNOCKDOWN
IN THE FRAME
THE DANGER*
RISK
SMOKESCREEN
RAT RACE
PROOF*
A JOCKEY'S LIFE: The Biography of Lester
    Piggott*
BREAK IN*
BOLT*
HOT MONEY*

*Published by Fawcett Books

THE EDGE

Dick Francis

FAWCETT CREST • NEW YORK

Library of Congress Catalog Card Number: 88-23806

ISBN 0-449-21783-3

This edition published by arrangement with G.P. Putnam's Sons, a division of the Putnam Berkley Group

Lines from *The Poems of Dylan Thomas* by Dylan Thomas. Copyright 1952 by Dylan Thomas. Reprinted by permission of New Directions Publishing Corporation.

Manufactured in the United States of America

First International Edition: October 1989

The villains in this story are imaginary.
The good guys may recognize their own virtues!

My thanks to

SHANNON WRAY
formerly of Penguin Books, Canada, who started
the train rolling

SHEILA BOWSLAUGH
and Sam Blyth of Blyth & Co., travel entrepreneurs

BILL COO
Manager of Travel Communications, VIA Rail, and the
staff of Union Station, Toronto

HOWARD SHRIER and **TED BISAILLION**
actor/writers

and

Col. Charles (Bud) Baker, Chairman of the Ontario Jockey
Club,

Krystina Schmidt, caterer; American Railtours Inc.,
operators of private rail cars,

and John Jennings, who traveled the trains with horses.

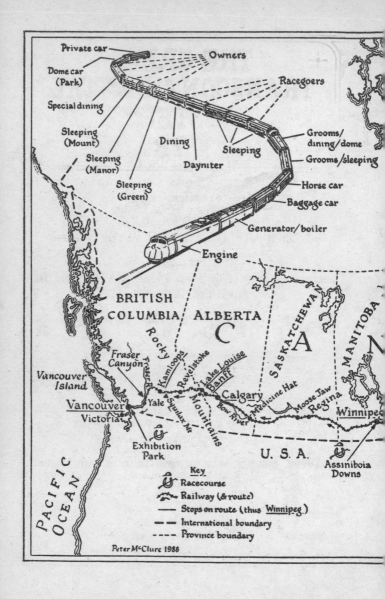

Private car
Dome car (Park)
Special dining
Sleeping (Mount)
Sleeping (Manor)
Sleeping (Green)
Owners
Racegoers
Dining
Dayniter
Sleeping
Grooms/dining/dome
Grooms/sleeping
Horse car
Baggage car
Generator/boiler
Engine

BRITISH COLUMBIA
ALBERTA
SASKATCHEWAN
MANITOBA

Rocky
Fraser Canyon
Vancouver Island
Vancouver
Victoria
Fraser
Kamloops
Yale
Sunlax Mt.
Revelstoke
Lake Louise
Banff
Mountains
Bow River
Calgary
Medicine Hat
Moose Jaw
Regina
Winnipeg

Exhibition Park

PACIFIC OCEAN

U.S.A.

Assiniboia Downs

Key
Racecourse
Railway (& route)
Stops on route (thus Winnipeg.)
International boundary
Province boundary

Peter McClure 1988

THE GREAT TRANSCONTINENTAL MYSTERY RACE TRAIN

THE EDGE

1

I was following Derry Welfram at a prudent fifty paces when he stumbled, fell face down on the wet tarmac and lay still. I stopped, watching, as nearer hands stretched to help him up, saw the doubt, the apprehension, the shock flower in the opening mouths of the faces around him. The word that formed in consequence in my own brain was violent, of four letters and unexpressed.

Derry Welfram lay face down, unmoving, while the fourteen runners for the three-thirty race at York stalked closely past him, the damp jockeys looking down and back with muted curiosity, minds on the business ahead, bodies shivering in the cold near-drizzle of early October. The man was drunk. One could read their minds. Midafternoon falling-down drunks were hardly unknown on racecourses. It was a miserable, uncomfortable afternoon. Good luck to him, the drunk.

I retreated a few unobtrusive steps and went on watching. Some of the group who had been nearest to Welfram when he fell were edging away, looking at the departing horses, wanting to leave, to see the race. A few shuffled from foot to foot, caught between a wish to desert and shame at doing so, and one, more civic-minded, scuttled off for help.

I drifted over to the open door of the paddock bar, from

1

where several customers looked out on the scene. Inside, the place was full of dryish people watching life on closed circuit television, life at second hand.

One of the group in the doorway said to me, "What's the matter with him?"

"I've no idea." I shrugged. "Drunk, I dare say."

I stood there quietly, part of the scenery, not pushing through into the bar but standing just outside the door under the eaves of the overhanging roof, trying not to let the occasional drips from above fall down my neck.

The civic-minded man came back at a run, followed by a heavy man in a St. John's Ambulance uniform. People had by now half-turned Welfram and loosened his tie, but seemed to step back gladly at the approach of officialdom. The St. John's man rolled Welfram fully onto his back and spoke decisively into a walkie-talkie. Then he bent Welfram's head backward and tried mouth to mouth resuscitation.

I couldn't think of any circumstance that would have persuaded me to put my mouth on Welfram's. Perhaps it was easier between absolute strangers. Not even to save his life, I thought, though I'd have preferred him alive.

Another man arrived in a hurry, a thin raincoated man I knew by sight to be the racecourse doctor. He tapped the paramedic on the shoulder, telling him to discontinue, and himself laid first his fingers against Welfram's neck, then his stethoscope against the chest inside the opened shirt. After a long listening pause, perhaps as much as half a minute, he straightened and spoke to the paramedic, meanwhile stuffing the stethoscope into his raincoat pocket. Then he departed, again at a hurry, because the race was about to begin and the racecourse doctor, during each running, had to be out on the course to succor the jockeys.

The paramedic held a further conversation with his walkie-talkie but tried no more to blow air into unresponsive lungs, and presently some colleagues of his arrived with a stretcher and covering blanket, and loaded up and carried away, decently hidden, the silver hair, the bulging navy-blue suit and the stilled heart of a heartless man.

The group that had stood near him broke up with relief, two or three of them heading straight for the bar.

The man who had earlier asked me, asked the newcomers the same question. "What's the matter with him?"

"He's dead," one of them said briefly and unnecessarily. "God, I need a drink." He pushed his way into the bar, with the doorway spectators, me among them, following him inside to listen. "He just fell down and died." He shook his head, "Strewth, it makes you think." He tried to catch the barman's eye. "You could hear his breath rattling . . . then it just stopped . . . he was dead before the St. John's man got there . . . Barman, a double gin . . . make it a treble . . ."

"Was there any blood?" I asked.

"Blood?" He half-looked in my direction, "Course not. You don't get blood with heart attacks . . . Barman, a gin and tonic . . . not much tonic . . . get a move on, will you?"

"Who was he?" someone said.

"Search me. Just some poor mug."

On the television the race began, and everyone, including myself, swiveled round to watch, though I couldn't have said afterward what had won. With Derry Welfram dead my immediate job was going to be much more difficult, if not temporarily impossible. The three-thirty in those terms was irrelevant.

I left the bar in the general break-up after the race and wandered inconclusively about for a bit, looking for other things that were not as they should be and, as on many days, not seeing any. I particularly looked for anyone who might be looking for Derry Welfram, hanging around for that purpose outside the ambulance-room door, but no one arrived to inquire. An announcement came over the loudspeakers presently asking for anyone who had accompanied a Mr. D. Welfram to the races to report to the clerk of the course's office, so I hung about outside there for a while also, but no one accepted the invitation.

Welfram the corpse left the racecourse in an ambulance en route to the morgue and after a while I drove away from York in my unremarkable Audi, and punctually at five o'clock telephoned on my car phone to John Millington, my immediate boss, as required.

"What do you mean, he's dead?" he demanded. "He can't be."

"His heart stopped," I said.

"Did someone kill him?"

Neither of us would have been surprised if someone had, but I said, "No, there wasn't any sign of it. I'd been following him for ages. I didn't see anyone bump into him, or anything like that. And there was apparently no blood. Nothing suspicious. He just died."

"*Shit.*" His angry tone made it sound as if it were probably my fault. John Millington, retired policeman (chief inspector), currently deputy head of the Jockey Club Security Service, had never seemed to come to terms with my covert and indeterminate appointment to his department, even though in the three years I'd been working for him we'd seen a good few villains run off the racecourse.

"The boy's a blasted amateur," he'd protested when I was presented to him as a fact, not a suggestion. "The whole thing's ridiculous."

He no longer said it was ridiculous but we had never become close friends.

"Did anyone make waves? Come asking for him?" he demanded.

"No, no one."

"Are you sure?" He cast doubt as always on my ability.

"Yes, positive." I told him of my vigils outside the various doors.

"Who did he meet, then? Before he snuffed it?"

"I don't think he met anybody, unless it was very early in the day, before I spotted him. He wasn't searching for anyone, anyway. He made a couple of bets on the Tote, drank a couple of beers, looked at the horses and watched the races. He wasn't busy today."

Millington let loose the four-letter word I'd stifled. "And we're back where we started," he said furiously.

"Mm," I agreed.

"Call me Monday morning," Millington said, and I said, "Right," and put the phone down. Tonight was Saturday. Sunday was my regular day off, and Monday too, except in times of trouble. I could see my Monday vanishing fast.

Millington, in common with the whole Security Service and the Stewards of the Jockey Club, was still smarting from the collapse in court of their one great chance of seeing behind bars arguably the worst operator still lurking in the undergrowth of racing. Julius Apollo Filmer had been accused of conspiring to murder a stable lad who had been unwise enough to say loudly and drunkenly in a Newmarket pub that he knew things about Mr. effing Filmer that would get the said arsehole chucked out of racing quicker than Shergar won the Derby.

The pathetic stable lad turned up in a ditch two days later with his neck broken, and the police (Millington assisting) put together a watertight-looking conspiracy case, establishing Julius Filmer as paymaster and planner of the crime. Then, on the day of his trial, odd things happened to the four prosecution witnesses. One had a nervous breakdown and was admitted in hysteria to a mental hospital, one disappeared altogether and was later seen in Spain, and two became mysteriously unclear about facts that had been razor-sharp in their memories earlier. The defense brought to the witness box a nice young man who swore on oath that Mr. Filmer had been nowhere near the Newmarket hotel where the conspiracy was alleged to have been hatched but had instead been discussing business with him all night in a motel (bill produced) three hundred miles away. The jury was not allowed to know that the beautifully mannered, well-dressed, blow-dried, quietly spoken youth was already serving time for confidence tricks and had arrived at court in a black maria.

Almost everyone else in the court—lawyers, police, the judge himself—knew that the nice young man had been out on bail on the night in question, and that even though the actual murderer was still unknown, Filmer had beyond doubt arranged the stable lad's killing.

Julius Apollo Filmer smirked with satisfaction at the "not guilty" verdict and clasped his lawyer in a bear hug. Justice had been mocked. The stable lad's parents wept bitter tears over his grave and the Jockey Club ground its collective teeth. Millington swore to get Filmer somehow, anyhow, in the future, and had made it into a personal vendetta, the pursuit of this one villain filling his mind to the exclusion of nearly everything else.

He had spent a great deal of time in the Newmarket pubs going over the ground the regular police had already covered, trying to find out exactly what Paul Shacklebury, the dead stable lad, had known to the detriment of Filmer. No one knew—or no one was saying. And who could blame anyone for not risking a quick trip to the ditch?

Millington had had more luck with the hysterical witness, now back home but still suffering fits of the shivers. She, the witness, was a chambermaid in the hotel where Filmer had plotted. She had heard and had originally been prepared to swear she heard Filmer say to an unidentified man, "If he's dead, he's worth five grand to you and five to the hatchet, so go and fix it."

She had been hanging fresh towels in the bathroom when the two men came in from the corridor, talking. Filmer had been abrupt with her and bundled her out and she hadn't looked at the other man. She remembered the words clearly but hadn't of course seen their significance until later. It was because of the word "hatchet" that she remembered particularly.

A month after the trial Millington got from her a half-admission that she'd been threatened not to give evidence.

Who had threatened her? A man she didn't know. But she would deny it. She would deny everything, she would have another collapse. The man had threatened to harm her sixteen-year-old daughter. Harm . . . he'd spelled out all the dreadful program lying ahead.

Millington, who could lay on the syrup if it pleased him, had persuaded her with many a honeyed promise (that he wouldn't necessarily keep) to come for several days to the races, and there, from the safety of various strategically placed security offices, he'd invited her to look out of the window. She would be in shadow, seated, comfortable, invisible, and he would point out a few people to her. She was nervous and came in a wig and dark glasses. Millington got her to remove the glasses. She sat in an upright armchair and twisted her head to look over her shoulder at me, where I stood quietly behind her.

"Never mind about him," Millington said. "He's part of the scenery."

All the world went past those windows on racing afternoons, which was why, of course, the windows were where they were. Over three long sessions during a single week on three different racecourses Millington pointed out to her almost every known associate and friend of Filmer's, but she shook her head to them all. At the fourth attempt, the following week, Filmer himself strolled past, and I thought we'd have a repeat of the hysterics: but though our chambermaid wobbled and wept and begged for repeated assurances he would never know she had seen him, she stayed at her post. And she astonished us, shortly after, by pointing toward a group of passing people we'd never before linked with Filmer.

"That's him," she said, gasping. "Oh, my God, that's him. I'd know him anywhere."

"Which one?" Millington said urgently.

"In the navy with the gray sort of hair. Oh my God, don't let him know. . ." Her voice rose with panic.

I could hear the beginnings of Millington's reassurances

as I fairly sprinted out of the office and through to the open air, slowing there at once to the much slower speed of the crowd making its way from paddock to stands for the next race. The navy suit with the silvery hair above it was in no hurry, going along with the press. I followed him discreetly for the rest of the afternoon, and only once did he touch base with Filmer, and then as if accidentally, as between strangers.

The exchange looked as if navy-suit asked Filmer the time. Filmer looked at his watch and spoke. Navy-suit nodded and walked on. Navy-suit was Filmer's man, all right, but was never to be seen to be that in public: just like me and Millington.

I followed navy-suit from the racecourse in the going-home traffic and telephoned from my car to Millington.

"He's driving a Jaguar," I said, "license number A576 FDD. He spoke to Filmer. He's our man."

"Right."

"How's the lady?" I asked.

"Who? Oh, her. I had to send Harrison all the way back to Newmarket with her. She was half off her rocker again. Have you still got our man in sight?"

"Yep."

"I'll get back to you."

Harrison was one of Millington's regular troops, an ex-policeman, heavy, avuncular, near to pensioned retirement. I'd never spoken to him, but I knew him well by sight, as I knew all the others. It had taken me quite a while to get used to belonging to a body of men who didn't know I was there; rather as if I were a ghost.

I was never noticeable. I was twenty-nine, six foot tall, brown-haired, brown-eyed, 165 pounds in weight with, as they say, no distinguishing features. I was always part of the moving race crowd, looking at my race-card, wandering about, looking at horses, watching races, having a bet or two. It was easy because there were always a great many other people around doing exactly the same thing. I was a grazing sheep in a flock. I changed my clothes and general appearance from day to day and never made acquaintances, and it was lonely quite often, but also fascinating.

I knew by sight all the jockeys and trainers and very many owners, because all one needed for that was eyes and race-cards, but also I knew a lot of their histories from long memory, as I'd spent much of my childhood and teens on racecourses, towed along by the elderly race-mad aunt who had brought me up. Through her knowledge and via her witty tongue I had become a veritable walking data bank; and then, at eighteen, after her death, I'd gone world-wandering for seven years. When I returned I no longer looked like the unmatured youth I'd been, and the eyes of the people who had known me vaguely as a child slid over me without recognition.

I returned to England finally because at twenty-five I'd come into the inheritances from both my aunt and my father, and my trustees were wanting instructions. I had been in touch with them from time to time, and they had dispatched funds to far-flung outposts fairly often, but when I walked into the hushed book-lined law office of the senior partner of Cornborough, Cross and George, old Clement Cornborough greeted me with a frown and stayed sitting down behind his desk.

"You're not...er..." he said, looking over my shoulder for the one he'd expected.

"Well, yes, I am. Tor Kelsey."

"Good Lord." He stood up slowly, leaning forward to extend a hand. "But you've changed. You...er..."

"Taller, heavier and older," I said, nodding. Also suntanned, at that moment, from a spell in Mexico.

"I'd...er...penciled in lunch," he said doubtfully.

"That would be fine," I said.

He took me to a similarly hushed restaurant full of other solicitors who nodded to him austerely. Over roast beef he told me that I would never have to work for a living (which I knew) and in the same breath asked what I was going to do with my life, a question I couldn't answer. I'd spent seven years learning how to live, which was different, but I'd had no formal training in anything. I felt claustrophobic in offices and I was not academic. I understood machines and was quick with my hands. I had no overpowering ambitions. I wasn't the entrepreneur my father had been, but nor would I squander the fortune he had left me.

"What have you been doing?" old Cornborough said, making conversation valiantly. "You've been to some interesting places, haven't you?"

Travelers' tales were pretty boring, I thought. It was always better to live it. "I mostly worked with horses," I said politely. "Australia, South America, United States, anywhere. Racehorses, polo ponies, a good deal in rodeos. Once in a circus."

"Good heavens."

"It's not easy now, though, and getting harder, to work one's passage. Too many countries won't allow it. And I won't go back to it. I've done enough. Grown out of it."

"So what next?"

"Don't know." I shrugged. "Look around. I'm not getting in touch with my mother's people, so don't tell them I'm here."

"If you say so."

My mother had come from an impoverished hunting family who were scandalized when at twenty she married a sixty-five-year-old giant of a Yorkshireman with an empire in secondhand car auctions and no relatives in *Burke's Peerage*. They'd said it was because he showered her with horses, but it always sounded to me as if she'd been truly attracted. He at any rate was besotted with her, as his sister, my aunt, had often told me, and he'd seen no point in living after she was killed in a hunting accident, when I was two. He'd lasted three years and died of cancer, and because my mother's family hadn't wanted me, my aunt Viv Kelsey had taken me over and made my young life a delight.

To Aunt Viv, unmarried, I was the longed-for child she'd

had no chance of bearing. She must have been sixty when she took me, though I never thought of her as old. She was always young inside; and I missed her dreadfully when she died.

Millington's voice said, "The car you are following... are you still following it?"

"Still in sight."

"It's registered to a Derry Welfram. Ever heard of him?"

"No."

Millington still had connections in the police force and seemed to get useful computerized information effortlessly.

"His address is down as Parkway Mansions, Maida Vale, London," he said. "If you lose him, try there."

"Right."

Derry Welfram obligingly drove straight to Parkway Mansions and others of Millington's minions later made a positive identification. Millington tried a photograph of him on each of the witnesses with the unreliable memories and, as he described to me afterward, "They both shit themselves with fear and stuttered they'd never seen the man, never, never." But they'd been so effectively frightened, both of them, that Millington could get nothing out of them at all.

Millington told me to follow Derry Welfram if I saw him again at the races, to see who else he talked to, which I'd been doing for about a month on the day the navy suit fell on its buttons. Welfram had talked intensely to about ten people by then and proved he was comprehensively a bearer of bad news, leaving behind him a trail of shocked, shivering, hollow-eyed stares at unwelcome realities. And because I had an ingenious camera built into binoculars (and another that looked like a cigarette lighter) we had recognizable portraits of most of Welfram's shattered contacts, though so far identifications for less than half. Millington's men were working on it.

Millington had come to the conclusion that Welfram was a frightener hired to shake out bad debts: a rent-a-thug in general, not solely Filmer's man. I had seen him speak to

Filmer only once since the first occasion, which didn't mean
he hadn't done so more often. There were usually race meetings at three or more different courses in England each day,
and it was a toss-up, sometimes, to guess where either of the
quarries would go. Filmer, moreover, went racing less often
than Welfram, two or three times a week at most. Filmer had
shares in a great many horses and usually went where they
ran, and I checked their destinations every morning in the
racing press.

The problem with Filmer was not what he did, but catching him doing it. At first sight, second sight, third sight he
did nothing wrong. He bought racehorses, put them in training, went to watch them run, enjoyed all the pleasures of an
owner. It was only gradually, over the ten years since Filmer
had appeared on the scene, that there had been eyebrows
raised, frowns of disbelief, mouths pursed in puzzlement.

Filmer bought horses occasionally at auction through an
agent or a trainer but chiefly acquired them by deals struck
in private, a perfectly proper procedure. Any owner was
always at liberty to sell his horses to anyone else. The surprising thing about some of Filmer's acquisitions was that no
one would have expected the former owner to sell the horse
at all.

I had been briefed about him by Millington during my
first few weeks in the Service, but then only as someone to
be generally aware of, not as a number-one priority.

"He leans on people," Millington said. "We're sure of it,
but we don't know how. He's much too sly to do anything
where we can see him. Don't think you'll catch him handing
out bunches of money for information, nothing crude like
that. Look for people who're nervous when he's near,
right?"

"Right."

I had spotted a few of those. Both of the trainers who
trained his horses treated him with caution, and most of the
jockeys who rode them shook his hand with their fingertips.
The press, who knew who wouldn't answer questions,

hardly bothered to ask them. A deferential decorative girl-friend jumped when he said jump, and the male companion frequently in attendance fairly scuttled. Yet there was nothing visibly boorish about his general manner at the races. He smiled at appropriate moments, nodded congratulations to other owners in the winners' enclosures and patted his horses when they pleased him.

He was in person forty-eight, heavy, about five foot ten in height. Millington said the weight was mostly muscle, as Filmer spent time three days a week raising a sweat in a gym. Above the muscle there was a well-shaped head, large flat ears and thick black hair flecked with gray. I hadn't been near enough to see the color of his eyes, but Millington had them down as greenish brown.

Rather to Millington's annoyance I refused to follow Filmer about much. For one thing, in the end he would have been certain to have spotted me, and for another it wasn't necessary. Filmer was a creature of habit, moving from car to lunch to bookmaker to grandstand to paddock at foreseeable intervals. At each track he had a favorite place to watch the races from, a favorite vantage point overlooking the parade ring and a favorite bar where he drank lager mostly and plied the girlfriend with vodka. He rented a private box at two racecourses and was on the waiting list at several more, where his aim seemed to be seclusion rather than the lavish entertainment of friends.

He had been born on the Isle of Man, that tax-haven rock out of sight of England in the stormy Irish Sea, and had been brought up in a community stuffed with millionaires fleeing the fleecing taxes of the mainland. His father had been a wily fixer admired for fleecing the fled. Young Julius Apollo Filmer (his real name) had learned well and outstripped his father in rich pickings until he'd left home for wider shores; and that was the point, Millington said gloomily, at which they had lost him. Filmer had turned up on racecourses sixteen or so years later giving his occupation as "company director" and maintaining a total silence about his source of considerable income.

During the run up to the conspiracy trial the police had done their best to unravel his background further, but Julius Apollo knew a thing or two about offshore companies and had stayed comfortably raveled. He still officially lived on the Isle of Man, though he was never there for long. During the Flat season he mostly divided his time between hotels in Newmarket and Paris, and in the winter he dropped entirely out of sight, as far as the Security Service was concerned. Steeplechasing, the winter sport, never drew him.

During my first summer with the Service he had bought, to everyone's surprise, one of the most promising two-year-olds in the country. Surprise, because the former owner, Ezra Gideon, was one of the natural aristocrats of racing, a much-respected elderly and extremely wealthy man who lived for his horses and delighted at their successes. No one had been able to persuade him to say why he had parted with the best of his crop or for what price: he bore its subsequent high-flying autumn, its brilliant three-year-old season and its eventual multimillion-pound syndication for stud with an unvaryingly stony expression.

After Filmer's acquittal, Ezra Gideon had again sold him a two-year-old of great promise.The Jockey Club mandarins begged Gideon practically on their knees to tell them why. He said merely that it was a private arrangement; and since then he had not been seen on a racecourse.

On the day Derry Welfram died I drove homeward to London wondering yet again, as so many people had wondered so often, just what leverage Filmer had used on Gideon. Blackmailers had gone largely out of business since adultery and homosexuality had blown wide open, and one couldn't see old-fashioned upright Ezra Gideon as one of the newly fashionable brands of transgressor: an insider-trader or an abuser of children. Yet without some overwhelming reason he would never have sold Filmer two such horses, denying himself what he most enjoyed in life.

Poor old man, I thought. Derry Welfram or someone like that had got to him, as to the witnesses, as to Paul Shacklebury dead in his ditch. Poor old man, too afraid of the consequences to let anyone help.

Before I reached home the telephone again purred in my car and I picked up the receiver to hear Millington's voice.

"The boss wants to see you," he said. "This evening at eight, usual place. Any problem?"

"No," I said. "I'll be there. Do you know . . . er . . . why?"

"I should think," Millington said, "because Ezra Gideon has shot himself."

2

The boss, Brigadier Valentine Catto, director of Security to the Jockey Club, was short, spare, and a commanding officer from his polished toecaps to the thinning blond hair on his crown. He had all the organizational skills needed to rise high in the army, and he was intelligent and unhurried and listened attentively to what he was told.

His motto, often repeated, was "Thought before action: if you've got time."

I met him first on a day when old Clement Cornborough asked me again to lunch to discuss in detail, as he said, the winding up of the trust he'd administered on my behalf for twenty years. A small celebration, he said. At his club.

His club turned out to be the Hobbs Sandwich Club, near the Oval cricket ground, a Victorian minimansion with a darkly opulent bar and club rooms, their oak-paneled walls decorated with endless pictures of gentlemen in small cricket caps, large white flannels and (quite often) side-whiskers.

The Hobbs Sandwich, he said, leading the way through stained-glass paneled doors, was named for two great Surrey cricketers from between the wars, Sir Jack Hobbs, one of the few cricketers ever knighted, and Andrew Sandham, who had scored 107 centuries in first-class cricket. Long before I was born, he said.

16

I hadn't played cricket since distant days at school, nor liked it particularly even then: Clement Cornborough proved to be a lifelong fanatic.

He introduced me in the bar to an equal fanatic, his friend Val Catto, who then joined us for lunch. Not a word about my trust was spoken. The two of them talked cricket solidly for fifteen minutes and then the friend Catto began asking questions about my life. It dawned on me uneasily after a while that I was being interviewed, though I didn't know for what; and I learned afterward that in conversation one day during the tea interval of a cricket match Catto had lamented to Cornborough that what he really needed was someone who knew the racing scene intimately, but whom the racing scene didn't know in return. An eyes and ears man. A silent, unknown investigator. A fly on racing's wall that no one would notice. Such a person, they had sighed together, was unlikely to be found. And that when a few weeks later I walked into Cornborough's office (or at least by the time I left it) the lawyer had suffered a brainwave, which he passed on to his friend Val.

The Hobbs Sandwich lunch (of anything but sandwiches) had lasted through a good chunk of the afternoon, and by the end of it I had a job. I hadn't taken a lot of persuading, as it seemed interesting to me from the start. A month's trial on both sides, Brigadier Catto said, and mentioned a salary that had Cornborough smiling broadly.

"What's so funny?" the Brigadier asked. "That's normal. We pay most of our men that at the start."

"I forgot to mention it. Tor here is . . . um . . ." He paused, perhaps wondering whether finishing the sentence came under the heading of breaking a client's right to confidentiality, because after a short while he went on, "He'd better tell you himself."

"I accept the salary," I said.

"What have you not told me?" Catto asked, suddenly very much the boss, his eyes not exactly suspicious but unsmiling; and I saw that I was not binding myself to some slightly eccentric friendly cricket nut, but to the purposeful, powerful man who had commanded a brigade and was currently keeping horseracing honest. I was not going to be playing a game, he was meaning, and if I thought so we would go no further.

I said wryly, "I have a private income after tax of about twenty times the salary you're offering, but I'll take your money all the same, sir, and I'll work for it."

He listened to the underlying declaration of commitment and good faith, and after a long pause he smiled briefly and nodded.

"Very well," he said. "When can you start?"

I had started the next day at Epsom races, relearning the characters, reawakening sleeping memories, hearing Aunt Viv's bright voice in my ear about as clearly as if she were alive. "There's Paddy Fredericks. Did I tell you he used to be married to Betsy who's now Mrs. Glovebinder? Brad Glovebinder used to have horses with Paddy Fredericks but when he pinched Betsy, he took his horses away too. No justice in the world. Hello, Paddy, how are things? This is my nephew Torquil, as I expect you remember, you've met him often enough. Well done with your winner, Paddy," and Paddy had taken us off for a drink, buying me a Coke.

I came face to face unexpectedly with the trainer Paddy Fredericks that first day at Epsom and he hadn't known me. There hadn't been a pause or a flicker. Aunt Viv had been dead nearly eight years and I had changed too much; and I had been reassured from that early moment that my weird new nonidentity was going to work.

On the grounds that racing villains made it their business to know the Security Service comprehensively by sight, Brigadier Catto said that if he ever wanted to speak to me himself, it would never be on a racecourse but always in the bar of the Hobbs Sandwich, and so it had been for the past three years. He and Clement Cornborough had sponsored me for full membership of the club and encouraged me to go there occasionally on other days on my own, and although

I'd thought the Brigadier's passion for secrecy a shade obsessive I had fallen in with his wishes and come to enjoy it, even if I'd learned a lot more about cricket than I really wanted to.

On the night of Derry Welfram's death I walked into the bar at ten to eight and ordered a glass of Burgundy and a couple of beef sandwiches, which came promptly because of the post-cricket-season absence of a hundred devotees discussing leg-breaks and insider politics at the tops of their voices. There were still a good number of customers, but from late September to the middle of April one could talk all night without laryngitis the next day, and when the Brigadier arrived he greeted me audibly and cheerfully as a fellow member well met and began telling me his assessment of the Test team just assembled for the winter tour abroad.

"They've disregarded Withers," he complained. "How are they ever going to get Balping out if they leave our best inswinger biting his knuckles at home?"

I hadn't the faintest idea, and he knew it. With a gleam of a smile he bought himself a double Scotch drowned in a large glass of water, and led the way to one of the small tables round the edge of the room, still chatting on about the whys and wherefores of the selected team.

"Now," he said without change of speed or volume, "Welfram's dead, Shacklebury's dead, Gideon's dead, and the problem is what do we do next."

The question, I knew, had to be rhetorical. He never called me to the Hobbs Sandwich to ask my advice but always to direct me toward some new course of action, though he would listen and change his requirements if I put forward any huge objections, which I didn't often. He waited for a while, though, as if for an answer, and took a slow contemplative mouthful of weak whisky.

"Did Mr. Gideon leave any notes?" I asked eventually.

"Not as far as we know. Nothing as helpful as telling us why he sold his horses to Filmer, if that's what you mean.

Not unless a letter comes in the post next week, which I very much doubt."

Gideon had been frightened beyond death, I thought. The threat must have been to the living: an ongoing perpetual threat.

"Mr. Gideon has daughters," I said.

The Brigadier nodded. "Three. And five grandchildren. His wife died years ago, I suppose you know. Am I reading you aright?"

"That the daughters and grandchildren were hostages? Yes. Do you think they could know it?"

"Positive they don't," the Brigadier said. "I talked with his eldest daughter today. Nice, sensible woman, about fifty. Gideon shot himself yesterday evening, around five, they think, but no one found him for hours as he did it out in the woods. I went down to the house today. His daughter, Sarah, said he's been ultra depressed lately, going deeper and deeper, but she didn't know what had caused it. He wouldn't discuss it. Sarah was in tears, of course, and also of course feeling guilty because she didn't prevent it, but she couldn't have prevented it, it's almost impossible to stop a determined suicide, you can't force people to go on living. Short of imprisonment, of course. Anyway, if she was any sort of a hostage, she didn't know it. It wasn't that sort of guilt."

I offered him one of my so far uneaten sandwiches. He took one absentmindedly and began to chew, and I ate one myself. The problem of what to do about Filmer lay in morose wrinkles across his brow and I'd heard he considered the collapse of the conspiracy trial a personal failure.

"I went to see Ezra Gideon myself after you and John Millington flushed out Welfram," he said. "I showed Ezra your photograph of Welfram. I thought he would faint, he went so white, but he still wouldn't speak. And now, God damn it, in one day we've lost both contacts. We don't know who Filmer will get to next, or if he's already active again, and we'll have the devil's own job spotting another frightener."

"He won't have found one himself yet, I shouldn't think," I said. "Certainly not one as effective. They aren't that common, are they?"

"The police say they're getting younger."

He looked unusually discouraged for someone whose success rate in all other fields was impressive. The lost battle rankled: the victories had been shrugged off. I drank some wine and waited for the commanding officer to emerge from the worried man, waited for him to unfold the plan of campaign.

He surprised me, however, by saying, "I didn't think you'd stick with this job this long."

"Why not?"

"You know damn well why not. You're not dim. Clement told me the pile your father left you simply multiplied itself for twenty years, growing like a mushroom. And still does. Like a whole field of mushrooms. Why aren't you out there picking them?"

I sat back in my chair wondering what to say. I knew very well why I didn't pick them, but I wasn't sure it would sound sensible.

"Go on," he said. "I need to know."

I glanced at his intent eyes and sensed his concentration, and realized suddenly that he might mean in some obscure way to base the future plan on my answer.

"It isn't so easy," I said slowly, "and don't laugh, it really isn't so easy to be able to afford anything you want. Short of the Crown Jewels and trifles like that. Well . . . I don't find it easy. I'm like a child loose in a sweet shop. I could eat and eat . . . and make myself sick . . . and greedy . . . and a jellyfish. So I keep my hands off the sweets and occupy my time following crooks. Is that any sort of answer?"

He grunted noncommittally. "How strong is the temptation?"

"On freezing cold days in sleet and wind at say Doncaster races, very strong indeed. At Ascot in the sunshine I don't feel it."

"Be serious," he said. "Put it another way. How strong is your commitment to the Security Service?"

"They're really two different things," I said. "I don't pick too many mushrooms because I want to retain order, to keep my feet well planted. Mushrooms can be hallucinogenic, after all. I work for you, for the Service, rather than in banking or farming and so on, because I like it and I'm not all that bad at what I do, really, and it's useful, and I'm not terribly good at twiddling my thumbs. I don't know that I'd die for you. Is that what you want?"

His lips twitched. He said, "Fair enough. How do you feel about danger nowadays? I know you did risky enough things on your travels."

After a brief pause I said, "What sort of danger?"

"Physical, I suppose." He rubbed a thumb and forefinger down his nose and looked at me with steady eyes. "Perhaps."

"What do you want me to do?"

We had come to the point of the meeting, but he backed away from it still.

I knew in a way that it was because of what he'd called the mushrooms that he'd grown into the way of speaking to me as he did, proposing but seldom giving straight orders. He would have been more forthright if I'd been a junior army officer in uniform. Millington, who didn't know about the mushrooms, could uninhibitedly boss me around like a sergeant-major, and did so pretty sharply under pressure.

Millington mostly called me Kelsey and only occasionally, on good days, Tor. ("Tor? What sort of name is that?" he'd demanded at the beginning. "Short for Torquil," I said. "*Torquil?* Huh. I don't blame you.") He always referred to himself as Millington ("Millington here," when he telephoned), and that was how I thought of him: he had never asked me to call him John. I supposed that a man who had served in a strongly hierarchical organization for a long time found surnames natural.

The Brigadier's attention still seemed to be focused on the

glass he was slowly revolving in his hands, but finally he put it down precisely in the center of a beer mat as if coming to a precise conclusion in his thoughts.

"I had a telephone call yesterday from my counterpart in the Canadian Jockey Club." He paused again. "Have you ever been to Canada?"

"Yes," I said. "Once, for a while, for maybe three months, mostly in the west. Calgary . . . Vancouver . . . I went up by boat from there to Alaska."

"Did you go to the races in Canada?"

"Yes, a few times, but it must be about six years ago and I don't know anyone. . . ." I stopped, puzzled, not knowing what kind of response he wanted.

"Do you know about this train?" he said. "The transcontinental mystery race train? Ever heard of it?"

"Um," I said, reflecting. "I read something about it the other day. A lot of top Canadian owners are going on a junket with their horses, stopping to race at tracks along the way. Is that the one you mean?"

"It is indeed. But the owners aren't all Canadian. Some of them are American, some are Australian and some are British. One of the passengers is Julius Filmer."

"Oh," I said.

"Yes, oh. The Canadian Jockey Club has given its blessing to the whole affair because it's attracting worldwide publicity and they are hoping for bumper attendances, hoping to give all Canadian racing an extra boost. Yesterday, my counterpart, Bill Baudelaire, told me he'd been talking with the company who are arranging everything and he found there was a late addition to the passenger list, Julius Filmer. Bill Baudelaire of course knows all about the conspiracy fiasco. He wanted to know if there wasn't some way we could keep the undesirable Mr. Filmer off that prestigious train. Couldn't we possibly declare him persona non grata on all racetracks, including and especially Canadian. I told him if we'd had any grounds to warn Filmer off we'd have done it already, but the man was acquitted. We can't be seen to disgrace him when he's been declared not guilty, we'd be in all sorts of trouble. We can't warn him off for buying two horses from Gideon. These days, we can't just warn him off because we want to. He can only be warned off for transgressing against the rules of racing."

All the frustrated fury of the Jockey Club vibrated in his voice. He wasn't a man to take impotence lightly.

"Bill Baudelaire knows all that, of course," he went on. "He said if we couldn't get Filmer off the train, would we please get one of our grandees *on.* Although the whole thing is sold out, he twisted the arms of the promoters to say they would let him have one extra ticket, and he wanted one of our Stewards, or one of the Jockey Club department heads, or me myself, to go along conspicuously, so that Filmer would know he was being closely watched and would refrain from any sins he had in mind."

"Are you going?" I asked, fascinated.

"No, I'm not. You are."

"Um . . ." I said a shade breathlessly, "I hardly fit the bill."

"I told Bill Baudelaire," the Brigadier said succinctly, "that I would send him a passenger Filmer *didn't* know. One of my men. Then if Filmer does try anything, and after all it's a big if, we might have a real chance of finding out how and what, and catching him at it."

My God, I thought. So simple, put like that. So absolutely impossible of performance.

I swallowed. "What did Mr. Baudelaire say?"

"I talked him into agreeing. He's expecting you."

I blinked.

"Well," the Brigadier said, "not you by name. Someone. Someone fairly young, I said, but experienced. Someone who wouldn't seem out of place . . ." his teeth gleamed briefly, ". . . on the millionaires' express."

"But," I said, and stopped dead, my mind full of urgent

reservations and doubts that I was good enough for a job like that. Yet on the other hand, what a lark.

"Will you go?" he asked.

"Yes," I said.

He smiled. "I hoped you might."

———————

Brigadier Catto, who lived ninety miles from London in Newmarket, was staying overnight, as he often did, in a comfortable bedroom upstairs in the club. I left him in the bar after a while and drove the last half-mile home to where I lived in a quiet residential street in Kennington.

I had looked in that district for somewhere to put down a few roots on the grounds that I wouldn't be bothered to use the club much if I lived on the other side of London. Kennington, south of the Thames, rubbing shoulders with the grittiness of Lambeth and Brixton, was not where the racing crowd panted to be seen, and in fact I'd never spotted anyone locally that I knew by sight on the racecourse.

I'd come across an advertisement: "House share available, for single presentable yuppie; 2 rooms, bath, share kit, mortgage and upkeep. Call evenings," and although I'd been thinking in terms of an apartment on my own, house sharing had suddenly seemed attractive, especially after the loneliness of work. I'd presented myself by appointment, been inspected by the four others in residence, and let in on trial, and it had all worked very well.

The four others were currently two sisters working in publishing (whose father had originally bought the house and set up the running-mortgage scheme), one junior barrister who tended to stutter, and an actor with a supporting role in a television series. The house rules were simple: pay on the dot, show good manners at all times, don't pry into the others' business, and don't let overnight girl/boyfriends clog up any of the three bathrooms for hours in the morning.

There was a fair amount of laughter and camaraderie, but we tended to share coffee, beer, wine and saucepans more than confidences. I told them I was a dedicated racegoer and no one asked whether I won or lost.

The actor, Robbie, on the top floor, had been of enormous use to me, though I doubted he really knew it. He'd invited me up for a beer early one evening a few days after I went to live there, and I'd found him sitting before a brightly lit theatrical dressing table creating, as he said, a new makeup for a part he'd accepted in a play. I'd been startled to see how a different way of brushing his hair, a large false moustache and heavier eyebrows had changed him.

"Tools of the trade," he said, gesturing to the greasepaints and false hair lying in neat rows and boxes before him. "Instant stubble, Fauntleroy curls—what would you like?"

"Curls," I said slowly.

"Sit down, then," he said cheerfully, getting up to give me his place, and he brought out a butane hair curler and wound my almost straight hair onto it bit by bit there and then, and within minutes I looked like a brown poodle, tousled, unbrushed, totally different.

"How's that?" he said, bending to look with me into the looking glass.

"Amazing." And easy, I thought. I could do it in the car, any time.

"It suits you," Robbie said. He knelt beside me, put his arm round my shoulders, gave me a little squeeze and smiled with unmistakable invitation into my eyes.

"No," I said matter-of-factly. "I like girls."

He wasn't offended. "Haven't you ever tried the other?"

"It's just not me, dear," I said, "as one might say."

He laughed and took his arm away. "Never mind, then. No harm in trying."

We drank the beer and he showed me how to shape and stick on a bold macho moustache, holding out a pair of thick-framed glasses for good measure. I regarded the stranger looking back at me from the glass and said I'd never realized how easy it was to mislead.

"Sure thing. All it takes is a bit of nerve."

And he was right about that. I bought a butane curler for myself, but I took it with me for a week in the car before I screwed myself up to stop in a rest area on the way to Newbury races and actually use it. In the three years since then, I'd done it dozens of times without a thought, brushing and damping out the effects on the way home.

Sundays I usually spent lazily in my two big bright rooms on the second floor (the barrister directly above, the sisters below) sleeping, reading, pottering about. For about a year some time earlier I'd spent my Sundays with the daughter of one of the Hobbs Sandwich members, but it had been a mutual passing pleasure rather than a grand passion for both of us, and in the end she'd drifted away and married someone else. I supposed I too would marry one day; knew I would like to; felt there was no hurry this side of thirty.

On the Sunday morning after meeting the Brigadier in the club I began to think about what I should pack for Canada. He'd told me to be what I spent so much time not being, a rich young loafer with nothing to do but enjoy himself. "All you need to do is talk about horses to the other passengers and keep your eyes open."

"Yes," I said.

"Look the part."

"Yes, right."

"I've caught sight of you sometimes at the races, you know, looking like a stockbroker one day and a hillbilly the next. Millington says he often can't see you, even though he knows you're there."

"I've got better with practice, I suppose, but I never really do much. Change my hair, change my clothes, slouch a bit."

"It works," he said. "Be what Filmer would expect."

It wasn't so much what Filmer would expect, I thought, looking at the row of widely assorted jackets in my ward-

27

robe, but what I could sustain over the ten days the party was due to take before it broke up.

Curls, for instance, were out, as they disappeared in rain. Stuck-on moustaches were out in case they came off. Spectacles were out, as one could forget to put them on. I would have to look basically as nature had ordained and be as nondescript and unnoticeable as possible.

I sorted out the most expensive and least worn of my clothes, and decided I'd better buy new shirts, new shoes and a cashmere sweater before I went.

I telephoned Millington on Monday morning as instructed and found him in a usual state of disgruntlement. He had heard about the train. He was not in favor of my going on it. The Security Service (meaning the Brigadier) should have sent a properly trained operative, an ex-policeman preferably. Like himself, for instance. Someone who knew the techniques of investigation and could be trusted not to destroy vital evidence through ignorance and clumsiness. I listened without interruption for so long that, in the end, he said sharply, "Are you still there?"

"Yes," I said.

"I want to see you, preferably later this morning. I'll have your air ticket. I suppose you do have an up-to-date passport?"

We agreed to meet, as often before, in a reasonably good small snack bar next to Victoria Station, convenient both for Millington, who lived a couple of miles southwest across Battersea Bridge, and for me a few stops down the line to the south.

I arrived ten minutes before the appointed time and found Millington already sitting at a table with a mug of brown liquid and several sausage rolls in progress. I took a tray, slid it along the rails in front of the glass-fronted serving display and picked a slice of cheesecake from behind one of the small hinged doors. I actually approved the glass-door arrangement: it meant that with luck one's cheesecake wouldn't have been sneezed on by the general public, but only by a cook or two and the snack-bar staff.

Millington eyed my partially hygienic wedge and said he preferred the lemon meringue pie, himself.

"I like that too," I said equably.

Millington was a big beer-and-any-kind-of-pie man who must have given up thankfully on weight control when he left the police. He looked as if he now weighed about 240 pounds, and while not gross was definitely a solid mass, but with an agility also that he put to good use in his job. Many petty racecourse crooks had made the mistake of believing Millington couldn't snake after them like an eel through the crowds, only to feel the hand of retribution falling weightily on their collar. I'd seen Millington catch a dipping pick-pocket on the wing: an impressive sight.

The large convenience-food snack bar, bright and clean, was always infernally noisy, pop music thumping away to the accompaniment of chairs scraping the floor and the clatter of meals at a gallop. The clientele were mostly travelers, coming or going on trains lacking buffet cars, starving or prudent; travelers checking their watches, gulping too-hot coffee, uninterested in others, leaving in a hurry. No one ever gave Millington and me a second glance, and no one could ever have overheard what we said.

We never met there when there was racing at places like Plumpton, Brighton, Lingfield and Folkestone: on those days the whole racing circus could wash through Victoria Station. We never met, either, anywhere near the Security Service head office in the Jockey Club, in Portman Square. It was odd, I sometimes thought, that I'd never once been through my employer's door.

Millington said, "I don't approve of you traveling with Filmer."

"So I gathered," I said. "You said so earlier."

"The man's a murderer."

He wasn't concerned for my safety, of course, but thought me unequal to the contest.

"He may not actually murder anyone on the train," I said flippantly.

"It's no joke," he said severely. "And after this he'll know you, and you'll be no use to us on the racecourse, as far as he's concerned."

"There are about fifty people going on the trip, the Brigadier said. I won't push myself into Filmer's notice. He quite likely won't remember me afterward."

"You'll be too close to him," Millington said obstinately.

"Well," I said thoughtfully, "it's the only chance we've ever had so far to get really close to him at all. Even if he's only going along for a harmless holiday, we'll know a good deal more about him this way."

"I don't like wasting you," Millington said, shaking his head.

I looked at him in real surprise. "That's a change," I said.

"I didn't want you working for us, to begin with," he said, shrugging. "Didn't see what good you could do, thought it was stupid. Now you're my eyes. The eyes in the back of my head, that the villains have been complaining about ever since you started. I've got the sense to know it. And if you must know, I don't want to lose you. I told the Brigadier we were wasting our trump card, sending you on that train. He said we might be playing it, and if we could get rid of Filmer, it was worth it."

I looked at Millington's worried face. I said slowly, "Do you, and does the Brigadier, know something about Filmer's travel plans that you've not told me?"

"When he said that," Millington said, looking down at his sausage rolls, "I asked him that same question. He didn't answer. I don't know of anything myself. I'd tell you, if I did."

Perhaps he would, I thought. Perhaps he wouldn't.

30

The next day, Tuesday, I drove north to Nottingham for a normal day's hard work hanging around doing nothing much at the races.

I'd bought the new clothes and a new suitcase and had more or less packed ready for my departure the next morning, and the old long-distance wanderlust that had in the past kept me traveling for seven years had woken from its recent slumber and given me a sharp nudge in the ribs. Millington shouldn't fear losing me to Filmer, I thought, so much as to the old seductive tug of moving on, moving on and seeing what lay round the next corner.

I could do it now, I supposed, in five-star fashion, not backpacking; in limousines, not on buses; eating haute cuisine, not hot dogs; staying in Palm Beach, not dusty backwoods. Probably I'd enjoy the lushness for a while, maybe even for a long while, but in the end, to stay real, I'd have to get myself out of the sweet shop and do some sort of work, and not put it off until I no longer had a taste for plain bread.

I was wearing, perhaps as a salute to plain bread, a well-worn leather jacket and a flat cloth cap, the binoculars-camera slung round my neck, a race-card clutched in my hand. I stood around vaguely outside the weighing room, watching who came and who went, who talked to whom, who looked worried, who happy, who malicious.

A young apprentice with an ascendant reputation came out of the weighing room in street clothes, not riding gear, and stood looking around as if searching for someone. His eyes stopped moving and focused, and I looked to see what had caught his attention. He was looking at the Jockey Club's paid steward, who was acting at the meeting as the human shape of authority. The steward was standing in social conversation with a pair of people who had a horse running that day, and after a few minutes he raised his hat to the lady and walked out toward the parade ring.

The apprentice calmly watched his departing back, then made another sweep of the people around. Seeing nothing to worry about he set off toward the stand the jockeys watched the races from and joined a youngish man with whom he walked briefly, talking. They parted near the stands, and I, following, transferred my attention from the apprentice and followed the other man instead; he went straight into the bookmakers' enclosure in front of the stands, and along the rows of bookmakers to the domain of Collie Goodboy, who was shouting his offered odds from the height of a small platform the size of a beer crate.

The apprentice's contact didn't place a bet. He picked up a ledger and began to record the bets of others. He spoke to Collie Goodboy (Les Morris to his parents), who presently wiped off the offered odds from his board and chalked up new ones. The new odds were generous. Collie Goodboy was rewarded by a rush of eager betters keen to accept the invitation. Collie Goodboy methodically took their money.

With a sigh I turned away and wandered off up to the stands to watch the next race, scanning the crowds as usual, watching the world revolve. I ended up standing not far from the rails dividing the bookmakers' section of the stands (called the Tattersalls enclosure) from the Club, the more expensive end. I often did that, as from there one could see the people in both enclosures easily. One could see also who came to the dividing rails to put bets on with the row of bookmakers doing business in that privileged position. The "rails" bookmakers were the princes of their trade, genial, obliging, fair, flint-hearted, brilliant mathematicians.

I watched as always to see who was betting with whom, and when I came to the bookmaker nearest to the stands, nearest to me, I saw that the present customer was Filmer.

I was watching him bet, thinking of the rail journey ahead, when he tilted his head back and looked straight up into my eyes.

3

I looked away instantly but smoothly, and presently
glanced back.

Filmer was still talking to the bookmaker. I edged upward
through the crowd behind me until I was about five steps
higher and surrounded by other racegoers.

Filmer didn't look back to where I'd been standing. He
didn't search up or down or sideways to see where I had
gone.

My thumping heart quietened down a bit. The meeting of
eyes had been accidental: had to have been. Dreadfully unwelcome, all the same, particularly at this point.

I hadn't expected him to have been at Nottingham, and
hadn't looked for him. Two of his horses were certainly
down to run, but Filmer himself almost never went to the
midland courses of Nottingham, Leicester or Wolverhamp-
ton. He had definite preferences in racecourses, as in so
much else: always a creature of habit.

I made no attempt to shadow him closely, as it wasn't
necessary: before the following race he would be down in
the parade ring to watch his horse walk round and I could
catch him up there. I watched him conclude his bet and walk
away to climb the stands for the race about to start, and as
far as I could see he was alone, which also was unusual, as

either the girlfriend or the male companion was normally in obsequious attendance.

The race began and I watched it with interest. The chatty apprentice wasn't riding in it himself, but the stable that employed him had a runner. The runner started third favorite and finished third last. I switched my gaze to Collie Goodboy, and found him smiling. A common, sad, fraudulent sequence that did racing no good.

Filmer stepped down from the stands and headed in the direction of the saddling boxes, to supervise, as he always did, the final preparation for his horse's race. I drifted along in his wake to make sure, but that was indeed where he went. From there to the parade ring, from there to place a bet with the same bookmaker as before, from there to the stands to watch his horse race. From there to the unsaddling enclosure allotted to the horse that finished second.

Filmer took his defeat graciously, making a point as always of congratulating the winning owner, in this case a large middle-aged lady who looked flushed and flattered.

Filmer left the unsaddling enclosure with a smirk of self-satisfaction and was immediately confronted by a young man who tried to thrust a briefcase into his hand.

Julius Apollo's face turned from smug to fury quicker than Shergar won the Derby, as Paul Shacklebury would have said. Filmer wouldn't take the case and he practically spat at the offerer, his black head going forward like a striking cobra. The young man with the briefcase retreated ultra-nervously and in panic ran away, and Filmer, regaining control of himself, began looking around in the general direction of stewards and pressmen to see if any of them had noticed. He visibly sighed with relief that none of them showed any sign of it—and he hadn't looked my way at all.

I followed the demoralized young man who still held on to the briefcase. He made straight for the men's cloakroom, stayed there for a fair time and came out looking pale. Filmer's effect on people's guts, I reflected, would put any laxative to shame.

The shaken youth with the briefcase then made his nervous way to a rendezvous with a thin, older man who was waiting just outside the exit gate, biting his nails. When the thin man saw the briefcase still in the nervous youth's possession he looked almost as furious as Filmer had, and a strong argument developed in which one could read the dressing-down in the vigorous chopping gestures, even if one couldn't hear the words.

Thin man poked nervous man several times sharply in the chest. Nervous man's shoulders dropped. Thin man turned away and walked off deep into the parking lot.

Nervous man brought the briefcase with him back through the gate and into the nearest bar, and I had to hang around for a long time in the small crowd there before anything else happened. The scattered clientele was watching the television: nervous man shuffled from foot to foot and sweated, and kept a sharp lookout at the people passing by outside in the open air. Then, sometime after Filmer's second runner had tried and (according to the closed-circuit commentary) lost, Filmer himself came past, tearing up betting tickets and not looking pleased.

Nervous man shot out from his waiting position just inside the door of the sheltering bar and offered the briefcase again, and this time Filmer took it, but in fierce irritation and with another sharp set of glances around him. He saw nothing to disturb him. He was leaving after the fifth of the six races and all forms of authority were still engaged to his rear. He gripped the case's handle and strode purposefully out on his way to his car.

Nervous man shuffled on the spot a bit more and then followed Filmer through the exit gate and into the parking lot. I tagged along again and saw both of them still making for their transport, though in different directions. I followed nervous man, not Filmer, and saw him get into the front passenger seat of a car already occupied by thin man, who still looked cross. They didn't set off immediately and I had time to walk at a steady pace past the rear of their car on the way to my own, which was parked strategically, as ever, near the gate to the road, for making quick following getaways. I memorized their number plate in case I later lost them; and out on the road, comfortably falling into place behind them, I telephoned to Millington.

I told him about the briefcase and read him the number plate still ahead in my sight.

"The car's going north, though," I said. "How far do you want me to go?"

"What time's your flight tomorrow?"

"Noon, from Heathrow. But I have to go home first to pick up my gear and passport."

He thought for a few moments. "You'd better decide for yourself. If he gets on the motorway to Scotland . . . well, don't go."

"All right."

"Very interesting," Millington said, "that he didn't want to be seen in public accepting that briefcase."

"Very."

"Anything special about it?"

"As far as I could see," I said, "it was black, polished, possibly crocodile, with gold clasps."

"Well, well," Millington said vaguely. "I'll get back to you with that car number."

The thin man's car aimed unerringly for the highway in the direction of Scotland. I decided to keep on going at least until Millington called back, which he did with impressive speed, telling me that my quarry was registered to I. J. Horfitz, resident of Doncaster, address supplied.

"All right," I said, "I'll go to Doncaster." An hour and a bit ahead, I thought, with plenty of time to return.

"Does that name Horfitz ring any bells with you?" Millington asked.

"None at all," I said positively. "And by the way, you know that promising young apprentice of Pete Shaw's? All that talent? The silly young fool passed some verbal info to a new character on the racecourse who turned out to be writing the book for Collie Goodboy. Collie Goodboy thought it good news."

"What was it, do you know?"

"Pete Shaw had a runner in the second race, third favorite, finished nearly last. The apprentice knew the score, though he wasn't riding it."

"Huh," Millington said. "I'll put the fear of God into the lot of them, Pete Shaw, the owner, the jockey, the apprentice and Collie Goodboy. Stir them up and warn them. I suppose," he said as an afterthought, "you didn't get any photos? We haven't any actual proof?"

"Not really. I took one shot of the apprentice talking to Collie's man, but they had their backs to me. One of Collie's man with Collie. One of Collie's board with the generous odds."

"Better than nothing," he said judiciously. "It'll give them all an unholy fright. The innocent ones will be livid and sack the guilty, like they usually do. Clean their own house. Save us a job. And we'll keep a permanent eye on that stupid apprentice. Ring me when you get to Doncaster."

"OK. And I took some more photos. One of the nervous young man with the briefcase, one of him with the thin man ... er ... I. J. Horfitz possibly, I suppose, and one of Filmer with the briefcase, though I'm not sure if that one will be very clear, I had almost no time and I was quite far away, and I was using the cigarette lighter camera, it's less conspicuous."

"All right. We need that film before you go. Um ... er ... you'd better give me a ring when you're on the way back, and I'll have thought of somewhere we can meet tonight. Right?"

"Yes," I said. "Right."

"This Horfitz person, what did he look like?"

"Thin, elderly, wore a dark overcoat and a black trilby, and glasses. Looked ready for a funeral, not the races."

Millington grunted in what seemed to me to be recognition.

"Do you know him?" I asked.

"He was before your time. But yes, I know him. Ivor Horfitz. It must be him. We got him warned off for life five years ago."

"What for?"

"It's a long story. I'll tell you later. And I don't think after all you need to spend all that time going to Doncaster. We can always find him, if we want to. Turn round at the next exit and come back to London, and I'll meet you in that pub at Victoria. Not the snack bar; the pub."

"Yes, right. See you in about . . . um . . . two and a half hours, with luck."

Two and a half hours later, it was beer and pork pie time in a dark far corner in a noisy bar, Millington's preferred sort of habitat.

I gave him the exposed but undeveloped film, which he put in his pocket saying, "Eyes in the back of my head," with conspicuous satisfaction.

"Who is Horfitz?" I said, quenching the long drive's thirst in a half-pint of draught. "Did you know he knew Filmer?"

"No," he said, answering the second question first. "And Filmer wouldn't want to be seen with him, nor to be seen in any sort of contact."

"What you're saying," I said slowly, "is that the messenger, the nervous young man, is also known by sight to the stewards, to you yourself probably. Because if he were an unidentifiable stranger, why should Filmer react so violently to being seen with him; to being seen accepting something from him?"

Millington gave me a sideways look. "You've learned a thing or two, haven't you, since you started." He patted the pocket containing the film. "This will tell us if we know him. What did he look like?"

"Fairly plump, fairly stupid. Sweaty. Unhappy. A worm between two hawks."

Millington shook his head. "Might be anyone," he said.

"What did Horfitz do?" I asked.

Millington bit into a pork pie and took his time, speaking eventually round escaping crumbs of pastry.

"He owned a small stableful of horses in Newmarket and employed his own trainer for them, who naturally did what he was told. Very successful little stable in a quiet way. Amazing results, but there you are, some owners are always lucky. Then the trainer got cold feet because he thought we were on to him, which we actually weren't, we'd never reckoned him for a villain. Anyway, he blew the whistle on the operation, saying the strain was getting too much for him. He said all the horses in the yard were as good as interchangeable. They ran in whatever races he and Horfitz thought they could win. Three-year-olds in two-year-old races, past winners in maidens-at-starting, any old thing. Horfitz bought and sold horses continually so the yard never looked the same from week to week, and the stable lads came and went like yo-yos, like they do pretty much anyway. They employed all sorts of different jockeys. No one cottoned on. Horfitz had some nice long-priced winners but no bookmakers hollered foul. It was a small, unfashionable stable, see? Never in the newspapers. Because they didn't run in big races, just small ones at tracks the press don't go to, but you can win as much by betting on those as on any others. It was all pretty low key, but we found out that Horfitz had made literally hundreds of thousands, not just by betting but by selling his winners. Only he always sold the real horses that fitted the names on the race-card, not the horses that had actually run. He kept those and ran them again, and sold the horses in whose names they'd run, and so on and so on. Audacious little fiddle, the whole thing."

"Yes," I agreed, and felt a certain amount of awe at the energy and organization put into the enterprise.

"So when the trainer ratted we set a few traps with his help and caught Horfitz with his pants down, so to speak. He got warned off for life and swore to kill his trainer, which he hasn't done so far. The trainer was warned off for three years with a severe caution, but he got his license back two years ago. Part of the bargain. So he's in business again in a small way but we keep his runners under a microscope, checking their passports every time they run. We're a lot hotter at checking passports randomly all over the place now, as of course you know."

I nodded. Then Millington's jaw literally dropped. I looked at the classic sign of astonishment and said, "What's the matter?"

"Gawd," he said. "What a turn up. Can you believe it? Paul Shacklebury, that murdered stable lad, he was working for Horfitz's old trainer."

I left Millington frowning with concentration over a replenished pint while he tried to work out the significance of Horfitz's old trainer employing a lad who was murdered for knowing too much about Filmer. What had Paul Shacklebury known? Millington demanded rhetorically for the hundredth time. And, more to the minute, what was in the briefcase, and why was Horfitz giving it to Filmer?

"Work on the sweating messenger," I suggested, getting up to go. "He might crack open like the trainer. You never know."

"Maybe we will," Millington said. "And Tor, look out for yourself on the train."

He could be quite human sometimes, I thought.

———

I flew to Ottawa the next day and gave in to temptation at Heathrow to the extent of changing my ticket from knees-against-chest economy to full-stretch-out first class. I also asked the Ottawa taxi driver who took me into the city from the airport to find me a decent hotel; he cast a rapid eye over my clothes and the new suitcase and said the Four Seasons should suit.

It suited. They gave me a small pleasant suite and I telephoned straightaway to the number I'd been given for Bill Baudelaire. He answered himself at the first ring, rather to my surprise, and said yes, he'd had a telex to confirm I was on my way. He had a bass voice with a lot of timbre even over the wires and was softly Canadian in accent.

He asked where I would be in an hour and said he would come around then to brief me on the matter in hand, and I gathered from his circumspect sentences that he wasn't alone and didn't want to be understood. Just like home, I thought comfortably, and unpacked a few things, showered off the journey and awaited events.

Outside, the deepening orange of the autumn sunshine was turning the green copper roofs of the turreted stone government buildings to a transient shimmering gold, and I reflected, watching from the windows, that I'd much liked this graceful city when I'd been here before. I was filled with a serene sense of peace and contentment, which I remembered a few times in the days lying ahead.

Bill Baudelaire came when the sky had grown dark and I'd switched on the lights, and he looked round the suite with quizzical eyebrows.

"I'm glad to see old Val has staked you to rooms befitting a rich young owner."

I smiled and didn't enlighten him. He'd shaken my hand when I opened the door to him and looked me quickly, piercingly up and down in the way of those used to assessing strangers instantly and with no inhibitions about letting them know it.

I saw a man of plain looks but positive charm, a solid man much younger than the Brigadier, maybe forty, with reddish hair, pale blue eyes and pale skin pitted by the scars of old acne. Once seen, I thought, difficult to forget.

He was wearing a dark gray business suit with a cream shirt and a red tie out of step with his hair, and I wondered if he were color-blind or simply liked the effect.

He walked straight across the sitting room, sat in the armchair nearest to the telephone and picked up the receiver.

"Room service?" he said. "Please send up as soon as possible a bottle of vodka and . . . er . . ." He raised his eyebrows in my direction, in invitation.

"Wine," I said. "Red. Bordeaux preferably."

Bill Baudelaire repeated my request with a ceiling price and disconnected.

"You can put the drinks on your expense sheet and I'll initial it," he said. "You do have an expense sheet, I suppose?"

"I do in England."

"Then start one here, of course. How are you paying the hotel bills?"

"By credit card. My own."

"Is that usual? Never mind. You give all the bills to me when you've paid them, along with your expense sheet, and Val and I will deal with it."

"Thank you," I said. Val would have a fit, I thought, but then on second thought, no, he probably wouldn't. He would pay me the agreed budget; fair was fair.

"Sit down," Bill Baudelaire said, and I sat opposite him in another armchair, crossing one knee over the other. The room seemed hot to me with the central heating, and I wasn't wearing a jacket. He considered me for a while, his brow furrowing with seeming uncertainty.

"How old are you?" he said abruptly.

"Twenty-nine."

"Val said you were experienced." It wasn't exactly a question, nor a matter of disbelief.

"I've worked for him for three years."

"He said you would look this part and you do." He sounded more puzzled than pleased, though. "You seem so polished. I suppose it's not what I expected."

I said, "If you saw me in the cheaper sections of a race-course you would think I'd been born there, too."

His face lightened into a smile. "Right, then. I'll accept that. Well, I've brought you a whole lot of papers." He glanced at the large envelope that he had put on the table beside the telephone. "Details about the train and about some of the people who'll be on it, and details about the horses and the arrangements for those. This has all been an enormous undertaking. Everyone has worked very hard on it. It's essential that it retains a good, substantial, untarnished image from start to finish. We're hoping for increased world-wide awareness of Canadian racing. Although we do of course hit world headlines with the Queen's Plate in June or July, we want to draw more international horses here. We want to put our programs more on the map. Canada's a great country. We want to maximize our impact on the international racing circuit."

"Yes," I said, "I do understand." I hesitated. "Do you have a public relations firm working on it?"

"What? Why do you ask? Yes, we do, as a matter of fact. What difference does it make?"

"None, really. Will they have a representative on the train?"

"To minimize negative incidents? No, not unless . . ." He stopped and listened to what he'd said. "I'm using their jargon, damn it. I'll watch that. So easy to repeat what they say."

A knock on the door announced the drinks in charge of an ultra-polite slow-moving waiter who knew where to find ice and mixers in the room's own refrigerator. The waiter took his deliberate time over uncorking the wine, and Bill Baudelaire, stifling impatience, said we would do the pouring ourselves. When the tortoise waiter had gone he gestured to me to help myself, and on his own account fixed a lengthy splash of vodka over a tumblerful of cubes.

He had suggested to the Brigadier that I should meet him first here in Ottawa, as he had business in that city that couldn't be postponed. It would also, they both thought, be more securely private, as everyone going on the train in the normal way would be collecting in Toronto.

"You and I," Bill Baudelaire said over his vodka, "will fly to Toronto tomorrow evening on separate planes, after you've spent the day absorbing all the material I've brought you and asking any questions that arise. I propose to drop by your sitting room here again at two o'clock for a final briefing."

"Will I be able to get in touch with you fairly easily after tomorrow?" I asked. "I'd like to be able to."

"Yes, indeed. I'm not going on the train myself, as of course you know, but I'll be at Winnipeg for the races there, and at Vancouver. And at Toronto, of course. I've outlined everything. You'll find it in the package. We can't really discuss anything properly until you've read it."

"All right."

"There's one unwelcome piece of news, however, that isn't in there because I heard it too late to include. It seems Julius Filmer has bought a share in one of the horses traveling on the train. The partnership was registered today and I was told just now by telephone. The Ontario Racing Commission is deeply concerned, but we can't do anything about it. No regulations have been broken. They won't let people who've been convicted of felonies such as arson, fraud or illegal gambling own horses, but Filmer hasn't been convicted of anything."

"Which horse?" I said.

"Which horse? Laurentide Ice. Quite useful. You can read about it in there." He nodded to the package. "The problem is that we made a rule that only owners could go along to the horse car to see the horses. We couldn't have everyone trampling about there, both for security reasons and for preventing the animals being upset. We thought the only comfort left to us about Filmer's being on the train was that he wouldn't have access to the horse car, and now he will."

"Awkward."

"Infuriating." He refilled his glass with the suppressed violence of his frustration. "Why for God's sake couldn't that goddamn crook have kept his snotty nose out. He's trouble. We all know it. He's planning something. He'll ruin the whole thing. He practically said as much." He looked me over and shook his head. "No offense to you, but how are you going to stop him?"

"It depends what needs to be stopped."

His face lightened suddenly to a smile as before. "Yes, all right, we'll wait and see. Val said you don't miss things. Let's hope he's right."

He went away after a while and with a great deal of interest I opened the package and found it absolutely fascinating from start to finish.

"The Great Transcontinental Mystery Race Train," as emblazoned in red on the gold cover of the glossy prospectus, had indeed entailed an enormous amount of organization. Briefly, the enterprise offered to the racehorse owners of the world a chance to race a horse in Toronto, to go by train to Winnipeg and race a horse there, to stop for two nights at a hotel high in the Rockies, and to continue by train to Vancouver, where they might again race a horse. There was accommodation for eleven horses on the train, and for forty-eight human VIP passengers.

At Toronto, Winnipeg and Vancouver there would be overnight stays in first-class hotels. Transport from train to hotels to races and back to the train was also included as required. The entire trip would last from lunch at Toronto races on the Saturday, to the end of the special race day at Vancouver ten days later.

On the train there would be special sleeping cars, a special dining car, two private chefs and a load of good wine. People who owned their own private rail cars could, as in the past, apply for them to be joined to the train.

Every possible extra luxury would be available if requested in advance, and in addition, for entertainment along the way, an intriguing mystery would be enacted on board and at the stopovers, which passengers would be invited to solve.

I winced a shade at that last piece of information: keeping eyes on Filmer would be hard enough anyhow without all sorts of imaginary mayhem going on around him. He himself was mystery enough.

Special races, I read, had been introduced into the regular programs at Woodbine racecourse, Toronto, at Assiniboia Downs, Winnipeg, and at Exhibition Park, Vancouver. The races had been framed to be ultra attractive to the paying public, with magnificent prize money to please the owners. The owners of the horses and indeed all the train passengers would be given VIP treatment at all the racecourses, including lunch with the presidents.

It wasn't to be expected that owners would want to run the horses on the train three times in so short a span. Any owner was free to run a horse just once. Any owner (or any other passenger on the train) was free to bring any others of his horses to Toronto, Winnipeg or Vancouver by road or by air to run in the special races. The trip was to be a lighthearted junket for the visitors, a celebration of racing in Canada.

In smaller print after all that trumpeting came the information that accommodation was available also for one groom for each horse. If owners wanted space for extra attendants, would they please specify early. Grooms and other attendants would have their own dining and sleeping cars and their own separate entertainments.

Stabling had been reserved at Toronto, Winnipeg and Vancouver for the horses going by train, and they would be able to exercise normally at all three places. In addition, during the passengers' visit to the mountains, the horses would be stabled and exercised in Calgary. The good care of the horses was of prime importance, and a veterinarian would be at once helicoptered to the train if his services should become necessary between scheduled stops.

Next in the package was a penciled note from Bill Baudelaire:

All eleven horse places were sold out within two weeks of the first major announcement.

All forty-eight VIP passenger places were sold within a month.

There are dozens of entries for the special races.

This is going to be a success!

After that came a list of the eleven horses, with past form, followed by a list of their owners, with nationalities. Two owners from England (including Filmer), one from Australia, three from the United States and six from Canada (including Filmer's partner).

The owners, with husbands, wives, family and friends, had taken up twenty-seven of the forty-eight passenger places. Four of the remaining twenty-one places had also been taken by well-known Canadian owners (identified by a star against their names), and Bill Baudelaire, in a note penciled at the bottom of this passenger list, had put, "Splendid response from our appeal to our owners to support the project!"

There were no trainers mentioned on the passenger list, and in fact I later learned that the trainers were making their own way by air as usual to Winnipeg and Vancouver, presumably because the train trip was too time-consuming and expensive.

Next in the package came a bunch of handouts from the three racecourses, from the Canadian railway company and from the four hotels, all shiny pamphlets extolling their individual excellencies. Finally, a fat brochure with good color plates put together by the travel organizers in charge of getting the show on the railroad, a job that seemed well within their powers since they apparently also arranged safaris to outer deserts, treks to the Poles and tours to anywhere anyone cared to go.

They also staged mysteries as entertainments; evenings, weekends, moving or stationary. They were experts from much practice.

For The Great Transcontinental Mystery Race Train, they said, they had arranged something extra-special. "A mystery that will grab you by the throat. A stunning experience. All around you the story will unfold. Clues will appear. BE ON YOUR GUARD."

Oh, great, I thought wryly. But they hadn't finished. There was a parting shot.

BEWARE. MANY PEOPLE ARE NOT WHAT THEY SEEM.

4

"How can they stage a play on a train?" I asked Bill Baudelaire the next day. "I wouldn't have thought it would work."

"Mysteries are very popular in Canada. Very fashionable," he said, "and they don't exactly stage a play. Some of the passengers will be actors and they will make the story evolve. I went to a dinner party, a mystery dinner party, not long ago, and some of the guests were actors, and before we knew where we were we were all caught up in a string of events, just as if it were real. Quite amazing. I went because my wife wanted to. I didn't think I would enjoy it in the least, but I did."

"Some of the passengers . . ." I repeated slowly. "Do you know which ones?"

"No, I don't," he said, more cheerfully than I liked. "That's part of the fun for everyone, trying to spot the actors."

I liked it less and less.

"And of course the actors may be hiding among the other lot of passengers until their turn to appear comes."

"What other lot of passengers?" I said blankly.

"The racegoers." He looked at my face. "Doesn't it say anything about them in the package?"

"No, it doesn't."

"Ah." He reflected briefly. "Well, in order to make the trip economically viable, the rail company said we should add our own party onto the regular train that sets off every day from Toronto to Vancouver, which is called the Canadian. We didn't want to do that because it would have meant we couldn't stop the train for two nights in Winnipeg and again for the mountains, and although the carriages could be unhitched and left in a siding, we'd be faced with security problems. But our own special train was proving extremely, almost impossibly, expensive. So we advertised a separate excursion . . . a racegoing trip . . . and now we have our own train. But it has been expanded, with three or four more sleeping cars, another dining car, and a dayniter or two according to how many tickets they sell in the end. We had an enormous response from people who didn't want to pay what the owners are paying but would like to go to the races across Canada on vacation. They are buying their tickets for the train at the normal fare and making their own arrangements at the stops; we call these passengers the racegoers, for convenience."

I sighed. I supposed it made sense. "What's a dayniter?" I said.

"A car with reclining seats, not bedrooms."

"And how many people altogether will be traveling?"

"Difficult to say. Start with forty-eight owners . . . we call them owners to distinguish them from the racegoers . . . and the grooms. Then the actors and the people from the travel company. Then the train crew and stewards, waiters, chefs and so on. With all the racegoers, well, perhaps about two hundred people altogether. We won't know until we start. Probably not then, unless we actually count."

I could get lost among two hundred more easily than among forty-eight, I thought. Perhaps it might not be too bad. Yet the owners would be looking for actors, for people who weren't what they seemed.

"You asked about contact," Bill Baudelaire said.

"Yes."

"I've discussed it with some of our Jockey Club, and we think you'll simply have to telephone us from the stops."

I said with some alarm, "How many of your Jockey Club know I'm going on the train?"

He looked surprised. "I suppose everyone in the executive office knows we'll have a man in place. They don't know exactly who. Not by name. Not yet. Not until I'd met you and approved. They don't and won't know what you look like."

"Would you please not tell them my name," I said.

He was half-bewildered, half-affronted. "But our Jockey Club are sensible men. Discreet."

"Information leaks," I said.

He looked at me broodingly, vodka and ice cubes tinkling in a fresh glass. "Are you serious?" he said.

"Yes, indeed."

His brow wrinkled. "I'm afraid I may have mentioned your name to one or two. But I will impress on them not to repeat it."

It was too late, I supposed, for much else. Perhaps I was getting too obsessed with secrecy. Still . . .

"I'd rather not telephone direct to the Jockey Club," I said. "Couldn't I leave messages where only you will get them? Like your own home?"

His face melted into an almost boyish grin. "I have three teenage daughters and a busy wife. The receiver is almost never in the cradle." He thought briefly, then wrote a number on a sheet of a small notepad and gave it to me.

"Use this one," he said. "It's my mother's number. She's always there. She's not well and spends a good deal of time in bed. But her brains are intact. She's quick-witted. And because she's ill, if she calls me at the office she gets put straight through to me or else she gets told where to find me. If you give her a message, it will reach me personally with minimum delay. Will that do?"

"Yes, fine," I said, and kept my doubts hidden. Carrier pigeons, I thought, might be better.

"Anything else?" he asked.

"Yes, do you think you could ask Laurentide Ice's owner why he sold a half-share to Filmer?"

"It's a she. I'll inquire." He seemed to have hesitations in his mind but he didn't explain them. "Is that all?" he said.

"My ticket?"

"Oh, yes. The travel company, Merry and Company, they'll have it. They're still sorting out who's to sleep where, since we've added you in. We'll have to tell *them* your name, of course, but all we've said so far is that we absolutely have to have another ticket and even if it looked impossible it would have to be done. They'll bring your ticket to Union Station in Toronto on Sunday morning and you can pick it up there. All the owners are picking theirs up then."

"All right."

He stood up to go. "Well, bon voyage," he said, and after a short pause added, "perhaps he won't try anything."

"Hope not."

He nodded, shook my hand, finished the last of his vodka at a gulp and left me alone with my thoughts.

The first of those was that if I were going across a whole continent by train I might as well start out as I meant to go on. If there was a train from Ottawa to Toronto I would take it instead of flying.

There was indeed a train, the hotel confirmed. Leaving at five-fifty, arriving four hours later. Dinner on board.

Ottawa had shoveled its center-of-town railway station under a rug, so to speak, as if railways should be kept out of sight like the lower orders, and built a great new station several miles away from anywhere useful. The station itself, however, proved a delight, a vast airy tent of glass set among trees with the sun flooding in with afternoon light and throwing angular shadows on the shiny black floor.

People waiting for the train had put their luggage down in

a line and gone to sit on the seats along the glass walls, and thinking it a most civilized arrangement I put my suitcase at the rear of the line and found myself a seat also. Filmer or not, I thought, I was definitely enjoying myself.

Dinner on the train was arranged as in airplanes with several stewards in shirtsleeves and deep yellow waistcoats rolling first a drinks trolley, then a food trolley down the center aisle, serving to right and left as they went. I watched them idly for quite a long time, and when they'd gone past me I couldn't remember their faces. I drank French wine as the daylight faded across the flying landscape and ate a better-than-many-airlines dinner after dark, and thought about chameleons; and at Toronto I took a cab and booked into another in the chain of the Four Seasons hotels, as I had told Bill Baudelaire I would.

In the morning, a few hundred thoughts later, I followed the hotel porter's directions and walked to the offices of the travel organizers, Merry and Company, as given in their brochure.

The street-level entrance was unimposing, the building deceptively small, but inside there seemed to be acres of space all brightly lit, with pale carpeting, blond woods and an air of absolute calm. There were some green plants, a sofa or two and a great many desks behind which quiet unhurried conversations seemed to be going on at a dozen telephones. All the telephonists faced the center of the huge room, looking out and not at the walls.

I walked to one desk whose occupant wasn't actually speaking on the wire, a purposeful-looking man with a beard who was cleaning his nails.

"Help you?" he asked economically.

I said I was looking for the person organizing the race train.

"Oh, yes. Over there. Third desk along."

I thanked him. The third desk along over there was unoccupied.

"She'll be back in a minute," comforted the second desk along. "Sit down if you like."

There were chairs, presumably for clients, on the near sides of the desks. Comfortable chairs, clients for the pampering of, I thought vaguely, sitting in one.

The empty desk had a piece of engraved plastic on it announcing its absent owner's name: Nell. A quiet voice behind me said, "Can I help you?" and I stood up politely and said, "Yes, please."

She had fair hair, gray eyes, a sort of clean look with a dust of freckles, but she was not as young, I thought, as her immediate impression, which was about eighteen.

"I came about the train," I said.

"Yes. Could you possibly compress it into five minutes? There's such a lot still to arrange." She walked round to the back of her desk and sat, looking down at an array of list upon list.

"My name is Tor Kelsey," I began.

Her head lifted fast. "Really? The Jockey Club told us your name this morning. Well, we've put you in because Bill Baudelaire said he'd cancel the whole production if we didn't." The unemphatic gray eyes assessed me, not exactly showing that she didn't think the person she saw to be worth the fuss, but pretty near. "It's the dining car that's the trouble," she said. "There are only forty-eight places. We have to have everyone seated at the same time because the mystery is acted before and after meals, and two or three of those places are taken by actors. Or are supposed to be, only now there isn't room for them either, as my boss sold too many tickets to late applicants, and you are actually number forty-nine." She stopped briefly. "I suppose that's our worry, not yours. We've given you a roomette for sleeping, and Bill Baudelaire says anything you ask for will we please let you have. We said what would you ask for and he didn't know. Maddeningly unhelpful. Do you yourself know what you want?"

"I'd like to know who the actors are, and the story they're going to enact."

"No, we can't do that. It'll spoil it for you. We never tell the passengers anything."

"Did Bill Baudelaire tell you," I asked, "why he so particularly wanted me on the train?"

"Not really." She frowned slightly. "I didn't give it much thought, I've so much else to see to. He simply insisted we take you, and since the Jockey Club is our client, we do what the client asks."

"Are you going on the train?" I asked.

"Yes, I am. There has to be someone from the company to sort out the crises."

"And how good are you at secrets?"

"I keep half a dozen before breakfast every day."

Her telephone rang quietly and she answered it in a quiet voice, adding her murmur to the hum of other murmurs all round the room. I realized that the quiet was a deliberate policy, as otherwise they would all have been shouting at the tops of their lungs and not hearing a word their callers said.

"Yes," she was saying, "out at Mimico before ten. Four dozen, yes. Load them into the special dining car. Right. Good." She put the phone down and without pause said to me, "What secret do you want kept?"

"That I'm employed by the Jockey Club . . . to deal with crises."

"Oh." It was a long sound of understanding. "All right, it's a secret." She reflected briefly. "The actors are holding a run-through right now, not far away. I've got to see them sometime today, so it may as well be at once. What do you want me to tell them?"

"I'd like you to say that your company are putting me on the train as a trouble-spotter, because a whole train of racing people is a volatile mass looking for an excuse to explode. Say it's a form of insurance."

"Which it is," she said.

"Well, yes. And I also want to solve your problem of the

forty-ninth seat. I want to go on the train as a waiter."

She didn't blink but nodded. "Yes, OK. Good idea. Quite often we put one of the actors in as a waiter, but not actually on this trip, luckily. The rail company are very helpful when we ask. I'll fix it. Come on, then, there's such a lot still to do."

She moved fast without seeming to, and presently we were skimming round corners in her small blue car, pulling up with a jerk outside the garage of a large house.

The rehearsal, if you could call it that, was actually going on in the garage itself, which held no car but a large trestle table, a lot of folding chairs, a portable gas heater and about ten men and women standing in groups.

Nell introduced me without mentioning my name. "We're taking him on the train as company eyes and ears. Anything you think might turn into trouble, tell him or me. He's going as a service attendant, which will mean he can move everywhere through the train without question. OK? Don't tell the paying passengers he's one of us."

They shook their heads. Keeping the true facts from the passengers was their daily occupation.

"OK," Nell said to me. "I'll leave you here. Phone me later." She put a large envelope she was carrying onto the table, waved to the actors and vanished, and one of them, a man of about my own age with a mop-head of tight, light brown curls, came forward, shook my hand and said, "She's the best in the business. My name's David Flynn, by the way, but call me Zak. That's my name in the mystery. From now on we call each other by the mystery names, so as not to make mistakes in front of the passengers. You'd better have an acting name, too. How about . . . um . . . Tommy?"

"It's all right by me."

"Right, everybody, this is Tommy, a waiter."

They nodded, smiling, and I was introduced to them one by one in the names they would use on the train.

"Mavis and Walter Bricknell, racehorse owners." They

were middle-aged, dressed like the others in jeans and casual sweaters. "They're married in real life too."

David/Zak went briskly along the row, an enormously positive person, wasting no time. "Ricky, a groom in the mystery, though he'll be traveling with the racegoers, not the grooms. His part in the mystery finishes at Winnipeg, and he'll be getting off there. This is Raoul, racehorse trainer for the Bricknells, their guest on the train. Ben, he's an old groom who has ridden a few races." Ben grinned from a small, deeply lined face, looking the part. "This is Giles: don't be taken in by his good looks, he's our murderer. This is Angelica, whom you won't see much of as she's the first victim. And Pierre, he's a compulsive gambler in love with the Bricknells' daughter, Donna, and this is Donna. And last, this is James Winterbourne, he's a big noise in the Ontario Jockey Club."

I don't think I jumped. The big name in the Ontario Jockey Club wore a three-day beard and a red trilby hat, which he lifted to me ceremoniously. "Alas," he said, "I'm not traveling. My part ends with giving the train an official blessing. Too bad."

David/Zak said to me, "We're walking through the first scene now. Everyone knows what to do. This is Union Station. This is the gathering point for the passengers. They're all here. Right, guys, off we go."

Mavis and Walter said, "We're chatting to other passengers about the trip."

Pierre and Donna said, "We're having a quiet row."

Giles said, "I'm being nice to the passengers."

Angelica: "I am looking for someone called Steve. I ask the passengers if they've seen him. He is supposed to be traveling, but he hasn't turned up."

Raoul said, "I put my two cents' worth into Pierre and Donna's quarrel as I want to break them up so I can marry her myself. For her father's money, of course."

Pierre said, "Which I furiously point out."

Donna: "Which I don't like, and am near to tears."

Ben: "I ask Raoul for a handout, which I don't get. I tell a lot of people he's stingy, after I worked for him all those years. The passengers are to find me a nuisance. I tell them I'm traveling on the racegoers' part of the train."

James Winterbourne said, "I ask for attention and tell everybody that we have horses, grooms, racegoers and all you owners and friends on the train. I hope everyone will have a great time on this historic re-enactment, etcetera, etcetera, for the glory of Canadian racing."

Ricky said, "I arrive. One of the station staff—who will be Jimmy (not here now) in staff uniform—tries to stop me, but I run in among the passengers, bleeding all over the place, shouting that some thugs tried to hijack one of the horses off the train, but I shouted and the maintenance men in the loading yard chased them away. I think the owners should know."

Zak said, "Jimmy runs off to fetch me and I stride in and tell everyone not to be worried, all the horses are safe and on the train, but to make sure things are all right in the future I will go on the train myself. I am the top security agent for the railway." He looked round the company. "All right so far? Then James Winterbourne calms everyone down and tells them to board the train at Gate Six, Track Seven. I'll check that that's still right, on Sunday morning, but that's what we've been told so far."

The Bricknells said, "We ask you which horse they were trying to hijack, but you don't know. We try to find Ricky, to ask him. He's not our groom, but we are always anxious sort of people."

"Right," Zak said. "So we all board. It'll take a good half hour. Ricky gets bandaged by Nell in plain view, beside the train. The train leaves at twelve. Then everyone gathers shortly afterward in the dining room for champagne. We do scene two next, just before lunch."

They "walked through" scene two, which was shorter and chiefly established Zak as being in charge, and had Ricky coming to say that he didn't know which of the horses the horsenappers had been making for . . . they had come into the horse car wearing masks, brandishing clubs . . . Ricky had been alone out there in the loading yard as all the other grooms had gone back to the station's coffee shop.

The Bricknells were atwitter. Angelica was distraught that Steve hadn't turned up. Who cared about a horse, where was Steve.

Who was Steve? Zak asked. Angelica said he was her business manager. What business? Zak asked. None of yours, Angelica tartly said.

"Right," Zak said, "about now it has dawned on the thickest passenger that this is all fiction. They'll be smiling. So lunch is next. Everyone gets the afternoon to relax. Our next scene is during drinks before dinner. That's the one we rehearsed before Nell came. Right. We may have to change things a bit as we go along, so we'll do the rest of the final walk-throughs in one of the bedrooms, a day at a time."

The others thought this reasonable and began to put on their coats.

"Don't you have a script?" I asked Zak.

"Not formal words to learn, if that's what you mean. No. We all know what we've got to establish in each scene, and we improvise. When we plan a mystery, the actors get a brief outline of what's going to happen and basically what sort of people they are, then they invent their own imaginary life stories, so that if any passenger asks questions in conversation, they have the answers ready. I'd advise you to do it too. Invent a background, a childhood. As near as possible to the real thing is always easiest."

"Thanks for the tip," I said. "Will you let me know your plans each day, and also tell me instantly if anything odd happens you don't expect? Even small things, really."

"Yes, sure. Ask Nell, too. She knows the story. And there are some actors who weren't here today because they don't get activated until later on the trip. They're on the passenger list. Nell will point them out."

He stifled a yawn and looked suddenly very tired, a complete contrast to two minutes earlier, and I suspected he was one of those people who could turn energy on and off like a tap. One of Aunt Viv's best friends had been an elderly actor who could walk down to the theater like a tired old pensioner and go out on the stage and make the audience's hair stand on end with his power.

David Flynn, offering me a lift if I needed one, was beginning to move with a sort of lassitude that one would never have seen in Zak. He picked up Nell's large envelope, opened it and distributed its contents to the others: luggage labels saying "Merry and Company" and photocopied sheets of "Information and Advice to Passengers."

Scene dressing, I supposed. I asked him if he would be going anywhere near the Merry and Company office and he said he would detour that way and was as good as his word.

"Do you do this all the time?" I asked on the way.

"Act, do you mean? Or mysteries?"

"Either."

"Anything I'm offered," he said frankly. "Plays. Commercials. Bit parts in series. But I do mostly mysteries now that they're so popular, and nearly all for Merry and Company. I write the stories to suit the occasion. I was engaged for a doctors' convention last week, so we did a medical crime. Just now it's racing. Next month I've got to think up something for a fishing club weekend train trip to Halifax. It keeps me employed. It pays the bills. It's quite good fun. It's not Stratford-upon-Avon."

"What about the other actors?" I asked. "The ones in the garage."

"Much the same. It's work. They like the train trips, even if it does mean shouting all the scenes against the wheel noise when we're going along, because the dining cars are so long. Not by any means the right shape for a stage. We don't always use the same actors, it depends on the characters, but they're all friendly, we never take anyone who can't get along. It's essential to be tolerant and generous, to make our sort of improvisation work."

"I'd no idea mysteries were such an industry."

He gave me a small sideways smile. "They have a lot in England too, these days."

"Um . . ." I said, as he braked to a halt outside the Merry and Company offices. "How English do I sound to you?"

"Very. An educated Englishman in an expensive suit."

"Well, the original plan was for me to go on the train as a wealthy owner. What would you think of my accent if I were dressed as a waiter in a deep yellow waistcoat?"

"Harvest gold, that's what they call that color," he said thoughtfully. "I wouldn't notice your accent so much, perhaps. There are thousands of English immigrants in this country, after all. You'll get by all right, I should think."

I thanked him for the lift and got out of the car. He yawned and turned that into a laugh, but I reckoned the tiredness was real. "See you Sunday, Tommy," he said, and I dryly said, "Sure thing, Zak." He drove away with a smile and I went into the Merry and Company office where the earlier calm had broken up into loud frenetic activity on several telephones.

"How *could* twenty-five of our bikers all burst their tires at once?"

"They won't reach Nuits St. George tonight."

"Any suggestions for alternative hotels?"

"Where do we *find* fifty new tires, assorted, in France? They've cut them to ribbons, they say."

"It was sabotage. It has to be."

"They rode over a cattle-grid that had spikes on it."

Nell was sitting at her desk talking on her telephone, one hand pressed to her free ear to block out the clamor.

"Why didn't the fools pick up their bikes and walk across?"

"Nobody told them. It was a new grid. Where *is* Nuits St. George? Can't we get a bus to go and pick up the bikes? What bus company do we use in that part of France?"

"Why isn't our French office dealing with all this?"

I sat on Nell's client chair and waited. The hubbub subsided: the crisis was sorted. Somewhere in Burgundy, the bikers would be transported to their dinners on sturdier wheels, and new tires would be found in the morning.

Nell put her receiver down.

"You arrange cycling tours?" I said.

"Sure. And trips up Everest. Not me personally, I do mysteries. Do you need something?"

"Instructions."

"Oh, yes. I talked to VIA. No problems."

VIA Rail, I had discovered, was the company that operated Canada's passenger trains, which didn't mean that it owned the rails or the stations. Nothing was simple on the railways.

"VIA," Nell said, "are expecting you to turn up at Union Station tomorrow morning at ten to get fitted for a uniform. Here's who you ask for." She passed me a slip of paper. "They've got hand-picked service people going on this trip, and they'll show you what to do when you meet them at the station on Sunday morning. You'll board the train with them."

"What time?" I asked.

"The train comes into the station soon after eleven. The chefs and crew board soon after. Passengers board at eleven-thirty, after the reception in the station itself. The train leaves at twelve. That's thirty-five minutes earlier than the regular daily train, the Canadian, which will be on our heels as far as Winnipeg."

"And the horses will have boarded, I gather, out in a loading area."

"Yes, at Mimico, about six miles away. That's where they do maintenance and cleaning and put the trains together. Everything will be loaded there. Food, wine, flowers, everything for the owners."

"And the grooms?"

"No, not them. They're being shipped back to the station by bus after they've settled the horses in. And you might like to know we've another addition to the train, a cousin of our boss, name of Leslie Brown, who's going as horse-master, to oversee the horses and the grooms and keep everything up that end in good order."

"Which end?"

"Behind the engine. Apparently horses travel better there. No swaying."

While she was talking she was sorting postcards into piles: postcards with names and numbers on them.

"Do you have a plan of the train?" I asked.

She glanced up briefly and didn't exactly say I was a thundering nuisance, but looked as if she thought it. Still, she shuffled through a pile of papers, pulled out a single sheet and pushed it across the desk toward me.

"This is what we've asked for, and what they say we'll get, but the people out at Mimico sometimes change things," she said.

I picked up the paper and found it was written in a column.

	Engine.		
	Generator/boiler.		
	Baggage car.		
	Horse car		
	Grooms/sleeping.		
	Grooms/dining/dome.		
(Racegoers)	Sleeping.		
"	Sleeping.		
"	Sleeping.		
"	Dayniter.		
"	Dining.		
(Owners)	Sleeping.	(Green)	26.
"	Sleeping.	(Manor)	24.
"	Sleeping.	(Mount)	16.
"	Special dining.		
"	Dome car.	(Park)	8.
"	Private car.		4.
			78, if full.

(Owners includes actors, Company and VIA executives, chefs and service crew, most in Green.)

"Do you have a plan of who sleeps where?" I asked.

For answer she shuffled through the same pile as before and gave me two sheets stapled together. I looked first, as one does, for my own name, and found it.

She had given me a room—a roomette—that was right next door to Filmer.

5

I walked back to the hotel and at two o'clock local time telephoned to England, reckoning that seven o'clock Friday evening was perhaps a good time to catch Brigadier Catto relaxing in his Newmarket house after a busy week in London. I was lucky to catch him, he said, and he had news for me.

"Remember Horfitz's messenger who gave the briefcase to Filmer at Nottingham?" he asked.

"I sure do."

"John Millington has identified him from your photographs. He is Ivor Horfitz's son, Jason. He's not bright, so they say. Not up to much more than running errands. Delivering briefcases would be just about his mark."

"And he got that wrong, too, according to his father."

"Well, there you are. It doesn't get us anywhere much, but that's who he is. John Millington has issued photos to all the ring inspectors, so that if they see him they'll report it. If Horfitz plans on using his son as an on-course errand boy regularly, we'll make sure he knows we're watching."

"He'd do better to find someone else."

"A nasty thought." He paused briefly. "How are you doing, your end?"

"I haven't seen Filmer yet. He's staying tomorrow night

at a hotel with most of the owners' group, according to the travel company's lists. Presumably he'll be at the official lunch with the Ontario Jockey Club at Woodbine tomorrow. I'll go to the races, but probably not to the lunch. I'll see what he's doing, as best I can." I told him about Bill Baudelaire's mother, and said, "After we've started off on the train, if you want to get hold of me direct, leave a message with her, and I'll telephone back to you or John Millington as soon as I'm able."

"It's a bit hit or miss," he grumbled, repeating the number after I'd dictated it.

"She's an invalid," I added, and laughed to myself at his reaction.

When he'd stopped spluttering, he said, "Tor, this is impossible."

"Well, I don't know. It's an open line of communication, after all. Better to have one than not. And Bill Baudelaire suggested it himself. He must know she's capable."

"All right then. Better than nothing." He didn't sound too sure, though, and who could blame him. Brigade commanders weren't accustomed to bedridden grandmothers manning field telephones. "I'll be here at home on Sunday," he said. "Get through to me, will you, for last-minute gen both ways, before you board?"

"Yes, certainly."

"You sound altogether," he said with a touch of disapproval, "suspiciously happy."

"Oh! Well, this train looks like being good fun."

"That's not what you're there for."

"I'll do my best not to enjoy it."

"Insubordination will get you a firing squad," he said firmly, and put down his receiver forthwith.

I put my own receiver down more slowly and the bell rang again immediately.

"This is Bill Baudelaire," my caller said in his deep-down voice. "So you arrived in Toronto all right?"

"Yes, thank you."

"I've got the information you asked for about Laurentide Ice. About why his owner sold a half-share."

"Oh, good."

"I don't know that it is, very. In fact, not good at all. Apparently Filmer was over here in Canada at the end of last week inquiring of several owners who had horses booked on the train if they would sell. One of them mentioned it to me this morning and now I've talked to the others. He offered a fair price for a half-share, they all say. Or a third-share. Any toehold, it seems. I would say he methodically worked down the list until he came to Daffodil Quentin."

"Who?"

"The owner of Laurentide Ice."

"Why is it bad news?" I asked, taking the question from the disillusionment in his voice.

"You'll meet her. You'll see," he said cryptically.

"Can't you tell me?"

He sighed audibly. "Her husband, Hal Quentin, was a good friend of Canadian racing, but he died this time last year and left his string of horses to his wife. Three of them so far have died in accidents since then, with Mrs. Quentin collecting the insurance."

"Three!" I said. "In a year?"

"Exactly. They've all been investigated but they all seem genuine. Mrs. Quentin says it's a dreadful coincidence and she is most upset."

"She would be," I said dryly.

"Anyway, that is who has sold a half-share to Julius Filmer. What a pair! I phoned just now and asked her about the sale. She said it suited her to sell, and there was no reason not to. She says she is going to have a ball on the train." He sounded most gloomy, himself.

"Look on the bright side," I said. "If she's sold a half-share she can't be planning to push Laurentide Ice off the train at high speed for the insurance."

"That's a scurrilous statement." He was not shocked, however. "Will you be at Woodbine tomorrow?"

"Yes, but not at the lunch."

"All right. If we bump into each other, of course it will be as strangers."

"Of course," I agreed; and we said goodbyes and disconnected.

Daffodil Quentin, I reflected, settling the receiver in its cradle, had at least not been intimidated into selling. No one on the business end of Filmer's threats could be looking forward to having a ball in his company. It did appear that in order to get himself on the train as an owner, he had been prepared to spend actual money. He had been prepared to fly to Canada to effect the sale, and to return to England to collect the briefcase from Horfitz at Nottingham on Tuesday, and to fly back to Canada, presumably, in time for tomorrow's races.

I wondered where he was at that moment. I wondered what he was thinking, hatching, setting in motion. It was comforting to think that he didn't know I existed.

———

I spent the rest of the afternoon doing some shopping and walking and taxi-riding around, getting reacquainted with one of the most visually entertaining cities in the world. I'd found it architecturally exciting six years earlier, and it seemed to me now not less but more so, with glimpses of its slender tallest-in-the-world free-standing tower with the onion bulge near its top appearing tantalizingly between angular high-rises covered with black glass and gold. And they had built a whole new complex, Harbourfront, since I'd been there, a new face turned to Lake Ontario and the world.

At six, having left my purchases at the hotel, I went back to Merry and Company's warm pale office and found many of the gang still working. Nell, at her desk, naturally on the telephone, pointed mutely to her client chair, and I sat there and waited.

Some of the murmurers were putting on coats, yawning,

switching off computers, taking cans of cold drinks out of the large refrigerator and opening them with the carbonation hisssing. Someone put out a light or two. The green plants looked exhausted. Friday night; all commercial passion spent. Thank God for Fridays.

"I have to come in here tomorrow," Nell said with resignation, catching my thought. "And why I ever said I'd have dinner with you tonight I cannot imagine."

"You promised."

"I must have been mad."

I'd asked her after she'd shown me the train's sleeping arrangements (which perhaps had been my subconscious making jumps unbeknown to me) and she'd said "Yes, all right, I have to eat," and that had seemed a firm enough commitment.

"Are you ready?" I asked.

"No, there are two more people I positively must talk to. Can you wait?"

"I'm quite good at it," I said equably.

A few more lights went out. Some of those remaining shone on Nell's fair hair, made shadows of her eyes and put hollows in her cheeks. I wondered about her, as one does. An attractive stranger; an unread book; a beginning, perhaps. But there had been other beginnings, in other cities, and I'd long outgrown the need to hurry. I might never yet have come to the conventional ending, but the present was greatly OK, and as for the future . . . we would see.

I listened without concentration to her talking to someone called Lorrimore. "Yes, Mr. Lorrimore, your flowers and your bar bottles will already be on the train when it comes into the station. . . . And the fruit, yes, that too. . . . The passengers are gathering at ten-thirty for the reception at the station. . . . Yes, we board at eleven-thirty and leave at twelve. . . . We're looking forward to meeting you too. . . . Goodbye, Mr. Lorrimore." She glanced over at me as she began to dial her next number, and said, "The Lorrimores have the private car, the last car on the train. Hello, is that Vancouver racecourse?"

I listened to her discussing entry arrangements for the owners. "Yes, we're issuing them all with the special club passes . . . and yes, the other passengers from the train will be paying for themselves individually, but we're offering them group transport . . ." She put down the receiver eventually and sighed. "We've been asked to fix moderate-price hotels and bus transport for so many of the racegoers that it's like duplicating the whole tour. Could you wait for just one more call or two?"

We left the darkened office almost an hour later and even then she was still checking things off in her mind and muttering vaguely about not forgetting scissors and clips to go with the bandages for Ricky. We walked not very far to a restaurant called the Fluted Point People that she'd been to before and whose menu I had prospected earlier. Not very large, it had tables crammed into every cranny, each dimly lit by a candle lantern.

"Who are the Fluted Point People," I asked, "in general?"

"Heaven knows," Nell said.

The waiter, who must have been asked a thousand times, said the fluted point people had lived on this land ten thousand years ago. Let's not worry about them, he said.

Nell laughed and I thought of ten thousand years and wondered who would be living on this land ten thousand years ahead. Fluted points, it transpired, described the stone tools in use over most of the continent: would our descendants call us the knife and fork people?

"I don't honestly care," Nell said, to those questions. "I'm hungry right now in Toronto today."

We did something about that in the shape of deviled smoked salmon followed by roast quail. "I hope this is all on your expense account," she said without anxiety as I ordered some wine, and I said, "Yes, of course," untruthfully and thought there was no point in having money if one didn't enjoy it. "Hamburgers tomorrow," I said, "to make up for it."

Nell nodded as if that were a normal bargain she well understood and said with a galvanic jump that she had forgotten to order a special limousine to drive the Lorrimores around at Winnipeg.

"Do it tomorrow," I said. "They won't run away."

She looked at me with a worried frown of indecision, and then round the comfortable little candlelit restaurant, and then at the shining glass and silver on the table and then back at me, and the frown dissolved into a smile of self-amusement.

"All right. Tomorrow. The Lorrimores may be the icing on this cake but they've meant a lot of extra work."

"Who are the Lorrimores?" I asked.

She looked at me blankly and answered obliquely, "Where do you live?"

"Ah," I said. "If I lived here, I would know the Lorrimores?"

"You certainly wouldn't ask who they are."

"I live in London," I said. "So please tell me."

She was wearing, as so many women in business tended to, a navy suit and white blouse of such stark simplicity as to raise questions about the warmth of the soul. Women who dressed more softly, I thought inconsequentially, must feel more secure in themselves, perhaps.

"The Lorrimores," Nell said, showing no insecurity, "are one of the very richest families of Toronto. Of Ontario. Of Canada, in fact. They are the society magazines' staple diet. They are into banking and good works. They own mansions, endow art museums, open charity balls and entertain heads of state. There are quite a few of them, brothers, sisters and so on, and I'm told that in certain circles, if Mercer Lorrimore accepts an invitation and comes to your house, you are made for life." She paused, smiling. "Also he owns great racehorses, is naturally a pillar of the Ontario Jockey Club and has this private rail car that used to be borrowed regularly by campaigning politicians." She paused again for breath. "That's who's honoring our train—Mercer Lorrimore, the big chief of the whole clan, also Bambi, his wife, and their son Sheridan and their daughter Xanthe. What have I left out?"

I laughed. "Do you curtsy?"

"Pretty nearly. Well, to be honest, Mercer Lorrimore sounds quite nice on the telephone but I haven't met him yet or any of the others. And he phones me himself. No secretaries."

"So," I said, "if Mercer Lorrimore is on the train it will be even more in the news from coast to coast?"

She nodded. "He's going For the Benefit of Canadian Racing in capital letters on the Jockey Club's PR handout."

"And is he eating in the dining car?" I asked.

"Don't!" She rolled her eyes in mock horror. "He is supposed to be. They all are. But we don't know if they'll retreat into privacy. If they stay in their own car there might just be enough room for everyone else to sit down. It's a shambles in the making, though, and it was made by my boss selling extra tickets himself when he knew we were full." She shook her head over it, but with definite indulgence. The boss, it appeared, ranked high in her liking.

"Who did he sell them to?" I asked.

"Just people. Two friends of his. And a Mr. Filmer, who offered to pay double when he found there was no room. No one turns down an extra profit of that sort." She broke open a roll with the energy of frustration. "If only there was more room in the dining car, we could have sold at least six more tickets."

"David . . . er . . . Zak was saying the forty-eight–seater was already stretching the actors' vocal cords to the limit against the noise of the wheels on the rails."

"It's always a problem." She considered me over the candle flame. "Are you married?" she said.

"No. Are you?"

"Actually, no." Her voice was very faintly defensive, but

her mouth was smiling. "I invested in a relationship that didn't work out."

"And which was some time ago?"

"Long enough for me to be over it."

The exchange cleared the ground, I thought, and maybe set the rules. She wasn't looking for another relationship that was going nowhere. But dalliance? Have to see.

"What are you thinking?" she asked.

"About life in general."

She gave me a dry look of disbelief but changed the subject back to the almost as compelling matter of trains, and after a while I asked her the question I'd had vaguely in my mind all day.

"Besides the special passes for the races, and so on," I said, "is there anything else an owner of a horse is entitled to? An owner, that is to say, of one of the horses traveling on the train?"

She was puzzled. "How do you mean?"

"Are they entitled to any privileges that the other people in the special dining car don't have?"

"I don't think so." Her brow wrinkled briefly. "Only that they can visit the horse car, if that's what you mean."

"Yes, I know about that. So there's nothing else?"

"Well, the racecourse at Winnipeg is planning a group photograph of owners only, and there's television coverage of that." She pondered. "They're each getting a commemorative plaque from the Jockey Club when we get back on the train at Banff after the days in the mountains." She paused again. "And if a horse that's actually on the train wins one of the special races, the owner gets free life membership of the clubs at all three racecourses."

The last was a sizeable carrot to a Canadian, perhaps, but not enough on its own, surely, to attract Filmer. I sighed briefly. Another good idea down the drain. So I was left with the two basic questions, why was Filmer on the train, and why had he worked so hard to be an owner? And the answers were still I don't know and I don't know. Highly helpful.

We drank coffee, dawdling, easy together, and she said she had wanted to be a writer and had found a job with a publisher ("which real writers never do, I found out") but was very much happier with Merry and Company, arranging mysteries.

She said, "My parents always told me practically from birth that I'd be a writer, that it ran in the family, and I grew up expecting it, but they were wrong, though I tried for a long time, and then I was also living with this man who sort of bullied me to write. But, you know, it was such a *relief* the day I said to myself, some time after we'd parted and I'd dried my eyes, that I was not really a writer and never would be and I'd much rather do something else. And suddenly I was liberated and happier than I could remember. It seems so stupid, looking back, that it took me so long to know myself. I was in a way brainwashed into writing, and I thought I wanted it myself, but I wasn't good enough when it came to the point, and it was such hard work, and I was depressed so much of the time." She half-laughed. "You must think I'm crazy."

"Of course not. What did you write?"

"I was writing for a woman's weekly magazine for a while, going to interview people and writing up their lives, and making up lives altogether sometimes if I couldn't find anyone interesting or lurid enough that week. Don't let's talk about it. It was awful."

"I'm glad you escaped."

"Yes, so am I," she said with feeling. "I look different, I feel different, and I'm much healthier. I was always getting colds and flu and feeling ill, and now I don't." Her eyes sparkled in the light, proving her right. "And you," she said, "you're the same. Lighthearted. It shows all over you."

"Does it, indeed?"

"Am I right?"

"On the button, I suppose."

And we were lucky, I thought soberly, paying the bill. Lightheartedness was a treasure in a world too full of sorrows, a treasure little regarded and widely forfeited to aggression, greed and horrendous tribal rituals. I wondered if the fluted point people had been lighthearted ten thousand years ago. But probably not.

Nell and I walked back to where she had parked her car near the office: she lived twenty minutes' drive away, she said, in a very small apartment by the lake.

To say goodnight we kissed cheeks and she thanked me for the evening, saying cheerfully that she would see me on Sunday if she didn't sink without trace under all the things she still had to do. I watched her taillights recede until she turned a corner, then I walked back to the hotel, slept an untroubled night, and presented myself next morning at ten sharp in the Public Affairs office, at Union Station.

The Public Affairs officer, a formidably efficient lady, had gathered from Nell that I was one of the actors, as they had helped with actors before, and I didn't change that understanding. She wheeled me back into the cavernous Great Hall of the station (which she briskly said was 250 feet long, 84 feet wide and had a tiled arched ceiling 88 feet above the floor) and led me through a heavy door into an undecorated downstairs duplication of the grandeur upstairs, a seemingly endless basic domain where people did the trains' laundry and food and odd jobs. There was a mini power station also, and painting and carpentering going on all over the place.

"This way," she said, clattering ahead on snapping heels. "Here is the uniform center. They'll see to you." She pushed open a door to let me through, said briefly, "Here's the actor," to the staff inside, and with a nod abandoned me to fate.

The staff inside were good-natured and equally efficient. One was working a sewing machine, another a computer and a third asked me what size collar I took.

There were shelves all round the room bearing hundreds of folded shirts of fine light gray and white vertical stripes, with striped collars, long striped sleeves and buttoned cuffs. "The cuffs must remain buttoned at all times unless you are washing dishes."

Catch me, I thought mildly, washing dishes.

There were two racks of the harvest-gold waistcoats on hangers. "All the buttons must be fastened at all times."

There were row on row of mid-gray trousers and mid-gray jackets tidily hung, and boxes galore of gray, yellow and maroon striped ties.

My helper was careful that everything he gave me should fit perfectly. "VIA Rail staff at all times are well turned out and spotlessly clean. We give everyone tips on how to care for the clothes."

He gave me a gray jacket, two pairs of gray trousers, five shirts, two waistcoats (which of course he called vests), two ties and a gray raincoat to go over all, and as he passed each garment as suitable he called out the size to the man with the computer. "We know the sizes of every VIA employee right across Canada."

I looked at myself in the glass in my shirtsleeves and yellow waistcoat, and the waiter Tommy looked back. I smiled at my reflection. Tommy looked altogether too pleased with himself, I thought.

"Comfortable?" my helper asked.

"Very."

"Don't vary the uniform at all," he said. "Any variation would mark you out straightaway as an actor."

"Thank you."

"This uniform," he said, "trousers, shirt, tie and vest, is worn by all male service attendants and assistant service attendants when on duty. That's to say, the sleeping car attendants and the dining car staff, except that sometimes they wear aprons in the dining car."

"Thank you," I said again.

"The chief service attendant, who is in charge of the dining car, wears a gray suit, not a vest or an apron. That's how you'll know him."

"Right."

He smiled. "They'll teach you what to do. Now, we'll lend you a locker for these clothes until Sunday morning. Collect the clothes and put them on in the changing room here before boarding, and take your own clothes with you onto the train. When you've finished with the VIA uniform, please see that we get it back."

"Right," I said again.

When I'd put my own clothes on once more, he took me along a few passages into a room with ultra-narrow lockers into which Tommy's clothes barely slotted. He locked the metal door, gave me the key, showed me the way back into the Great Hall and smiled briefly.

"Good luck," he said. "Don't spill anything."

"Thank you," I said, "very much."

———

I went back to the hotel and had them arrange a car with a driver to take me to Woodbine, wait through the afternoon and bring me back. No trouble at all, they said, so as it was a nice bright autumn day with no forecast of rain I curled my hair and put on some sunglasses and a Scandinavian patterned sweater to merge into the crowd at the races.

It actually isn't easy to remember a stranger's face after a fleeting meeting unless one has a special reason for doing so, or unless there is something wholly distinctive about it, and I was reasonably certain no one going on the train would know me again even if I inadvertently stood next to him on the stands. I had spectacular proof of this, in fact, almost as soon as I'd paid my way into the paddock, because Bill Baudelaire was standing nearby, watching the throng coming in, and his eyes paused on me for a brief second and slid away. With his carroty hair and the acne scars, I thought, *he* would have trouble getting lost in a crowd.

I walked over to him and said, "Could you tell me the time, sir, please?"

He glanced at his watch but hardly at me and said, "One-twenty-five," in his gravelly voice, and looked over my shoulder toward the gate.

"Thank you," I said. "I'm Tor Kelsey."

His gaze sharpened abruptly on my face and he almost laughed.

"When Val told me about this I scarcely believed him."

"Is Filmer here?" I asked.

"Yes. He arrived for the lunch."

"OK," I said. "Thanks again." I nodded and walked on past him and bought a race-card, and when in a moment or two I looked back, he had gone.

The racecourse was packed with people and there were banners everywhere announcing that this was the opening event of The Great Transcontinental Mystery Race Train's journey. Race Train Day, they economically said. There was a splendid color photograph of a train crossing a prairie on the race-card's cover. There were stalls selling red and white Race Train T-shirts, with a horse face to face with a locomotive across the chest. There were Race Train flags and scarves and baseball caps; and a scatter of young ladies with Support Canadian Racing sashes across their bosoms were handing out information leaflets. The PR firm, I thought with amusement, were leaving no one in any doubt.

I didn't see Filmer until just before the Race Train's special race, which had been named without subtlety The Jockey Club Race Train Stakes at Woodbine. I'd spent some of the afternoon reading the information in the race-card about the owners and their horses and had seen that whereas all the owners were on the train's passenger list, none of the horses were. We would be taking fresh animals to Winnipeg and Vancouver.

Filmer wasn't on the race-card as an owner, but Mrs. Daffodil Quentin was, and when she came down to see the saddling of her runner, Filmer was with her, assiduous and smiling.

Daffodil Quentin had a big puffball hair arrangement of

blond curls above a middle-aged face with intense shiny red lipstick. She wore a black dress with a striped chinchilla coat over it: too much fur, I briefly thought, for the warmth of the afternoon sun.

There was hardly time to identify all the other owners as the prerace formalities were over much more quickly than in England, but I did particularly look for and sort out Mercer Lorrimore.

Mercer Lorrimore, darling of the glossy mags, was running two horses in the race, giving it his loyal support. He was a man of average height, average build, average weight, and was distinguishable chiefly because of his well-cut, well-brushed full head of white hair. His expression looked reasonable and pleasant, and he was being nice to his trainer.

Beside him was a thin well-groomed woman whom I supposed to be his wife, Bambi; and in attendance were a supercilious-looking young man and a sulking teenage girl. Son and daughter, Sheridan and Xanthe, no doubt.

The jockeys were thrown up like rainbow thistledown onto the tiny saddles and let their skinny bodies move to the fluid rhythm of the walking thoroughbreds. Out on the track with the horses' gait breaking into a trot or canter they would be more comfortable standing up in the stirrups to let the bumpier rhythms flow beneath them, but on the way out from the parade ring they swayed languorously like a camel train. I loved to watch them: never grew tired of it. I loved the big beautiful animals with their tiny brains and their overwhelming instincts and I'd always, all over the world, felt at home tending them, riding them and watching them wake up and perform.

The Lorrimore colors were truly Canadian, bright red and white like the maple-leaf flag. Daffodil Quentin's colors weren't daffodil yellow but pale blue and dark green, a lot more subdued than the lady.

She and Filmer and all the other owners disappeared upstairs behind glass to watch the race, and I went down toward the track to wait and watch from near where the lucky owner would come down to greet his winner.

There were fourteen runners for the mile-and-a-half race and I knew nothing about the form of any of them except for the information on the race-card. In England I knew the current scene like a magnified city map, knew the thoroughfares, the back alleys, the small turnings. Knew whom people knew, whom they would turn to and turn away from, whom they lusted after. In Canada, I was without radar and felt blind.

The Race Train Stakes at Woodbine, turning out to be hot enough in the homestretch to delight the Ontario Jockey Club's heart, was greeted with roars and screams of encouragement from the stands. Lorrimore's scarlet-and-white favorite was beaten in the last stride by a streak in pale blue and dark green and a good many of the cheers turned to groans.

Daffodil Quentin came down and passed close by me in clouds of chinchilla, excitement and a musky scent. She preened coquettishly, receiving compliments and the trophy, and Filmer, ever at her side, gallantly kissed her hand.

A let-off murderer, I thought, kissing an unproven insurance swindler. How very nice. Television cameras whirred and flash photographers outdid the sun.

I caught sight of Bill Baudelaire scowling, and I knew what John Millington would have said.

It was enough to make you sick.

6

On Saturday evening and early Sunday morning I packed two bags, the new suitcase from England and a softer holdall bought in Toronto.

Into the first I put the rich young owner's suit, cashmere pullover and snowy shirts and into the second, the new younger-looking clothes for off-duty Tommy, jeans, sweatshirts, woolly hat and trainers. I packed the Scandinavian jersey I'd worn at Woodbine into the suitcase just in case it jogged anyone's memory, and got dressed in dark trousers, open-necked shirt and a short zipped navy jacket with lighter blue bands round waist and wrists.

The rich young owner's expensive brown shoes went away. Tommy, following instructions from the uniform department, had shiny new black ones, with black socks.

Into Tommy's holdall went the binoculars-camera and the hair curler (one never knew), and I had the cigarette lighter camera as always in my pocket. Tommy also had the rich young owner's razor and toothbrush, along with his underclothes, pajamas and stock of fresh film. The suitcase, which held my passport, had a Merry and Company label on it addressed to the Vancouver Four Seasons Hotel; the holdall had no identification at all.

With everything ready I telephoned Brigadier Catto in

England and told him about Daffodil Quentin and the touching little scene in the winners' circle.

"Damn!" he said. "Why does that sort of thing always happen? Absolutely the wrong person winning."

"The general public didn't seem to mind. The horse was third favorite, quite well backed. Daffodil Quentin seems to be acceptable to the other owners, who of course probably don't know about her three dead horses. They're bound to take to Filmer too, you know how civilized he can seem, and I don't suppose news of the trial got much attention here since it collapsed almost before it began. Anyway, Filmer and Daffodil left the races together in what looked like her own car, with a chauffeur."

"Pity you couldn't follow them."

"Well, I did actually, in a hired car. They went to the hotel, where Filmer and the other owners from the train are staying, and they went into the bar for a drink. After that, Daffodil left in her Rolls and Filmer went upstairs. Nothing of note. He looked relaxed."

The Brigadier said, "You're sure they didn't spot you at the hotel?"

"Quite sure. The entrance hall of the hotel was as big as a railway station itself. There were dozens of people sitting around waiting for other people. It was easy."

It had even been easy following them from the racecourse, as when I went out to where my driver had parked his car I had a clear view from a distance of Daffodil at the exit gate being spooned into a royal-blue Rolls-Royce by Filmer and her chauffeur. My driver, with raised eyebrows but without spoken question, agreed to keep the Rolls in sight for as long as possible, which he did without trouble all the way back to the city. At the hotel I paid him in cash with a bonus and sent him on his way, and was in time to see Filmer's back view receding into a dark-looking bar as I walked into the big central hall lobby.

It had been an exercise without much in the way of results, but then many of my days were like that, and it was only by knowing the normal that the abnormal, when it happened, could be spotted.

"Would you mind telling me," I said diffidently to the Brigadier, "whether Filmer has made a positive threat to disrupt this train?"

There was a silence, then, "Why do you ask?"

"Something Bill Baudelaire said."

After a pause he answered, "Filmer didn't directly threaten the train. He said the world's racing authorities could threaten him all they liked but he would find a spanner to throw into their international works, and they'd regret it."

"When did he say that?" I asked. "And who to?"

"Well ... er ..." He hesitated and sighed. "Things go wrong, you know. After the acquittal, the Disciplinary Committee of the Jockey Club called Filmer to Portman Square to warn him as to his future behavior, and Filmer said they couldn't touch him, and was generally unbearably arrogant. As a result, one of the committee lost his temper and told Filmer he was the scum of the earth and no one in racing would sleep well until he was warned off, which was the number-one priority of the world's racing authorities."

"That's a bit of an exaggeration," I commented, sighing in my turn. "I suppose you were there?"

"Yes. You could have cut the fury on both sides with a knife. Very vicious, all of it."

"So," I said regretfully, "Filmer might indeed see the train as a target."

"He might."

The trouble and expense he had gone to get himself on board looked increasingly ominous, I thought.

"There's one other thing you might care to know," the Brigadier said. "John saw Ivor Horfitz's son Jason hanging around outside the weighing room at Newmarket yesterday and had a word with him."

When Millington had a word with people they could take days to recover. In his own way, he could be as frightening as Derry Welfram or Filmer himself.

"What happened?" I asked.

"John spoke to him about the inadvisability of running errands on racecourses for his warned-off father, and said that if Jason had any information, he should pass it on to him, John Millington. And apparently Jason Horfitz then said he wouldn't be passing on the information he had to anybody else as he didn't want to end up in a ditch."

"What?" I said.

"John Millington pounced on that but he couldn't get another word out of the wretched Jason. He turned to jelly and literally ran away, John says."

"Does Jason really know," I said slowly, "what Paul Shacklebury knew? Did he *tell* Paul Shacklebury whatever it was he knew? Or was it just a figure of speech?"

"God knows. John's working on it."

"Did he ask Jason what was in the briefcase?"

"Yes, he did, but Jason either didn't know or was too frightened to speak. John says he was terrified that we even knew about the briefcase. He couldn't believe we knew."

"I wonder if he'll tell his father."

"Not if he has any sense."

He hadn't any sense, I thought, but he did have fear, which was almost as good a life preserver.

"If I hear anything more," the Brigadier said, "I'll leave a message with..." his voice still disapproved, "...with Mrs. Baudelaire senior. Apart from that, good luck."

I thanked him and hung up, and with considerable contentment took my two bags in a taxi to Union Station.

The train crew were already collecting in the locker room when I made my way there and introduced myself as Tommy, the actor.

They smiled and were generous. They always enjoyed the mysteries, they said, and had worked with an actor among them before. It would all go well, I would see.

The head waiter, head steward, chief service attendant, whatever one called him, was a neat small Frenchman named Emil. Late thirties, perhaps, I thought, with dark bright eyes.

"Do you speak French?" he asked first, shaking my hand. "All VIA employees have to be able to speak French. It is a rule."

"I do a bit," I said.

"That is good. The last actor, he couldn't. This time the chef is from Montreal, and in the kitchen we may speak French."

I nodded and didn't tell him that, apart from school days, my working French had been learned in stables, not kitchens, and was likely to be rusty in any case. But I'd half-learned several languages on my travels, and somehow they each floated familiarly back at the first step onto the matching soil. Everything in bilingual Canada was written in both English and French and I realized that since my arrival I'd been reading the French quite easily.

"Have you ever worked in a restaurant?" Emil asked.

"No, I haven't."

He shrugged good-humoredly. "I will show you how to set the places, and to begin with, this morning, perhaps you will serve only water. When you pour anything, when the train is moving, you pour in small amounts at a time, and you keep the cup or glass close to you. Do you understand? It is always necessary to control, to use small movements."

"I understand," I said, and indeed I did.

He put a copy of the timetable into my hands and said, "You will need to know where we stop. The passengers always ask."

"OK. Thanks."

He nodded with good humor.

I changed into Tommy's uniform and met some others of the crew; Oliver, who was a waiter in the special dining car, like myself, and several of the sleeping car attendants, one to each car the whole length of the train. There was a smiling Chinese gentleman who cooked in the small forward dining car where the grooms, among others, would be eating, and an unsmiling Canadian who would be cooking in the main central dining car for the bulk of the racegoers and the crew themselves. The French chef from Montreal was not there, I soon discovered, because he was a she, and could be found in the women's changing room.

Everyone put on the whole uniform including the gray raincoat on top, and I put on my raincoat also; I packed Tommy's spare garments and my own clothes into the hold-all, and was ready.

Nell had said she would meet me this Sunday morning in the coffee shop in the Great Hall, and had told me that the crews often went there to wait for train time. Accordingly, accompanied by Emil and a few of the others, I carried my bags to the coffee shop where everyone immediately ordered huge carrot cakes, the specialty of the house, as if they were in fear of famine.

Nell wasn't there, but Zak and some of the other actors were, sitting four to a table, drinking pale-looking orange juice and not eating carrot cake because of the calories.

Zak said Nell was along with the passengers in the reception area, and that he wanted to go and see how things were shaping.

"She said something about you checking a suitcase through to Vancouver in the baggage car," he added, standing up.

"Yes, this one."

"Right. She said to tell you to bring it along to where the passengers are. I'll show you."

I nodded, told Emil I'd be back, and followed Zak down the Great Hall and round a corner or two and came to a buzzing gathering of people in an area like an airport departure lounge.

An enormous banner across a latticed screen left no one in any doubt. Stretching for a good twelve feet it read in red on white THE GREAT TRANSCONTINENTAL MYS-

TERY RACE TRAIN, and in blue letters a good deal smaller underneath, THE ONTARIO JOCKEY CLUB, MERRY AND COMPANY AND VIA RAIL PRESENT A CELEBRATION OF CANADIAN RACING.

The forty or so passengers already gathered in happy anticipation wore name badges and carnations and held glasses of orange juice convivially.

"There was supposed to be champagne in the orange juice," Zak said dryly. "There isn't. Something to do with the Sunday drink law." He searched the throng with his eyes from where we stood a good twenty paces away out in the station. "There's Ben doing his stuff, see? Asking Raoul to lend him money?"

I could indeed see. It looked incredibly real. People standing around them were looking shocked and embarrassed.

Zak was nodding his mop of curls beside me and had begun snapping his fingers rather fast. I could sense the energy starting to flow in him now that his fiction was coming alive, and I could see that he had used makeup on himself, not greasepaint or anything heavy, more a matter of darkening and thickening his eyebrows and darkening his mouth, emphasizing rather than disguising. An actor in the wings, I thought, gathering up his power.

I spotted Mavis and Walter Bricknell being fussy and anxious as intended, and saw and heard Angelica asking if anyone had seen Steve.

"Who's Steve?" I asked Zak. "I forget."

"Her lover. He misses the train."

Pierre and Donna began to have their row, which made a different bunch of passengers uncomfortable. Zak laughed. "Good," he said, "that's great."

Giles (the murderer), who had been in the coffee shop, strolled along into the melee and started being frightfully nice to old ladies. Zak snapped his fingers even faster and started humming.

The crowd parted and shifted a little and through the gap

I saw Julius Apollo Filmer, another murderer, being frightfully nice to a not-so-old lady, Daffodil Quentin.

I took a deep breath, almost of awe, almost on a tremble. Now that it was really beginning, now that I was going to be near him, I felt as strung up and as energized as Zak, and no doubt suffered the same compelling anxiety that things shouldn't go wrong.

Daffodil was playfully patting Filmer's hand.

Yuk, I thought.

Ben the actor appeared beside them and started his piece, and I saw Filmer turn a bland face toward him and watched his mouth shape the unmistakable words, "Go away."

Ben backed off. Very wise, I thought. The crowd came together again and hid Filmer and his flower and I felt the tension in my muscles subside, and realized I hadn't known I had tensed them. Have to watch that, I thought.

The Lorrimores had arrived, each wearing yesterday's expression: pleasant, aloof, supercilious, sulky. Mercer was entering into the spirit of things, Bambi also but more coolly. Sheridan looked as if he thought he was slumming. The young daughter, Xanthe, could have been quite pretty if she'd smiled.

James Winterbourne, actor, had discarded his red felt trilby and had shaved off the stubble and was drifting around being welcoming in his role as a member of the Jockey Club. And the real Jockey Club was there, I saw, in the person of Bill Baudelaire, who was known to one or two of the owners with whom he was chatting. I wondered how much he would fret if he didn't see me among the passengers, and I hoped not much.

Nell emerged from the noise of the crowd and came across toward us, a clipboard clasped to her chest, her eyes shining. She wore another severe suit, gray this time over a white blouse, but perhaps in honor of the occasion had added a long twisted rope of coral, pearls and crystal.

"It's all happening," she said. "I can hardly believe it, after all these months. I won't kiss you both, I'm not supposed to know you yet, but consider yourselves kissed. It's all going very well. Pierre and Donna are having a humdinger of a row. How does she manage to cry whenever she wants to? Is that the suitcase for Vancouver? Put it over there with those others that are being checked right through. Mercer Lorrimore is sweet, I'm so relieved. We haven't had any disasters yet, but there must be one on the way. I'm as high as a kite and there's no champagne in the orange juice."

She stopped for breath and a laugh and I said, "Nell, if Bill Baudelaire asks you if I'm here, just say yes, don't say where."

She was puzzled but too short of time to argue. "Well, OK."

"Thanks."

She nodded and turned to go and take care of the passengers, and the James Winterbourne character came out to meet her and also to talk to Zak.

"It's too much," he complained, "the real goddamn chairman of the Ontario Jockey Club has turned up to do the 'bon voyage' bit himself. I'm out of a job."

"We did ask him first," Nell said. "We suggested it right at the beginning, before it all grew so big. He's obviously decided he should be here after all."

"Yes, but what about my fee?"

"You'll get it," Zak said resignedly. "Just go back and jolly things along and tell everyone what a great trip they're going to have."

"I've been doing that," he grumbled, but returned obediently to his task.

"As a matter of fact," Nell said, her brow wrinkling, "I suppose I did get a message days ago to say the chairman was coming, but I didn't know it meant him. I didn't know who it meant. It was a message left for me while I was out. 'The Colonel is coming.' I didn't know any colonels. Is the Chairman a colonel?"

"Yes," I said.

"Oh, well, no harm done. I'd better go and see if he

needs anything." She hurried off, unperturbed.

Zak sighed. "I could have saved myself that fee."

"How do you mean?"

"Oh, Merry and Company pay me a lump sum to stage the mystery. I engage the actors and pay them, and whatever is left at the end is mine. Not much, sometimes."

Voices were suddenly raised over in the crowd and people began scattering to the edges of the area, clearing the center and falling silent. Zak and I instinctively went nearer, he in front, I in his shadow.

On the floor, sprawling, lay the actor Raoul, with Donna and Pierre bending down to help him up. Raoul dabbed at his nose with the back of his hand, and everyone could see the resulting scarlet streak.

Mavis Bricknell began saying loudly and indignantly, "He hit him. He hit him. That young man hit our trainer in the face. He had no right to knock him down."

She was pointing at Sheridan Lorrimore, who had turned his back on the scene.

I glanced at Zak for enlightenment.

"That," he said blankly, "wasn't in the script."

———

Nell smoothed it over.

Sheridan Lorrimore could be heard saying furiously and fortissimo to his father, "How the hell could I know they were acting? The fellow was being a bore. I just bopped him one. He deserved it. The girl was crying. And he was crowding me, pushing against me. I didn't like it."

His father murmured something.

"Apologize?" Sheridan said in a high voice. "Apol—oh, all right. I apologize. Will that do?"

Mercer drew him away to a corner, and slowly, haltingly, the general good humor resurfaced. Ironic compliments were paid to Pierre, Donna and Raoul for the potency and effect of their acting and Raoul played for sympathy and looked nobly forgiving, holding a handkerchief to his nose and peering at it for blood, of which there seemed to be not much.

Zak cursed and said that Pierre had in fact been going to knock Raoul to the ground at a slightly later time, and now that would have to be changed. I left him to his problems because it was coming up to the time when Emil had said the crew should board the train, and I was due back in the coffee shop.

The carrot cakes had been reduced to crumbs and the coffee cups were empty. The bussed consignment of grooms had arrived and were sitting in a group wearing Race Train T-shirts above their jeans. Emil looked at his watch and another crew member arrived and said the computer in the crews' room downstairs was showing that the special train had just pulled into the station, Gate Six, Track Seven, as expected.

"*Bon,*" Emil said, smiling. "Then, Tommy, your duties begin."

Everyone picked up their traveling bags and in a straggle more than a group walked back toward the passengers' assembly area. As we approached we could hear the real chairman of the Ontario Jockey Club welcoming everyone to the adventure and we could see Zak and the other actors waiting for him to finish so that they could get on with the mystery.

Jimmy the actor was dressed in a maroon VIA Rail station uniform, Zak was intent, and Ricky, due on in gory glory at any moment, was checking in a small hand mirror that "blood" was cascading satisfactorily from a gash on his head.

Zak flashed a glance at the crew, saw me and gave me a thumbs-up sign. The chairman wound up to applause. Zak tapped Ricky, who had put the mirror into his pocket, and Ricky went into the "I've been attacked" routine most convincingly.

Emil, the crew and I wasted no time watching. We went

on past and came to Gate Six, which was basically a stair-case leading to ground level, where the rails were. Even though it was high morning, the light was dim and artificial outside as acres of arched roof far above kept out the Canadian weather.

The great train was standing there, faintly hissing, silver, immensely heavy, stretching away in both directions for as far as one could see in the gloom. In the Merry and Company office, I'd learned that each carriage (built of strong unpainted corrugated aluminum with the corrugations lying horizontally) was eighty-five feet long; and there were fifteen carriages in all, counting the horses, the baggage and the Lorrimores. With the engines as well, this train covered more than a quarter of a mile standing still.

Two furlongs, I thought frivolously, to put it suitably. Three times round the train more than equaled the Derby.

There was another long banner, a duplication of the one in the station, fastened to the side of the train, telling all the passengers what they were going on, if they were still in any doubt. The crew divided to right and left according to where their jobs were and, following Emil, I found myself climbing up not into the dining car but into one of the sleeping cars.

Emil briefly consulted a notebook, stowed his travel bag on a rack in a small bedroom and directed me to put my bag in the one next door. He said I should remove my raincoat and my jacket and hang them on the hangers provided. That done, he closed both doors and we descended again to the ground.

"It's easier to walk along outside while we are in the station," he explained. He was ever precise. We walked along beside the wheels until the end of the train was in sight and finally walked past the dining car and at the end of it swung upward through its rear door into the scene of operations.

The special dining car lived up to its name with a blue-and-red carpet, big blue padded leather chairs, polished wood gleaming in the lights and glass panels engraved with birds. There were windows all down both sides with blue patterned curtains at intervals and green plants lodged above, behind pelmets. Ten feet wide, the car was long enough to accommodate six oblong tables down each side of a wide aisle with four chairs at each: forty-eight seats, as promised. All quiet, all empty. All waiting.

"Come," Emil said, leading the way forward through the splendor, "I show you the kitchen."

The long, silvery, all-metal kitchen was already occupied by two figures dressed in white trousers and jackets topped by high white paper hats: the diminutive lady chef from Montreal and a tall willowy young man who introduced himself as Angus, the special chef employed by the outside firm of first-class caterers who were providing for this journey the sort of food not usually served on trains.

It seemed to my amused eyes that the two chefs were in chilly unfriendliness, marking out their territories, each, in the normal course of events, being accustomed to being the boss.

Emil, who must have picked up the same signals, spoke with a true leader's decisiveness. "In this kitchen this week," he said to me, "Angus is to command. Simone will assist." Angus looked relieved, Simone resentful. "This is because," Emil said, as if it clinched matters, which it did, "Angus and his company have designed le menu and provided the food."

The matter, everyone could see, was closed. Emil explained to me that on this trip the linen, cutlery and glasses had been provided by the caterers, and without more ado he showed me first, where to find everything and second, how to set a table.

He watched me do the second table in imitation of his manner. "You learn fast," he said approvingly. "If you practice, they will not tell you are not a waiter."

I practiced on about half of the remaining tables while two other dining room stewards, the real regular service attendants, Oliver and Cathy, set the rest. They put things right with a smile when I got them wrong, and I fell into their ways and rhythm of working as well as I could. Emil surveyed the finished dining room with a critical eye and said that after a week I would probably be able to fold a napkin tidily. They all smiled: it seemed that my napkins were already OK, and I felt quite ridiculously pleased, and also reassured.

Outside the windows the red hat of a porter trundling luggage went by, with, in its wake, the Lorrimores.

"They're boarding," Emil said. "When the train departs, our passengers will all come here for the champagne." He bustled about with champagne flutes and ice and showed me how to fold a napkin round the neck of a bottle and how to pour without drips. He seemed to have forgotten about only letting me loose on water.

There were voices outside as the train came alive. I put my head out of the rear door of the dining car and looking forward saw all the passengers climbing upward into the sleeping cars, with porters following after with their bags. Several people were embarking also into the car behind the dining car, into the car that comprised three bedrooms, a bar, a large lounge area and an upstairs glass-domed observation deck, the whole lot known, I'd discovered, as the dome car.

Forward by the gate through which the passengers were crowding, Nell was doing her stuff with bandages on the convincing bloodiness of Ricky. The little scene concluded, she walked aft, looking inward through the windows, searching for someone, who in fact turned out to be me.

"I wanted to tell you," she said, "the conductor—he's like the captain of a ship—knows that you're our security guard, sort of, and he's agreed to help you with anything you want, and to let you go everywhere in the train without question, including the engines, as long as the two engineers permit it, which he says they will once he's talked to them. Say you are Tommy, when you see him."

I gazed at her with admiration. "You're marvelous," I said.

"Yes, aren't I?" She smiled. "Bill Baudelaire did ask about you. I said you were here and you'd boarded early. He seemed satisfied. Now I've got to sort out all the people who persist in putting themselves into the wrong bedrooms." She had gone before she'd finished the sentence, climbing into the sleeping car forward of the kitchen and vanishing from view.

Filmer's bedroom was in that car.

It had been easy to get myself moved away from next door to him: it had happened naturally with my demotion to crew. However much I might want to keep tabs on him, bumping into him several times a day in the corridor hardly seemed the best route to anonymity.

People started coming into the dining room and sitting at the tables regardless of the fact that we were still in the station.

"Where do we sit?" a pleasant-faced woman asked Emil, and he said "Anywhere, madam." The man with her demanded a double scotch on the rocks, and Emil told him that alcohol was available only after departure. Emil was courteous and helpful. I listened, and I learned.

Mercer Lorrimore came through into the dining car followed by his wife, who looked displeased.

"Where do we sit?" Lorrimore said to me, and I answered "Anywhere, sir" in best Emil fashion, which drew a fast appreciative grin from Emil himself.

Mercer and Bambi chose a centrally located table and were soon joined by their less than happy offspring, Sheridan audibly saying, "I don't see why we have to sit here when we have our own private car."

Both mother and daughter looked as if they agreed with him but Mercer, smiling round clenched molars, said with surprising bitterness, "You will do what I ask or accept the consequences." And Sheridan looked furious but also afraid.

They had spoken as if I weren't there, which in a way I wasn't, as other passengers were moving round me, all asking the same questions. "Anywhere, madam. Anywhere, sir," I said, and "I'm afraid we can't serve alcohol before departure."

Departure came from one instant to the next, without any whistles blowing, horns sounding or general ballyhoo. One moment we were stationary, the next sliding forward smoothly, the transition from rest to motion of a quarter of a mile of metal achieved as if on silk.

We emerged from the shadow of the station into the bright light of noon, and Daffodil Quentin under her sunburst of curls made an entrance from the dome car end, looking about her as if accustomed to people leaping up to help.

"Where do we sit?" she asked, not quite looking at me, and I said "Anywhere, madam. Wherever you like."

She found two seats free not far from the Lorrimores and, putting herself on one chair and her handbag on the other said with bonhomie to the elderly couple already occupying the table, "I'm Daffodil Quentin. Isn't this fun?" They agreed with her warmly. They knew who she was: she was yesterday's winner. They started talking with animation, like almost everyone else in the car. There was no cool period here of waiting for the ice to break. Any ice left after the previous day's racing had been broken conclusively in the scenes out in the station, and the party had already jelled and was in full swing.

Emil beckoned me toward the kitchen end, and I went up there into the small lobby with a serving counter, a space that made a needed gap between the hot glittering galley and the actual dining area. The lobby led on the left to the kitchen and on the right to the corridor to the rest of the train, along which desultory passengers were appearing, swaying gently now to the movement of gathering speed.

Behind the counter Emil was opening bottles of Pol Roger. Oliver and Cathy were still taking glasses from a cardboard container and arranging them on small trays.

"Would you mind polishing some of these smeary

glasses?" Emil said to me, pointing at a trayful. "It would be of great help."

"Just tell me," I said.

"Polish them," he said.

"That's better."

They all laughed. I picked up a cloth and began polishing the tall flutes, and Filmer emerged from the corridor and crossed into the dining room without glancing our way.

I watched him walk toward Daffodil, who was waving to him vigorously, and take the place saved by her handbag. He had his back to me, for which I was grateful. Prepared for the closeness of him, I was still unprepared, still missing a breath. It wouldn't do, I thought. It was time for a bit of bottle, not for knocking knees.

Every seat in the dining car filled up and still people were coming. Nell, arriving, took it in her stride. "Bound to happen. All the actors are here. Give everyone champagne." She went on down the car, clipboard hugged to her chest, answering questions, nodding and smiling, keeping the class in order.

Emil gave me a tray of glasses. "Put four on each table. Oliver will follow you to fill them. Start at the far end and work back."

"OK."

Carrying a tray of glasses would have been easier if the floor had been stable but I made it to the far end with only a lurch or two and delivered the goods as required. Three or four people without seats were standing at the far dome car end, including the actress Angelica. I offered them all glasses as well, and Angelica took one and went on bellyaching to all around her about how Steven had let her down and she should never have trusted the louse, and it was a tribute to her acting that there was a distinct drawing aside of skirts in the pursed mouths of those around her who were fed up with hearing about it.

Oliver, on my heels, was delivering them solace in Pol Roger's golden bubbles.

I came with acute awareness to the table where Filmer was sitting with Daffodil and, careful not to look directly at either of them, put my last four glasses in a row on the tablecloth.

At once Filmer said, "Where have I seen you before?"

7

About fifty conclusions dashed through my head, all of them disastrous. I had been so sure he wouldn't know me. Stupid, arrogant mistake.

"I expect it was when we were over in Europe and went to the Derby Eve dinner in London," the elderly woman said. "We sat at the head table. We were guests of dear Ezra Gideon, poor man."

I moved away sending wordless prayers of thankfulness to anyone out there listening. Filmer hadn't even glanced at me, still less had known me. His head, when I'd finally looked at him, was turned away from me toward his companions, as was Daffodil's also.

Filmer's own thoughts must anyway have been thrown in a tangle. He was himself directly responsible for Gideon's suicide, and now he found himself sitting with Gideon's friends. Whether or not he felt an ounce of embarrassment (probably not), it had to be enough to make him unaware of waiters.

I fetched more glasses and dealt some of them to the Lorrimores, who were an oasis of silence in the chattering mob and paid me absolutely no attention; and from then on I felt I had indeed chosen the right role and could sustain it indefinitely.

When everyone was served, Zak the investigator appeared like a gale-force wind and moved the mystery along through scene two, disclosing the details of the attempted kidnapping of one of the horses and leaving a tantalizing question mark in the shape of *which one*? To the amusement of the audience, he quizzed several of the real passenger owners: "Which is your horse, sir? Did you say Upper Gumtree?" He consulted a list. "Ah yes. You must be Harvey Unwin from Australia? Do you have any reason to believe that your horse might be the target of international intrigue?"

It was skillfully and entertainingly acted. Mercer Lorrimore in his turn and with a smile said his horse was called Voting Right, and no, he'd had no advance notice of any attack. Bambi smiled thinly, and Sheridan said in a loud voice that he thought the whole thing was stupid; everyone knew there hadn't been any goddamn kidnap attempt and why didn't Zak stop messing around and piss off.

Into a gasping horrified silence while Mercer struggled for words, Zak smiled brilliantly and said, "Is it indigestion? We'll get you some tablets," and he patted Sheridan compassionately on the shoulder.

It brought the house, or rather the train, down. People laughed and applauded and Sheridan looked truly murderous.

"Now, Sparrowgrass," Zak said, consulting his list and very smoothly carrying on, "who owns Sparrowgrass?"

The elderly gentleman sitting with Filmer said, "I do. My wife and I."

"So you are Mr. and Mrs. Young? Any relation to Brigham? No? Never mind. Isn't it true that someone tried to burn down the barn your Sparrowgrass was stabled in a month ago? Could the two attacks be linked, would you say?"

The Youngs looked astounded. "How ever did you know that?"

"We have our sources," Zak said loftily, and told me afterward his source was the *Daily Racing Form*, busily read recently for background help with his story. It impressed the passengers most satisfactorily.

"I'm sure no one's trying to kidnap my horse," Young said, but with a note of doubt in his voice that was a triumph for Zak.

"Let's hope not," he said. "And finally, who owns Calculator?"

The actors Walter and Mavis Bricknell put up their hands in agitation. "We do. What's wrong with him? We must go at once to make sure. The whole thing's most upsetting. Have you proper guards now looking after the horses?"

"Calm down, sir, calm down, madam," Zak said as to children. "Merry and Company have a special horse-master looking after them. They will all be safe from now on."

He concluded the scene by saying that we would soon be stopping at Newmarket, but that British owners shouldn't get off the train as they would find no races there (laughter). Lunch was now on its way, he added, and he hoped everyone would return for drinks at five-thirty when there would be Interesting Developments as per their printed programs. The passengers clapped very loudly, to encourage him. Zak waved, retreated and set off down the corridor, flat-footed almost at once after his bounce in the dining car, and already with drooping shoulders consulting his notebook about what he needed to do next. How often, I wondered, had he had to deal with the likes of Sheridan? From his demeanor, often enough.

Emil told me to collect the champagne glasses, pour the water and put a pot of breadsticks on each table. He himself was opening wine. Oliver and Cathy began bringing plates of smoked salmon and bowls of vichyssoise on trays from the kitchen and offering a choice.

The seating problem more or less sorted itself out. Mavis and Walter, pretending "their horse's welfare meant more to them than eating," set off up the train to eat in the racegoers' dining car, and so did Angelica, "too upset to sit down." A few others, like Raoul, Pierre and Donna, left discreetly, until Nell, counting heads, could match all paying passengers with a place. Giles the murderer, I was interested to see, was still in the dining room, still being overpoweringly nice: it was apparently essential to the drama that he should be liked.

We stopped at Newmarket briefly. No British owners got off (a pity). The soup gave place to a fricassee of chicken with lemon and parsley.

I was promoted from Aquarius to Ganymede, forsaking water for wine. Emil quite rightly didn't trust me to clear dirty plates, which involved fancy juggling with knives and forks. I was allowed with the others to change ashtrays, to deliver maple hazelnut praline mousse and to take tea and coffee to the cups, already laid. Filmer ignored my presence throughout and I was extremely careful not to draw his attention by spilling things.

By the end I had a great admiration for Emil, Oliver and Cathy, who had neatly served and cleared three full courses with the floor swaying beneath their feet and who normally would have taken my few jobs also in their stride.

When nearly all the passengers (including Filmer) had left, heading for their own rooms or the observation car, we cleared the tables, spread fresh cloths and began thinking of food for ourselves. At least, I did. The others made for the kitchen with me following, but once there Oliver took off his waistcoat, donned an apron and long yellow gloves, and began washing dishes. A deep endless sinkful of three courses for forty-eight people.

I watched him in horror. "Do you always do this?" I asked.

"Who else?"

Cathy took a cloth to do some drying.

"No machines?" I protested.

"We're the machines," she said.

Catch me, I thought ruefully, washing dishes. I picked up one of the cloths and helped her.

"You don't have to," she said. "But thanks."

Angus the chef was cleaning up his realm at the far end of the long hot kitchen and Simone was unpacking fat beef sandwiches, which we all ate standing up while working. There was an odd sort of camaraderie about it all, as if we were the front-line troops in battle. They were entitled to eat after the last sitting in the central dining car, Emil said, rinsing glasses, but usually they went only for dinner, if then; I could see why, as after the sandwiches on that first day we ate the all-too-few leftover portions of the Lucullan lunch we had served. "There's never anything thrown away," Cathy said, "when we do trips like this."

The dishes finally finished and stowed in their racks, it appeared that we were free for a blessed couple of hours: reassembly on the dot of five-thirty.

I don't know what the others did but I made straight toward the front of the packed train, threading an unsteady way through seemingly endless sleeping cars (passing my own berth), through the still busy central dining car, the full and raucous open-seat dayniter, three more sleeping cars, the crowded forward dome car, another sleeping car, and finally reaching the horses. In all, a little less than a quarter of a mile's walk, though it felt like a marathon.

I was stopped at the horse car entrance by a locked door and, in response to my repeated knocking, by a determined female who told me I wasn't welcome.

"You can't come in," she said bluntly, physically barring my way. "The train crew aren't allowed in here."

"I'm working for Merry and Company," I said.

She looked me up and down. "You're an attendant," she said flatly. "You're not coming in."

She was quivering with authority, the resolute governess guarding the pass. Maybe forty, I judged, with regular features, no makeup and a slim wiry figure in shirt, sweater and jeans. I knew an immovable object when I saw it, and I retreated through the first sleeping car, where grooms in T-shirts lolled in open day compartments (shut off by heavy felt curtains for sleeping), on my way to consult with the Chinese chef in the forward dome car's kitchen.

"The conductor?" he said in answer to my question. "He is here." He pointed along the corridor toward the dining section. "You're lucky."

The conductor, in his gray suit with gold bars of long service on his left sleeve, was sitting at the first table past the kitchen, finishing his lunch. There were other diners at other tables, but he was alone, using his lunch break to fill in papers laid out on the cloth. I slid into one of the seats opposite him and he raised his eyes inquiringly.

"I'm from Merry and Company," I said. "I believe you know about me."

"Tommy?" he said, after thought.

"Yes."

He put a hand across the table, which I shook.

"George Burley," he said. "Call me George."

He was middle-aged, bulky, close-cropped as to hair and mustache and with, I discovered, a nice line in irony.

I explained about the impasse at the door of the horse car.

His eyes twinkled, "You've met the dragon-lady, eh? Ms. Leslie Brown. They sent her to keep the grooms in order. Now she tries to rule the train, eh?"

He had the widespread Canadian habit of turning the most ordinary statement into a question. It's a nice day, eh?

"I hope," I said politely, "that your authority outranks hers."

"You bet your life," he said. "Let me finish these papers and my lunch and we'll go along there, eh?"

I sat for a while watching the scenery slide by, wild uninhabited stretches of green and autumn-blazing trees, gray rocks and blue lakes punctuated by tiny hamlets and lonely houses, all vivid in the afternoon sunshine, a panorama impression of the vastness of Canada and the smallness of her population.

"Right," George said, shuffling his papers together. "I'll just finish my coffee, eh?"

"Is there," I asked, "a telephone on the train?"

He chuckled. "You bet your life. But it's a radio phone, eh? It only works near cities where they have receiver/transmitters. At small stations we have to get off and use the regular phones on the ground, like the passengers do at longer stops."

"But can anyone use the train telephone?" I asked.

He nodded. "It's a pay phone by credit card, eh? Much more expensive. Most people stretch their legs and go into the stations. It's in my office." He anticipated my question. "My office is in the first sleeping car aft of the central dining car."

"My roomette is there," I said, working it out.

"There you are, then. Look for my name on the door."

He finished his coffee, slid his papers into a folder and took me forward again to the horse car. The dragon answered belligerently to his knock and stared at me disapprovingly.

"He is Tommy," George said. "He is a security guard for Merry and Company, eh? He has the run of the *whole* train under my authority."

She bowed in her turn to an irresistible force and let us in with raised eyebrows and an air of power suspended, not abdicated. She produced a clipboard with a sheet of ruled paper attached. "Sign here," she said. "Everyone who comes in here has to sign. Put the date and time."

I signed Tommy Titmouse in a scrawl and put the time. Filmer, I was interested to see, had been to see his horse before departure.

We walked forward into the horse car with George pointing things out.

"There are eleven stalls, see? In the old days they carried twenty-four horses in a car, but there was no center aisle, eh? No passage for anyone between stops. They don't carry horses by train much now. This car was built in 1958. One of the last, one of the best."

There was a single stall lengthwise against the wall on

each side of the entrance door, then a space, then two more box-stalls, one on each side, then a space where big sliding doors gave access to the outer world for loading and unloading. Next came a wider central space with a single box on one side only. Then two more boxes and another space for loading, then two more boxes and a space, and finally another box on each side of the far forward door. Eleven boxes, as promised, with a central aisle.

The boxes were made of heavy green-painted panels of metal slotted and bolted together; dismantleable. In the wide center space, where one box alone stood along one wall, there was a comfortable chair for the redoubtable Ms. Brown, along with a table, equipment lockers, a refrigerator and a heavy plastic water tank with a tap low down for the filling of buckets. George opened the top lid of the tank and showed me a small plank floating on the surface.

"It stops the water sloshing about so much, eh?"

Eh, indeed, I thought.

There were dozens of bales of hay everywhere possible, and a filled hay-net swinging gently above each horse's head. A couple of grooms sat around on bales while their charges nibbled their plain fare and thought mysterious equine thoughts.

Each box had the name of its occupant thoughtfully provided on a typewritten card slotted into a holder on the door. I peered at a few of them, identifying Filmer and Daffodil's Laurentide Ice as a light gray colt with brittle-looking bones, the Lorrimores' Voting Right as an unremarkable bay, and the Youngs' Sparrowgrass as a bright chestnut with a white star and sock.

"Come on," George said. "Meet the engineers, eh?" He wasn't a horse man, himself.

"Yes. Thank you."

He opened the forward door of the horse van with a key, and with a key also let us through into the baggage car.

"The doors are kept locked, eh?"

I nodded. We swayed down the long baggage car, which

was half empty of freight and very noisy, and George, having told me to remove and lay aside my waistcoat so as not to get oil on it, unlocked the door at the far end. If I'd thought it noisy where we were, where we went made talking impossible.

George beckoned and I followed through a door into the heat of the rear section of the engines, the section containing among other things the boiler that provided steam to heat the whole train. George pointed wordlessly to an immense tank of water and with amusement showed me the system for telling the quantity of the contents. At intervals up the huge cylinder there were normal taps, the sort found over sinks. George pointed to the figures beside each, which were in hundreds of gallons, and made tap-turning motions with his hands. One turned on the taps, I understood with incredulity, to discover the level of the contents. Supremely logical, I supposed, if one had never heard of gauges.

We went on forward into a narrow passage beside yards of hot hammering engine of more than head height, throbbingly painful to the senses, and then passed over a coupling into another engine, even longer, even noisier, even hotter, the very stuff of hell. At the forward end of that we came to a glass-paneled door, which needed no key, and suddenly we were in the comparative quietness of the drivers' cab, right at the front of the train.

There was fresh cool air there, as the small right-hand window, next to the bank of controls in front of the engineer's seat, was wide open. When I commented on it, George said that that window was open always except in blizzards, eh?

Through the wide forward unopening windows there was a riveting view of the rails stretching ahead, signals shining green in the distance, trees flashing back at a useful seventy miles an hour. I'd never been in a cab of a moving train before, and I felt I could have stayed there all day.

At the controls sat a youngish man in no sort of uniform,

and beside him sat an older man in cleanish overalls with grease on his fingers.

George made introductions. "Robert," that was the younger, and "Mike" the elder. They nodded and shook hands when George explained my position. "Give him help, eh? if he asks for it."

They said they would. George patted Robert on the shoulder and pointed out to me a small white flag blowing stiffly outside to the right of the front windows.

"That flag shows this is a special train. Not in the timetable, eh? It's so all railwaymen along the way don't think the Canadian is running thirty minutes early."

They all thought it a great joke. Trains never ran early the world over. Late was routine.

Still chuckling, George led the way back through the glass door into the inferno. We inched again past the thundering monster and its second string to the rear, and emerged at last into the clattering reverberating peace of the baggage car where I was reunited with my waistcoat. My suitcase, I was interested to see, stood in a quiet row of others, accessible enough if I wanted it.

George locked the baggage car door behind us and we stood again in the quiet horse car, which looked homely and friendly with the horses' heads poking forward over the doors. It was interesting, I thought, that as far as they were able in their maybe four-foot-wide stalls, most of them were standing diagonally across the space, the better to deal with the motion; and they all looked alert and interested, sure signs of contentment.

I rubbed the noses of one or two under the frowning suspicious gaze of Ms. Brown, who was not pleased to be told that she should let me in whenever I asked, eh?

George chuckled his way out of the horse car and we meandered back down the train together, George stopping to check for news with each sleeping car attendant and to solve any problems. There was a sing-song in progress in the forward dome car and the racegoers in the dayniter had formed about four separate card games with cash passing briskly.

The overworked and gloomy chef in the main dining car had not lost his temper altogether and only a few passengers had grumbled that the roomettes were too cramped; the most usual disgruntlement, George said.

No one was ill, no one was drunk, no one was fighting. Things, George said eventually, were going so smoothly that one should expect disaster any time now, eh?

We came at last to his office, which was basically a roomette like my own: that is to say it was a seven-by-four space on one side of a central corridor, containing a washbasin, a folding table and two seats, one of which concealed what the timetable coyly called "facilities." One could either leave the sliding door open and see the world go by down the corridor, or close oneself into a private cocoon; and at night one's bed descended from the ceiling and onto the seat of the facilities, which effectively put them out of use.

George invited me in and left the door open.

"This train," he said, settling himself into the armchair and indicating the facilities for me, "is a triumph of diplomacy, eh?"

He had a permanent smile in his eyes, I thought, much as if he found the whole of life a joke. I learned later that he thought stupidity the norm for human behavior, and that no one was as stupid as passengers, politicians, pressmen and the people who employed him.

"Why," I asked, "is it a triumph?"

"Common sense has broken out."

I waited. He beamed and in a while went on, "Except for the engineers, the same crew will stay with the train to Vancouver!"

I didn't to his eyes appear sufficiently impressed.

"It's unheard of, eh?" he said. "The unions won't allow it."

"Oh."

"Also the horse car belongs to Canadian Pacific."

I looked even blanker.

He chuckled. "The Canadian Pacific and VIA Rail, who work so closely together, get along like sandpaper, good at friction. Canadian Pacific trains are freight trains, eh?, and VIA trains carry passengers, and never the two shall mix. This train is a mix. A miracle, eh?"

"Absolutely," I said encouragingly.

He looked at me with twinkling pity for my lack of understanding of the really serious things in life.

I asked if his telephone would work at the next big stop, which came under the heading of serious to me.

"Sudbury?" he said. "Certainly. But we will be there for an hour. It's much cheaper from the station. A fraction of the price."

"But more private here."

He nodded philosophically. "Come here as soon as we slow down coming to Sudbury, eh? I'll leave you here. I have to be busy in the station."

I thanked him for everything and left the orbit of his beaming smile knowing that I was included in the universality of stupid behavior. I could see a lot more of George, I thought, before I tired of him.

My own door, I found, was only two doors along from his, on the right-hand side of the train when facing forward. I went past without stopping, noting that there were six roomettes altogether at the forward end of the car: three each side. Then the corridor bent to the side to accommodate four enclosed double bedrooms and bent back again through the center of open seating with sleeping curtains, called sections. The six sections of that car were allocated to twelve assorted actors and crew, most of them at that point reading, talking or fast asleep.

"How's it going?" Zak said, yawning.

"All quiet on the western front."

"Pass, friend."

I smiled and went on down the train, getting the feel of it now, understanding the way it was put together, beginning to wonder about things like electricity, water supply and sewage. A small modern city on the move, I thought, with all the necessary infrastructure.

All the doors were closed in the owners' sleeping cars (there were almost no open sections in those), the inhabitants there having the habit of privacy. The rooms could have been empty, it was impossible to tell, and in fact when I came to the special dining car I found a good number of the passengers sitting at the unlaid tables, just chatting. I went on through into the dome car where there were three more bedrooms before one came to the bar, which was furnished with tables, seating and barman. A few people sat there also, talking, and some again were sitting around in the long lower lounge to the rear.

From there a short staircase went up to the observation lounge, and I went up there briefly. The many seats there were almost full, the passengers enjoying their uninterrupted view of a million brilliant trees under blue skies and baking in the hot sunshine streaming through the glass roof.

Mr. Young was up there, asleep. Julius Apollo wasn't, nor anywhere else in public view.

I hadn't seen Nell at all either. I didn't know where she'd put herself finally on her often-revised allocation of sleeping space, but wherever she was, it was behind a closed door.

To the rear of the dome car there was only the Lorrimores' private car, which I could hardly enter, so I retraced my steps, intending to retreat to my own roomette and watch the scenery do its stuff.

In the dining car I was stopped by Xanthe Lorrimore, who was sitting alone at a table looking morose.

"Bring me some Coke," she said.

"Yes, certainly," I said, and went to fetch some from the cold locker in the kitchen, thanking my stars that I'd happened to see where the soft-drink cans were kept. I put the can and a glass on one of the small trays (Emil's voice in my ear saying, "Never ever carry the object. Carry the tray") and returned to Xanthe.

"I'm afraid this is on a cash bar basis," I said putting the glass on the table and preparing to open the can.

"What does that mean?"

"Things from the bar are extra. Not included in the fare."

"How ridiculous. And I haven't any money."

"You could pay later, I'm sure."

"I think it's stupid."

I opened the can and poured the Coke, and Mrs. Young, who happened to be sitting alone at the next table, turned round and said to Xanthe sweetly that she, Mrs. Young, would pay for the Coke, and wouldn't Xanthe come and join her?

Xanthe's first instinct was clearly to refuse but, sulky or not, she was also lonely, and there was an undemanding grandmotherliness about Mrs. Young that promised an uncritical listening ear. Xanthe moved herself and her Coke and unburdened herself of her immediate thought.

"That brother of mine," she said, "is an asshole."

"Perhaps he has his problems," Mrs. Young said equably, digging around in her capacious and disorganized handbag for some money.

"If he was anyone else's kid, he'd be in jail."

The words came out as if propelled irresistibly from a well of compressed emotion. Even Xanthe herself looked shocked at what she'd let out, and feebly tried to weaken the impact. "I didn't mean literally, of course," she said. But she had.

Mrs. Young, who had paused in her search, finally found her purse and gave me a dollar.

"If there's any change, keep it," she said.

"Thank you, madam."

I had no choice but to leave and I made for the kitchen carrying the dollar on the tray like a trophy anchored by a thumb. From there I looked back to see Xanthe begin to talk to Mrs. Young, at first slowly, with brakes on, and then faster and faster, until all the unhappiness was pouring out like a flood. I could see Xanthe's face and the back of Mrs. Young's head. Xanthe, it seemed to me, was perhaps sixteen, but probably younger: certainly not older. She still had the facial contours of childhood, with a round chin and big-pupiled eyes; also chestnut hair in abundance and a growing figure hidden within a bulky white top with a pink glittering pop-group slogan on the front, the badge of youth.

They were still talking when I continued on my way back to my roomette, where I sat in comfortable privacy for a while reading the timetable and also reflecting that although I still had no answers to the questions, I now had a whole crop of new ones, the most urgent being whether or not Filmer had already known the Youngs were friends of Ezra Gideon. Whether the Youngs were, in fact, a target of some kind. Yet Filmer hadn't chosen to sit at their table; it had been the random fortuitous decision of Daffodil. Perhaps if it hadn't happened so handily by chance, he would have engineered a meeting. Or was the fact of their friendship with Gideon just an unwelcome coincidence, as I had at first supposed? Time, perhaps, would tell.

Time told me more immediately that it was five-thirty, the hour of return to the dining room, and I returned to find every single seat already taken, the passengers having learned fast. Latecomers stood in the entrances, looking forlorn.

Filmer, I saw at once, was placed opposite Mercer Lorrimore. Daffodil, beside him, was opposite Bambi, who was being coolly gracious.

Xanthe was still sitting across from Mrs. Young, now rejoined by her husband. Sheridan, as far as I could see, was absent. Giles the murderer was present, sitting with the Youngs and Xanthe, being nice.

Emil, Oliver, Cathy and I went round the tables pouring wine, tea or coffee into glasses or cups on small trays with small movements, and when that was done Zak bounded into the midst of things, vibrating with fresh energy, to get on with the mystery.

I didn't listen in detail to it all, but it revolved round Pierre and Donna, and Raoul the racehorse trainer who wanted to marry her money. Zak had got round the pre-empted Pierre-hitting-Raoul-to-the-ground routine by having Donna slap Raoul's face instead, which she did with a gusto that brought gasps from the audience. Donna was clearly established as the fussy Bricknells' besotted daughter, with Raoul obviously Mavis's favorite, and Pierre despised as a no-good compulsive gambler. Mother and daughter went into a sharp slanging match, with Walter fussing and trying to stop them. Mavis, in the end, started crying.

I looked at the passengers' faces. Even though they knew this lot were all actors, they were transfixed. Soap opera had come to life within touching distance. Racing people, I'd always thought, were among the most cynical in the world, yet here some of the most experienced of them were moved and involved despite themselves.

Zak, keeping up the tension, said that at the last of our brief stops at minor stations he had been handed a telex about Angelica's missing friend, Steve. Was Angelica present? Everyone looked around, and no, she wasn't. Never mind, Zak said, would someone please tell her that she must telephone Steve from Sudbury, as he had serious news for her.

A lot of people nodded. It was amazing.

Dressed in silk and ablaze with jewelry, apparently to prove that Donna's inheritance was no myth, Mavis Bricknell stumbled off toward the toilet room at the dome car's entrance saying she must repair the ravages to her face, and presently she came back, screaming loudly.

Angelica, it appeared, was lying on the bathroom floor, extremely dead. Zak naturally bustled to investigate, followed by a sizeable section of the audience. Some of them soon came back smiling weakly and looking unsettled.

"She can't really be dead," someone said solemnly. "But she certainly looks it."

There was a lot of "blood" all over the small compartment, it appeared, with Angelica's battered head in shadow beyond the essential facility. Angelica's eyes were just visible staring at the wall, unblinking. "How can she do that?" several said.

Zak came back, looked around him and beckoned to me.

"Stand in front of that door, will you, and don't let anyone go in?"

I nodded and went through the crowd toward the dome car. Zak himself was calling everyone back into the dining room, saying they should all stay together until we reached Sudbury, which would be soon. I could hear Nell's voice announcing calmingly that everyone had time for another drink. There would be an hour's stop in Sudbury for everyone to stretch their legs if they wanted to, and dinner would be served as soon as the train started again.

I went across the clattering, windy linkage space between the dining and dome cars and stood outside the toilet room. I wasn't actually pleased with Zak as I didn't want to risk being identified as an actor, but that, I supposed, would be a great deal better than the truth.

It was boring in the passage but also, it proved, necessary, as one or two passengers came back for a look at the corpse. They were good-humored enough when turned away. Meanwhile the corpse, who must have had to blink in the end, could be heard flushing water within.

When we began to slow down I knocked on the door. "Message from Zak," I said.

The door opened a fraction. Angelica's greasepaint makeup was a pale bluish gray, her hair a mass of tomato ketchup.

"Lock the door," I said. "Zak will be along. When you hear his voice outside, unlock it."

"Right," she said, sounding cheerfully alive. "Have a nice trip."

8

Angelica left the train on a stretcher in the dusk under bright station lights, her tomato head half-covered by a blanket and one lifeless hand, with red fingernails and sparkling rings, artistically drooping out of concealment on the side where the train's passengers were able to look on with fascination.

I watched the scene through the window of George Burley's office while I talked to Bill Baudelaire's mother on the telephone.

The conversation had been a surprise from the beginning, when a light young female voice had answered my call.

"Could I speak to Mrs. Baudelaire, please?" I said.

"Speaking."

"I mean . . . Mrs. Baudelaire senior."

"Any Mrs. Baudelaire who is senior to me is in her grave," she announced. "Who are you?"

"Tor Kelsey."

"Oh, yes," she replied instantly. "The invisible man."

I half-laughed.

"How do you do it?" she asked. "I'm dying to know."

"Seriously?"

"Of course, seriously."

"Well . . . say if someone serves you fairly often in a

116

shop, you recognize them when you're in the shop, but if you meet them somewhere quite different, like at the races, you can't remember who they are."

"Quite right. It's happened to me often."

"To be easily recognized," I said, "you have to be in your usual environment. So the trick about invisibility is not to have a usual environment."

There was a pause, then she said, "Thank you. It must be lonely."

I couldn't think of an answer to that, but was astounded by her perception.

"The interesting thing is," I said, "that it's quite different for the people who work in the shop. When they get to know their customers, they recognize them easily anywhere in the world. So the racing people I know, I recognize everywhere. They don't know that I exist. And that's invisibility."

"You are," she said, "an extraordinary young man."

She stumped me again.

"But Bill knew you existed," she said, "and he told me he didn't recognize you face to face."

"He was looking for the environment he knew . . . straight hair, no sunglasses, a good gray suit, collar and tie."

"Yes," she said. "If I meet you, will I know you?"

"I'll tell you."

"Pact."

This, I thought with relief and enjoyment, was some carrier pigeon.

"Would you give Bill some messages?" I asked.

"Fire away. I'll write them down."

"The train reaches Winnipeg tomorrow evening at about seven-thirty, and everyone disembarks to go to hotels. Please would you tell Bill I will not be staying at the same hotel as the owners, and that I will again not be going to the president's lunch, but that I will be at the races, even if he doesn't see me."

I paused. She repeated what I'd said.

"Great," I said. "And would you ask him some questions?"

"Fire away."

"Ask him for general information on a Mr. and Mrs. Young who own a horse called Sparrowgrass."

"It's on the train," she said.

"Yes, that's right." I was surprised, but she said Bill had given her a list to be a help with messages.

"Ask him," I said, "if Sheridan Lorrimore has ever been in any trouble that he knows of, apart from assaulting an actor at Toronto, that should have resulted in Sheridan going to jail."

"Gracious me. The Lorrimores don't go to jail."

"So I gathered," I said dryly, "and would you also ask which horses are running at Winnipeg and which at Vancouver, and which in Bill's opinion is the really best horse on the train, not necessarily on form, and which has the best chance of winning either race."

"I don't need to ask Bill the first question, I can answer that for you right away, it's on this list. Nearly all the eleven horses, nine to be exact, are running at Vancouver. Only Upper Gumtree and Flokati run at Winnipeg. As for the second, in my own opinion neither Upper Gumtree nor Flokati will win at Winnipeg because Mercer Lorrimore is shipping in his great horse Premiere by horse-van."

"Um . . ." I said. "You follow racing quite a bit?"

"My dear young man, didn't Bill tell you? His father and I owned and ran the *Ontario Raceworld* magazine for years before we sold it to a conglomerate."

"I see," I said faintly.

"And as for the Vancouver race," she went on blithely. "Laurentide Ice might as well melt right now, but Sparrowgrass and Voting Right are both in with a good chance. Sparrowgrass will probably start favorite as his form is consistently good, but as you ask, very likely the best horse, the one with most potential for the future, is Mercer Lorrimore's Voting Right, and I would give that one the edge."

"Mrs. Baudelaire," I said, "you are a gem."

"Beyond the price of rubies," she agreed. "Anything else?"

"Nothing, except . . . I hope you are well."

"No, not very. You're kind to ask. Goodbye, young man. I'm always here."

She put her receiver down quickly as if to stop me from asking anything else about her illness, and it reminded me sharply of my Aunt Viv, bright, spirited and horse mad to the end.

I went back to the dining car to find Oliver and Cathy laying the tables for dinner, and I helped them automatically, although they said I needn't. The job done, we repaired to the kitchen door to see literally what was cooking and to take the printed menus from Angus to put on the tables.

Blinis with caviar, we read, followed by rack of lamb or cold poached salmon, then chocolate mousse with cream.

"There won't be any over," Cathy sighed, and she was right as far as the blinis went, though we all ate lamb in the end.

With ovens and gas burners roaring away, it was wiltingly hot even at the dining room end of the kitchen. Down where the chef worked, a temperature gauge on the wall stood at 102 Fahrenheit, but tall willowy Angus, whose high hat nearly brushed the ceiling, looked cool and unperturbed.

"Don't you have air-conditioning?" I asked.

Angus said, "In summer, I daresay. October is, however, officially winter, even though it's been warm this year. The air-conditioning needs freon gas, which has all leaked away, and it won't be topped up again until spring. So Simone tells me."

Simone, a good foot shorter and with sweat trickling down her temples, mutely nodded.

The passengers came straggling back shedding overcoats

and saying it was cold outside, and again the dining car filled up. The Lorrimores this time were all sitting together. The Youngs were with the Unwins from Australia and Filmer and Daffodil shared a table with a pair Nell later identified to me as the American owners of the horse called Flokati.

Filmer, extremely smooth in a dark suit and gray silk tie, solicitously removed Daffodil's chinchillas and hung them over the back of her chair. She shimmered in a figure-hugging black dress, diamonds sparkling whenever she moved, easily outstripping the rest of the company (even Mavis Bricknell) in conspicuous expenditure.

The train made its smooth inconspicuous departure and I did my stuff with water and breadsticks.

Bambi Lorrimore put her hand arrestingly on my arm as I passed. She was wearing a mink jacket and struggling to get out of it.

"Take this back into our private car, will you?" she said. "It's too hot in here. Put it in the saloon, not the bedroom."

"Certainly, madam," I agreed, helping her with alacrity. "I'd be glad to."

Mercer produced a key and gave it to me, explaining that I would come to a locked door.

"Lock it again when you come back."

"Yes, sir."

He nodded and, carrying the coat away over my arm, I went back through the dome car and with a great deal of interest into the private quarters of the Lorrimores.

There were lights on everywhere. I came first to a small unoccupied sleeping space, then a galley, cold and lifeless. Provision for private food and private crew, but no food, no crew. Beyond that was the locked door, and beyond that a small handsome dining room to seat eight. Through there, down a corridor, there were three bedrooms, two with the doors open. I took a quick peek inside: bed, drawers, small bathroom with shower. One was clearly Xanthe's, the other by inference Sheridan's. I didn't go into the parents' room but went on beyond it to find myself in the rear part of the carriage, at the very end of the train.

It was a comfortable drawing room with a television set and abundant upholstered armchairs in pastel blues and greens. I went over to the rear door and looked out, seeing a little open boarding platform with a polished brass-topped balustrade and, beyond, the Canadian Pacific's single pair of rails streaming away into darkness. The railroad across Canada, I'd learned, was single-track for most of the way. Only in towns and at a few other places could trains going in opposite directions pass.

I put the mink coat on a chair and retraced my journey, locking the door again and eventually returning the key to Mercer, who nodded without speech and put it in his pocket.

Emil was pouring wine. The passengers were scoffing the blinis. I eased into the general picture again and became as unidentifiable as possible. Few people, I discovered, looked directly at a waiter's eyes, even when they were talking to him.

About an hour after we'd left Sudbury we stopped briefly for under five minutes at a place called Cartier and then went on again. The passengers, replete with the lamb and chocolate mousse, lingered over coffee, and began to drift away to the dome car's bar and lounge. Xanthe Lorrimore got up from the table after a while and went that way, and presently came back screaming.

This time, the real thing. She came stumbling back into the dining car followed by a commotion of people yelling behind her.

She reached her parents, who were bewildered as well as worried.

"I was nearly killed," she said frantically. "I nearly stepped off into space. I mean, I was *nearly killed*."

"Darling," Mercer said calmingly, "what has exactly happened?"

"You don't understand." She was screaming, trembling,

hysterical. "I nearly stepped into space because our private car *isn't there*."

It brought both of the Lorrimores to their feet in an incredulous rush, but they had only to look at the faces crowding behind her to know it was true.

"And they say, all those people say. . ." She was gasping, half-unable to get the words out, terribly frightened. ". . . they say the other train, the regular Canadian, is only half an hour behind us, and will smash into . . . will smash into . . . Don't you *see*?"

The Lorrimores, followed by everyone still in the dining room, went dashing off into the dome car, but Emil and I looked at each other, and I said, "How do we warn that train?"

"Tell the conductor. He has a radio."

"I'll go," I said. "I know where his office is. I'll find him."

"Hurry then."

"Yes."

I hurried. Ran. Reached George's office.

No one there.

I went on, running where I could, and found him walking back toward me through the dayniter. He instantly took in that I brought bad news and steered me at once into the noisy outside coupling space between the dayniter and the central dining car.

"What is it?" he shouted.

"The Lorrimores' private car is unhitched. It's somewhere back on the track, and the Canadian is coming."

He moved faster than I would have thought anyone could on a train and was already talking into a radio headset when I reached his office.

"The private car was there at Cartier," he said. "I was off the train there and saw it. Are you sure it's not in sight?" He listened. "Right, then radio to the Canadian and warn the conductor he'll not be leaving Cartier, eh? I'll get this train stopped and we'll go back for the lost car. See what's what. You'd better inform Toronto and Montreal. They won't think this is very funny on a Sunday evening, eh?" He chuckled and looked at me assessingly as I stood in his doorway. "I'll leave someone here manning the radio," he continued. "Tell him when you've got the Canadian understanding the situation, eh?"

He nodded at the reply he heard, took off the headset and gave it to me.

"You are talking to the dispatcher in Schreiber," he said. "That's ahead of us, this side of Thunder Bay—and he can radio straight to the Canadian following us. You can hear the dispatcher without doing anything. To transmit, press the button." He pointed, and was gone.

I put on the headset and sat in his chair and presently into my ears a disembodied voice said, "Are you there?"

I pressed the button, "Yes."

"Tell George I got the Canadian and it will stop in Cartier. There's a CP freight train due behind it but I got Sudbury in time and it isn't leaving there. No one is happy. Tell George to pick up that car and get the hell out."

I pressed the button. "Right," I said.

"Who are you?" asked the voice.

"One of the attendants."

He said "Huh," and was quiet.

The Great Transcontinental Mystery Race Train began to slow down and soon came to a smooth stop. Almost in the same instant, George was back in his doorway.

"Tell the dispatcher we've stopped and are going back," he said, when I'd relayed the messages. "We're eleven-point-two miles out of Cartier, between Benny and Stralak, which means in an uninhabited wilderness. You stay here, eh?" And he was gone again, this time toward the excitement in the tail.

I gave his message to the dispatcher and added, "We're reversing now, going slowly."

"Let me know when you find the car."

"Yes."

It was pitch dark through the windows; no light in the wilderness. I heard afterward from a lot of excited chattering in the dining room that George had stood alone outside the rear door of the dome car on the brink of space, directing a bright hand-held torch beam down the track. Heard that he had a walkie-talkie radio on which he could give the engineer instructions to slow further, and to stop.

He found the Lorrimores' car about a mile and a half out of Cartier. The whole train stopped while he jumped down from the dome car and went to look at the laggard. There was a long pause from my point of view, while the lights began flickering in the office and the train exceedingly slowly reversed, before stopping again and going into a sudden jerk. Then we started forward slowly, and then faster, and the lights stopped flickering, and soon after that George appeared in his office looking grim, all chuckles extinguished.

"What's the matter," I said.

"*Nothing,*" he said violently, "that's what's the matter." He stretched out a hand for the headset, which I gave him.

He spoke into it. "This is George. We picked up the Lorrimores' car at one-point-three miles west of Cartier. There was no failure in the linkage." He listened. "That's what I said. Who the hell do they have working in Cartier, eh? Someone uncoupled that car at Cartier and rigged some way of pulling it out of the station into the darkness before releasing it. The brakes weren't on. You tell Cartier to send someone right away down the track looking for a rope or some such, eh? The steam heat pipe wasn't broken, it had been unlocked. That's what I said. The valve was closed. It was no goddamn accident, no goddamn mechanical failure, someone deliberately unhitched that car. If the Lorrimore girl hadn't found out, the Canadian would have crashed into it. No, maybe not at high speed, but at twenty-five, thirty miles an hour the Canadian can do a lot of damage. Would have made matchsticks of the private car. Might have killed the Canadian engineers, or even derailed the train. You tell them to start looking, eh?"

He took off the headset and stared at me with rage.

"Would you," he said, "know how to uncouple one car from another?"

"No, of course not."

"It takes a railwayman." He glared. "A railwayman! It's like a mechanic letting someone drive off in a car with loose wheel nuts. It's criminal, eh?"

"Yes."

"A hundred years ago," he said furiously, "they designed a system to prevent cars that had broken loose from running backward and crashing into things. The brakes go on automatically in a runaway." He glared. "That system had been bypassed. The Lorrimores' brakes weren't on. That car was deliberately released on level ground, eh? I don't understand it. What was the point?"

"Maybe someone doesn't like the Lorrimores," I suggested.

"We'll find the bastard," he said, not listening. "There can't be many in Cartier who know trains."

"Do you get much sabotage?" I asked.

"Not like this. Not often. Once or twice in the past. But it's mostly vandals. A kid or two throwing rocks off a bridge. Some stealing, eh?"

He was affronted, I saw, by the treachery of one of his own kind. He took it personally. He was in a way ashamed, as one is if one's countrymen behave badly abroad.

I asked him about his communication system with the engineer. Why had he gone up the train himself to get it stopped if he had a walkie-talkie?

"It crackles if we're going at any speed. It's better to talk face to face."

A light flashed on the ship-to-shore radio and he replaced his headset.

"George here," he said, and listened. He looked at his watch and frowned. "Yes. Right. Understood." He took off the headset, shaking his head. "They're not going to go along the track looking for a rope until both the Canadian and the freight train have been through. If our saboteur's got an ounce of sense, by that time there won't be anything incriminating to find."

"Probably not already," I said. "It's getting on for an hour since we left Cartier."

"Yeah," he said. His good humor was trickling back despite his anger, the gleam of irony again in his eye. "Better than that fellow's fake mystery, eh?"

"Yes . . ." I said, thinking. "Is the steam pipe the only thing connecting one car to the next? Except the links, of course."

"That's right."

"What about electricity . . . and water?"

He shook his head. "Each car makes its own electricity. Self-contained. They have generators under the floors—like dynamos on bicycles—that make electricity from the wheels going round. The problem is that when we're going slowly, the lights flicker. Then there are batteries for when we're stopped, but they'd only last for forty-five minutes, eh?, if we weren't plugged into the ground supply at a station. After that we're down to emergency lighting, just the aisle lights and not much else for about four hours, then we're in the dark."

"And water?" I asked.

"It's in the roof."

"Really?" I said, surprised.

He patiently explained. "At city stations, we have water hydrants every eighty-five feet, the length of the cars. One to each car. Also the main electricity, same thing, eh? Anyway, the water goes up under pressure into the tanks in the roof and feeds down again to the washrooms by gravity."

Fascinating, I thought. And it had made unhitching the Lorrimores' car a comparatively quick and easy job.

"The new cars," George said, "will be heated by electricity, not steam, so we'll be doing away with the steam pipe, eh? And they'll have tanks for the sewage, which now drops straight down onto the tracks, of course."

"Canada's railways," I said politely, "will be the envy of the world."

He chuckled. "The trains between Montreal and Toronto are late three-quarters of the time, and the new engines break down regularly. The old rolling stock, like this train, is great."

He picked up the headset again. I raised a hand in farewell and went back to the dining room where the real mystery had easily usurped Zak's, though some were sure it was part of the plot.

Xanthe had cheered up remarkably through being the center of sympathetic attention, and Filmer was telling Mercer Lorrimore he should sue the railway company for millions of dollars for negligence. The near-disaster had galvanized the general consciousness to a higher adrenaline level, probably because Xanthe had not, in fact, been carried off like Angelica.

Nell was sitting at a table with a fortyish couple who she later told me owned one of the horses in the boxcar, a dark bay called Redi-Hot. The man beckoned to me as I stood around vaguely, and asked me to fetch cognac for him, vodka with ice for his wife and . . . what for Nell?

"Just Coke, please," she said.

I went to the kitchen where I knew the Coke was, but made frantic question mark signals to Nell about the rest. Emil, the chefs, Oliver and Cathy had finished cleaning up and had all gone off duty. I had no alcohol divining rod to bend a twig in the direction of brandy or Smirnoff.

Nell said something to the owners and came to join me, stifling laughter.

"Yes, very funny," I said, "but what the hell do I do?"

"Take one of the small trays and get the drinks from the bar. I'll explain they have to pay for them."

"I haven't seen you for five minutes alone today," I complained.

"You're downstairs, I'm up."

"I could easily hate you."

"But do you?"

"Not yet," I said.

"If you're a good little waiter, I'll leave you a tip."

She went back to her place with a complacent bounce to her step, and with a curse, but not meaning it, I took the Coke and a glass to her table and went on into the dome car for the rest. After I'd returned and delivered the order someone else asked for the same service, which I willingly performed again, and yet again.

On each trip I overheard snatches of the barroom conversations and could hear the louder buzz of continuing upheaval along in the lounge, and I thought that after I'd satisfied everyone in the dining room I might drift along to the far end with my disarming little tray.

The only person not wholly in sympathy with this plan was the bartender, who complained that I was supposed to be off duty and that the passengers should come to the bar to buy the drinks themselves; I was siphoning off his tips. I saw the justice of that and offered to split fifty-fifty. He knew very well that, without my running to and fro, the passengers mostly wouldn't be bothered to move to drink, so he accepted fast, no doubt considering me a mug as well as an actor.

Sheridan Lorrimore, who was sitting at a table apart from his parents, demanded I bring him a double scotch at once. He had a carrying voice, and his sister from two tables away turned round in disapproval.

"No, no, you're not supposed to," she said.

"Mind your own business." He turned his head slightly toward me and spoke in the direction of my tie. "Double scotch, at the double."

"Don't get it," Xanthe said.

I stood irresolute.

Sheridan stood up, his ready anger rising. He put out a hand and pushed my shoulder fiercely.

"Go on," he said. "Damn well do as I say. Go and get my drink."

He pushed again quite hard and as I turned away I heard him snigger and say, "You have to kick 'em, you know."

I went into the dome car and stood behind the bar with the bartender, and felt furious with Sheridan, not for his outrageous behavior but because he was getting me noticed. Filmer had been sitting with his back to me, it was true, but near enough to overhear.

Mercer Lorrimore appeared tentatively in the bar doorway and came in when he saw me.

"I apologize for my son," he said wearily, and I had a convincing impression that he'd apologized countless times before. He pulled out his wallet, removed a twenty-dollar bill from it and offered me the money.

"Please don't," I said. "There's no need."

"Yes, yes. Take it."

I saw he would feel better if I did, as if paying money would somehow excuse the act. I thought he should stop trying to buy pardons for his son and pay for mental treatment instead. But then, perhaps he had. There was more wrong with Sheridan than ill-temper, and it had been obvious to his father for a long time.

I didn't approve of what he was doing, but if I refused his money I would be more and more visible, so I took it, and when he had gone off in relief back toward the dining car I gave it to the barman.

"What was that all about?" he asked curiously, pocketing the note without hesitation. When I explained, he said, "You should have kept the money. You should have charged him triple."

"He would have felt three times as virtuous," I said, and the barman looked at me blankly.

I didn't go back to the dining car but forward into the lounge, where again the sight of my yellow waistcoat stirred a few thirsts, which I did my best to accommodate. The barman was by now mellow and helpful and said we were rapidly running out of the ice that had come aboard in bags in Sudbury.

Up in the dome, the uncoupling of the private car had given way to speculation about whether the northern lights would oblige: the weather was right, apparently. I took a few drinks up there (including some for Zak and Donna, which amused them), and on my way down the stairs saw the backs of Mercer and Bambi, Filmer and Daffodil, as they walked through the lounge toward the door to the private car. Mercer stood aside to let Bambi lead the other two through the short noisy joining section, and then, before going himself, he looked back, saw me and beckoned.

"Bring a bowl of ice, will you?" he said when I reached him. "To the saloon."

"Yes, sir," I said.

He nodded and departed, and I relayed the request to the barman, who shook his head and said he was down to six cubes. I knew there were other bags of cubes in the kitchen refrigerator, so, feeling that I had been walking the train for a lifetime, I went along through the dining room to fetch some.

There weren't many people still in there, though Xanthe was still being comforted and listened to by Mrs. Young. Nell sat opposite Sheridan Lorrimore, who seemed to be telling her that he had wrapped his Lamborghini round a tree recently and had ordered a new one.

"Tree?" Nell said, smiling.

He looked at her uncomprehendingly. Sheridan wasn't a great one for jokes. I fetched a bag of ice and a bowl from the kitchen, swayed back to the bar and in due course took the bowl of ice (on a tray) to the saloon.

The four of them were sitting in armchairs, Bambi talking to Daffodil, Mercer to Filmer.

Mercer said to me, "You'll find glasses and cognac in the cupboard in the dining room. And Benedictine. Bring them along here, will you?"

"Yes, sir."

Filmer paid me no attention. In the neat dining room, the cupboards had glass fronts with pale green curtains inside them. In one I found the bottles and glasses as described, and took them aft.

Filmer was saying, "Will Voting Right go on to the Breeders' Cup if he wins at Winnipeg?"

"He's not running at Winnipeg," Mercer said. "He runs at Vancouver."

"Yes, I meant Vancouver."

Daffodil with enthusiasm was telling a cool Bambi that she should try some face cream or other that helped with wrinkles.

"Just leave everything," Mercer said to me. "We'll pour."

"Yes, sir," I said, and retreated as he began the ultimate heresy of sloshing Remy Martin's finest onto rocks.

Mercer would know me everywhere on the train, I thought, but none of the other three would. I hadn't met Filmer's eyes all day; had been careful not to; and it seemed to me that his attention had been exclusively focused upon what he had now achieved, a visiting-terms acquaintance-ship with Mercer Lorrimore.

There was now loud music in the lounge, with two couples trying to dance and falling over with giggles from the perpetual motion of the dance floor. Up in the dome, aurora borealis was doing its flickering fiery best on the horizon, and in the bar there was a group playing poker in serious silent concentration. Playing for thousands, the barman said.

Between the bar and the dining room there were three bedrooms, and in one of those, with the door open, was a sleeping car attendant, dressed exactly like myself.

"Hello," he said, as I paused in the doorway. "Come to help?"

"Sure," I said. "What do I do?"

"You're the actor, aren't you?" he asked.

"It's hush hush."

He nodded. "I won't say a word."

He was of about my own age, perhaps a bit older, pleasant-looking and cheerful. He showed me how to fold up the ingenious mechanism of the daytime armchairs and slide them under a bed that pulled out from the wall. A top bunk was then pulled down from the ceiling, complete with ladder. He straightened the bedclothes and laid a wrapped chocolate truffle on each pillow, a goodnight blessing.

"Neat," I said.

He had only one more room to do, he said, and he should have finished long before this but he'd been badly delayed in the car on the other side of the dining car, which he had in his care also.

I nodded—and several thoughts arrived simultaneously in a rush on my mental doorstep. They were that Filmer's bedroom was in that car. Filmer was at that moment with the Lorrimores. The only locks on the bedroom doors were inside, in the form of bolts to insure privacy. There was no way of preventing anyone from walking in if a room were empty.

I went along to the sleeping car on the far side of the kitchen and opened the door of the abode of Julius Apollo.

9

By virtue of having paid double and possibly treble, Filmer had a double bedroom all to himself. Only the lower bunk had been prepared for the night: the upper was still in the ceiling.

For all that he could be expected to stay in the Lorrimores' car for at least fifteen more minutes I felt decidedly jittery, and I left the door open so that if he did come back unexpectedly I could say I was merely checking that everything was in order. My uniform had multiple advantages.

The bedrooms were small, as one would expect, though in the daytime, with the beds folded away, there was comfortable space. There was a washbasin in full view, with the rest of the plumbing in a discreet little closet. For hanging clothes there was a slot behind the bedheads about eight inches wide, enough in Filmer's case for two suits. Another two jackets hung on hangers on pegs on the wall.

I searched quickly through all the pockets, but they were mostly empty. There was only, in one inner pocket, a receipt for a watch repair which I replaced where I found it.

There were no drawers: more or less everything else had to be in his suitcase, which stood against the wall. With an eye on the corridor outside, I tried one of the latches and wasn't surprised to find it locked.

That left only a tiny cupboard above the hanging space, in which Julius Apollo had stored a black leather toilet bag and his brushes.

On the floor below his suits, pushed to the back of the hanging space, I found his briefcase.

I put my head out of the door which was directly beside the hanging space, and looked up and down the corridor.

No one in sight.

I went down on hands and knees, half in and half out of the doorway, with an excuse ready of looking for a coin I'd dropped. I put a hand into the hanging space and drew the briefcase to the front; and it was of black crocodile skin with gold clasps, as I'd seen at Nottingham races.

The fact of its presence was all I was going to learn, however, as it had revolving combination locks, which were easy enough to undo, but only if one had two hours to spend on each lock, which I hadn't. Whether the briefcase still contained whatever Horfitz had given Filmer at Nottingham was anyone's guess, and dearly though I would have liked to look at the contents, I didn't want to risk any more at that point. I pushed the black case deep into the hanging space again, stood up outside the door, closed it and went back to the scenes of jollity to the rear.

It was, by this time, nearly midnight. The Youngs were standing up in the dining room, ready to go to bed. Xanthe however, alarmed by the departure of her newfound friend, was practically clinging to Mrs. Young and with an echo of the earlier hysteria was saying that she couldn't possibly sleep in the private car, she would have nightmares, she would be too scared to stay, she was sure whoever had uncoupled the car before would do it again in the middle of the night, and they would all be killed when the Canadian crashed into them, because the Canadian was still there behind us, wasn't it, wasn't it?

Yes, it was.

Mrs. Young did her best to soothe her, but it was impossible not to respect her fears. She had undoubtedly nearly been killed. Mrs. Young told her that the madman who had mischievously unhitched the car was hours behind us in Cartier, but Xanthe was beyond reassurance.

Mrs. Young appealed to Nell, asking if there was anywhere else that Xanthe could sleep, and Nell, consulting the ever-present clipboard, shook her head doubtfully.

"There's an upper berth in a section," she said slowly, "but it only has a curtain, and no facilities except at the end of the car, and it's hardly what Xanthe's used to."

"I don't care," Xanthe said passionately. "I'll sleep on the floor or on the seats in the lounge, or *anywhere*. I'll sleep in that upper berth . . . please let me."

"I don't see why not, then," Nell said. "What about night things?"

"I'm not going into our car to fetch them. I'm *not*."

"All right," Nell said. "I'll go and ask your mother."

Mrs. Young stayed with Xanthe, who was again faintly trembling, until at length Nell returned with both a small grip and Bambi.

Bambi tried to get her daughter to change her mind, but predictably without success. I thought it unlikely that Xanthe would ever sleep in that car again, so strong was her present reaction. She, Bambi, Nell and the Youngs made their way past me without looking at me and continued along the corridor beside the kitchen, going to inspect the revised quarters, which I knew were in the sleeping car forward of Filmer's.

After a while Bambi and Nell returned alone, and Bambi with an unexcited word of gratitude to Nell walked a few paces forward and stopped beside her son, who had done nothing to comfort or help his sister and was now sitting alone.

"Come along, Sheridan," she said, her tone without peremptoriness but also without affection. "Your father asks you to come."

Sheridan gave her a look of hatred that seemed not in the least to bother her. She stood patiently waiting until, with

135

exceedingly bad grace, he got to his feet and followed her homeward.

Bambi, it seemed to me, had taught herself not to care for Sheridan so as not to be hurt by him. She too, like Mercer, must have suffered for years from his boorish behavior in public, and she had distanced herself from it. She didn't try to buy the toleration of the victims of his rudeness, as Mercer did: she ignored the rudeness instead.

I wondered which had come first, the chill and disenchantment of her worldly sophistication, or the lack of warmth in her son: and perhaps there was ice in both of them, and the one had reinforced the other. Bambi, I thought, was a highly inappropriate name for her; she was no innocent wide-eyed smooth-skinned fawn but an experienced, aloof, good-looking woman in the skin of minks.

Nell, watching them go, sighed and said, "She didn't kiss Xanthe good night, you know, or give her even a hug to comfort her. Nothing. And Mercer's so nice."

"Forget them."

"Yes. You do realize the press will be down on this train like a pack of hunting lions at the next stop."

"Lionesses," I said.

"What?"

"It's the females who hunt in a pack. One male sits by, watching, and takes the lion's share of the kill."

"I don't want to know that."

"Our next stop," I said, "will be fifteen minutes at White River in the middle of the night. After the delay, we'll aim to arrive at four-oh-five, depart four-twenty."

"And after that?"

"Except for a three-minute pause in a back-of-beyond, we stop at Thunder Bay for twenty-five minutes at ten-fifty tomorrow morning."

"Do you know the whole timetable by heart?"

"Emil told me to learn it. He was right when he said the question I would have to answer most was 'When do we reach so and so.' And if I were a regular waiter he said I would know the answers, even though we're thirty-five minutes earlier everywhere than the regular Canadian."

"Emil is cute," she said.

I looked at her in surprise. I wouldn't have thought of Emil as cute. Small, neat, bright and generous, yes. "Cute?" I asked.

"I would hope," she said, "that you don't think so."

"No."

"Good." She was relieved, I saw.

"Weren't you sure?" I asked curiously. "Am I so . . . ambivalent?"

"Well . . ." There was a touch of embarrassment. "I didn't mean to get into this sort of conversation, really I didn't. But if you want to know, there's something about you that's secret . . . ultra private. As if you didn't want to be known too well. So I just wondered. I'm sorry."

"I shall shower you with ravening kisses."

She laughed. "Not your style."

"Wait and see." And two people didn't, I thought, drift into talking like that after knowing each other for such a short while unless there was immediate trust and liking.

We were standing in the tiny lobby between the kitchen and the dining room, and she still had the clipboard clasped to her chest. She would have to put it down, I thought fleetingly, before any serious ravening could take place.

"You always have jokes in your eyes," she said. "And you never tell them."

"I was thinking about how you use your clipboard as chain mail."

Her own eyes widened. "A lousy man in the magazine office squeezed my breast . . . Why am I telling you? It was years ago. Why should I care? Anyway, where else would you carry a clipboard?"

She put it down, all the same, on the counter, but we didn't talk much longer as the revelers from the rear began coming through to go to the bedrooms. I retreated into the kitchen and I could hear people asking Nell what time they could have breakfast.

"Between seven and nine-thirty," she said. "Sleep well, everybody." She put her head into the kitchen. "Same to you, sleep well. I'm off to bed."

"Goodnight," I said, smiling.

"Aren't you going?"

"Yes, in a while."

"When everything's safe?"

"You might say so."

"What exactly does the Jockey Club expect you to *do*?"

"See trouble before it comes."

"But that's practically impossible."

"Mm," I said. "I didn't foresee anyone uncoupling the Lorrimores."

"You'll be fired for that," she said dryly, "so if you sleep, sleep well."

"Tor would kiss you," I said. "Tommy can't."

"I'll count it done."

She went away blithely, the clipboard again in place: a habit, I supposed, as much as a defense.

I walked back to the bar and wasted time with the barman. The intent poker group looked set for an all-night session, the dancing was still causing laughter in the lounge and the northern lights were entrancing the devotees in the dome. The barman yawned and said he'd be closing the bar soon. Alcohol stopped at midnight.

I heard Daffodil's voice before I saw her, so that when Filmer came past the door of the bar I was bending down with my head below the counter as if to be tidying things there. I had the impression they did no more than glance in as they passed, as Filmer was saying "When we get to Winnipeg..." "You mean Vancouver," Daffodil said. "Yes, Vancouver." "You always get them mixed." Her voice, which had been raised, as his had been, so as to be heard while one of them walked ahead of the other, died away as they passed down the corridor, presumably en route to bed.

Giving them time to say goodnight, as Daffodil's room was one of the three just past the bar, I slowly followed. They were nowhere in sight as I went through to the dining car, and Filmer seemed to have gone straight to his room, as there was a thread of light shining along the bottom of his door; but Daffodil, I discovered, had after all not. Instead of being cozily tucked up in her bunk near the bar, she surprisingly came walking toward me from the sleeping car forward of Filmer's, her diamonds lighting small bright fires with every step.

I stood back to let her pass, but she shimmered to a stop before me and said, "Do you know where Miss Lorrimore is sleeping?"

"In the car you've just come from, madam," I answered helpfully.

"Yes, but where? I told her parents that I would make sure she was all right."

"The sleeping car attendant will know," I said. "If you would like to follow me?"

She nodded assent and as I turned to lead the way I thought at close quarters that she was probably younger than I'd assumed, or else that she was older but immature: an odd impression, fleeting and gone.

The middle-aged sleeping car attendant was dozing but dressed. He obligingly showed Daffodil the upper berth where Xanthe was sleeping, but the thick felt curtains were closely fastened, and when Daffodil called the girl's name quietly, there was no response. The slightly fatherly attendant said he was sure she was safely asleep, as he'd seen her returning from the washroom at the end of the car and climbing up to her bunk.

"I guess that will do," Daffodil said, shrugging off someone else's problem. "Goodnight, then, and thank you for your help."

We watched her sway away holding on to the rails, her high curls shining, her figure neat, her intense musky scent lingering like a memory in the air after she herself had gone.

139

The sleeping car attendant sighed deeply at so much opulent femininity and philosophically returned to his roomette, and I went on up the train into the next car, where my own bed lay.

George Burley's door, two along from mine, was wide open, and I found he was in residence, dressed but asleep, quietly snoring in his armchair. He jerked awake as if with a sixth sense as I paused in his doorway and said, "What's wrong, eh?"

"Nothing that I know of," I said.

"Oh, it's you."

"I'm sorry I woke you."

"I wasn't asleep . . . well, napping, then. I'm used to that. I've been on the railways all my life, eh?"

"A love affair?" I said.

"You can bet your life." He rubbed his eyes, yawning. "In the old days there were many big railway families. Father to son, cousins, uncles . . . it got handed down. My father, my grandfather, they were railwaymen. But my sons, eh? They're behind desks in big cities tapping at computers." He chuckled. "They run the railways too now from behind desks, eh? They sit in Montreal making decisions and they've never heard a train's call at night across the prairie. They've missed all that. These days the top brass fly everywhere." His eyes twinkled. Anyone who wasn't a wheel-on railwayman was demonstrably stupid. "I'll tell you," he said, "I hope to die on the railways."

"Not too soon, though."

"Not before White River, at any rate."

I said goodnight and went to my own room where I found the sleeping car attendant had duly lowered my bed and laid a chocolate truffle on the pillow.

I ate the chocolate. Very good.

I took off the yellow waistcoat with its white lining and hung it on a hanger, and I took off my shoes, but, rather like George, I still felt myself to be on duty, so I switched off the light and lay on top of the bedclothes watching the black

Canadian land slide by, while the free northern show went on above for hours in the sky. There seemed to be wide horizontal bands of light that slowly changed in intensity, with brighter spots growing and fading in places mysteriously against the deeps of eternity. It was peaceful more than frenetic, a mirage of slow dawns and sunsets going back to the Fluted Point People: humbling. In the context of ten thousand years, I thought, what did Filmer and his sins matter? Yet all we had was here and now, and here and now was always where the struggle toward goodness had to be fought. Toward virtue, morality, uprightness, order: call it what one liked. A long, ever-recurring battle.

In the here and now we stopped without incident at White River. I saw George outside under the station lights and watched him set off toward the rear of the train. Apparently the Lorrimores were still safely with us as he came back presently without haste or alarm, and after a while the train made its usual unobtrusive departure westward.

I slept for a couple of hours and was awakened while it was still dark by a gentle rapping on my door: it proved to be Emil, fully dressed and apologetic.

"I didn't know if I should wake you. If you are serious about this, it is time to set the tables for breakfast."

"I'm serious," I said.

He smiled with seeming satisfaction. "It is much easier with four of us."

I said I would come at once and made it, washed, shaved and tidy, in roughly ten minutes. Oliver and Cathy were already there, wide awake. The kitchen was filled with glorious smells of baking and Angus, with languid largesse, said he wouldn't notice if we ate a slice or two of his raisin bread, or of his apple and walnut. Simone said dourly that we were not to eat the croissants as there wouldn't be enough. It was all rather like school.

We set the places, put fresh water and carnations in bud vases, one flower to each table, and folded pink napkins with precision. By seven-fifteen, the first breakfasters were addressing themselves to eggs benedict and I was pouring tea and coffee as to the service born.

At seven-thirty, in struggling daylight, we stopped briefly in a place identified in suitably small letters on the small station as Schreiber.

It was from here, I reflected, looking through the windows at a small scattered town, that the dispatcher had spoken to George and me the previous evening: and while I watched, George appeared outside and was met by a man who came from the station. They conferred for a while, then George returned to the train, and the train went quietly on its way.

A spectacular way: all through breakfast, the track ran along the north shore of Lake Superior, so close that at times the train seemed to be overhanging the water. The passengers oohed and aahed, the Unwins (Upper Gumtree) sitting with the owners of Flokati, the Redi-Hots with a couple talking incessantly of the prowess of their horse, Wordmaster, also on the train.

Filmer came alone to sit at an untenanted table, ordering eggs and coffee from Oliver without looking at him. Presently the Youngs appeared and with smiling acquaintance-ship joined Filmer. I wondered if he thought immediately of Ezra Gideon, the Youngs' dear friend, but his face showed nothing but politeness.

Xanthe ambled in in a tousled yawning state and yesterday's clothes and flopped into the empty chair beside Filmer. Interestingly he made no attempt to save the seat for Daffodil, but seemed to echo Mrs. Young's inquiries about how Xanthe had slept.

Like a log, it appeared, although she seemed to regret not reporting constant nightmares. Mr. Young looked bored, as if he had tired of the subject a long time ago, but his wife retained her sweet comforting expression without any visible effort.

I waited with hovering impatience for Nell to arrive, which she did at length in a straight black skirt (worse and

worse) with a prim coffee blouse and unobtrusive gold ear-
rings. She had drawn her fair hair high into an elaborate plait
down the back of her head and fastened it at the bottom with
a wide tortoiseshell clasp: it looked distinguished and competent, but nowhere near cuddly.

People I hadn't yet identified beckoncd her eagerly to join
them, which she did with the ravishing smile she had loosed
once or twice in my direction. She told Cathy she would
pass on the eggs but would like croissants and coffee, and
presently I was bringing them to her as she sat with eyes
demurely downward, studiously ignoring my existence. I set
butter, jam and breads before her. I poured into her cup. She
told her table companions it was nice having hand-picked
attendants all thc way to Vancouver.

I knew it was a game but I could cheerfully have stran-
gled her. I didn't want them noticing me even a little. I went
away and looked back, and met her eyes, which were laughing. It was the sort of look between us that would have
started alert interest in me if I'd spotted it between others,
and I thought I was near to losing my grip on what I was
supposed to be doing, and that I'd better be more careful. I
hadn't needed to serve her: I'd taken the tray from Cathy.
Temptation will be your downfall, Tor, I thought.

Except for Xanthe, Mercer was the only Lorrimore to
surface for breakfast, and he came not to eat but to ask Emil
to send trays through to his own private dining room. Emil
himself and Oliver delivered the necessary, although Emil on
his return said he hoped this wasn't going to happen at lunch
and dinner also, because it took too much time. Room service was strictly not available, yet one didn't disoblige the
Lorrimores if one could help it.

Daffodil arrived after everyone else with each bright curl
in place and pleasantly sat across the aisle from the Filmer/
Young table, asking for news of Xanthe's night. The only
people not bothering to ask, it seemed, were the near-vic-
tim's own family. Xanthe chattered and could be heard telling Daffodil she felt snug and safe behind her curtain. The

next time I went slowly past their table, refill coffee pot at the ready, the conversation was back to the journey, with Xanthe this time saying she basically thought horseracing boring and she wouldn't have come on this trip if her father hadn't made her.

"How did he make you?" Filmer said interestedly.

"Oh!" She sounded suddenly flustered and evaded an answer. "He made Sheridan come, too."

"But why, if you both didn't want to?" That was Daffodil's voice, behind my back.

"He likes us where he can see us, he says." There was a note of grudge and bitterness but also, it seemed to me, a realistic acknowledgment that father knew best: and judging from Sheridan's behavior to date, under his father's long-suffering eye was certainly the son's safest place.

The conversation faded into the distance and I paused to refill the Unwins' cups, where the talk was about Upper Gumtree having the edge over Mercer's Premiere that was coming to Winnipeg by road.

George Burley presently came into the dining car and spoke for a while to Nell, who subsequently went from table to table, clipboard in place, repeating what he'd said.

"We're stopping at Thunder Bay for longer than scheduled, as there'll be an investigation there about the Lorrimores' car being uncoupled. We'll be there about an hour and a half, as we're not going on until after the regular Canadian has gone through. The Canadian will be ahead of us then all the way to Winnipeg."

"What about lunch?" Mr. Young asked. Mr. Young, though thinnish, had a habit of eating half his wife's food as well as his own.

"We'll leave Thunder Bay at about a quarter to one," Nell said, "so we'll have lunch soon after. And a more leisurely dinner before we get to Winnipeg, instead of having to crowd it in early. It will all fit in quite well." She was smiling, reassuring, keeping the party from unraveling. "You'll be glad to stretch your legs for a bit longer in Thunder Bay, and some of you might visit your horses."

The owner of Redi-Hot, who seemed to spend most of his time reading a guide book, told Mr. and Mrs. Wordmaster, who looked suitably impressed, that Thunder Bay, one of Canada's largest ports, was at the far west end of the St. Lawrence–Great Lakes seaway and should really be called what the locals called it, The Lakehead. Grain from the prairies was shipped from there throughout the world, he said.

"Fancy that," said Mrs. Wordmaster, who was English.

I retreated from this scintillating conversation and helped Oliver and Cathy clear up in the kitchen, and shortly before eleven we slid to a halt in the port that was halfway across Canada on some rails parallel with but a little removed from the station buildings.

Immediately a double posse of determined-looking men advanced from the station across two intervening tracks, one lot sprouting press cameras, the other notebooks. George stepped down from the train to meet the notebook people, and the others fanned out and began clicking. One of the notebook crowd climbed aboard and came into the dining car, inviting anyone who had seen anyone or anything suspicious the previous evening to please unbutton, but of course no one had, or no one was saying, because otherwise the whole train would have known about it by now.

The investigator said he would try his luck with the scenery-watchers in the dome car, with apparently the same result, and from there he presumably went in to see the Lorrimores, who apart from Xanthe were still in seclusion. He then reappeared in the dining car with an interested crowd of people following him and asked to speak to Xanthe, who up until then had kept palely quiet.

He identified her easily because everyone looked her way. Filmer was still beside her: the passengers generally tended to linger at the tables, talking, after the meals had been cleared, rather than return to the solitude of their bedrooms. Nearly everyone, I would have guessed, had been either in the dining room or the dome car all morning.

Mrs. Young squeezed Xanthe's hand encouragingly from across the table while the half-child half-young-woman shivered her way through the dangerous memory.

"No," she said, with everyone quiet and attentively listening, "no one suggested I go to our car . . . I just wanted to use the bathroom. And I could . . . I . . . could have been killed."

"Yes." The investigator, middle-aged and sharp-eyed, was sympathetic but calming, speaking in a distinct voice that carried easily through the dining car, now that we weren't moving. "Was there anyone in the dome car lounge when you went through?"

"Lot's of people." Xanthe's voice was much quieter than his.

"Did you know them?"

"No. I mean, they were on this trip. Everyone there was." She was beginning to speak more loudly, so that all could hear.

A few heads nodded.

"No one you now know was a stranger?"

"No."

Mrs. Young, intelligent as well as comforting, asked, "Do you mean it's possible to uncouple a car while you're actually on the train? You don't have to be on the ground to do it?"

The investigator gave her his attention and everyone leaned forward slightly to hear the answer.

"It's possible. It can be done also while the train is moving, which is why we want to know if there was anyone in the dome car who was unknown to you all. Unknown to any of you, I should say."

There was a long, respectful, understanding silence.

Nell said, "I suppose I know most of our passengers by sight by now. I identified them all at Toronto station when I was allocating their sleeping quarters. I didn't see anyone yesterday evening who puzzled me."

"You don't think," Mrs. Young said, putting her finger unerringly on the implication, "that the car was unhitched by *someone in our party*?"

"We're investigating all possibilities," the investigator said without pomposity. He looked around at the ranks of worried faces and his slightly severe expression softened. "The private car was deliberately uncoupled," he said, "but we're of the preliminary opinion that it was an act of mischief committed by someone in Cartier, the last place you stopped before Miss Xanthe found the car was missing. But we do have to ask if the saboteur could have been on the train, just in case any of you noticed anything wrong."

A man at the back of the crowd said, "I was sitting in the dome car lounge when Xanthe came through, and I can tell you that no one had come the other way. I mean, we all know that only the Lorrimores' car was behind the dome car. If anyone except the Lorrimores had gone that way and come back again . . . well . . . we would have noticed."

Another nodding of heads. People noticed everything to do with the Lorrimores.

I was watching the scene from the kitchen end of the dining car, standing just behind Emil, Cathy and Oliver. I could see Xanthe's troubled face clearly, and also Filmer's beside her. He seemed to me to be showing diminishing interest in the inquiry, turning his tidily brushed head away to look out of the window instead. There was no tension in him: when he was tense there was a rigidity in his neck muscles, a rigidity I'd watched from the depths of the crowd during the brief day of his trial and seen a few times since, as at Nottingham. When Filmer felt tense, it showed.

Even as I watched him, his neck went rigid.

I looked out of a window to see what he was looking at, but there seemed to be nothing of great note, only the race-going passengers streaming off their forward carriages en route to write postcards home from the station.

Filmer looked back toward Xanthe and the investigator and made a small gesture of impatience, and it seemed to trigger a response from the investigator because he said that if anyone remembered any helpful detail, however small, would they please tell him or one of his colleagues, but meanwhile everyone was free to go.

There was a communal sigh as the real-life investigation broke up. Zak, I thought, would be finding the competition too stiff, the fiction an anticlimax after the fact. He hadn't appeared for this scene: none of the actors had.

Most of the passengers went off to don coats against what appeared to be a cold wind outside, but Filmer climbed down from the door at the dome car end of the dining car without more protection than his carefully casual shirt and aristocratic tweed jacket. He paused irresolutely, not hurrying, as the others were beginning to, across the two sets of rails between our train and the station but meandering at an angle forward in the direction of the engine.

Inside, I followed him, easily keeping pace with his slow step. I thought at first that he was merely taking an open-air path to his own bedroom, but he went straight past the open door at the end of his sleeping car, and straight on past the next car also. Going to see his horse, no doubt. I went on following: it had become a habit.

At the end of the third car, just past George Burley's office, he stopped, because someone was coming out from the station to meet him: a gaunt man in a padded short coat with a fur collar, with gray hair blowing in disarray in the wind.

They met between George's window and the open door at the end of the car and although at first they looked moderately at peace with each other, the encounter deteriorated rapidly.

I risked them seeing me so as to try to hear, but in fact by the time I could hear them they were shouting, which meant I could listen through the doorway without seeing them or being seen.

Filmer was yelling furiously, "I said before Vancouver."

The gaunt man with a snarl in his Canadian voice said, "You said before Winnipeg, and I've done it and I want my money."

"Coo-ee" trilled Daffodil, teetering toward them in chinchillas and high-heeled boots. "Are we going to see Laurentide Ice?"

10

Blast her, I thought intensely. Triple bloody shit, and several other words to that effect.

I watched through George's window as Filmer made great efforts to go toward her with a smile, drawing attention away from the gaunt-faced man, who returned to the station.

Before Winnipeg, before Vancouver. Julius Apollo had mixed them up yet again. "You said before Winnipeg, and I've done it and I want my money." Heavy words, full of threat.

What before Winnipeg? What had he done?

What indeed.

It couldn't have been the Lorrimores' car, I thought. Filmer had shown no interest and no tension; had been obviously uninvolved. But then he would have been calm, I supposed, if he hadn't been expecting anything to happen except before Vancouver. He hadn't been expecting the Lorrimores' car to be uncoupled before either city, of that I was certain. He had instead been cultivating his acquaintanceship with Mercer, a game plan that would have come to an abrupt end if the Lorrimores had deserted the trip, which they would have done at once if the Canadian had ploughed into their home-from-home.

If not the Lorrimores' car, what else had happened? What

had happened before Winnipeg that Filmer had intended to happen before Vancouver? In what way had the gaunt man already earned his money?

Anyone's guess, I thought.

He could have robbed someone, bribed a stable lad, nobbled a horse . . .

Nobbled a horse that was going to run at Winnipeg, instead of one running at Vancouver?

From the fury in their voices, the mistake had been devastating.

Only Flokati and Upper Gumtree were due to run at Winnipeg. Laurentide Ice was running at Vancouver against Voting Right and Sparrowgrass. Could Filmer have been so stupid as to get the horses' names wrong in addition to the cities? No, he couldn't.

Impasse. Yet gaunt-face had done *something*.

Sighing, I watched the Youngs walk past the window en route, I supposed, to the horse car. Soon after, the Unwins followed. I would have liked to have checked at once on the state of the horses, but I supposed if there were something wrong with any of them I would hear soon enough.

I wished I'd been able to take a photograph of gaunt-face, but I'd been more keen to listen.

If he'd done something to or around the horses, I thought, then he had to have traveled with us on the train. He hadn't just met us in Thunder Bay. If he'd been on the train and had walked with the other racegoers toward the station, Filmer could have seen him through the window . . . and just the sight of him had caused the tensing of the neck muscles . . . and if Filmer hadn't yet paid him for whatever . . . then he would come back to the train . . .

I left George's office and went two doors along to my roomette to dig my telescopic-lens binoculars-camera out of Tommy's holdall, and I sat and waited by the window for gaunt-face's return.

What happened instead was that after a while Filmer and Daffodil appeared in my view, making a diagonal course toward the station buildings, and pretty soon afterward, accompanied by a lot of bell-ringing and warning hooters, a huge bright yellow diesel engine came grinding and groaning past my window followed by long corrugated silver coaches as the whole of the regular Canadian rolled up the track next to the race train and stopped precisely alongside.

Instead of a nice clear photographic view of the station I now faced the black uninformative window of someone else's roomette.

Frustration and damnation, I thought. I tucked the binoculars into the holdall again and without any sensible plans wandered back toward the dining car. If I went on like this, I would fulfill the gloomiest fears of Bill Baudelaire, the Brigadier and, above all, John Millington. "I *told* you we should have sent an ex-policeman." I could hear his voice in my ear.

It occurred to me, when I reached Julius Apollo's door, that the Canadian would be standing where it was for the whole of the twenty-five minutes of its daily scheduled stop. For twenty-five minutes . . . say twenty-two by now . . . Filmer would stay over in the station. He would not walk around either end of the lengthy Canadian to return to his room.

Would he?

No, he would not. Why should he? He had only just gone over there. I had twenty minutes to see what I could do about his combination locks.

If I'd paused for more thought I perhaps wouldn't have had the nerve, but I simply opened his door, checked up and down the corridor for observers (none) and went inside, shutting myself in.

The black briefcase was still on the floor at the back of the hanging space, under the suits. I pulled it out, sat on one of the armchairs, and with a feeling of unreality started on the right-hand lock. If anyone should come in, I thought confusedly . . . if the sleeping car attendant for instance came in . . . whatever excuse could I possibly find?

None at all.

The right-hand combination wheels were set at one-three-seven. I methodically went on from there, one-three-eight, one-three-nine, one-four-zero, trying the latch after each number change.

My heart hammered and I felt breathless. I was used to long-distance safety in my work, and in the past to many physical dangers, but never to this sort of risk.

One-four-one, one-four-two, one-four-three . . . I tried the latch over and over and looked at my watch. Only two minutes had gone. It felt like a lifetime. One-four-four, one-four-five . . . There were a thousand possible combinations. One-four-six, one-four-seven . . . In twenty minutes I could perhaps try a hundred and fifty numbers. I had done this process before, once, but not under pressure, when Aunt Viv had set a combination on a new suitcase and then forgotten it. One-four-eight, one-four-nine . . . My face was sweating, my fingers slipping on the tiny wheels from haste. One-five-zero, one-five-one . . .

With a snap the latch flew open.

It was incredible. I could hardly believe it. I had barely started. All I needed now was double the luck.

The left-hand combination numbers stood at seven-three-eight. I tried the latch. Nothing.

With just a hope that both locks opened to the same sesame, I turned the wheels to one-five-one and tried it. Nothing. Not so easy. I tried reversing it to five-one-five. Nothing. I tried comparable numbers, one-two-one, two-one-two, one-three-one, three-one-three, one-four-one, four-one-four . . . six . . . seven . . . eight . . . nine . . . three zeros.

Zilch.

My nerve deserted me. I rolled the left-hand wheels back to seven-three-eight and with the latch closed again set the right-hand lock to one-three-seven. I polished the latches a bit with my shirtsleeve, then I put the briefcase back exactly as I'd found it and took my leaf-trembling self along to the dining car, already regretting, before I got there, that I hadn't stayed until the Canadian left, knowing that I'd wasted some of the best and perhaps the only chance I would get of seeing what Filmer had brought with him on the train.

Perhaps if I'd tried one-one-five, or five-five-one, or five-one-one, or five-five-five . . .

Nell was sitting alone at a table in the dining car working on her interminable lists (those usually clipped to the clipboard) and I sat down opposite her feeling ashamed of myself.

She glanced up. "Hello," she said.

"Hi."

She considered me. "You look hot. Been running?"

I'd been indulging in good heart exercise while sitting still. I didn't think I would confess.

"Sort of," I said. "How's things?"

She glanced sideways with disgust at the Canadian.

"I was just about to go over to the station when *that* arrived."

That, as if taking the hint, began quietly to roll, and within twenty seconds we again had a clear view of the station. Most of the train's passengers, including Filmer and Daffodil, immediately started across the tracks to reboard. Among them, aiming for the racegoers' carriages, was gaunt-face.

God in heaven, I thought. I forgot about him. I forgot about photographing him. My wits were scattered.

"What's the matter?" Nell said, watching my face.

"I've earned a D minus. A double D minus."

"You probably expect too much of yourself," she said dispassionately. "No one's perfect."

"There are degrees of imperfection."

"How big is the catastrophe?"

I thought it over more coolly. Gaunt-face was on the train, and I might have another opportunity. I could undo one of the latches of Filmer's briefcase and, given time, I might do the other. Correction: given nerve, I might do the other.

"OK," I said. "let's say C minus, could do better. Still not good." Millington would have done better.

Zak and Emil arrived together at that point, Emil ready to set the tables for lunch, Zak in theatrical exasperation demanding to know if the actors were to put on the next scene before the meal, as originally planned, and if not, when?

Nell looked at her watch and briefly thought. "Couldn't you postpone it until cocktail time this evening?"

"We're supposed to do the following scene then," he objected.

"Well, couldn't you run them both together?"

He rather grumpily agreed and went away saying they would have to rehearse. Nell smiled sweetly at his departing back and asked if I'd ever noticed how *important* everything was to actors? Everything except the real world, of course.

"Pussycat," I said.

"But I have such tiny, indulgent claws."

Oliver and Cathy arrived and with Emil began spreading tablecloths and setting places. I got to my feet and helped them, and Nell with teasing amusement watched me fold pink napkins into water lilies and said, "Well, well, hidden depths," and I answered "You should see my dishwashing," which were the sort of infantile surface remarks of something we both guessed might suddenly become serious. The surface meanwhile was safe and shimmering and funny, and would stay that way until we were ready for change.

As usual, the passengers came early into the dining car, and I faded into the scenery in my uniform and avoided Nell's eyes.

The passengers hadn't over-enjoyed their sojourn in the station, it appeared, as they had been fallen upon by the flock of pressmen who had taken Xanthe back again to the brink of hysteria, and had asked Mercer whether it wasn't unwise to flaunt the privilege of wealth in his private car, and hadn't he invited trouble by adding it to the train. Indignation on his behalf was thick in the air. Everyone knew he was public-spiritedly on the trip For the Sake of Canadian Racing.

The Lorrimores, all four of them, arrived together to murmurs of sympathy, but the two young ones split off immediately from their parents and from each other, all of them gravitating to their various havens: the parents went to join Filmer and Daffodil of their own free will, Xanthe made a straight piteous line to Mrs. Young, and Sheridan grabbed hold of Nell, who was by this time standing, saying that he needed her to sit with him, she was the only decent human being on the whole damn train.

Nell, unsure of the worth of his compliment, nevertheless sat down opposite him, even if temporarily. Keeping Sheridan on a straight or even a wavy line definitely came into the category of crisis control.

Sheridan had the looks that went with Julius's name, Apollo: he was tall, handsome, nearly blond, a child of the sun. The ice, the arrogance, the lack of common sense and of control, these were the darkside tragedy. A mini psychopath, I thought, and maybe not so mini, at that, if Xanthe thought he should be in jail.

The Australian Unwins, sitting with the rival owners of Flokati, were concerned about a lifelessness they had detected in Upper Gumtree due to the fact that on the train their horse had been fed a restricted diet of compressed food nuts and high-grade hay, and the Flokati people were cheerfully saying that on so long a stretch without exercise, good hay was best. Hay was calming. "We don't want them climbing the walls," Mr. Flokati said. Upper Gumtree had looked asleep, Mrs. Unwin remarked with disapproval. The Flokati people beamed while trying to look sympathetic. If Upper Gumtree proved listless, so much the better for Flokati's chances.

It seemed that all of the owners had taken the opportunity of visiting the horses while the train was standing still, and listen though I might I could hear no one else reporting trouble.

Upper Gumtree, it seemed to me, might revive spectacularly on the morrow, given oats, fresh air and exercise. His race was still more than forty-eight hours away. If gaunt-face had in fact given Upper Gumtree something tranquilizing, the effects would wear off long before then.

On reflection, I thought it less and less probable that he had done any such thing: he would have to have by-passed the dragon-lady, Leslie Brown, for a start. Yet presumably at times she left her post to eat and sleep.

"I said," Daffodil said to me distinctly, "would you bring me a clean knife? I've dropped mine on the floor."

"Certainly, madam," I said, coming back abruptly to the matter in hand and realizing with a shock that she had already asked me once. I fetched her a knife fast. She nodded merely, her attention again on Filmer, and he, I was mightily relieved to see, had taken no notice of the small matter. But how could I, I thought ruefully, how could I have possibly stopped concentrating when I was so close to him? Only one day ago the proximity had had my pulse racing.

The train had made its imperceptible departure and was rolling along again past the uninhabited infinity of rocks and lakes and conifers that seemed to march on to the end of the world. We finished serving lunch and coffee and cleared up, and as soon as I decently could I left the kitchen and set off forward up the train.

George, whom I looked for first, was in his office eating a fat ragged beef sandwich and drinking diet Coke.

"How did it go?" I asked, "in Thunder Bay?"

He scowled, but halfheartedly. "They found out nothing I hadn't told them. There was nothing to see. They're thinking now that whoever uncoupled the private car was on it when the train left Cartier."

"On the private car?" I said in surprise.

"That's right. The steam tube could have been disconnected in the station, eh? Then the train leaves Cartier with the saboteur in the Lorrimores' car. Then less than a mile out of Cartier, our saboteur pulls up the rod that undoes the coupling. Then the private car rolls to a stop, and he gets off and walks back to Cartier."

"But why should anyone do that?"

"Grow up, sonny. There are people in this world who cause trouble because it makes them feel important. They're ineffective, eh?, in their lives. So they burn things and smash things, paint slogans on walls . . . leave their mark on something, eh? And wreck trains. Put slabs of concrete on the rails. I've seen it done. Power over others, that's what it's about. A grudge against the Lorrimores, most like. Power over them, over their possessions. That's what those investigators think."

"Hm," I said. "If that's the case, the saboteur wouldn't have walked back to Cartier but up to some vantage point from where he could watch the smash."

George looked startled. "Well, I suppose he might."

"Arsonists often help to put out the fires they've started."

"You mean he would have waited around to help with the wreck? Even to help with casualties?"

"Sure," I said. "Pure, heady power, to know you'd caused such a scene."

"I didn't see anyone around," he said thoughtfully, "when we went back to the car. I shone the lamp. There wasn't anyone moving, eh?, or anything like that."

"So, what are the investigators going to do?" I asked.

His eyes crinkled and the familiar chuckle escaped. "Write long reports, eh? Tell us never to take private cars. Blame me for not preventing it, I daresay."

He didn't seem worried at the idea. His shoulders and his mind were broad.

I left him with appreciation and went forward into the central dining car where all the actors were sitting in front of coffee cups and poring over typed sheets of stage directions, muttering under their breaths and sometimes exclaiming aloud.

Zak raised his eyes vaguely in my direction but it would have been tactless to disrupt the thoughts behind them, so I pressed on forward, traversing the dayniter and the sleeping cars and arriving at the forward dome car. There were a lot of people about everywhere, but no one looked my way twice.

I knocked eventually on the door of the horse car and, after inspection and formalities that would have done an Iron Curtain country proud, was admitted again by Ms. Brown to the holy of holies.

Rescrawling Tommy Titmouse on her list I was interested to see how long it had grown, and I noticed that even Mercer hadn't been let in without signing. I asked the dragon-lady if anyone had come in who wasn't an owner or a groom, and she bridled like a thin turkey and told me that she had conscientiously checked every visitor against her list of bonafide owners, and only they had been admitted.

"But you wouldn't know them all by sight," I said.

"What do you mean?" she demanded.

"Supposing for instance someone came and said they were Mr. Unwin, you would check that his name was on the list and let him in?"

"Yes, of course."

"And suppose he wasn't Mr. Unwin, although he said he was?"

"You're just being difficult," she said crossly. "I cannot refuse entry to the owners. They were given the right to visit, but they don't have to produce passports. Nor do their wives or husbands."

I looked down her visitors' list. Filmer appeared on it twice, Daffodil once. Filmer's signature was large and flamboyant, demanding attention. No one had written Filmer in any other way: it seemed that gaunt-face hadn't gained entry by giving Filmer's name, at least. It didn't mean he hadn't given someone else's.

I gave Leslie Brown her list back and wandered around under her eagle eye looking at the horses. They swayed peacefully to the motion, standing diagonally across the stalls, watching me incuriously, seemingly content. I couldn't perceive that Upper Gumtree looked any more sleepy than any of the others: his eyes were as bright, and he pricked his ears when I came near him.

All of the grooms, except one who was asleep on some hay bales, had chosen not to sit in the car with their charges, and I imagined it was because of Leslie Brown's daunting presence: racing lads on the whole felt a companionable devotion to their horses, and I would have expected more of them to be sitting on the hay bales during the day.

"What happens at night on the train?" I asked Leslie Brown. "Who guards the horses then?"

"I do," she said tartly. "They've given me a roomette or some such, but I take this thing seriously. I slept in here last night, and will do so again after Winnipeg, and after Lake Louise. I don't see why you're so worried about anyone slipping past me." She frowned at me, not liking my suspicions. "When I go to the bathroom, I leave one groom in here and lock the horses' car door behind me. I'm never away more than a few minutes. I insist on one of the grooms being in here at all times. I am very well aware of the need for security, and I assure you that the horses are well guarded."

I regarded her thin obstinate face and knew she believed to her determined soul in what she said.

"As for the barns at Winnipeg and the stabling at Calgary," she added righteously, "they are someone else's responsibility. I can't answer for what happens to the horses there." She was implying, plain enough, that no one else could be trusted to be as thorough as herself.

"Do you ever have any fun, Ms. Brown?" I asked.

"What do you mean," she said, raising surprised eyebrows. "All this is fun." She waved a hand in general round the horse car. "I'm having the time of my life." And she wasn't being ironic: she truly meant it.

"Well," I said a little feebly, "then that's fine."

She gave two sharp little nods, as if that finished the matter, which no doubt it did, except that I still looked for gaps in her defenses. I wandered one more time round the whole place, seeing the sunlight slant in through the barred unopenable windows (which would keep people out as well as horses in), smelling the sweet hay and the faint musty odor of the horses themselves, feeling the swirls of fresh air coming from the rows of small ventilators along the roof, hearing the creaking and rushing noises in the car's fabric and the grind of the electricity-generating wheels under the floor.

In that long, warm, friendly space there were animals worth at present a total of many millions of Canadian dollars: worth more if any of them won at Winnipeg or Vancouver. I stood for a long while looking at Voting Right. If Bill Baudelaire's mother knew her onions, in this undistinguished-looking bay lay the dormant seed of greatness.

Maybe she was right. Vancouver would tell.

I turned away, cast a final assessing glance at Laurentide Ice, who looked coolly back, thanked the enthusiastic dragon for her cooperation (prim acknowledgment) and began a slow walk back through the train, looking for gaunt-face.

I didn't see him. He could have been behind any of the closed doors. He wasn't in the forward dome car, upstairs or down, nor in the open dayniter. I sought out and consulted separately with three of the sleeping car attendants in the racegoers' sleeping cars who frowned in turn and said that first, the sort of jacket I was describing was worn by thousands, and second, everyone tended to look gaunt outside in the cold air. All the same, I said, if they came across anyone fitting that description in their care, please would they tell George Burley his name and room number.

Sure, they each said, but wasn't this an odd thing for an actor to be asking? Zak, I improvised instantly at the first inquiry, had thought the gaunt man had an interesting face and he wanted to ask if he could use him in a scene. Ah, yes, that made sense. If they found him, they would tell George.

When I got back to George, I told him what I'd asked. He wrinkled his brow. "I saw a man like that at Thunder Bay," he said. "But I probably saw several men like that in all this trainload. What do you want him for?"

I explained that I'd told the sleeping car attendants that Zak wanted to use him in a scene.

"But you?" George said. "What do you want him for yourself?"

I looked at him and he looked back. I was wondering how far I should trust him and had an uncomfortable impression that he knew what I was thinking.

"Well," I said finally, "he was talking to someone I'm interested in."

I got a long bright beam from the shiny eyes.

"Interested in . . . in the line of duty?"

"Yes."

He didn't ask who it was and I didn't tell him. I asked him instead if he himself had talked to any of the owners' party.

"Of course I have," he said. "I always greet passengers, eh?, when they board. I tell them I'm the conductor, tell them where my office is, tell them if they've any problems to bring them to me."

"And do they? Have they?"

He chuckled. "Most of the complaints go to your Miss Richmond, and she brings them to me."

"Miss Richmond," I repeated.

"She's your boss, isn't she? Tall pretty girl with her hair in a plait today, eh?"

"Nell," I said.

"That's right. Isn't she your boss?"

"Colleague."

"Right, then. The sort of problems the owners' party have had on this trip so far are a tap that won't stop dripping, a blind that won't stay down in one of the bedrooms, eh?, and a lady who thought one of her suitcases had been stolen, only it turned up in someone else's room." He beamed.

"Most of the owners have been along to see the horses. When they see me, they stop to talk."

"What do they say?" I asked. "What sort of things?"

"Only what you'd expect. The weather, the journey, the scenery. They ask what time we get to Sudbury, eh? Or Thunder Bay, or Winnipeg, or wherever."

"Has anyone asked anything that was different, or surprised you?"

"Nothing surprises me, sonny." He glowed with irony and bonhomie. "What would you expect them to ask?"

I shrugged in frustration. "What happened before Thunder Bay that shouldn't have?"

"The Lorrimores' car, eh?"

"Apart from that."

"You think something happened?"

"Something happened, and I don't know what, and it's what I'm here to prevent."

He thought about it, then said, "When it turns up, you'll know, eh?"

"Maybe."

"Like if someone put something in the food, eh?, sooner or later everyone will be ill."

"George!" I was dumbstruck.

He chuckled. "We had a waiter once years ago who did that. He had a grudge against the world. He put handfuls of ground-up laxative pills into the chocolate topping over ice cream and watched the passengers eat it, and they all had diarrhea. Dreadful stomach pains. One woman had to go to hospital. She'd had two helpings. What a to-do, eh?"

"You've frightened me stiff," I said frankly. "Where do they keep the fodder for the horses?"

He stared, his perpetual smile fading.

"Is that what you're afraid of? Something happening to the horses?"

"It's a possibility."

"All the fodder is in the horse car," he said, "except for some extra sacks of those cubes most of the horses are having, which are in the baggage car. Some of the horses have their own special food brought along with them, sent by their trainers. One of the grooms has a whole set of separate bags labeled 'Sunday evening,' 'Monday morning' and so on. He was showing them to me."

"Which horse was that for?"

"Um . . . the one that belongs to that Mrs. Daffodil Quentin, I think. The groom said one of her horses died of colic or some such recently, from eating the wrong things, and the trainer didn't want any more accidents, so he'd made up the feeds himself."

"You're brilliant, George."

His ready laugh came back.

"Don't forget the water tank, eh? You can lift the lid where the plank floats, remember? You could dope all those horses at once with one quick cupful of mischief, couldn't you?"

11

Leslie Brown told us adamantly that no one could possibly have tampered with either the fodder or the water.

"When did the grooms last fill the buckets?" I asked.

During the morning, she said. Each groom filled the bucket for his own horse, when he wanted to. All of them had been in there, seeing to their charges.

The horses' drinking water tank had been topped up, she said, by a hosepipe from the city's water supply during the first twenty minutes of our stop in Thunder Bay, in a procedure that she herself had supervised.

George nodded and said the whole train had been rewatered at that point.

"Before Thunder Bay," I said, "could anyone have put anything in the water?"

"Certainly not. I've told you over and over again, I am here all the time."

"And how would you rate all the grooms for trustworthiness?" I said.

She opened her mouth and closed it again and gave me a hard look.

"I am here to supervise them," she said. "I didn't know any of them before yesterday. I don't know if any of them could be bribed to poison the water. Is that what you want?"

"It's realistic," I said with a smile.

She was unsoftened, unsoftenable.

"My chair, as you see," she said carefully, "is next to the water tank. I sit there and watch. I do not think, I repeat, I do not believe, that anyone has tampered with the water."

"Mm," I said calmingly. "But you could ask the grooms, couldn't you, if they've seen anything wrong?"

She began to shake her head automatically, but then stopped and shrugged. "I'll ask them, but they won't have."

"And just in case," I said, "in case the worst happens and the horses prove to have been interfered with, I think I'll take a sample of what's in the tank and also what's in their buckets at this moment. You wouldn't object to that, Ms. Brown, would you?"

She grudgingly said she wouldn't. George elected himself to go and see what could be done in the way of sample jars and presently returned with gifts from the Chinese cook in the dome car, in the shape of four rinsed-out plastic tomato sauce bottles rescued from the rubbish bin.

George and Leslie Brown took a sample from the tank, draining it, at the dragon's good suggestion, from the tap lower down, where the buckets were filled. I visited Voting Right, Laurentide Ice and Upper Gumtree, who all graciously allowed me to dip into their drink. With Leslie Brown's pen, we wrote the provenance of each sample on the sauce label and put all four containers into a plastic carrier bag that Leslie Brown happened to have handy.

Carrying the booty, I thanked her for her kindness in answering our questions, and helping, and George and I retreated.

"What do you think?" he said, as we started back through the train.

"I think she now isn't as sure as she says she is."

He chuckled. "She'll be doubly careful from now on."

"As long as it's not already too late."

He looked as if it were a huge joke. "We could get the tank emptied, scrubbed and refilled at Winnipeg," he said.

"Too late. If there's anything in it, it was there before Thunder Bay, and the horses will have drunk some of it. Some horses drink a lot of water, but they're a bit fussy. They won't touch it if they don't like the smell. If there's traces of soap in it for instance, or oil. They'd only drink doped water if it smelled all right to them."

"You know a lot about it," George commented.

"I've spent most of my life near horses, one way and another."

We reached his office where he said he had some paperwork to complete before we stopped fairly soon for ten minutes at Kenora. We would be there at five-twenty, he said. We were running thirty minutes behind the Canadian. There were places the race train didn't really need to stop, he said, except to keep pace with the Canadian. We needed always to stop where the trains were serviced for water, trash and fuel.

I had nowhere on our journey to and from the horse car seen the man with the gaunt face. George had pointed someone out to me in the dayniter, but he was not the right person: gray-haired, but too ill-looking, too old. The man I was looking for, I thought, was fifty-something, maybe less, still powerful; not in decline.

In a vague way, I thought, he had reminded me of Derry Welfram. Less bulky than the dead frightener, and not as smooth, but the same stamp of man. The sort Filmer seemed to seek out naturally.

I sat for an hour in my roomette looking out at the unvarying scenery and trying to imagine anything else that Filmer might have paid to have done. It was all the wrong way round, I thought: it was more usual to know the crime and seek the criminal, than to know the criminal and seek his crime.

The four sample bottles of water stood in their plastic carrier on my roomette floor. To have introduced something noxious into that tank, gaunt-face would certainly have to have bribed a groom. He wasn't one of the grooms himself, though perhaps he had been one, somewhere, sometime.

The grooms on the train were all younger, thinner and from what I'd seen of them in their uniform T-shirts, less positive. I couldn't imagine any of them having the nerve to stand up to Filmer and demand their money.

I spent the brief stop at the small town of Kenora hanging out of the open doorway past George's office, watching him, on the station side of the train, walk a good way up and down outside while he checked that all looked well. The Lorrimores' car, it appeared, was still firmly tacked on. Up behind the engine, two baggage handlers were loading a small pile of boxes. I hung out of the door on the other side of the train for a while, but no one was moving out there at all.

George climbed back on board and closed the doors, and presently we set off again from our last stop before Winnipeg.

I wished intensely that I had the power to see into Filmer's mind. I ached to foresee what he was planning. I felt blind, and longed for second sight. Failing such superhuman qualities, however, there was only usual ordinary observation and patience, and they both seemed inadequate and tame.

I went along to the dining car where I found that Zak had already positioned some of the actors at the tables for the cocktail-hour double-length scene. He and Nell were agreeing that after the scene the actors would leave again (all except Giles the murderer), even though they didn't like being banished all the time and were complaining about it.

Emil, laying tablecloths, said that wine alone was included in the fare, all other cocktails having to be paid for, and perhaps I'd better just serve the wine; he and Oliver and Cathy would do the rest. Fine by me, I said, distributing ashtrays and bud vases. I could set the wineglasses also, Emil said. Glasses for red wine and for white at each place.

The passengers drifted in from their rooms and the dome car and fell into by now predictable patterns of seating. Even though to my mind Bambi Lorrimore and Daffodil Quentin were as compatible as salt and strawberries, the two women were again positioned opposite each other, bound there by the attraction between their men. When I put the wineglasses on their table, Mercer and Filmer were discussing world-wide breeding in terms of exchange rates. Daffodil told Bambi there was a darling little jewelry store in Winnipeg.

Xanthe was still clinging to Mrs. Young. Mr. Young looked exceedingly bored.

Sheridan had struck up an acquaintanceship with the actor-murderer Giles, a slightly bizarre eventuality that might have odd consequences.

The Upper Gumtree Unwins and the Flokati couple seemed locked in common interest: whether the instant friendship would wither after their mutual race would be Wednesday evening's news.

Most of the other passengers I knew only vaguely, by face more than by name. I'd learned their names only to the extent that they owned horses in the horse car or had touched bases with Filmer, which came to only about half. They were all in general pleasant enough, although one of the men sent nearly everything back to the kitchen to be reheated, and one of the women pushed the exceptional food backward and forward across her plate with flicking movements of her fork, sternly remarking that plain fare was all anyone needed for godliness. What she was doing among the racing fraternity, I never found out.

Zak's long scene began with impressive fireworks as soon as everyone had been served with a drink.

A tall man dressed in the full scarlet traditional uniform of the Royal Canadian Mounted Police strode into the dining car and in a conversation-stopping voice said he had some serious information for us. He had come aboard at Kenora, he said, because the body of a groom from this train called Ricky had been found lying beside the railway lines near Thunder Bay. He had been wearing his Race Train T-shirt, and he had identification in his pocket.

The passengers looked horrified. The Mountie's impres-

sive presence dominated the whole place and he sounded
undoubtedly authentic. He understood, he said, that the
groom had been attacked earlier, in Toronto, when he foiled
the kidnaping of a horse, but he had insisted on making the
journey nevertheless, having been bandaged by a Miss Richmond. Was that correct?

Nell demurely said that it was.

Among the actual owners of the horses, disbelief had set
in the quickest. Mercer Lorrimore enjoyed the joke. Mounties, when investigating, didn't nowadays go around dressed
for parades.

"But we are in Manitoba," Mercer could be heard saying
in a lull, "they've got that right. We passed the boundary
with Ontario a moment ago. The Mounted Police's territory
starts right there."

"You seem to know all about it," our Mountie said.
"What do you know about this dead groom?"

"Nothing," Mercer said cheerfully.

I glanced briefly at Filmer. His face was hard, his neck
rigid, his eyes narrow; and I thought in a flash of Paul
Shacklebury, the lad dead in his ditch. Stable lads in England, grooms in Canada: same job. What had Paul Shacklebury known about Filmer? Same old unanswerable
question.

"And why was he killed?" the Mountie asked. "What did
he know?"

I risked a glance, looked away. Filmer's mouth was a
tight line. The answer to the question had to be in his tautly
held head at that moment and it was as inaccessible to me as
Alpha Centauri.

Zak suggested that Ricky had identified one of the hijackers. Perhaps, he said, the hijackers had come on the
train. Perhaps they were among the racegoers, waiting another chance to kidnap their quarry.

Filmer's neck muscles slowly relaxed, and I realized that
for a moment he must have suspected that the scene had
been specifically aimed at him. Perhaps he spent a lot of his

time reacting in that way to the most innocent of remarks.

Mavis and Walter Bricknell demanded that the Mountie should keep their own precious horse safe.

The Mountie brushed them aside. He was taking over the inquiry into the death of Angelica Standish, he said. Two deaths connected to the same train could be no coincidence. What was the connection between Angelica and Ricky?

Zak said that *he* was in charge of the Angelica investigation.

No longer, said the Mountie. We were now in the province of Manitoba, not Ontario. His territory, exclusively.

Zak's intended scene of investigation into Angelica's murder had been upstaged by the reality of the Lorrimores' car and then aborted by the long stop at Thunder Bay. Passing the questioning to the Mountie bridged the void neatly, and the Mountie told us that the reason that Steve, Angelica's business manager, also her lover, had not turned up at Toronto station was that he too was dead, struck down in his apartment by blows to the head with a mallet.

The audience received the news of still more carnage with round eyes. The said Steven, the Mountie went on, seemed to have been in bed asleep at the time of his murder, and the Ontario police were wanting to interview Angelica Standish as a suspect.

"But she's dead!" Mavis Bricknell said.

After a pause, Donna said she and Angelica had talked for maybe two hours between Toronto and Sudbury, and Donna was sure Angelica couldn't have murdered Steve, she was lost without him.

Maybe, the Mountie said, but if she was as upset as all that, why had she come on the train at all? Couldn't it have been to escape from having to realize that she'd killed her lover?

Giles-the-murderer calmly inquired whether any murder weapon had been found after Angelica had been killed.

Also, Pierre asked, wouldn't Angelica's murderer have

been covered with blood? The whole toilet compartment had been splashed.

Zak and the Mountie exchanged glances. The Mountie said grudgingly that a blood-covered rolled-up sheet of plastic had been found on the track near the area where Angelica must have been battered, and it could have been used as a poncho, and it was being investigated for blood type and fingerprints.

Donna said couldn't Steve and Angelica both have been killed by a mallet? That would make her innocent, wouldn't it? She couldn't believe that anyone as nice as Angelica could have been mixed up in an insurance swindle.

What? What insurance swindle?

I glanced involuntarily at Daffodil, but if there had been a flicker of her eyelids, I had missed it.

Donna in confusion said she didn't know what insurance swindle. Angelica had just mentioned that Steve was mixed up in an insurance swindle, and she was afraid that was why he had missed the train. Donna hadn't liked to probe any further.

Sheridan Lorrimore, saying loudly that Angelica had been a bitch, made a lunging grab at the pistol sitting prominently in a holster on the Mountie's hip. The Mountie, feeling the tug, turned fast and put his hand down on Sheridan's wrist. It was a movement in a way as dexterous as John Millington on a good day, speaking of razor-sharp reactions, more like an athlete than an actor.

"That gun's mine, sir," he said, lifting Sheridan's wrist six inches sideways and releasing it. "And, everybody, it's not loaded."

There was a general laugh. Sheridan, universally unpopular and having made a boorish fool of himself yet again, looked predictably furious. His mother, I noticed, had turned her head away. Mercer was shaking his.

The Mountie, unperturbed, said he would be proceeding vigorously with the inquiries into both Angelica's and Ricky's deaths and perhaps he would have news for everyone in Winnipeg. He and Zak went away together, and Donna drifted around from table to table for a while telling everyone that poor Angelica had really been very sweet, not a murderess, and she, Donna, was dreadfully upset at the suggestion. She wrung out a real tear or two. She was undoubtedly an effective actress.

"What do you care?" Sheridan asked her rudely. "You only met her yesterday morning and she was dead before dinner."

Donna looked at him uncertainly. He'd sounded as if he really believed in Angelica's death.

"Er . . ." she said, "some people you know at once." She moved on gently and presently disappeared with disconsolate-looking shoulders down the corridor beside the kitchen. Sheridan muttered under his breath several times, making the people he was sitting with uncomfortable.

Emil and his crew, including me, immediately began setting the table round the passengers for dinner, and were soon serving warm goat's cheese and radicchio salads followed by circles of rare Chateaubriand with snow peas and matchstick carrots and finally rich orange sorbets smothered in fluffy whipped cream and nuts. Most of the passengers persevered to the end and looked as though it were no torture.

My suggestion to Angus, while we were dishwashing after the battle, that maybe his food could have been injected somehow with a substance that even now could be working away to the detriment of everyone's health was received by him with frosty amusement. Absolutely impossible, he assured me. I had surely noticed that nearly all the ingredients had come onto the train *fresh*? He was *cooking* this food, not bringing it in prefrozen packs.

I assured him truthfully that I had been impressed by his skill and speed, and I thought his results marvelous.

"You actors," he said more indulgently, "will think of any impossible thing for a plot."

Everyone got off the train at Winnipeg, 1,413 miles along the rails from Toronto.

Two large motor horse-vans were waiting for the horses, which were unloaded down and loaded up ramps. The grooms and Leslie Brown led the horses across from train to van and saw them installed and then, carrying holdalls, themselves trooped onto a bus, which followed the horse-vans away toward the racetrack.

A row of buses waited outside the station to take the racegoers away to a variety of outlying motels, and a long new coach with darkly tinted windows was set aside for the owners. A few of the owners, like the Lorrimores and Daffodil and Filmer, had arranged their own transport separately in the shape of chauffeur-driven limousines, their chauffeurs coming over to the train to carry their bags.

The crew, after everyone else had left, tidied away into secure lockers every movable piece of equipment and goods, and then joined the actors in the last waiting bus. The Mountie, I was interested to see, was among us, tall and imposing even with his scarlet and brass buttons tucked away in his bag.

George came last, carrying an attaché case of papers and looking over his shoulder at the train as if wondering if he'd forgotten anything. He sat in the seat across the aisle from me and said the cars would be backed into a siding for two days, the engine would be removed and used elsewhere, and there would be a security guard on duty. In the siding, the carriages would be unheated and unlit and would come to life again only about an hour before we left on the day after tomorrow. We'd been able to keep the same crew from coast to coast, he said, only because of the two rest breaks along the way.

The owners and some of the actors were staying in the Westin Hotel, which had, Nell had told everyone during dinner, a ballroom and an indoor pool. There was a breakfast room set aside for the train party where a piece of the mystery would unravel each morning. Apart from that, everyone was on their own: there were good shops, good restaurants and good racing. Transport had been arranged to and from the racecourse. We would all come back to reboard the train after the Jockey Club Race Train Stakes on Wednesday, and cocktails and dinner would be served as soon as we'd rolled out of the station. The party, in good humor, applauded.

I had decided not to stay in the same hotel as any of the groups of owners, actors, racegoers or crew, and asked Nell if she knew of anywhere else. A tall order, it seemed.

"We've put people almost everywhere," she said doubtfully, "but only a few actors will be at the Holiday Inn. Why don't you try there? Although actually there *is* one place we haven't booked anyone into, and that's the Sheraton. But it's like the Westin—expensive."

"Never mind, I'll find somewhere," I said, and when the crew bus after a short drive stopped and disgorged its passengers, I took my grip and vanished on foot and, after asking directions, made a homing line to where no one else was staying.

In my buttoned-up gray VIA raincoat, I was unexceptional to the receptionists of the Sheraton: the only problem, they said, was that they were full. It was late in the evening. The whole city was full.

"An annex?" I suggested.

Two of them shook their heads and consulted with each other in low voices. Although they had no single rooms left, they said finally, they had had a late cancellation of a suite. They looked doubtful. I wouldn't be interested in that, they supposed.

"Yes, I would," I said and gave them my American Express card with alacrity. So Tommy the waiter carefully hung up his yellow waistcoat with its white lining and ordered some wine from room service and in a while after a long easing shower slept for eight solid hours and didn't dream about Filmer.

————

In the morning, I telephoned Mrs. Baudelaire and listened again to the almost girlish voice on the wire.

"Messages for the invisible man," she said cheerfully. "Er . . . are you still invisible?"

"Mostly, yes, I think."

"Bill says Val Catto would like to know if you are still invisible to the quarry. Does that make sense to you?"

"It makes sense, and the answer is yes."

"They're both anxious."

"And not alone," I said. "Will you tell them the quarry has an ally on the train, traveling I think with the racegoers. I've seen him once and will try to photograph him."

"Goodness!"

"Also will you ask them whether certain numbers, which I'll tell you, have any significance in the quarry's life."

"Intriguing," she said. "Fire away."

"Well . . . three numbers I don't know. Three question marks, say. Then one-five-one."

"Three question marks, then one-five-one. Right?"

"Right. I know it's not his car's number plate, or not the car he usually travels in, but ask if it fits his birthday in any way, or his phone number, or anything at all they can think of. I want to know what the first three digits are."

"I'll ask Bill right away, when I've finished talking to you. He gave me some answers to give you about your questions yesterday evening."

"Great."

"The answers are that Mr. and Mrs. Young who own Sparrowgrass are frequent and welcome visitors to England and are entertained by the Jockey Club at many racemeetings. They were friends of Ezra Gideon. Val Catto doesn't know if they know why Ezra Gideon sold two horses to a Mr. J. A. Filmer. Does that make sense?"

"Yes," I said.

"I'm glad you understand what I'm talking about. How about this one, then?" She paused for breath. "Sheridan Lorrimore was sent down—expelled—from Cambridge University, England, last May, amid some sort of hushed-up scandal. Mercer Lorrimore was over in England at that time, and stayed and went racing at Newmarket in July, but the Jockey Club found him grimmer than his usual self and understood it was something to do with his son, although he didn't say what. Val Catto is seeing what he can find out from Cambridge."

"That's fine," I said.

"Sheridan Lorrimore!" she said, sounding shocked. "I hope it's not true."

"Brace yourself," I said dryly.

"Oh, dear."

"How well do you know him?" I asked.

"Hardly at all. But it does no good, does it, for one of our golden families to hit the tabloids."

I loved the expression, and remembered she'd owned a magazine.

"It demeans the whole country," she went on. "I just hope whatever it was will stay hushed up."

"Whatever it was?"

"Yes," she said firmly. "For his family's sake. For his mother's sake. I know Bambi Lorrimore. She's a proud woman. She doesn't deserve to be disgraced by her son."

I wasn't so sure about that: didn't know to what extent she was responsible for his behavior. But perhaps not much. Perhaps no one deserved a son like Sheridan. Perhaps people like Sheridan were born that way, as if without arms.

"Are you still there?" Mrs. Beaudelaire asked.

"I sure am."

"Bill says the Lorrimores' private car got detached from

the train on Sunday evening. Is that really true? There's a great fuss going on, isn't there? It's been on the television news and it's all over the papers this morning. Bill says it was apparently done by some lunatic for reasons unknown, but he wants to know if you have any information about it that he doesn't have."

I told her what had happened: how Xanthe had casually nearly walked off into space.

"Tell Bill the quarry sat relaxed and unconcerned throughout both the incident and the inquiry held at Thunder Bay yesterday morning, and I'm certain he didn't plan the uncoupling. I think he did plan *something* though, with his ally on the train, and I think Bill should see that they guard the train's horses very carefully out at the track."

"I'll tell him."

"Tell him there's a slight possibility that the horses' drinking water was tampered with on the train, before it got to Thunder Bay. But I think that if it had been, the horses should have been showing distress by last night, which they weren't. I can't check them this morning. I suppose if there's anything wrong with them, Bill will know pretty soon. Anyway, I took four samples of the drinking water, which I will take to the races this evening."

"Good heavens."

"Tell Bill I'll get them to him somehow. They'll be in a package with his name on it."

"Let me write some of this down. Don't go away."

There was a quiet period while she put down the receiver and wrote her notes. Then she came back on the line and faithfully repeated everything I'd told her, and everything I'd asked.

"Is that right?" she demanded, at the end.

"Perfect," I said fervently. "When in general is it a good time for me to phone you? I don't like to disturb you at bad moments."

"Phone any time. I'll be here. Have a good day. Stay invisible."

I laughed, and she'd gone off the line before I could ask her about her health.

A complimentary copy of a Winnipeg newspaper had been slipped under my sitting-room door, and I picked it up and checked on what news it gave of the train. The story wasn't exactly all over the front page, but it started there with photographs of Mercer and Bambi and continued inside, with a glamorous backlit formal shot of Xanthe, which made her look a lot older than her published age, fifteen.

I suspected ironically that the extra publicity given to the Great Transcontinental Mystery Race Train hadn't hurt the enterprise in the least. Blame hadn't been fastened on anyone except some unknown crazy back in the wilds of Ontario. Winnipeg was full of racegoing visitors who were contributing handsomely to the local economy. Winnipeg was pleased to welcome them. Don't forget, the paper prominently said, that the first of the two Celebration of Canadian Racing meetings would be held this evening with the regular post time of 7:00, while the second meeting, including the running of the Jockey Club Race Train Stakes, would be tomorrow afternoon, post time 1:30. The afternoon had been declared a local holiday, as everyone knew, and it would be a fitting finale to the year's thoroughbred racing program at Assiniboia Downs. (Harness racing, it said in brackets, would hold the first meeting of its winter season on the following Sunday.)

I spent most of the day mooching around Winnipeg, seeing a couple of owners once in a shop selling Eskimo sculptures, but never coming face to face with anyone who might know me. I didn't waste much time trying to see what Filmer did or where he went, because I'd quickly discovered that the Westin Hotel was sitting over an entrance to a subterranean shopping mall that stretched like a rabbit warren in all directions. Shopping, in Canada, had largely gone underground to defeat the climate. Filmer could go in and out of the Westin without a sniff of fresh air, and probably had.

There were racetrack express buses, I found, going from

the city to the Downs, so I went on one at about six o'clock and strolled around at ground level looking for some way of conveying to Bill Baudelaire the water samples that were now individually wrapped inside the nondescript plastic carrier.

It was made easy for me. A girl of about Xanthe's age bounced up to my side as I walked slowly along in front of the grandstand, and said, "Hi. I'm Nancy. If that's for Clarrie Baudelaire, I'll take it up if you like."

"Where is she?" I asked.

"Dining with her dad up there by a window in the Clubhouse." She pointed to a part of the grandstand. "He said you were bringing her some thirst quenchers, and he asked me to run down and collect them. Is that right?"

"Spot on," I said appreciatively.

She was pretty, with freckles, wearing a bright-blue track suit with a white-and-gold studded belt. I gave her the carrier and watched her jaunty backview disappear with it into the crowds, and I was more and more sure that what she was carrying was harmless. Bill Baudelaire wouldn't be calmly eating dinner with his daughter if there were a multihorse crisis going on over in the racecourse stables.

The Clubhouse, from where diners could watch the sport, took up one whole floor of the grandstand, glassed in along its whole length to preserve summer indoors. I decided not to go in there on the grounds that Tommy would not, and Tommy off duty in Tommy's off-duty clothes was what I most definitely wanted to be at that moment. I made some Tommy-sized bets and ate very well in the (literally) below-stairs bar, and in general walked around, race-card in hand, binoculars around neck, exactly as usual.

The daylight faded almost imperceptibly into night, electricity taking over the sun's job smoothly. By seven, when the first race was run, it was under floodlighting, the jockeys' colors brilliant against the backdrop of night.

There were a lot of half-familiar faces in the crowds; the enthusiastic racegoers from the train. The only one of them that I was interested in, though, was either extremely elusive, or not there. All the techniques I knew of finding people were to no avail: the man with his gaunt face, gray hair and fur-collared parka was more invisible than I.

I did see Nell.

In her plain blue suit she came down from the Clubhouse with two of the owners who seemed to want to be near the horses at ground level. I drifted after the three of them to watch the runners come out for the third race and wasn't far behind them when they walked right down to the rails to see the contest from the closest possible quarters. When it was over the owners turned toward the stands talking animatedly about the result, and I contrived to be where Nell would see me, with any luck, making a small waving motion with my race-card.

She noticed the card, noticed me with widening eyes, and in a short while detached herself from the owners and stood and waited. When without haste I reached her side she gave me a sideways grin.

"Aren't you one of the waiters from the train?" she said.

"I sure am."

"Did you find somewhere to sleep?"

"Yes, thank you. How's the Westin?"

She was staying with the owners; their shepherd, their smoother-of-the-way, their information booth.

"The hotel's all right—but someone should strangle that rich . . . that arrogant . . . that *insufferable* Sheridan." Disgust vibrated in her voice as she suddenly let go of some clearly banked-up and held-back emotion. "He's unbearable. He's spoiling it for the others. They all paid a fortune to come on this trip and they're entitled not to be upset."

"Did something happen?" I asked.

"Yes, at breakfast." The memory displeased her. "Zak put on the next scene of the mystery and Sheridan shouted him down *three* times. I went over to Sheridan to ask him to be quiet and he grabbed my wrist and tried to pull me onto his lap, and I overbalanced and fell and hit the table hard where he was sitting, and I caught the cloth somehow and pulled it with me and everything on it landed on the floor. So you can imagine the fuss. I was on my knees, there was orange juice and broken plates and food and coffee everywhere and Sheridan was saying loudly it was my fault for being clumsy."

"And I can imagine," I said, seeing resignation more than indignation now in her face, "that Bambi Lorrimore took no notice, that Mercer hurried to help you up and apologize, and Mrs. Young inquired if you were hurt."

She looked at me in amazement. "You were there!"

"No. It just figures."

"Well, that's exactly what happened. A waiter came to deal with the mess, and while he was kneeling there Sheridan said loudly that the waiter was sneering at him and he would get him fired." She paused. "And I suppose you can tell me again what happened next?"

She was teasing, but I answered, "I'd guess Mercer assured the waiter he wouldn't be fired and took him aside and gave him twenty dollars."

Her mouth opened. "You *were* there."

I shook my head. "He gave me twenty dollars when Sheridan shoved me the other evening."

"But that's awful."

"Mercer's a nice man caught in an endless dilemma. Bambi's closed her mind to it. Xanthe seeks comfort somewhere else."

Nell thought it over and delivered her judgment, which was much like my own.

"One day beastly Sheridan will do something his father can't pay for."

"He's a very rich man," I said.

12

"It's nothing to do with his birthday, nor with his telephone numbers, nor addresses, past or present, nor his bank accounts, nor his national insurance."

Mrs. Baudelaire's light voice in my ear, passing on the bad news on Wednesday morning.

"Val Catto is working on your quarry's credit card numbers now," she said. "And he wants to know why he's doing all this research. He says he's looked up your quarry's divorced wife's personal numbers also and he cannot see one-five-one anywhere, with or without three unknown digits in front."

I sighed audibly, disappointed.

"How important is it?" she asked.

"It's impossible to tell. It could be pointless, it could solve all our problems. Empty box or jackpot, or anywhere in between. Please would you tell the Brigadier that one-five-one is the combination that unlocks the right-hand latch of a black crocodile briefcase. We have three unknowns on the left."

"Good gracious," she said.

"Could you say I would appreciate his instructions?"

"I could, young man. Why don't you just steal the briefcase and take your time?"

I laughed. "I've thought of that, but I'd better not. Or not yet, anyway. If the numbers have any logic, this way is safest."

"Val would presumably prefer you didn't get arrested."

Or murdered, perhaps, I thought.

"I would say," I agreed, "that getting myself arrested would lose me my job."

"You'd no longer be invisible?"

"Quite right."

"And I'm afraid," she said, "that I have some more negative news for you."

"What is it?" I asked.

"Bill says the samples of water you sent him were just that, water."

"That's good news, actually."

"Oh? Well, good, then."

I reflected. "I think I'll phone you again this evening before we leave Winnipeg."

"Yes, do," she agreed. "The further west you go the bigger the time change and the longer it takes to get replies from Val Catto."

"Mm."

Mrs. Baudelaire couldn't ring the Brigadier in the middle of his night, nor in the middle of hers. Toronto, where she lived, was five hours behind London, Winnipeg six, Vancouver eight. At breakfast time in Vancouver, London's office workers began traveling home. Confusing for carrier pigeons.

"Good luck," she said. "I'll talk to you later."

I was used by now to her abrupt disappearances. I put my receiver down, hearing only silence on the line, and wondered what she looked like, and how deeply she was ill. I would go back to Toronto, I thought, and see her.

I sped again on the bus to the races and found that overnight Assiniboia Downs had sprouted all the ballyhoo of Woodbine; T-shirt stalls, banners and besashed bosoms Supporting Canadian Racing.

I again spent most of the afternoon looking for gaunt-face, coming in the end to the conclusion that whatever he was doing on the train he wasn't traveling because of an overpowering interest in racing. The racegoers from the train were on the whole easily identifiable, as they all seemed to have been issued large red-and-white rosettes with Race Train Passengers emblazoned on them in gold: and the rosettes proved not to be confined to those in the front half of the train, because I came across Zak wearing one too, and he told me that everyone had been given one, the owners included, and where was mine?

I didn't know about them, I said. Too bad, he said, because they entitled everyone to free entry, free race-cards and free food. They were gifts from the racecourse, he said. Nell should have one for me, he thought.

I asked him how the scene from the mystery had fared that morning, as Nell had described what had happened the day before.

"A lot better without that bastard Sheridan."

"Wasn't he there?"

"I got Nell to tell his father that if Sheridan came to breakfast we wouldn't be putting on our scene, and it did the trick. No Sheridan." He grinned. "No Lorrimores at all, in fact." He looked around. "But they're all here, Sheridan included. They were getting out of a stretch limo when we rolled up in our private bus. That's where we were given these rosettes; on the bus. How did you get here, then?"

"On a public bus."

"Too bad."

His batteries were running at half-speed, neither highly charged up nor flat. Under the mop of curls his face, without the emphasizing makeup he wore perpetually on the train, looked younger and more ordinary: it was David Flynn who was at the races, not Zak.

"Are all the actors here?" I asked.

"Oh, sure. We have to know what happens here today.

Have to be able to talk about it to the owners tonight. Don't forget, it's a racing mystery, after all."

I thought that I had forgotten, in a way. The real mystery that I was engaged in tended to crowd the fiction out.

"What are you betting on in our race?" he asked. "I suppose Premiere will win. What do you think?"

"Upper Gumtree," I said.

"It's supposed to be half-asleep," he objected.

"It's got a nice face," I said.

He looked at me sideways. "You're crazy, you know that?"

"I am but mad north-north-west."

"When the wind is southerly," he said promptly, "I know a hawk from a handsaw." He laughed. "There isn't an actor born who doesn't hope to play Hamlet."

"Have you ever?"

"Only in school. But once learned, never forgotten. Shall I give you my 'To be or not to be'?"

"Not."

"You slay me. See you tonight."

He went off with a medium spring to his step and I saw him later with his arm round Donna's shoulders, which wasn't (as far as I knew) in his script.

Most of the owners came down from the Clubhouse to watch the saddling of the runners in the Jockey Club Race Train Special, and all the sportier of them wore the rosettes.

Filmer didn't: there was no lightheartedness in him. Daffodil, however, had fastened hers to her cleavage, the red, white and gold popping out now and again past the long-haired chinchillas. Mrs. Young wore hers boldly on her lapel. Mr. Young's wasn't in sight.

The Unwins, rosetted, were showing uninhibited pleasure in Upper Gumtree, who did in fact have a nice face, and wasn't unacceptably sleepy. Upper Gumtree's trainer hadn't made the journey from Australia, nor had his usual jockey: Canadian substitutes had been found. The Unwins beamed and patted everyone within reach including the horse, and

Mr. Unwin in his great antipodean accent could be heard calling his jockey "son," even though the rider looked older by far than the owner.

In the next stall along things were a great deal quieter. Mercer Lorrimore, unattended by the rest of his family, talked pleasantly with his trainer, who had come from Toronto, and shook hands with his jockey, the same one who had ridden for him at Woodbine. Premiere, the favorite, behaved like a horse that had had a fuss made of him all his life; almost, I thought fancifully, as arrogantly as Sheridan.

The owners of Flokati were showing Mavis and Walter Bricknell-type behavior, fluttering about in a nervous anxiety that would be bound to affect the horse if it went on too long. Their ineffective-looking trainer was trying to stop the owners from straightening the number cloth, tidying the forelock over the headband, tweaking at the saddle and shoving their big rosettes with every ill-judged movement near the horse's affronted nostrils. A riot, really. Poor Mr. and Mrs. Flokati; owning the horse looked an agony, not a joy.

Mr. and Mrs. Young, like Mercer Lorrimore, had shipped their Winnipeg runners, two of them, by road. They, old hands at the owning game, stood by with calm interest while their pair, Soluble and Slipperclub, were readied; Mrs. Young speaking with her sweet expression to one of the jockeys, Mr. Young more impassively to the other.

Daffodil Quentin's runner, Pampering, had been flown in with five others owned by people on the train, all of whom were strolling around with rosettes and almost permanently smiling faces. This was, after all, one of the highlights of their journey, the purpose behind the pizzazz. I learned that the Manitoba Racing Commission had moreover by midafternoon given each of them not only a champagne reception and a splendid lunch but also as a memento a framed group photograph of all the owners on the trip. They were living their memories, I thought, here and now.

Television cameras all over the place recorded everything

both for news items that evening and for the two-hour Support Canadian Racing program, which posters everywhere announced was being made for a gala showing coast to coast after the triple had been completed in Vancouver.

The Winnipeg runners went out onto the track to bugle fanfares and cheers from the stands and were pony-escorted to the starting gate.

Mercer Lorrimore's colors, red and white like the rosette he had pinned on gamely For the Sake of Canadian Racing, could be seen entering the outermost stall. Daffodil's pale blue and dark green were innermost. Upper Gumtree, carrying orange and black, started dead center of the eleven runners and came out of the stalls heading a formation like an arrow.

I was watching from the upper part of the grandstand, just above the Clubhouse floor to which the owners had returned in a chattering flock to watch the race. Through my binoculars-camera the colors down on the track in the chilly sunshine looked sharp and bright, the race easy on that account to read.

The arrow formation soon broke up into a ragged line, with Premiere on the outside, Pampering on the inner and Upper Gumtree still just in front. The Youngs' pair, split by the draw, nevertheless came together and raced the whole way side by side like twins. Flokati, in pink, made for the rails as if needing them to steer by, and four of the other runners boxed him in.

Going past the stands for the first time, the Unwins' Upper Gumtree still showed in front but with Premiere almost alongside; Pampering on the inside tugging his jockey's arms out. Doing their best for the glory of Canada, the whole field of eleven swept round the bend and went down the far side as if welded together, and it still seemed when they turned for home that that was how they might finish, in a knot.

They split apart in the straight, one group swinging wide, the red and white of Premiere spurting forward with the

Youngs' pair at his quarters and Upper Gumtree swerving dramatically through a gap to take the rails well ahead of Pampering.

The crowd bounced up and down. The money was on Premiere. The yelling could have been heard in Montreal. The Canadian racing authorities were again getting a rip-roaring brilliant finish to a Race Train Stakes . . . and Mercer, putting his brave face on it, again came in second.

It was the Unwins, in the stratosphere of ecstasy, who led Upper Gumtree into the winners' circle. The Unwins from Australia who were hugging and kissing everyone near enough (including the horse). The Unwins who had their photographs taken each side of their panting winner, now covered across the shoulders by a long triumphant blanket of flowers. The Unwins who received the trophy, the check and the speeches from the president of the racecourse and the top brass of the Jockey Club; whose memories of the day would be the sweetest.

Feeling pleased for them, I lowered the binoculars, through which I'd been able to see even the tears on Mrs. Unwin's cheeks, and there below me and in front of the grandstand was the man with the gaunt face looking up toward the Clubhouse windows.

Almost trembling with haste, I put the binoculars up again, found him, activated the automatic focus, pressed the button, heard the quiet click of the shutter: had him in the bag.

It had been my only chance. Even before the film had wound on, he'd looked down and away, so that I could see only his forehead and his gray hair; and within two seconds he'd walked toward the grandstand and out of my line of vision.

I had no idea how long he'd been standing there. I'd been too diverted by the Unwins' rejoicings. I went down from the upper grandstand as fast as I could, which was far too slowly because everyone else was doing the same thing.

Down on ground level again, I couldn't see gaunt-face

anywhere. The whole crowd was on the move: one could get no length of view. The Race Train event had been the climax of the program and although there was one more race on the card, no one seemed to be much interested. A great many red-and-white rosettes, baseball caps, T-shirts and balloons were on their way out of the gates.

The Unwins' entourage was disappearing into the Clubhouse entrance, no doubt for more champagne and press interviews, and probably all the other owners would be in there with them. If gaunt-face had been looking up at the Clubhouse windows in the hope of seeing Filmer—or of Filmer seeing him—maybe Filmer would come down to talk to him and maybe I could photograph them both together, which might one day prove useful. If I simply waited, it might happen.

I simply waited.

Filmer did eventually come down, but with Daffodil. They weren't approached by gaunt-face. They climbed into their chauffeured car and were whisked away to heaven knew where, and I thought frustratedly about time and the little of it there was left in Winnipeg. It was already nearly six o'clock, and I wouldn't be able to find a one-hour photo lab open anywhere that evening: and I had to return to the Sheraton to collect my bag, and be back on the train by seven-thirty or soon after.

I retreated to the men's room and took the film out of the binoculars-camera, and wrote a short note to go with it. Then I twisted the film and note together into a paper towel and went out to try to find Bill Baudelaire, reckoning it might be all right to speak to him casually down on ground level since Filmer wasn't there to see. I'd caught sight of him in the distance from time to time all afternoon, but now when I wanted him his red hair wasn't anywhere around.

Zak came up to me with Donna and offered me a lift back to the city in their bus, and at that exact moment I saw not Bill Baudelaire himself but someone who might go among the owners, where Tommy couldn't.

"When does the bus go?" I asked Zak rapidly, preparing to leave him.

"Twenty minutes . . . out front. It's got a banner on."

"I'll come. Thanks."

I covered a good deal of ground rapidly but not running and caught up with the shapely back view of a dark-haired girl in a red coat with a wide gold-and-white studded belt.

"Nancy?" I said from behind her.

She turned, surprised, and looked at me inquiringly.

"Er . . ." I said, "yesterday you collected some thirst quenchers from me for Bill Baudelaire's daughter."

"Oh, yes." She recognized me belatedly.

"Do you happen to know where I could find him now?"

"He's up in the Clubhouse, drinking with the winners."

"Could you . . . could you possibly deliver something else to him?"

She wrinkled the freckled teenage nose. "I just came down, for some fresh air." She sighed. "Oh, all right. I guess he'd want me to, if you asked. You seem to be OK with him. What do you want me to give him this time?"

I passed over the paper-towel bundle.

"Instructions?" she asked.

"There's a note inside."

"Real cloak-and-dagger goings-on."

"Thanks, truly, and . . . er . . . give it to him quietly."

"What's in it?" she asked.

"A film, with photos of today's events."

She didn't know whether or not to be disappointed.

"Don't lose it," I said.

She seemed to be more pleased with that, and flashing me a grin from over her shoulder went off toward the Clubhouse entrance. I hoped she wouldn't make a big production out of the delivery upstairs, but just in case she did I thought I wouldn't go anywhere where she could see me and point me out to any of the owners, so I left through the front exit gates and found the actors' bus with its Mystery Race Train banner and faded inside into the reassembling troupe.

In general, the cast had backed Premiere (what else) but were contented to have been interviewed on television at some length. A lot of Winnipeg's race crowd, Zak said, had asked how they could get on the train. "I must say," he said, yawning, "with all the publicity it's had, it's really caught on."

In the publicity and the success, I thought, lay the danger. The more the eyes of Canada and Australia and England were directed to the train, the more Filmer might want to discredit it. Might ... might. I was guarding a moving shadow; trying to prevent something that might not happen, searching for the intention so as to stop it occurring.

The bus letting me off at a convenient corner in the city, I walked to the Sheraton and from a telephone there spoke to Mrs. Baudelaire.

"Bill called me ten minutes ago from the track," she said. "He said you sent him a film and you didn't say where you wanted the pictures sent."

"Is he calling you back?" I asked.

"Yes, I told him I'd be speaking to you soon."

"Right, well, there's only one picture on the film. The rest is blank. Please tell Bill the man in the photo is the ally of our quarry. His ally on the train. Would you ask if Bill knows him? Ask if anyone knows him. And if there's something about him that would be useful if I knew, please will he tell you, to tell me."

"Heavens," she said. "Let me get that straight." She paused, writing. "Basically, who is he, what does he do, and is what he does likely to be of help."

"Yes," I said.

"And do you want a copy of the photo?"

"Yes, please. Ask if there's any chance of his getting it to Nell Richmond at Château Lake Louise by tomorrow night or the next morning."

"Difficult," she commented. "The mail is impossible."

"Well, someone might be flying to Calgary tomorrow

morning," I suggested. "They might even meet our train there. We get there at twelve-forty, leave at one-thirty. I suppose the time's too tight, but if it's possible, get Bill to address the envelope to the conductor of the train, George Burley. I'll tell George it might come."

"Dear young man," she said, "let me write it all down."

I waited while she did it.

"Let me check," she said. "Either George Burley on the train or Nell Richmond at Château Lake Louise."

"Right. I'll call you soon."

"Don't go," she said. "I have a message for you from Val Catto."

"Oh, good."

"He said . . . now these are his exact words . . . 'Stolen evidence cannot be used in court but facts learned can be verified.'" The understanding amusement was light in her voice. "What he means is, have a look-see but hands off."

"Yes."

"And he said to tell you to remember his motto."

"OK," I said.

"What is his motto?" she asked curiously, obviously longing to know.

"Thought before action, if you have time."

"Nice," she said, pleased. "He said to tell you he was working hard on the unknown numbers, and you are not to put yourself in danger of arrest."

"All right."

"Phone me from Calgary tomorrow," she said. "By then it will be evening in England. Val will have had a whole day on the numbers."

"You're marvelous."

"And I'll be able to tell you when you'll get your photos."

There was a click and she'd gone, and I could hardly believe that I'd ever doubted her as a relay post.

The train had come in from the sidings and stood in the station, warm and pulsing, its engines reattached, the horses and grooms on board and fresh foods and ice loaded.

It was like going back to an old friend, familiar and almost cozy. I changed into Tommy's uniform in my roomette and went along to the dining car where Emil, Oliver and Cathy welcomed me casually as if I were an accepted part of the crew. We began immediately laying the pink cloths and putting fresh flowers in the vases, and Angus in his tall white hat, whistling "Speed Bonny Boat" amid clouds of steam, addressed his talents to wild rice and scallops in Parmesan sauce while Simone rather grimly chopped lettuce.

The passengers returned well before eight o'clock in very good spirits, Mercer bringing with him a porter wheeling a case of highly superior bubbles for toasting the Unwins' success. The Unwins themselves—and it was impossible for anyone to grudge them their moment—said over and over that it was great, just great that one of the horses actually on the train had won one of the races, it made the whole thing worthwhile, and the whole party, drifting into the dining car in true party mood, agreed and applauded.

Filmer, I was interested to see as I distributed glasses, was smiling pleasantly in all directions, when the last thing he probably wanted was the enormous smash-hit the train enterprise was proving.

Daffodil had changed into a sparkling crimson dress and showed no pique over Pampering finishing fifth. She was being friendly as usual to Bambi, frostier in pale turquoise with pearls.

Mercer came to Emil and worried that the wine wasn't cold enough, but Emil assured him he had lodged all twelve bottles among the many plastic bags of ice cubes: by the time the train left the station, all would be well.

The Youngs, whose Slipperclub had finished third, were

embraced by the hyperjoyous Unwins and were invited to their table, leaving the poor Flokatis to seek solace with others whose hopes had died on the last bend. Sheridan Lorrimore was telling a long-suffering good-natured couple all about his prowess at ice hockey and Xanthe, pouting and put out at having been temporarily deserted by Mrs. Young, had ended up next to Giles-the-murderer, whose real-life preference, I'd gathered, was for boys.

The train slid out of Winnipeg on time at eight-twenty and I put my energies and attention all into being an unexceptional and adequate waiter, even though always conscious of the ominous presence in the aisle seat, facing forward, three tables back from the kitchen end. I never met his eyes and I don't think he noticed me much, but we were all, Emil, Oliver, Cathy and I, becoming slowly and inevitably more recognizable to the passengers. Several of them inquired if we'd been to the races (we all had) and had backed the winner (no, we hadn't). Fortunately Mercer himself had had this conversation with Emil, which meant he felt no need to ask me also, so I escaped having to speak too much in my English accent at his table.

The party atmosphere went on all through dinner, prevailed through a short scene put on by Zak to explain that the Mountie had been left behind in Winnipeg for investigations on the ground and heated up thoroughly afterward with more unsteady dancing and laughter in the dome car.

Nell wandered about looking slightly less starchy in a fuller-cut black skirt with her tailored white silk blouse, telling me in passing that Cumber and Rose wanted to give a similar party at Château Lake Louise.

"Who?" I said.

"Cumber and Rose. Mr. and Mrs. Young."

"Oh."

"I've spent most of the day with them." She smiled briefly and went on her way. No clipboard, I noticed.

Cumber and Rose, I thought, collecting ashtrays. Well, well. Rose suited Mrs. Young fine. Cumber was appropriate also, I supposed, though Mr. Young wasn't cumbersome; perhaps a shade heavy in personality, but not big, not awkward.

Mercer and Bambi again invited Filmer and Daffodil into their private car, although it was Oliver, this time, who obliged them with a bowl of ice. Mercer came back after a while to collect the Unwins and the Youngs, and the general jollifications everywhere wore on without any alarms.

After midnight Nell said she was going to bed, and I walked up the train with her to her roomette, almost opposite mine. She paused in the doorway.

"It's all going well, don't you think?" she said.

"Terrific." I meant it. "You've worked very hard."

We looked at each other, she in executive black and white, I in my yellow waistcoat.

"What are you really?" she said.

"Twenty-nine."

Her lips twitched. "One day I'll crack your defenses."

"Yours are half-down."

"What do you mean?"

I made a hugging movement across my own chest. "No clipboard," I said.

"Oh, well, I didn't need it this evening."

She wasn't exactly confused. Her eyes were laughing.

"You can't," she said.

"Can't what?"

"Kiss me."

I'd wanted to. She'd seen it unerringly.

"If you come into my parlor, I can," I said.

She shook her head, smiling. "I am not going to lose my credibility on this train by being caught coming out of the help's bedroom."

"Talking in the corridor is almost as bad."

"Yes, it is," she said, nodding. "So goodnight."

I said with regret, "Goodnight," and she went abruptly into her own domain and closed the door.

With a sigh I went on a few steps farther to George's

office and found him as I'd expected, fully dressed, lightly napping, with worked-on forms pushed to one side beside an empty coffee cup.

"Come in," he said, fully alert in an instant. "Sit down. How's it going?"

"So far, so good."

I sat on the facilities, and told him that the water samples from the horse car had been pure and simple H_2O.

"That'll please the dragon-lady, eh?" he said.

"Did you go to the races?" I asked.

"No, I've got family in Winnipeg, I went visiting. And I slept most of today, as I'll be up all night, with the stops." He knew, however, that Upper Gumtree had won. "You should see the party going on in the forward dome car. All the grooms are drunk. The dragon-lady's in a sober tizzy, eh, because they tried to give a bucket of beer to the horse. They're singing gold-rush songs at the tops of their voices in the dayniter and it's a wonder they haven't all rocked the train right off the rails, with the noise and the booze."

"I guess it wouldn't be easy to rock the train off the rails," I said thoughtfully.

"Easy?" George said. "Of course it is. Go too fast round the curves."

"Well . . . suppose it was one of the passengers who wanted to stop the train getting happily to Vancouver, what could he do?"

He looked at me with bright eyes, unperplexed. "Besides doping the horses' water? Do what they're doing in the mystery, I'd say. Throw a body off the train, eh? That would stop the parties pretty quick." He chuckled. "You could throw someone off the Stoney Creek bridge—that's a high, curved bridge over Roger's Pass. It's a long way down into the gulch. Three hundred feet and a bit more. If the fall didn't kill them, the bears would."

"Bears!" I exclaimed.

He beamed. "Grizzly bears, eh? The Rocky Mountains aren't anyone's tame backyard. They're raw nature. So are the bears. They kill people, no trouble." He put his head on one side. "Or you could throw someone out into the Connaught Tunnel. That tunnel's five miles long with no lights. There's a species of blind mice that live in there, eating the grain that falls from the grain trains."

"Jolly," I said.

"There's a wine storage space under the floor of your dining car," he said with growing relish. "They decided not to use it on this trip because opening it might disrupt the passengers. It's big enough to hide a body in."

His imagination, I saw, was of a scarier dimension than my own.

"Hiding a body in the wine store," I said politely, "might indeed disrupt the passengers."

He laughed. "Or how about someone alive and tied up in there, writhing in agony?"

"Shouting his head off?"

"Gagged."

"If we miss anyone," I promised, "that's where we'll look." I stood up and prepared to go. "Where exactly is the Stoney Creek bridge," I asked, pausing in the doorway, "over Roger's Pass?"

His eyes gleamed, the lower lids pouching with enjoyment. "About a hundred miles further on from Lake Louise. High up in the mountains. But don't you worry, eh?, you'll be going across it in the dark."

13

Everyone survived the night, although there were a few obvious hangovers at breakfast. Outside the windows, the seemingly endless rock, lakes and conifer scenery had dramatically given way to the wide sweeping rolling prairies, not yellow with the grain, which had already been harvested, but greenish gray, resting before winter.

There was a brief stop during breakfast at the town of Medicine Hat, which lay in a valley and looked a great deal more ordinary than its name. The passengers dutifully put back their watches when Nell told them we were now in Mountain Time, but where, they asked, were the mountains?

"This afternoon," she answered, and handed out the day's printed program, which promised Dreadful Developments in The Mystery at eleven-thirty, followed by an early lunch. We would reach Calgary at twelve-forty, where the horse car would be detached, and leave at one-thirty, heading up into the Rockies to Banff and Lake Louise. At Lake Louise, the owners would disembark and be ferried by bus to the Château, the huge hotel sitting on the lake's shore, amid Snowy Scenes of Breathtaking Beauty. Cocktails and Startling Discoveries would be offered at six-thirty in a private conference room in the hotel. Have a nice day.

Several people asked if we were now in front of or behind the regular Canadian.

"We're in front," I said.

"If we break down," Mr. Unwin said facetiously, "it will be along to help us out."

Xanthe, sitting next to him, didn't laugh. "I wish we were behind it," she said. "I'd feel safer."

"Behind the Canadian there are freight trains," Mr. Unwin said reasonably, "and ahead of us there are freight trains. And coming the other way there are freight trains. We're not all alone on these rails."

"No, I suppose not." She seemed doubtful still and said she had slept much better again that past night in her upper bunk than she would have done in her family's own quarters.

I brought her the French toast and sausages she ordered from the menu and filled her coffee cup, and Mr. Unwin, holding out his own cup for a refill, asked if I had backed his horse to win at Winnipeg.

"I'm afraid not, sir," I said regretfully. I put his cup on the tray and poured with small movements. "But congratulations, sir."

"Did you go to the races?" Xanthe asked me without too much interest.

"Yes, miss," I said.

I finished pouring Mr. Unwin's coffee and put it by his place, then took my tray and coffee pot along to the next table where the conversation seemed to be about Zak's mystery rather than directly about horses.

"I think the trainer killed Angelica. And the groom too."

"Why ever should he?"

"He wants to marry Donna for her money. Angelica knew something that would make the marriage impossible, so he killed her."

"Knew what?"

"Maybe that he's already married."

"To Angelica?"

"Well, why not?"

"But where does the dead groom come in?"

"He saw the murderer getting rid of the blood-spattered plastic."

They laughed. I filled their cups and moved on and poured for Daffodil, who had an empty place on her far side. Daffodil, smoking with deep sucking lungfuls, sat with the Flokatis, and nobody else.

No Filmer.

I glanced back along the whole dining car, but couldn't see him anywhere. He hadn't come in while I was serving others, and he hadn't been at the kitchen end when I'd started.

Daffodil said to me, "Can you bring me some vodka? Ice and lemon."

"I'll ask, madam," I said, and asked Emil, and it was he who civilly explained to her that the barman wouldn't be back on duty until eleven, and meanwhile everything was locked up.

Daffodil received the bad news without speaking but jabbed the fire out of her cigarette with some violent stabs and a long final grind. The Flokatis looked at her uncertainly and asked if they could help.

She shook her head. She seemed angry and near tears, but determinedly in control.

"Give me some coffee," she said to me, and to the Flokatis she said, "I think I'll get off the train at Calgary. I think I'll go home."

Small movements saved the day, as I would have spilled the brown liquid all over her hand.

"Oh, no!" exclaimed the Flokatis, instantly distressed. "Oh, don't do that. Your horse ran splendidly yesterday, even if it was only fifth. Ours was nearly last and we are going on. You can't give up. And you have Laurentide Ice, besides, for Vancouver."

Daffodil looked at them as if bemused. "It's not because of yesterday," she said.

"But why, then?"

Daffodil didn't tell them. Maybe wouldn't; maybe couldn't. She merely pursed her lips tight, shook her curly head and dug out another cigarette.

The Flokatis having declined more coffee, I couldn't stay to listen any further. I moved across the aisle and stretched my ears, but the Flokatis seemed to get nothing extra from Daffodil except a repeated and stronger decision to go home.

Nell, in her straight gray skirt, clipboard in attendance, was still talking to passengers up by the kitchen end. I took my nearly empty coffee pot up there and made a small gesture onward to the lobby, to where presently she came with inquiring eyebrows.

"Daffodil Quentin," I said, peering into the coffee pot, "is upset to the point of leaving the train. She told the Flokatis, not me, so you don't know, OK?"

"Upset about what?" Nell was alarmed.

"She wouldn't tell them."

"Thanks," she said. "I'll see what I can do."

Smoothing ruffled feelings, keeping smiles in place; all in her day's work. She started casually on her way through the dining car and I went into the kitchen to complete my mission. By the time I was out again with a full pot, Nell had reached Daffodil and was standing by her, listening. Nell appealed to the Youngs and the Unwins at adjacent tables for help, and presently Daffodil was out of sight in a bunch of people trying to persuade her to change her mind.

I had to wait quite a while to hear what was happening, but finally the whole little crowd, Daffodil among them, went out at the far end into the dome car and Nell returned to the lobby, relaying the news to me in snatches as I paused beside her on to-and-fro journeys to clear away the breakfast debris.

"Cumber and Rose . . ." The Youngs, I thought. "Cumber and Rose and also the Unwins say there was nothing wrong last night, they all had a splendid time in the Lorrimores' car. Daffodil finally said she'd had a disagreement with Mr. Filmer after the party had broken up. She said she had hardly slept and wasn't sure what to do, but there was no fun left in taking Laurentide Ice to Vancouver, and she couldn't face the rest of the journey. The Youngs have persuaded her to go up into the dome with them to think things over, but I honestly think she's serious. She's very upset."

"Mm." I put the last of the debris into the kitchen and excused myself apologetically from washing the dishes.

"How can Mr. Filmer have upset Daffodil so much?" Nell exclaimed. "She's obviously been enjoying herself, and he's such a nice man. They were getting on together so well, everyone thought." She paused. "Mr. Unwin believes it's a lovers' quarrel."

"Does he?" I pondered. "I think I'll wander up the train. See if anything else is happening."

Maybe Daffodil had made advances and been too roughly repulsed, I thought. And maybe not.

"Mr. Filmer hasn't been in to breakfast," Nell said. "It's all very worrying. And last night everyone was so happy."

If Daffodil's leaving the train was the worst thing that happened, I thought, we would have got off lightly. I left Nell and set off up the corridor, coming pretty soon to Filmer's bedroom door, which was uninformatively closed.

I checked with the sleeping car attendant farther along the car, who was in the midst of folding up the bunks for the day and unfolding the armchairs.

"Mr. Filmer? He's in his room still, as far as I know. He was a bit short with me, told me to hurry up. And he's not usually like that. He was eating something, and he had a thermos too. But then we do get passengers like that sometimes. Can't get through the night without raiding the icebox, that sort of thing."

I nodded noncommittally and went onward, but I thought that if Filmer had brought food and a thermos on board for breakfast, he must have known in Winnipeg that he would need them, which meant that last night's quarrel had been planned and hadn't been caused by Daffodil.

George Burley was in his office, writing his records.

"Morning," he said, beaming.

"How's the train?"

"The forward sleeping car attendants are threatening to resign, eh?, over the vomit in the bathrooms."

"Ugh."

He chuckled. "I brought extra disinfectant aboard in Winnipeg," he said. "Train-sickness gets them, you know."

I shook my head at his indulgence and pressed forward, looking as always for gaunt-face but chiefly aiming for the horses.

Leslie Brown, hollow-eyed from lack of sleep, regarded me with only half the usual belligerence.

"Come in," she said, stepping back from her door. "To be honest, I could do with some help."

As I'd just passed several green-looking grooms being sorry for themselves in their sections, I supposed at first she meant simply physical help in tending the horses, but it appeared that she didn't.

"Something's going on that I don't understand," she said, locking the entrance door behind me and leading the way to the central space where her chair stood beside the innocent water tank.

"What sort of thing?" I asked, following her.

She mutely pointed farther forward up the car, and I walked on until I came to the final space between the stalls, and there, in a sort of nest made of hay bales, one of the grooms half-lay, half-sat, curled like an embryo and making small moaning noises.

I went back to Leslie Brown. "What's the matter with him?" I said.

"I don't know. He was drunk last night, they all were, but this doesn't look like an ordinary hangover."

"Did you ask the others?"

She sighed. "They don't remember much about last night. They don't care what's the matter with him."

"Which horse is he with?"

"Laurentide Ice."

I'd have been surprised, I supposed, if she'd said anything else.

"That's the horse, isn't it," I asked, "whose trainer sent separate numbered individual bags of food, because another of Mrs. Quentin's horses had died because of eating the wrong things?"

She nodded. "Yes."

"And this boy was with the horse all the time in the barns at Winnipeg?"

"Yes, of course. They exercised the horses and looked after them, and they all came back to the train in horse-vans yesterday after the races, while the train was still in the siding. I came with them. There's nothing wrong with any of the horses, I assure you."

"That's good," I said. "Laurentide Ice as well?"

"See for yourself."

I walked round looking at each horse but in truth they all appeared healthy and unaffected, even Upper Gumtree and Flokati, who would have been excused seeming thin and fatigued after their exertions. Most of them had their heads out over the stall doors, sure sign of interest: a few were a pace or two back, semidreaming. Laurentide Ice watched me with a bright glacial eye, in far better mental health than his attendant.

I returned to Leslie Brown and asked her the groom's name.

"Lenny," she said. She consulted a list. "Leonard Higgs."

"How old is he?"

"About twenty, I should think."

"What's he like, usually?"

"Like the others. Full of foul language and dirty jokes." She looked disapproving. "Every other word beginning with *f*."

"When did all this moaning start?"

"He was lying there all night. The other boys said it was his turn to be in here, but it wasn't really, only he was paralytic, and they just dumped him in the hay and went back to the party. He started the moaning about an hour ago and he won't answer me at all." She was disturbed by him, and worried, I thought, that his behavior might be held to be her responsibility.

Rather to her surprise I took off my yellow waistcoat and striped tie and gave them to her to hold. If she would sit down for a while, I suggested, I would try to sort Lenny out.

Meekly for her, she agreed. I left her perching with my badges of office across her trousered knees and returned to the total collapse in the hay.

"Lenny," I said, "give it a rest."

He went on with the moaning, oblivious.

I sat down beside him on one of the hay bales and put my mouth near his one visible ear.

"Shut up," I said, very loudly.

He jumped and he gasped and after a short pause he went back to moaning, though artificially now, it seemed to me.

"If you're sick from beer," I said forcefully, "it's your own bloody fault, but I'll get you something to make you feel better."

He curled into a still tighter ball, tucking his head down into his arms as if shielding it from a blow. It was a movement impossible to misconstrue: what he felt, besides alcohol sickness, was fear.

Fear followed Julius Apollo Filmer like a spoor; the residue of his passing. Lenny, frightened out of his wits, was a familiar sight indeed.

I undid the top buttons of my shirt, loosening the collar, and rolled up my cuffs, aiming for informality, and I slid down until I was sitting on the floor with my head on the same level as Lenny's.

"If you're shit scared," I said distinctly, "I can do something about that, too."

Nothing much happened. He moaned a couple of times and fell silent and after a long while, I said, "Do you want help, or don't you? This is a good offer. If you don't take it, whatever you're afraid of will probably happen."

After a lengthy pause he rolled his head round, still wrapped in his arms, until I could see his face. He was red-eyed, bony, unshaven and dribbling, and what came out of his slack mouth wasn't a groan but a croak.

"Who the bleeding hell are you?" He had an English accent and a habitual pugnacity of speech altogether at odds with his present state.

"Your bit of good luck," I said calmly.

"Piss off," he said.

"Right." I got to my feet. "Too bad," I said. "Go on feeling sorry for yourself, and see where it gets you."

I walked away from him, out of his sight.

"Here," he said, croaking, making it sound like an order.

I stayed where I was.

"Wait," he said urgently.

I did wait, but I didn't go back to him. I heard the hay rustling and then a real groan as the hangover hit him, and finally he came staggering into view, keeping his balance with both hands on the green outside of Flokati's stall. He stopped when he saw me. Blinking, swaying, the Race Train T-shirt torn and filthy, he looked stupid, pathetic and spineless.

"Go back and sit down," I said neutrally. "I'll bring you something."

He sagged against the green stall but finally turned round and shuffled back the way he'd come. I went down to Leslie Brown and asked if she had any aspirins.

"Not aspirins, but these," she said, proffering a box from a canvas holdall. "These might do."

I thanked her, filled a polystyrene cup with water and went back to see how Lenny was faring: he was sitting on the hay with his head in his hands looking a picture of misery and a lot more normal.

"Drink," I said, giving him the water. "And swallow these."

"You said you could help me."

"Yes. Take the pills for a start."

He was accustomed, on the whole, to doing what he was told, and he must have been reasonably good at his job, I supposed, to have been sent across Canada with Laurentide Ice. He swallowed the pills and drank the water and not surprisingly they made no immediate difference to his physical woes.

"I want to get out of here," he said with a spurt of futile violence. "Off this bleeding train. Off this whole effing trip. And I've got no money. I lost it. It's gone."

"All right," I said. "I can get you off."

"Straight up?" He was surprised.

"Straight up."

"When?"

"At Calgary. In a couple of hours. You can leave then. Where do you want to go?"

He stared. "You're having me on," he said.

"No. I'll get you taken care of, and I'll see you get a ticket to wherever you want."

The dawning hope in his face became clouded with confusion.

"What about old Icy?" he said. "Who'll look after him?"

It was the first thought he'd had that hadn't been raw self-pity, and I felt the first flicker of compassion.

"We'll get another groom for old Icy," I promised. "Calgary's full of horse people."

It wasn't exactly true. The Calgary I'd known had been one of the six biggest cities in Canada, half the size of Montreal and on a population par with central Toronto. Time might have changed the statistics slightly, but probably not much. Calgary was no dusty old-west cattle town, but a skyscrapered modern city set like a glittering oasis in the skirts of the prairies: and the Stampede, in which one July I'd worked as a bronco rider, was a highly organized ten-day rodeo with a stadium, adjacent art and stage shows and all the paraphernalia and razzmatazz of big-time tourist entertainment. But Calgary, even in October, definitely had enough horse people around to provide a groom for Laurentide Ice.

I watched Lenny Higgs decide to jettison his horse, his job and his unbearable present. Fearful that I would bungle the whole business, because I'd never before actually tried this sort of unscrambling myself, I strove to remember John Millington's stated methods with people like the chambermaid at Newmarket. Offer protection, make any promise that might get results, hold out carrots, be supportive, ask for help.

Ask for help.

"Could you tell me why you don't want to go on to Vancouver?" I said.

I made the question sound very casual, but it threw him back into overall panic, even if not into the fetal position.

"No." He shivered with intense alarm. "Piss off. It's none of your effing business."

Without fuss I withdrew from him again, but this time I went farther away, beyond Leslie Brown, right down to the exit door.

"Stay there," I said to her, passing. "Don't say anything to him, will you?"

She shook her head, folding her thin arms over my waistcoat and across her chest. The dragon, I thought fleetingly, with the fire in abeyance.

"Here," Lenny shouted behind me. "Come back."

I didn't turn round.

He wailed despairingly at the top of his voice, "I want to get off this train."

It was, I thought, a serious cry for help.

I went back slowly. He was standing between Flokati's stall and Sparrowgrass's, swaying unsteadily, watching me with haggard eyes.

When I was near him, I said simply, "Why?"

"He'll kill me if I tell you."

"That's rubbish," I said.

"It isn't." His voice was high. "He said I'd effing die."

209

"Who said?"

"Him." He was trembling. The threat had been of sufficient power for him to believe it.

"Who is him?" I asked. "One of the owners?"

He looked blank, as if I were talking gibberish.

"Who is him?" I asked again.

"Some bloke. I never saw him before."

"Look," I said calmly, "let's go back, sit on the hay, and you tell me why he said he'd kill you." I pointed over his shoulders toward the bales and with a sort of exhausted compliance he stumbled that way and flopped into a huddled mess.

"How did he frighten you?" I asked.

"He . . . came to the barns . . . asked for me."

"Asked for you by name?"

He nodded glumly.

"When was this?"

"Yesterday," he said hoarsely. "During the races."

"Go on."

"He said he knew all about old Icy's food being in numbered bags." Lenny sounded aggrieved. "Well, it wasn't a secret, was it?"

"No," I said.

"He said he knew why . . . because Mrs. Quentin's other horse died . . ." Lenny stopped and looked as if an abyss had opened before him. "He started saying I done it."

"Done what?"

Lenny was silent.

"Said you'd poisoned Mrs. Quentin's other horse?" I suggested.

"I never did it. I didn't." He was deeply agitated. "I never."

"But this man said you did?"

"He said I would go to jail for it, and they do bad things to boys like you in jail, he said." He shivered. "I know they do. And he said, 'Do you wants AIDS, because you'll get it in jail, a pretty boy like you.'"

Pretty, at that moment, he did not look.

"So what next?" I prompted.

"Well, I . . . Well, I . . ." he gulped. "I said I never did it, it wasn't me. And he went on saying I'd go to jail and get AIDS and he went on and and on . . . and I told him . . . I told him . . ."

"Told him what?"

"She's a nice lady," he wailed. "I didn't want to . . . he made me . . ."

"Was it Mrs. Quentin," I asked carefully, "who poisoned her horse?"

He said miserably, "Yes. No. See . . . she gave me this bag of treats . . . that's what she said they were, treats . . . and to give them to her horse when no one was looking. See, I didn't look after that horse of hers, it was another groom. So I gave her horse the bag of treats private, like, and it got colic and blew up and died. Well, I asked her, after. I was that scared . . . but she said it was all dreadful, she'd no idea her darling horse would get colic, and let's not say anything about it, she said, and she gave me a hundred dollars, and I didn't. I didn't want to be blamed, see?"

I did see.

I said, "So when you told this man about the treats, what did he say?"

Lenny looked shattered. "He grinned like a shark . . . all teeth . . . and he says . . . if I say anything about him to anybody . . . he'll see I get . . . I'll get . . ." He finished in a whisper, "AIDS."

I sighed. "Is that how he threatened to kill you?"

He nodded weakly, as if spent.

"What did he look like?" I asked.

"Like my dad." He paused. "I hated my dad."

"Did he sound like your dad?" I asked.

He shook his head. "He wasn't a Brit."

"Canadian?"

"Or American."

"Well," I said, running out of questions, "I'll see you

don't get AIDS." I thought things over. "Stay in the car until we get to Calgary. Ms. Brown will get one of the other grooms to bring your bag here. The horse car is going to be unhitched from the train, and the horses are going by motor van to some stables for two days. All the grooms are going with them, as I expect you know. You go with the other grooms. And don't worry. Someone will come to find you and take you away, and bring another groom for Icy." I paused to see if he understood, but it seemed he did. "Where do you want to go from Calgary?"

"I don't know," he said dully. "Have to think."

"All right. When the someone comes for you, tell him then what you want to do."

He looked at me with a sort of wonderment. "Why are you bothering?" he asked.

"I don't like frighteners."

He shuddered. "My dad frightened the living daylights out of people . . . and me and Mum . . . and someone stabbed him, killed him . . . served him right." He paused. "No one ever helped the people he frightened." He paused again, struggling for the unaccustomed word, and came up with it. "Thanks."

With tie and buttons all correctly fastened, Tommy went back to the dining car. Zak was just finishing a scene in which old Ben, the groom who had been importuning Raoul for money at Toronto station, had been brought in from the racegoers' part of the train to give damning (false) evidence against Raoul for having doped the Bricknells' horses, a charge flatly denied by Raoul, who contrived to look virtuous and possibly guilty, both at the same time. Sympathy on the whole ended on Raoul's side because of Ben's whining nastiness, and Zak told everyone that a Most Important Witness would be coming to Château Lake Louise that evening to give Damaging Testimony. Against whom? some people asked. Ah, said Zak mysteriously, vanishing toward the corridor, only time would tell.

Emil, Oliver, Cathy and I set the tables for lunch and served its three courses. Filmer didn't materialize, but Daffodil did, still shaken and angry as at breakfast. Her suitcase was packed, it appeared, and she was adamant about leaving the party at Calgary. No one, it seemed, had been able to find out from her exactly what the matter was, and the lovers' tiff explanation had gained ground.

I served wine carefully and listened, but it was the appealing prospect of two days in the mountains rather than Daffodil's troubles that filled most of the minds.

When Calgary appeared like sharp white needles on the prairie horizon and everyone began pointing excitedly, I told Emil I would do my best to return for the dishwashing and sloped off up the train to George's office.

Would the credit-card telephone work in Calgary? Yes, it would. He waved me toward it as the train slowed and told me I'd got fifty minutes. He himself, as usual, would be outside, supervising.

I got through to Mrs. Baudelaire, who sounded carefree and sixteen.

"Your photograph is on its way," she said without preamble. "But it won't get to Calgary in time. Someone will be driving from Calgary to Château Lake Louise later this afternoon, and they are going to take it to your Miss Richmond."

"That's great," I said. "Thank you."

"But I'm afraid there's been no word from Val Catto about your numbers."

"It can't be helped."

"Anything else?" she asked.

"Yes," I said. "I need to talk to Bill direct."

"What a shame, I've been enjoying this."

"Oh," I said. "Please, so have I. It's only that it's more than a message and question and answer. It's long and complicated."

"My dear young man, don't apologize. Bill was still in Winnipeg ten minutes ago. I'll call him straightaway. Do you have a number?"

"Um, yes." I read her the number on the train's handset. "The sooner the better, would you tell him?"

"Talk to you later," she said, and went away.

I waited restlessly through ten wasted minutes before the phone rang.

Bill's deep voice reverberated in my ear. "Where are you?"

"On the train in Calgary station."

"My mother says its urgent."

"Yes, but chiefly because this cellular telephone is in the conductor's office and only works in cities."

"Understood," he said. "Fire away."

I told him about Daffodil's threatened departure and Lenny Higgs's frightened collapse; about what she had not said, and he had.

Bill Baudelaire at length demanded, "Have I got this straight? This Lenny Higgs said Daffodil Quentin got him to give her horse something to eat, from which the horse got colic and died?"

"Strong supposition of cause and effect, but unprovable, I should think."

"Yes. They had an autopsy and couldn't find what caused the colic. It was the third of her dead horses. The insurers were very suspicious, but they had to pay."

"Lenny says she told him she would never do any harm to her darling horses, but she gave him a hundred dollars to keep quiet."

Bill groaned.

"But," I said, "it might have been because she'd had two dead horses already and she was afraid everyone would think exactly what they did think anyway."

"I suppose so," he said. "So where are we now?"

"Going on past experience," I said, "I would think—and this is just guessing—that after midnight last night, our quarry told Daffodil that her groom had spilled the beans, and would spill them again to order in public, and that he, our quarry, would see she was warned off at the very least if she didn't sell him—or give him—her remaining share in Laurentide Ice."

He said gloomily, "You all know him better than I do, but on form I'd think you may be right. We'll know for sure, won't we, if he applies to change the partnership registration before the Vancouver race."

"Mm," I agreed. "Well, if you—the Ontario Racing Commission—feel like giving Daffodil the benefit of the doubt over her horses . . . and of course you know her better than I do, but it seems to me she may not be intentionally wicked, but more silly. I mean there's something immature about her, for all her fifty years or so . . . and some people don't think it's all that wicked to defraud insurance companies, perfectly respectable people sometimes do it . . . and I believe all three horses would have been put down sooner than later, wouldn't they? Anyway, I'm not excusing her if she's guilty, but explaining how she might feel about it."

"You've got to know her remarkably well."

"Er . . . I've just . . . noticed."

"Mm," he said dryly. "Val Catto said you notice things."

"Well, I, er, don't know how you feel about this, but I thought that if we spirited Lenny Higgs away, sort of, he wouldn't be around to be threatened, or to be a threat to Daffodil, and if you could tell her somehow that Lenny Higgs had vanished and will not be spilling any beans whatsoever . . . if you could square it with your conscience to do that . . . then she doesn't need to part with her half-share and we will have foiled at least one of our quarry's rotten schemes. And that's my brief, isn't it?"

He breathed out lengthily, as a whistle.

I held the line and waited.

"Is Lenny Higgs still on the train?" he asked eventually.

"Unless he panics, he's going with the other grooms and horses to their stabling here. I told him someone would come to fetch him and look after him and give him a free ticket to wherever he wants to go."

"Now, hold on . . ."

"It's the least we can do. But I think we should follow it up, and positively know his exact ultimate destination, even fix him up with a job, because we in our turn may want him to give evidence against the man who frightened him. If we do, we don't want to have to do a world-wide search. And if you can send someone to help him, get them to take along a copy of the photo you've had printed for me, because I'm pretty certain that's the man who frightened him. Lenny should turn to jelly, if it is."

14

There was unfortunately a fair amount of dishwashing still to do when I returned to the kitchen so I lent a slightly guilty hand but kept walking out with glasses and cloths into the dining car so that I could see what was going on outside the windows.

Daffodil, attended by Nell and Rose and Cumber Young (he carrying her two suitcases), was helped down from the dome car by station staff and went off slowly into the main part of the station. Daffodil's curls were piled as perkily high as usual but her shoulders drooped inside the chinchillas, and the glimpse I had of her face showed a forlorn lost-child expression rather than that of a virago bent on revenge. Nell was being helpful. Rose Young exuded comfort: Cumber Young looked grim.

"Are you drying glasses or are you not?" Cathy demanded. She was pretty, bright-eyed and quick, and also, at that moment, tired.

"Intermittently," I said.

Her momentary ill-temper dissolved. "Then get an intermittent move on or I won't be able to go over to the station before we leave."

"Right," I said, and dried and polished several glasses devotedly.

Cathy giggled. "How long are you going to keep this up?"

"To the end, I guess."

"But when is your scene?"

"Ah," I said, "that's the trouble. Right at the end. So I'll be drying dishes to Vancouver."

"Are you the murderer?" she asked teasingly.

"Most definitely not."

"The last time we had an actor pretending to be a waiter, he was the murderer."

"The murderer," I said, "is that passenger you give the best portions to. That good-looking single man who's nice to everyone."

Her eyes stretched wide. "He's an owner," she said.

"He's an actor. And don't give him away."

"Of course I won't." She looked slightly dreamy-eyed, though, as if I'd passed on good news. I didn't like to disillusion her about her or any girl's prospects with the gorgeous Giles; she would find out soon enough.

The chores finally done, Cathy skipped away to the delights of the station and in her place I helped Emil and Oliver stow and lock up all the equipment, as when everyone disembarked at Lake Louise the train was again going to be standing cold and silent in sidings for two days before the last stretch westward to the Pacific.

Some but not all of the passengers had gone ashore, so to speak, at Calgary, and those who had been in the station came wandering back in good time, including the Youngs. Of Filmer there was no sign, nor of the gaunt-faced man. The dining car half-filled again with people who simply preferred sitting there, and from those I heard that the horse car had been safely detached from the train and had been towed away by the engine, leaving the rest of us temporarily stranded.

The regular Canadian, they told each other, which had arrived on time thirty-five minutes after us, was the train standing three tracks away, its passengers stretching their legs like our own. The Canadian, it seemed, had changed from threat to friend in the general perception; our doppel-ganger and companion on the journey. The passengers from both had mingled and compared notes. The conductors had met for a talk.

There was a jerk and a shudder through the train as the engine returned and reattached, and soon afterward we were on our way again, with passengers crowding now toward the dome car's observation deck to enjoy the ascent into the mountains.

Filmer, slightly to my surprise, was among those going through the dining car, and right behind him came Nell, who looked over Filmer's shoulder at me and said, "I've got a message for you from George Burley."

"Excuse me, miss," I said abruptly, standing well back between two tables to let Filmer go by, "I'll be right with you."

"What?" She was puzzled, but paused and stepped side-ways also to let others behind her walk on through the car. Filmer himself had gone on without stopping, without pay-ing Nell or me the least attention, and when his back was way down the car and well out of earshot of a quiet conver-sation, I turned back to Nell with inquiry.

"It's a bit of a mix-up," she said. She was standing on the far side of the table from me, and speaking across it. "Ap-parently the telephone in George Burley's office was ringing when he got back on board, and it was a woman wanting to speak to a Mr. Kelsey. George Burley consulted his lists and said there was no Mr. Kelsey on board. So whoever it was asked him to give a message to me, which he did."

It must have been Mrs. Baudelaire phoning, I thought: no one else knew the number. Bill himself could never be mis-taken for a woman. Not his secretary. . .? Heaven forbid.

"What's the message?" I asked.

"I don't know if between us George Burley and I have got it right." She was frowning. "It's meaningless, but— zero-forty-nine. That's the whole message, zero-forty-nine."

She looked at my face. "You look happy enough about it, anyway."

I was also appalled, as a matter of fact, at how close Filmer had come to hearing it.

I said, "Yes, well, please don't tell anyone else about the message, and please forget it if you can."

"I can't."

"I was afraid not." I hunted around if not for explanations at least for a reasonable meaning. "It's to do," I said, "with the border between Canada and America, with the forty-ninth parallel."

"Oh, sure." She was unsure by the look of things, but willing to let it go.

I said, "Someone will bring a letter to the Château some-time this evening addressed to you. It will have a photo in it. It's for me, from Bill Baudelaire. Will you see that I get it?"

"Yes, OK." She briefly glanced at her clipboard. "I wanted to talk to you anyway about rooms." A passenger or two walked past, and she waited until they had gone. "The train crew are staying in the staff annex at Château Lake Louise and the actors will be in the hotel itself. Which do you want? I have to write the list."

"Our passengers will be in the hotel?"

"Ours, yes, but not the racegoers. They're all getting off in Banff. That's the town before Lake Louise. The owners are all staying in the Château. So am I. Which do you want?"

"To be with you," I said.

"Seriously."

I thought briefly. "Is there anywhere else?"

"There's a sort of village near the station about a mile from the Château itself, but it's just a few shops, and they're closing now at this time of the year, ready for winter. A lot of places are closed by this time, in the mountains." She paused. "The Château stands by itself on the lake shore. It's beautiful there."

"Is it big?" I asked.

"Huge."

"OK. I'll stay there and risk it."

"Risk what?"

"Being stripped of my waistcoat."

"But you won't wear it there," she assured me.

"No . . . metaphorically."

She lowered the clipboard and clicked her pen for writing.

"Tommy Titmouse," I said.

Her lips curved. "T. Titmuss." She spelled it out. "That do?"

"Fine."

"What are you really?"

"Wait and see," I said.

She gave me a dry look but no answer because some passengers came by with questions, and I went forward into the dome car to see how firmly Julius Apollo would appear to be seated, wondering whether it would be safe to try to look inside his briefcase or whether I should most stringently obey the command not to risk being arrested. If he hadn't hoped I would look, the Brigadier wouldn't have relayed the number. But if I looked and got caught looking, it would blow the whole operation.

Filmer was nowhere to be seen.

From the top of the staircase, I searched again through the rows of backs of heads under the dome. No thick black well-brushed thatch with a scattering of gray hairs. Bald, blond, tangled and trimmed, but no Filmer.

He wasn't in the downstairs lounge, and he wasn't in the bar where the poker group was as usual in progress, oblivious to the scenery. That left only the Lorrimores' car. He had to be with Mercer, Bambi and Sheridan. Xanthe was with Rose and Cumber Young, watching the approach of the distant white peaks under a cloudless sky.

I walked irresolutely back toward Filmer's bedroom, wondering whether the disinclination I felt to enter it was merely prudence or otherwise plain fear, and being afraid it was the latter.

I would have to do it, I thought, because if I didn't I'd spend too much of my life regretting it. A permanent D minus in the balance sheet. By the time I left the dining room and started along the corridor past the kitchen, I was already feeling breathless, already conscious of my heart, and it was not in any way good for self-confidence. With a dry mouth I crossed the chilly shifting join between cars, opening and closing the doors, every step bringing me nearer to the risky commitment.

Filmer's was the first room in the sleeping car beyond the kitchen. I rounded the corner into the corridor with the utmost reluctance and was just about to put my hand to the door handle when the sleeping car attendant, dressed exactly as I was, came out of his roomette at the other end of the car, saw me, waved and started walking toward me.

With craven relief I went slowly toward him, and he said, "Hi," and how was I doing.

He was the familiar one who'd told me about Filmer's private breakfast, who'd shown me how to fold and unfold the armchairs and bunks, the one who looked after both the car we were in and the three bedrooms, Daffodil's among them, in the dome car. He had all afternoon and nothing to do and was friendly and wanted to talk, and he made it impossible for me to shed him and get back to my nefarious business.

He talked about Daffodil and the mess she had made of her bedroom.

Mess?

"If you ask me," he said, nodding, "she'd had a bottle of vodka in her suitcase. There was broken glass all over the place. Broken vodka bottle. And the mirror over the washbasin. In splinters. All over the place. I'd guess she threw the vodka bottle at the mirror and they both broke."

"A bore for you to have to clear that up," I said.

He seemed surprised. "I didn't clear it. It's still like that.

George can take a look at it." He shrugged. "I don't know if the company will charge her for it. Shouldn't be surprised."

He looked over my shoulder at someone coming into the car from the dining car.

"Afternoon, sir," he said.

There was no reply from behind me. I turned my head and saw Filmer's backview going into his bedroom.

Dear God, I thought in horror: I would have been in there with his briefcase open, reading his papers. I felt almost sick.

I sensed more than saw Filmer come out of his bedroom again and walk toward us.

"Can I help you, sir?" the sleeping car attendant said, going past me, toward him.

"Yes. What do we do about our bags at Lake Louise?"

"Leave it to me, sir. We're collecting everyone's cases and transporting them to the Château. They'll be delivered to your room in the Château, sir."

"Good," Filmer said, and went back into his lair, closing the door. Beyond the merest flicker of a glance at about waist level, he hadn't looked at me at all.

"We did the same with the bags at Winnipeg," the sleeping car attendant said to me resignedly. "You'd think they'd learn."

"Perhaps they will by Vancouver."

"Yeah."

I left him after a while and went and sat in my own roomette and did some deep breathing and thanked every guardian angel in the firmament for my deliverance, and in particular the angel in the sleeping car attendant's yellow waistcoat.

Outside the window, the promise of the mountains became an embrace, rocky hillsides covered with tall narrow pines crowding down to the railway line winding through the valley of the Bow River. There were thick untidy collections of twigs sitting like Ascot hats on the top of a good many telegraph poles, which looked quite extraordinary; one of the passengers had said the hats were osprey nests, and that the poles were made with platforms on especially to accommodate them. Brave birds, I thought, laying their eggs near to the roaring trains. Hair-raising entertainment for the hatchlings.

Our speed had slowed from the brisk prairie rattle to a grunting uphill slither, the train taking two hours to cover the seventy miles from Calgary to Banff. When it stopped there, in the broad part of the valley, the snow-topped peaks were suddenly revealed as standing around in a towering, glistening, uneven ring, the quintessential mountains rising in bare majestic rocky grandeur from the thronging forested courtier foothills. I felt then, as most people do, the strong lure of high mysterious frozen places and, Filmer or not, I found myself smiling with pleasure, lighthearted to the bone.

It had been noticeably warm in Calgary, owing, it was said, to the föhn winds blowing down from the mountains, but in Banff it was suitably cold. The engine huffed and puffed about and split the train in two, taking the racegoers and all the front part off to a siding and coming back to pick up just the owners' quarters; the three sleeping cars, the dining, the dome, and the Lorrimores' cars. Abbreviated and much lighter, the remains of the train climbed at good speed for another three-quarters of an hour and triumphantly drew up beside the log cabin station of Lake Louise.

With great cheerfulness the passengers disembarked, shivering even in their coats after the warmth of the cars, but full of expectation, Daffodil forgotten. They filed onto a waiting bus, while their suitcases were loaded into a separate truck. I clung to a fraction of hope that Filmer would leave his briefcase to be ferried in that fashion, but when he emerged from the train the case went with him, clutched firmly in his fist.

I told Nell I would walk up the mile or so from the station so as not to arrive until everyone had booked in and cleared the lobby. She said I could travel up anyway with the crew in their own bus, but I entrusted my bag to her keeping and in my gray regulation raincoat, buttoned to the neck, I enjoyed the fresh cold air and the deepening harvest gold of the late afternoon sunlight. When I reached the lobby of the grand Château it was awash with polite young Japanese couples on honeymoon, not the Unwins, the Youngs and the Flokatis.

Nell was sprawled in a lobby armchair as if she would never be able to summon the energy to rise again, and I went and sat beside her before she'd realized I was there.

"Is everyone settled?" I asked.

She sighed deeply and made no attempt at moving. "The suite I had reserved for the Lorrimores had been given to someone else half an hour before we got here. The people are not budging, the management are not apologizing, and Bambi is not pleased."

"I can imagine."

"On the other hand, we are sitting with our backs to one of the greatest views on earth."

I twisted round and looked over the back of the chair, and saw, between thronging Japanese, black and white mountains, a turquoise-blue lake, green pines and an advancing glacier, all looking like painted stage scenery, awesomely close and framed by the windows.

"Wow," I said, impressed.

"It won't go away," Nell said, after a while. "It'll all still be there tomorrow."

I flopped back into the chair. "It's amazing."

"It's why people have been coming here to stare for generations."

"I expected altogether more snow," I said.

"It'll be knee-deep by Christmas."

"Do you have any time off here?" I asked.

She looked at me sideways. "Five seconds now and then, but almost no privacy."

I sighed lightly, having expected nothing else. She was the focus, the center round which the tour revolved: the most visible person, her behavior vivisected.

"Your room is in one of the wings," she said, handing me a card with a number on it. "You just have to sign in at the desk and they'll give you the key. Your bag should be up there already. Most of the actors are in that wing. None of the owners."

"Are you?"

"No."

She didn't say where her room was, and I didn't ask.

"Where will you eat?" she said doubtfully. "I mean, will you sit with the actors in the dining room?"

I shook my head.

"But not with the owners . . ."

"It's a lonely old life," I said.

She looked at me with sudden sharp attention, and I thought ruefully that I'd told her a good deal too much.

"Do you mean," she asked slowly, "that you do this all the time? Play a part? Not just on the train?"

"No," I smiled. "I work alone. That's all I meant."

She almost shivered. "Are you ever yourself?"

"Sundays and Mondays."

"Alone?"

"Well, yes."

Her eyes, steady and gray, looked only moderately troubled. "You don't seem unhappy," she observed, "being lonely."

"Of course not. I choose it, mostly. But not when there's an alluring alternative hiding behind a clipboard."

The armor lay on her lap at that moment, off duty. She smoothed a hand over it, trying not to laugh.

"Tomorrow," she said, retreating into common sense, "I'm escorting a busload of passengers to a glacier, then to lunch in Banff, then up a mountain in cable cars."

"And may it keep fine for you."

"The Lorrimores have a separate chauffeur-driven car."

"Has anyone else?"

"Not since Mrs. Quentin's left."

"Poor old Daffodil," I said.

"Poor?" Nell exclaimed. "Did you know she smashed the mirror in her room?"

"Yes, I heard. Is Mr. Filmer going on the bus trip?"

"I don't know yet. He wanted to know if there's an exercise gym because he likes lifting weights. The bus is simply available for anyone who wants to go. I won't know everyone who'll be on it until we set off."

I would have to watch the departure, I thought, and that could be difficult as I would be half-familiar to all of them by now and could hardly stand invisibly around for very long.

"The Unwins have come down into the hall and are heading toward me," Nell said, looking away from me.

"Right."

I stood up without haste, took the card she'd given me to the desk and signed the register. Behind me, I could hear the Unwins' Australian voices telling her they were going for a stroll by the shore and it was the best trip they'd ever taken. When I turned round, holding my own key, they were letting themselves out through the glass doors to the garden.

I paused again beside Nell, who was now standing up. "Maybe I'll see you," I said.

"Maybe."

I smiled at her eyes. "If anything odd happens . . ."

She nodded. "You're in room six-sixty-two."

"After Vancouver," I said, "what then?"

"After the races I'm booked straight back to Toronto on the red-eye special."

"What's the red-eye special?"

"The overnight flight."

"So soon?"

"How was I to know I wouldn't want to?"

"That'll do fine," I said, "for now."

"Don't get ideas," Nell said sedately, "above your lowly station."

She moved away with a mischievous glint and I went contentedly up to the sixth floor in the wing where there were no owners, and found that the room allocated to me was near the end of the passage and next door to Zak's.

His door was wide open with Donna and Pierre standing half-in, half-out.

"Come on in," Donna said, seeing me. "We're just walking through tonight's scene."

"And we've a hell of a crisis on our hands," Pierre said. "We need all the input we can get."

"But Zak might not—" I began.

He came to the door himself. "Zak is taking suggestions from chimpanzees," he said.

"OK. I'll just take off my coat." I pointed. "I'm in the room next along."

I went into my room, which proved to have the same sweeping view of the mountains, the lake, the trees and the glacier, and it was if anything more spectacular than in the lobby from being higher up. I took off the raincoat and the uniform it had hidden, put on a tracksuit and trainers, and returned to Zak's fray.

The crisis was the absence of an actor who was supposed to have arrived but had sent apologies instead.

"Apologies!" Zak fumed. "He broke his bloody arm this morning and he's not coming. I ask you! Is a broken arm any sort of excuse?"

The others, the whole troupe, were inclined to think not.

"He was supposed to be Angelica's husband," Zak said.

"What about Steve?" I asked.

"He was her lover, and her business partner. They were both killed by Giles because they had just found out he had embezzled all the capital and the bloodstock business was bankrupt. Now Angelica's husband comes on the scene to ask where her money is, as she hasn't changed her will and he inherits. He decided to investigate her death himself because he doesn't think either the Mounties or I have done a good enough job. And now he isn't even *here*."

"Well," I said, "why don't you discover that it is *Raoul* who is really Angelica's husband and who stands to inherit, which gives him a lot of motive as he doesn't know yet that Giles has embezzled the money, does he? No one does. And also Raoul is only free to marry Donna because Angelica is now dead, which can give the Bricknells hysterics. And how about if Raoul says the Bricknells themselves have been doping their horses, not Raoul, but they deny it and are very pleased that he should be judged guilty of everything now they know he can't marry their daughter because he is probably a murderer and will go to jail. And how about if it was the Bricknells' horse that was really supposed to be kidnaped, but by Giles, as you can later discover, so that he could sell it and gain enough to skip the country once he got safely to Vancouver."

They opened their mouths.

"I don't know that it actually makes sense," Zak said eventually.

"Never mind, I don't suppose they'll notice."

"You cynical son-of-a . . ."

"I don't see why not," Donna said. "And I can have a nice weepy scene with Pierre."

"Why?" Zak said.

"I like doing them."

They all fell about, and in a while walked through dramatic revelations (received by Zak from Outside Sources) of Raoul's marriage to Angelica five years earlier, which neither had acknowledged at Toronto station because, Raoul said unconvincingly, they were both shocked to find the other there, as he wanted to meld with Donna as she with Steve.

They all went away presently to get into their character clothes, and from Zak, very much later, I heard that the whole thing, played at the tops of their voices, had been a galvanic riot. He came to my door with a bottle in each hand, scotch for him, red wine for me, and sank exhaustedly into an armchair with an air of having nobly borne the weight of the world on his shoulders and bravely survived.

"Did you have any dinner?" he said, yawning. "Didn't see you."

"I had some sent up."

He looked at the television program with which I'd passed the time.

"Rotten reception in these mountains," he said. "Look at that idiot." He stared at the screen. "Couldn't act his way out of a paper bag."

We drank companionably and I asked if the party were all generally happy without Daffodil Quentin.

"The dear in the Mont Blanc curls?" he said. "Oh, sure. They were all in a great mood. That man who used to be with her all the time was dripping charm all over Bambi Lorrimore and that crazy son of hers didn't open his mouth once. Those Australians are still in the clouds."

He described the reactions of some of the others to the evening's scene and then said he would rely on me for another scintillating bit of scrambled plot for the next night. Not to mention, he added, a denouement and finale for the night after, our last on the train. The mystery had to be solved then before a Gala Dinner of epic proportions comprising five courses produced by Angus by sleight of hand.

"But I only said it all off the top of my head," I said.

"The top of your head will do us all fine." He yawned. "Tell you the truth, we need a fresh mind."

"Well . . . all right."

"So how much do I pay you?"

I was surprised. "I don't want money."

"Don't be silly."

"Um," I said. "I do earn more than Tommy."

He looked at me over his whisky glass. "You don't really surprise me."

"So thanks a lot," I said, meaning it, "but no thanks."

He nodded and left it: the offer honorably made, realistically declined. Anything he would have paid me would have come directly out of his own pocket: impossible to accept.

"Oh!" he said, clearly hit by a shaft of memory, "Nell

asked me to give you this." He dug into a pocket and produced a sealed envelope, which he handed over. It said "Nell Richmond" on the outside, and "Photographs, do not bend."

"Thanks," I said, relieved. "I was beginning to think it hadn't got here."

I opened the envelope and found three identical prints inside, but no letter. The pictures were clear, sharp and in black and white owing to the fast high-definition film I habitually used in the binoculars-camera. The subject, taken from above, was looking upward and to one side to a point somewhere below the lens, so that one couldn't see his eyes clearly; but the sharply jutting cheekbones, the narrow nose, the deep eye sockets, the angled jawbone and the hairline retreating from the temples, all were identifiable at a glance. I handed one of the prints to Zak, and he looked at it curiously.

"Who is it?" he said.

"That's the point. Who is he? Have you seen him on the train?"

He looked again at the picture, which showed, below the head, the shoulders and neck, with the sheepskin collar of the padded jacket over a sweater of some sort and a checked shirt unbuttoned at the top.

"A tough-looking man," Zak said. "Is he a militant union agitator?"

I was startled. "Why do you say that?"

"Don't know. He has the look. All intensity and aggression. That's what I'd cast him as."

"And is that how you'd also act a union agitator?"

"Sure." He grinned. "If he was described in the script as a troublemaker." He shook his head. "I haven't seen him on the train or anywhere else that I know of. Is he one of the racegoers, then?"

"I don't know for sure, but he was at Thunder Bay station and also at Winnipeg races."

"The sleeping car attendants will know."

I nodded. "I'll ask them."

"What do you want him for?"

"Making trouble."

He handed back the photograph with a smile. "Typecast," he said, nodding.

He ambled off to bed, and early the next morning I telephoned Mrs. Baudelaire, who sounded as if she rose with the lark.

I asked her to tell Bill the photos had arrived safely.

"Oh, good," she said blithely. "Did you get my message with the numbers?"

"Yes, I did, thank you very much."

"Val called with them from London, sounding very pleased. He said he wasn't having so much success with whatever it was that Sheridan Lorrimore did at Cambridge. No one's talking. He thinks the gag is cash for the new library being built at Sheridan's old college. How immoral can academics get? And Bill said to tell you that they went round to the Winnipeg barns with that photo, but no one knew who the man was, except that he did go there asking for Lenny Higgs. Bill says they will ask all the Ontario racing people they can reach and maybe print it in the racing papers coast to coast."

"Great."

"Bill wants to know what name you're using on the train."

I hesitated, which she picked up at once with audible hurt. "Don't you trust us?"

"Of course I do. But I don't trust everyone on the train."

"Oh, I see."

"You were right to send the message to Nell."

"Good, then."

"Are you well?" I asked.

The line said, "Have a nice day, young man," and went dead.

I listened to her silence with regret. I should have known better. I did know better, but it seemed discourteous never to ask.

With her much in mind I dressed for outdoors, hopped down the fire stairs and found an inconspicuous way out so as not to come face to face with any passengers who were en route to breakfast. In my woolly hat, well pulled down, and my navy zipped jacket, I found a good vantage point for watching the front door, then wandered round a bit and returned to the watching point a little before bus-boarding time for the sightseeing trip to Banff. Under the jacket I had slung the binoculars, just in case I could get nowhere near, but in fact, from leaning against the boot of an empty, parked, locked car where I hoped I looked as if waiting for the driver to return, I had a close enough view not to need them.

A large ultra-modern bus with tinted windows rolled in and stationed itself obligingly so that I could see who walked from the hotel to board it, and very soon after, when the driver had been into the hotel to report his arrival, Nell appeared in a warm jacket, trousers and boots and shepherded her flock with smiles into its depths. Most of the passengers were going sightseeing, it seemed, but not all.

Filmer didn't come out. I willed him to: to appear without his briefcase and roll away for hours: to give me a chance of thinking of some way to get into his room in safety. Willing didn't work. Julius Apollo didn't seem to want to walk on a glacier or dangle in a cable car, and stayed resolutely indoors.

Mercer, Bambi and Sheridan came out of the hotel together, hardly looking a lighthearted little family, and inserted themselves into a large waiting chauffeur-driven car, which carried them off immediately.

No Xanthe. No Xanthe on the bus either. Rose and Cumber Young had boarded without her. Xanthe, I surmised, was back in the sulks.

Nell, making a note on her clipboard and looking at her watch, decided there were no more customers for the bus. She stepped inside it and closed the door and I watched it roll away.

15

I walked about on foot in the mountains thinking of the gifts that had been given me.

Lenny Higgs. The combinations of the locks of the brief-case. Nell's friendship. Mrs. Baudelaire. The chance to invent Zak's scripts.

It was the last that chiefly filled my mind as I walked round the path that circled the little lake; and the plans I began forming for the script had a lot to do with the end of my conversation with Bill Baudelaire, which had been disturbing.

After he'd agreed to arrange a replacement groom for Laurentide Ice, he said he'd tried to talk to Mercer Lorrimore at Assiniboia Downs but hadn't had much success.

"Talk about what?" I asked.

"About our quarry. I was shocked to find how friendly he had become with the Lorrimores. I tried to draw Mercer Lorrimore aside and remind him about the trial, but he was quite short with me. If a man was found innocent, he said, that was an end of it. He thinks good of everyone, it seems —which is saintly but not sensible." Bill's voice went even deeper with disillusion. "Our quarry can be overpoweringly pleasant, you know, if he puts his mind to it, and he had certainly been doing that. He had poor Daffodil Quentin practically eating out of his hand, too, and I wonder what she thinks of him now."

I could hear the echo of his voice in the mountains. "More saintly than sensible." Mercer was a man who saw good where no good existed. Who longed for goodness in his son, and would pay forever because it couldn't be achieved.

The path round the lake wound up hill and down, sometimes through close-thronging pines, sometimes with sudden breath-stopping views of the silent giants towering above, sometimes with clear vistas of the deep turquoise water below in its perfect bowl. It had rained during the night so that the whole scene in the morning sunshine looked washed and glittering; and the rain had fallen as snow on the mountaintops and the glacier, which now appeared whiter, cleaner and nearer than the day before.

The air was cold, a cold descending perceptibly like a tide from the frozen peaks, but the sun, at its autumn highest in the sky, still kept enough warmth to make walking a pleasure, and when I came to a place where a bench had been placed before a stunning panorama of lake, the Château and the mountain behind it, it was warm enough also to pause and sit down. I brushed some raindrops off the seat and slouched on the bench, hands in pockets, gaze vaguely on the picture-postcard spectacle, mind in second gear on Filmer.

I could see figures walking about by the shore in the Château garden, and thought without hurry of perhaps bringing out the binoculars to see if any of them was Julius Apollo. Not that it would have been of much help, I supposed, if he'd been there. He wouldn't be doing anything usefully criminal under the gaze of the Château's serried ranks of windows.

Someone with quiet footsteps came along the path from the shelter of the trees and stopped, looking down at the lake. Someone female.

I glanced at her incuriously, seeing a backview of jeans,

blue parka, white trainers and a white woollen hat with two scarlet pompoms: and then she turned round, and I saw that it was Xanthe Lorrimore.

She looked disappointed to find the bench already occupied.

"Do you mind if I sit here?" she said. "It's a long walk. My legs are tired."

"No, of course not." I stood up and brushed the raindrops off the rest of the bench, making a drier space for her.

"Thanks." She flopped down in adolescent gawkiness and I took my own place again, with a couple of feet between us.

She frowned. "Haven't I seen you before?" she asked. "Are you on the train?"

"Yes, miss," I said, knowing that there was no point in denying it, as she would see me again and more clearly in the dining room. "I'm one of the crew."

"Oh." She began as if automatically to get to her feet, and then, after a moment, decided against it out of tiredness and relaxed. "Are you," she said slowly, keeping her distance, "one of the waiters?"

"Yes, Miss Lorrimore."

"The one who told me I had to pay for a Coke?"

"Yes, I'm sorry."

She shrugged and looked down at the lake. "I suppose," she said in a disgruntled voice, "all this is pretty special, but what I really feel is *bored*."

She had thick almost straight chestnut hair, which curved at the ends over her shoulders, and she had clear fine skin and marvelous eyebrows. She was going to be beautiful, I thought, with maturity, unless she let the sulky cast of her mouth spoil not just her face but her life.

"I sometimes wish I was poor like you," she said. "It would make everything simple." She glanced at me. "I suppose you think I'm crazy to say that." She paused. "My mother would say I shouldn't be talking to you anyway."

I moved as if to stand up. "I'll go away, if you like," I said politely.

"No, don't." She was unexpectedly vehement and surprised even herself. "I mean, there's no one else to talk to. I mean . . . well."

"I do understand," I said.

"Do you?" She was embarrassed. "I was going to go on the bus, really. My parents think I'm on the bus. I was going with Rose . . . Mrs. Young . . . and Mr. Young. But he—" She almost stopped, but the childish urge in her to talk was again running strong, sweeping away discretion. "He's never as nice to me as she is. I think he's tired of me. Cumber, isn't that a stupid name? It's Cumberland, really. That's somewhere in England where his parents went on their honeymoon, Rose says. Albert Cumberland Young, that's what his name is. Rose started calling him Cumber when they met because she thought it sounded cozier, but he isn't cozy at all, you know, he's stiff and stern." She broke off and looked down toward the Château. "Why do all those Japanese go on their honeymoons together?"

"I don't know," I said.

"Perhaps they'll all call their children Lake Louise."

"They could do worse."

"What's your name?" she asked.

"Tommy, Miss Lorrimore."

She made no comment. She was only half-easy in my company, too conscious of my job. But above all, she wanted to talk.

"You know my brother, Sheridan?" she said.

I nodded.

"The trouble with Sheridan is that we're too rich. He thinks he's better than everyone else because he's richer." She paused. "What do you think of that?" It was part a challenge, part a desperate question, and I answered her from my own heart.

"I think it's very difficult to be very rich very young."

"Do you really?" She was surprised. "It's what everyone wants to be."

"If you can have everything, you forget what it's like to need. And if you're given everything, you never learn to save."

She brushed that aside. "There's no point in saving. My grandmother left me millions. And Sheridan too. I suppose you think that's awful. He thinks he deserves it. He thinks he can do anything he likes because he's rich."

"You could give it away," I said, "if you think it's awful."

"Would you?"

I said regretfully, "No."

"There you are, then."

"I'd give some of it away."

"I've got trustees and they won't let me."

I smiled faintly. I'd had Clement Cornborough. Trustees, he'd told me once austerely, were there to preserve and increase fortunes, not to allow them to be squandered, and no, he wouldn't allow a fifteen-year-old boy to fund a farm for pensioned-off racehorses.

"Why do you think it's difficult to be rich?" she demanded. "It's easy."

I said neutrally, "You said just now that if you were poor, life would be simple."

"I suppose I did. I suppose I didn't mean it. Or not really. I don't know if I meant it. Why is it difficult to be rich?"

"Too much temptation. Too many available corruptions."

"Do you mean drugs?"

"Anything. Too many pairs of shoes. Self-importance."

She put her feet up on the bench and hugged her knees, looking at me over the top. "No one will believe this conversation." She paused. "Do you wish you were rich?"

It was an unanswerable question. I said truthfully in evasion, "I wouldn't like to be starving."

"My father says," she announced, "that one's not better because one's richer, but richer because one's better."

"Neat."

"He always says things like that. I don't understand them sometimes."

"Your brother, Sheridan," I said cautiously, "doesn't seem to be happy."

"Happy!" She was scornful. "He's never happy. I've hardly seen him happy in his whole life. Except that he does laugh at people sometimes." She was doubtful. "I suppose if he laughs he must be happy. Only he despises them, that's why he laughs. I wish I *liked* Sheridan. I wish I had a terrific brother who would look after me and take me places. That would be fun. Only it wouldn't be with Sheridan, of course, because it would end in trouble. He's been terrible on this trip. Much worse than usual. I mean, he's embarrassing." She frowned, disliking her thoughts.

"Someone said," I said without any of my deep curiosity showing, "that he had a bit of trouble in England."

"Bit of trouble! I shouldn't tell you, but he ought to be in jail, only they didn't press charges. I think my father bought them off. Anyway, that's why Sheridan does what my parents say, right now, because they threatened to let him be prosecuted if he as much as squeaks."

"Could he still be prosecuted?" I asked without emphasis.

"What's a statute of limitations?"

"A time limit," I said, "after which one cannot be had up for a particular bit of lawbreaking."

"In England?"

"Yes."

"You're English, aren't you?" she asked.

"Yes."

"He said, 'Hold your breath, the statute of limitations is out of sight.'"

"Who said?"

"An attorney, I think. What did he mean? Did he mean Sheridan is . . . is . . ."

"Vulnerable?"

She nodded. "Forever?"

"Maybe for a long time."

"Twenty years?" An unimaginable time, her voice said.

"It would have to have been bad."

"I don't know what he did," she said despairingly. "I only know it's ruined this summer. Absolutely ruined it. And I'm supposed to be in school right now, only they made me come on this train because they wouldn't leave me in the house alone. Well, not alone, but alone except for the servants. And that's because my cousin Susan Lorrimore, back in the summer, she's seventeen, she ran off with their chauffeur's son and they got married and there was an *earthquake* in the family. And I can see why she did, they kept leaving her alone in that huge house and going to Europe and she was bored out of her skull, and anyway it seems their chauffeur's son is all brains and cute, too, and she sent me a card saying she didn't regret a thing. My mother is scared to death that I'll run off with some—"

She stopped abruptly, looking at me a little wildly and sprang to her feet.

"I forgot," she said. "I sort of forgot you are . . ."

"It's all right," I said, standing also. "Really all right."

"I guess I talk too much." She was worried and unsure. "You won't . . ."

"No. Not a word."

"Cumber told me I ought to mind my tongue," she said resentfully. "He doesn't know what it's like living in a mausoleum with everyone glowering at each other and Daddy trying to smile." She swallowed. "What would you do?" she demanded, "if you were me?"

"Make your father laugh."

She was puzzled. "Do you mean . . . make him happy?"

"He needs your love," I said. I gestured to the path back to the Château. "If you'd like to go on first, I'll follow after."

"Come with me," she said.

"No. Better not."

In an emotional muddle that I hadn't much helped, she tentatively set off, looking back twice until a bend in the path took her out of sight, and I sat down again on the bench, although growing cold now, and thought about what she'd said, and felt grateful, as ever and always, for Aunt Viv.

There wasn't much wrong with Xanthe, I thought. Lonely, worried, only half-understanding the adult world, needing reassurance, she longed primarily for exactly what Mercer himself wanted, a friendly united family. She hadn't thought of affronting her parents by cuddling up to a waiter: very much the reverse. She hadn't tried to put me into a difficult position: had been without guile or tricks. I wouldn't have minded having a younger sister like her that I could take places for her to have fun. I hoped she would learn to live in peace with her money, and thought that a month or so of serving other people in the good company of people like Emil, Oliver and Cathy would be the best education she could get.

After a while I scanned the whole Château and its gardens with the binoculars but I couldn't see Filmer, which wasn't really surprising, and in the end I set off again to walk, and detoured up onto the foot of the glacier, trudging on the cracked, crunchy, gray-brown-green fringe of the frozen river.

Laurentide Ice, one of the passengers had knowledgeably said early on, was the name given to one of the last great polar ice sheets to cover most of Canada twenty thousand years before. Daffodil, nodding, had said her husband had named the horse because he was interested in prehistory, and she was going to call her next horse Cordilleran Ice, the sheet that had covered the Rockies. Her husband would have been pleased, she said. I could be standing at that moment on prehistoric Cordilleran Ice, perhaps, I thought, but if glaciers moved faster than history, perhaps not. Anyway, it gave a certain perspective to the concerns of Julius Apollo.

Back at the Château, I went upstairs and drafted a new scene for the script, and I'd barely finished when Zak came knocking to inquire for it. We went into his room where the cast had already gathered for the rehearsal, and I looked round their seven faces and asked if we still had the services of begging Ben, who was missing from the room. No, we didn't, Zak said. He had gone back to Toronto. Did it matter?

"No, not really. He might have been useful as a messenger, but I expect you can pretend a messenger."

They nodded.

"Right," Zak said, looking at his watch. "We're on stage in two and a half hours. What do we do?"

"First," I said, "Raoul starts a row with Pierre. Raoul is furious to have been discovered to be Angelica's husband, and he says he positively knows Pierre owes thousands in gambling debts, which he can't pay, and he knows who he owes it to, and he says that the man is known to beat people up who don't pay."

Raoul and Pierre nodded. "I'll put in some detail," Raoul said. "I'll say the debts are from illegal racing bets, and I've been told because they were on the Bricknells' horses, OK?"

"OK?" Zak said to me.

"Yes, OK. Then Raoul taunts Pierre that his only chance of getting the money is to marry Donna, and Walter Bricknell says that if Donna's so stupid as to marry Pierre, he will not give her a penny. He will in no circumstances pay Pierre's debts."

They all nodded.

"At that point, Mavis Bricknell comes screaming into the cocktail room saying that all her beautiful jewels have been stolen."

They all literally sat up. Mavis laughed and clapped her hands. "Who's stolen them?" she said.

"All in good time," I smiled. "Raoul accuses Pierre, Pierre accuses Raoul, and they begin to shove each other around, letting all their mutual hatred hang out. Finally Zak steps in, breaks it up, and says they will all go and search both Pierre's room and Raoul's room for the jewels. Zak, Raoul, Pierre and Mavis go off."

They nodded.

"That leaves," I said, "Donna, Walter Bricknell and Giles in the cocktail room. Donna and Walter have another argument about Pierre, Donna stifles a few tears and then Giles comes out of the audience to support Donna and say she's been having a bad experience, and he thinks it's time for a little good feeling all round."

Giles said, "OK, good. Here we go."

"Then," I said, "Zak and the others return. They haven't found the jewels. Giles begins to comfort Mavis as well. Mavis says she lived for her collection, she loved every piece. She's distraught. She goes on a bit."

"Lovely," Mavis said.

"Walter," I went on, "says he can't see any point in jewelry. His jewelry is his horses. He lives for his horses. He says extravagantly that if he couldn't go racing to watch his horses, he'd rather die. He'd kill himself if he couldn't have horses."

Walter frowned but eagerly nodded. He hadn't had much of a part so far: it would give him a big scene of his own, even if one difficult to make convincing.

"Walter then says Raoul is ruining his pleasure in his horses, and ruining the journey for everyone, and he gives him the formal sack as his trainer. Raoul protests, and says he hasn't deserved to be fired. Walter says Raoul is probably a murderer and a jewel thief and has been cheating him with his horses. Raoul in a rage tries to attack Walter. Zak hauls him off. Zak tells everyone to cool down. He says he will organize a search of everyone's bedrooms to see if the jewels can be found, and he will consult with the hotel's detective and call in the police if necessary. Everyone looks as if they don't want the police. End of scene."

I waited for their adverse comments and altering suggestions, but there were very few. I handed my outline to Zak who went over it again bit by bit with the actors concerned, and they all started murmuring, making up their own words.

"And what happens tomorrow?" Zak asked finally. "How do we sort it all out?"

"I haven't written it down yet," I said.

"But you do have it in mind? Could you write it this evening?"

I nodded twice.

"Right," he said. "We'd better all meet here tomorrow after breakfast. We'll have to do a thorough walk-through, maybe two or even three, to make sure we get it all right. Tie up the loose ends, that sort of thing. And don't forget, everybody, tomorrow we'll be back in the dining car. Not so much room for fighting and so on, so make it full of action tonight."

"Tomorrow Pierre gets shot," I said.

"Oh boy, oh boy," Pierre said.

"But not fatally. You can go on talking."

"Better and better."

"But you'll need some blood."

"Great," Pierre said. "How much?"

"Well," I laughed. "I'll let you decide where the bullet goes, and how much gore you think the passengers can stand, but you'd better be going to live, at the end of it."

They wanted to know what else I had in store, but I wouldn't tell them: I said they might give the future away by accident if they knew, and they protested they were too professional to do that. But I didn't altogether trust their improvising tongues, and they shrugged and gave way with fair grace.

I watched the walk-through, which seemed to go pretty well, but it was nothing, Zak assured me afterward, to the actual live performance among the cocktails.

He came back to my room at eleven, as on the previous night, drinking well-earned whisky exhaustedly.

"Those two, Raoul and Pierre, they really gave it a go," he said. "They both learned stage fighting and stunts at drama school, you know. They'd worked out the fight beforehand, and it was a humdinger. All over the place. It was a shame to break it up. Half the passengers spilled their cocktails with Raoul and Pierre rolling and slogging on the floor near their feet and we had to give everyone free refills." He laughed. "Dear Mavis put on the grand tragedy for reporting the theft of the jewels and poured on some tremendous pathos later over losing all her happy memories of the gifts that were bound up in them. Had half the audience in tears. Marvelous. Then Walter did his thing quite well considering he complained to me that no one in their right mind would kill themselves because they couldn't go racing. And afterward, would you believe it, one of the passengers asked me where we got the idea from, about someone killing themselves because they couldn't go racing."

"What did you say?" I asked with a jerk of anxiety.

"I said I picked it out of the air." He watched me relax a shade and asked, "Where *did* you get it from?"

"I knew of someone not long ago who did just that." Thirteen days ago . . . a lifetime.

"Crazy."

"Mm." I paused. "Who asked you?"

"Can't remember." He thought. "It might have been Mr. Young."

Indeed it might, I thought. Ezra Gideon had been his friend.

It might have been Filmer. Ezra Gideon had been his victim.

"Are you sure?" I asked.

He thought some more. "Yep, Mr. Young. He was sitting with that sweet wife of his, and he got up and came across the room to ask."

I drank some wine and said conversationally, "Did anyone else react?"

Zak's attention, never far below the surface, came to an intuitive point.

"Do I detect," he said, "a hint of Hamlet?"

"How do you mean?" I asked, although I knew exactly what he meant.

"The play's the thing, wherein I'll catch the conscience of the king? Right? Is that what you were up to?"

"In a mild way."

"And tomorrow?"

"Tomorrow too," I agreed.

He said broodingly, "You're not going to get any of us into trouble, are you? Not sued for slander, or anything?"

"I promise not."

"Perhaps I shouldn't let you write tomorrow's script."

"You must do what you think best." I picked the finished script off the table beside me and stretched forward to hand it to him. "Read it first, then decide."

"OK."

He put his glass down and began reading. He read to the end and finally raised a smiling face.

"It's great," he said. "All my original ideas with yours on top."

"Good." I was much relieved that he liked it, and thought him generous.

"Where's the Hamlet bit?" he asked.

"In loving not wisely but too well."

"That's Othello."

"Sorry."

He thought it over. "It seems harmless enough to me, but . . ."

"All I want to do," I said, "is open a few specific eyes. Warn a couple of people about the path they're treading. I can't, you see, just walk up to them and say it, can I? They wouldn't take it from Tommy. They probably wouldn't take it from anybody. But if they see something acted, they can learn from it."

"Like Hamlet's mother."

"Yes."

246

He sipped his whisky. "Who do you want to warn about what?" he said.

"Better I don't tell you, then nothing's your fault."

"What are you really on the train for?" he asked, frowning.

"You know what. To keep everyone happy and foil the wicked."

"And this scene will help?"

"I hope so."

"All right." He made up his mind. "I don't object to foiling the wicked. We'll give it our best shot." He grinned suddenly. "The others will love the Hamlet angle."

I was alarmed. "No, please don't tell them."

"Why ever not?"

"I want the passengers to think that any similarity of the plot to their own lives is purely coincidental. I don't want the actors telling them afterward that it was all deliberate."

He smiled twistedly. "Are we back to slander?"

"No. There's no risk of that. It's just . . . I don't want them identifying me as the one who knows so much about them. If anyone asks the actors where the plot came from, I'd far rather they said it was you."

"And dump me in the shit?" He was good-humored, however.

"No one could have suspicions about you." I smiled faintly. "Apart from foiling villainy, success for me means hiding in Tommy to the end and getting off the train unexposed."

"Are you some sort of spy?"

"A security guard, that's all."

"Can I put you in my next plot? In my next train mystery?"

"Be my guest."

He laughed, yawned, put down his glass and stood up.

"Well, pal, whoever you are," he said, "it's been an education knowing you."

Nell telephoned to my room at seven in the morning. "Are you awake?" she said.

"Wide."

"It snowed again in the night. The mountains are white."

"I can see them," I said, "from my bed."

"Do you sleep with your curtains open?"

"Always. Do you?"

"Yes."

"Are you dressed?" I asked.

"Yes, I am. What's that to do with anything?"

"With defenses, even over the telephone."

"I hate you."

"One can't have everything."

"Listen," she said severely, smothering a laugh. "Be sensible. I phoned to ask if you wanted to walk down again to the station this afternoon when we board the train, or go down on the crew bus?"

I reflected. "On the bus, I should think."

"OK. That bus goes from outside the staff annex at three-thirty-five. Take your bag with you."

"All right. Thanks."

"The whole train, with the horses and racegoers and everything, comes up from Banff to arrive at Lake Louise station at four-fifteen. That gives the passengers plenty of time to board and go to their bedrooms again and begin to unpack comfortably before we leave Lake Louise on the dot of four-thirty-five. The regular Canadian comes along behind us as before and leaves Lake Louise at ten past five, so we have to make sure everyone is boarded early so that our train can leave right on time."

"Understood."

"I'm going to tell all this to the passengers at breakfast, and also that at five-thirty we're serving champagne and canapés to everyone in the dining car, and at six we'll have the solution to the mystery, and after that cocktails for those who want them, and then the gala banquet. Then the actors return for photos and post-mortems over cognac. It all sounds like hell."

I laughed. "It will all work beautifully."

"I'm going into a nunnery after this."

"There are better places."

"Where, for instance?"

"Hawaii?"

There was a sudden silence on the line. Then she said, "I have to be back at my desk . . ."

"We could take the desk too."

She giggled. "I'll find out about shipment."

"Done, then?"

"No . . . I don't know . . . I'll let you know in Vancouver."

"Vancouver," I said, "is tomorrow morning."

"After the race, then."

"And before the red-eye special."

"Do you ever give up?"

"It depends," I said, "on the signals."

16

Filmer clung closely to his briefcase during the transit from Château to train at Lake Louise, although he had allowed his larger suitcase to be brought down with everyone else's to be arranged side by side in a long line at the station, waiting to be lifted aboard by porters.

From among the bunch of crew members, Emil, Oliver, Cathy, Angus, Simone, the barman and the sleeping car attendants, I watched Filmer and most of the passengers disembark from the bus and check that their bags were in the lineup. The Lorrimores, arriving separately with the chauffeur, brought their cases with them, the chauffeur stacking them in an aloof little group.

A freight train clanked by, seemingly endless. A hundred and two grain cars, Cathy said, counting. A whole lot of bread.

I thought about Mrs. Baudelaire, to whom I'd been talking just before leaving the Château.

"Bill said to tell you," she said, "that Lenny Higgs did turn to jelly and is being safely taken care of, and a new groom has been engaged for Laurentide Ice with the approval, by telephone, of his trainer. They told the trainer that Lenny Higgs had done a bunk. Bill has left Winnipeg and has come back to Toronto. He says he has been consulting with the Brigadier as a matter of urgency, and they agree that Bill will see Mrs. Daffodil Quentin as soon as possible. Does that all make sense?"

"Indeed it does," I said fervently.

"Good, then."

"Is Bill still going to Vancouver?" I asked.

"Oh, yes, I think so. Monday evening, I believe, ready for the race on Tuesday. He said he would be back here again on Wednesday. All these time changes can't be good for anybody."

"Canada is so huge."

"Five thousand five hundred and fourteen kilometers from side to side," she said primly.

I laughed. "Try me in miles."

"You'll have to do your own sums, young man."

I did them later, out of curiosity: 3,426 miles, and a quarter.

She asked if I had any more questions, but I couldn't think of any, and I said I would talk to her from Vancouver in the morning.

"Sleep well," she said cheerfully.

"You too."

"Yes." There was reservation in her voice, and I realized that she probably never slept well herself.

"Sweet dreams, then," I said.

"Much easier. Goodnight."

She gave me no time, as usual, to answer.

The train hooted in the distance: one of the most haunting of seductive sounds to a wanderer. That, and the hollow breathy boom of departing ships. If I had any addiction, it was to the setting off, not the arrival.

Headlights bright in the ripening afternoon sunlight, the huge yellow-fronted engine slowed into the station with muted thunder. One of the engineers, as he passed us, looked down from his open window. The engineers were the only crew that hadn't come the whole way from Toronto, each stretch of track having its own specialists.

There being no sidings at Lake Louise, the abbreviated train that had brought us there had been returned to Banff for the two mountain days, with George Burley going with it, in charge. He returned now with the whole train, his cheerful round figure climbing down in the station and greeting the passengers like long-lost friends.

With a visible lifting of spirits and freshening enjoyment, the whole party returned upward to their familiar quarters; the Lorrimores, a glum quartet stepping onto their private railed platform entrance at the rear of everything, were the only sad note. Nell went along to speak to them, to try to cheer them up. Mercer stopped, answered, smiled: the others simply went on inside. Why bother with them? I thought. One would get no thanks. Yet one would always bother, somehow, for Mercer, the blind saint.

Filmer boarded through the open door at the end of his sleeping car and through his window I saw him moving about in his room. Hanging up jackets. Washing his hands. Ordinary things. What made one man good, I wondered, and another man bad: one man to seek to build, the other to frighten and destroy. The acid irony was that the bad might feel more satisfied and fulfilled than the good.

I walked along to the car where my roomette was, dumped my bag there and took off my raincoat to reveal the familiar livery beneath. Only one more night of Tommy. One dinner, one breakfast. Pity, I thought: I'd been getting quite fond of him.

George came swinging aboard as the train moved off in its quiet way, and he greeted me with a pleased chuckle.

"We're lucky to have heat on this train, eh?" he said.

"Why?" I asked. "It's very warm."

"They couldn't start the boiler." He seemed to think it a great joke. "You know why?"

I shook my head.

"No fuel."

I looked blank. "Well, they could surely fill up?"

"You bet your life," he said. "Only the tank had been

filled two days ago, eh?, when we went down to Banff. Or was supposed to have been. So we had a look, and there were a few drips trickling from the bottom drain, which is only opened for sluicing through the tank, which isn't done often, eh?" He looked at me expectantly, his eyes bright.

"Someone stole the fuel?"

He chuckled. "Either stole it from the tank, or never loaded it in the first place, and opened the drain to be misleading."

"Was there a lot of oil on the ground?" I asked.

"Not a bad detective, are you? Yes, there was."

"What do you think, then?"

"I think they never loaded the right amount, probably just enough to get us a fair way out of Lake Louise, then they opened the drain a bit to persuade us the fuel had run away by accident along the track, eh? Only they got it wrong. Opened the drain too much." The laugh vibrated in his throat. "What a fuss, eh?, if the train went cold in the mountains! The horses would freeze. What a panic!"

"You don't seem too worried."

"It didn't happen, did it."

"No, I guess it didn't."

"We would have filled the tank again at Revelstoke, anyway," he said. "It would have ruined this gala banquet of yours, eh? But no one would have died. Doubt if they'd even have got frostbite, not like they might in January. The air temperature up here will fall below zero after sunset, soon, but the track goes through the valleys, not up the peaks, eh? And there'd be no wind chill factor, inside the cars."

"Very uncomfortable, though."

"Very." His eyes gleamed. "I left them all buzzing around like a wasp's nest in Banff, trying to find out who did it."

I wasn't as insouciant as he was. I said, "Is there anything else that can go wrong with this train? Is there for instance any *water* in the boiler?"

"Never you mind," he said comfortingly. "We checked

the water. The top tap ran. That tank's full, just as it should be. The boiler won't blow up."

"What about the engine?"

"We checked every inch of everything, eh? But it was just some greedy ordinary crook stealing that oil."

"Like the ordinary crook who unhitched the Lorrimores' car?"

He thought it over skeptically. "I'll grant you that this particular train might attract psychos, as the publicity would be that much greater, and more pleasing to them, but there is no visible connection between the two things." He chuckled. "People will steal anything, not just oil. Someone stole eight of those blue leather chairs in the dining car, once. Drove up to the dining car while it was standing unused in the sidings at Mimico in Toronto, drove up in a van saying Furniture Repairs on the side, and simply loaded up eight good chairs, eh? Last that was ever seen of them."

He turned away toward the paperwork spread out on his table, and I left him to go along to the dining car, but I'd taken only two paces when I remembered gaunt-face, and I fetched his photograph and went back to George.

"Who is he?" he asked, frowning slightly. "Yes, I'd say he might be on the train. He was down in Banff, in the sidings." He thought, trying to remember. "This afternoon, eh?" he exclaimed suddenly. "That's it. While they were joining up the train. See, the horses had come up from Calgary this morning as the first car of a freight train. They dropped the horse car in the sidings. Then our engine picked up the horse car and then the racegoers' cars." He concentrated. "This man, he was down on the ground, rapping on the horse car door with a stick, and when the dragon-lady came to the door and asked what he wanted, he said he had a message for the groom looking after the gray horse, so the dragon-lady told him to wait and she came back with a groom, only he said it wasn't the right groom, and he, the groom, eh?, said the other groom had left in Calgary and he had taken over, and then your man in the photo walked off. I didn't see where he went to. I mean, it wasn't important."

I sighed. "Did the man look angry, or anything?"

"I didn't notice. I was there to ask Ms. Brown if everything was in order in the horse car before we set off, and she said it was. She said all the grooms were in the horse car with their horses, looking after them, as they had been all day, and they would stay there until after we left. She looks after the horses well, eh?, and the grooms, too. Can't fault her, eh?"

"No."

He held out the photograph for me to take back, but I told him to keep it, and asked diffidently if he would check with the racegoers' sleeping car attendants, if he had time, to find out for sure whether or not gaunt-face had come all the way from Toronto among the passengers.

"What's he done? Anything yet?"

"Frightened a groom into leaving."

He stared. "Not much of a crime, eh?" His eyes laughed. "He won't do much jail time for that."

I had to agree with him. I left him to his enjoyment of human failures and went toward the dining car, passing as I did so the friendly sleeping car attendant who was again resting himself in the corridor, watching the changing perspectives of the snowy giants.

"I don't see this usually," he said in greeting. "I don't usually come further west than Winnipeg. Grand, isn't it?"

I agreed. Indeed it was.

"What time do you bring the beds down?" I asked.

"Any time after the passengers have all gone along to the dining car. Half of them are in their rooms here, now, changing. I've just taken extra towels to two of them."

"I'll give you a hand with the beds later, if you like."

"Really?" He was surprised and pleased. "That would be great."

"If you do your dome car rooms first," I said, "then when you come back through the dining car, I'll follow you and we can do these."

"You don't have to, you know."

"Makes a nice change from waiting at tables."

"And your scene," he said, smiling in understanding, "what about that?"

"That comes later," I promised him.

"All right, then. Thanks very much."

"Pleasure," I said, and swung along past Filmer's closed door, through the heavy doors of the cold draughty join, into the heat of the corridor beside the kitchen, and finally to the little lobby between kitchen door and tables where Emil, Oliver and Cathy were busy unboxing the champagne flutes.

I picked up a cloth and began polishing. The other three smiled.

In the hissing heat of the kitchen, Angus and Simone were arguing, Angus having asked Simone to shell a bowlful of hard-boiled eggs, which she refused to do, saying he must do it himself.

Emil raised amused eyebrows. "She is getting crosser as time goes by. Angus is a genius and she doesn't like it."

Angus, as usual seeming to have six hands all busy at once, proved to be making dozens of fresh canapés on baking trays ready for ten minutes in a scorching oven. Crab and brie together in thin layers of pastry, he said of one batch, and chicken and tarragon in another, cheese and bacon in a third. Simone stood with her hands on her hips, a hoity-toity tilt to her chin. Angus had begun ignoring her completely, which was making things worse.

The passengers as usual came to the dining car well before the appointed hour, but seemed perfectly happy just to sit and wait. The theatrical entertainment outside the windows anyway claimed all eyes and tongues until the shadows grew long in the valleys and only the peaks were lit with slowly fading intensity, until they too were extinguished into darkness. Evening came swift and early in the mountains, twilight being a matter of lingering lightness in the sky, night growing upward from the earth.

A real shame, most of the passengers complained to Nell,

that the train went through the best scenery in Canada in the dark. Someone in a newspaper, they were saying as I distributed the champagne glasses, had said that it was as if the French kept the lights off in the Louvre, in Paris. Nell said she was really sorry, she didn't write the timetables, and she hoped everyone had been able to see a mountain or two at Lake Louise, which everyone had, of course. Most had gone up one, Sulphur Mountain, to the windy summit, in four-seater glass containers on wires. Others had said no way, and stayed at the bottom. Filmer, sitting this time with the ultra-rich owners of Redi-Hot, was saying pleasantly that no, he hadn't been on the bus tour, he'd been content to take his exercise in the gym at Lake Louise.

Filmer had come into the dining room from the dome car end, not from his bedroom, and he arrived wearing a private smirk that sent uncomfortable shivers along my nerves. Any time Julius Apollo looked as pleased with himself as that, it was sure to mean trouble.

The Lorrimores arrived in a group and sat together at one table, the offspring both looking mutinous and the parents glum. Xanthe, it was clear, hadn't yet made Mercer laugh. Rose and Cumber Young were with the Upper Gumtree Unwins and the Flokati people were with the owners of Wordmaster. It was interesting, I thought, that the owners of the horses tended to be attracted to each other, much as if they belonged to a brotherhood that clung naturally together.

Perhaps Filmer had understood that. Perhaps it was why he had made such efforts to go on the train as an owner: because being an owner of one of the horses gave him standing, gave him credibility, gave him a power base. If that was what he intended, he had achieved it. Everyone on the train knew Mr. Julius Filmer.

Emil popped the champagne corks. Angus whizzed his succulent hot appetizers from oven to serving trays, seeming to summon from nowhere the now peeled and sliced eggs topped with caviar and lemon-skin twists on melba toast circles. We set off from the kitchen in a small procession, Emil and I pouring the bubbles, Oliver and Cathy doing the skillful stuff with silver tongs, giving everyone little platefuls of the hors d'oeuvre they preferred.

Nell was laughing at me silently. Well, she would. I kept a totally straight face while filling her glass and also that of Giles, who was sitting beside her in the aisle seat, ready for action.

"Thank you," Giles said in a bored voice when his glass was full.

"My pleasure, sir," I said.

He nodded. Nell smothered her laughing mouth against her glass and the people sitting opposite her noticed nothing at all.

When I reached the Lorrimores, Xanthe was perceptibly anxious. I poured into Bambi's glass and said to Xanthe, "For you, miss?"

She gave me a flicker of a glance. "Can I have a Coke?"

"Certainly, miss."

I poured champagne for Mercer and for Sheridan, and went back to the kitchen for the Coke.

"You have to pay for it," Xanthe said jerkily to her father when I returned.

"How much?" Mercer asked. I told him, and he paid. "Thank you," he said.

"A pleasure, sir."

He looked abstracted, not his usual placatory self. Xanthe risked another semifrightened glance at me and seemed to be greatly reassured when I didn't refer in any way to our encounter above the lake. The most I gave her was the faintest of deferential smiles, which even her mother couldn't have disapproved of, if she had seen it: but she, like Mercer, seemed more than unusually preoccupied.

I went on to the next table and hoped that Filmer's smirk and Mercer's gloom were not connected, although I was afraid that they might be. The smirk had been followed into the dining room by the gloom.

When Angus's canapés had been devoured to the last

melting morsel and the champagne glasses refilled, Zak arrived with a flourish for the long wrap-up scene. First of all, he said, he had to announce that a thorough search of the rooms in the Château had produced no sign of Mavis Bricknell's jewels.

Commiserations were expressed for Mavis, the passengers entering into the fantasy with zest. Mavis accepted them gracefully.

Raoul came bursting into the dining car, furious with Walter Bricknell, who was looking upset enough already.

It was too much, Raoul loudly said. It was bad enough Walter firing him as his trainer when he had done nothing to deserve it, but now he had found out that Walter had sent a letter from the Château to the racing authorities saying his horse, Calculator, wouldn't be running in his, Walter's, name at Vancouver, and that Raoul wouldn't be credited as trainer.

"It's unfair," he shouted. "I've trained the horse to the minute for that race. I've won five races with him for you. You're cheating me. You're damned ungrateful. I'm going to complain to the Jockey Club."

Walter looked stony. Raoul had another go. Walter said he would do what he liked, Calculator was his. If he wanted to sell it—or give it away—that was entirely his own business and nobody else's.

"You said yesterday," Raoul yelled, "that if you didn't have your horses, if you couldn't go racing, you'd kill yourself. Is that what you're going to do?"

Everyone looked at Walter in shocked disbelief.

Zak invited Walter to explain. Walter said it was none of Zak's business. Everything on the train was his business, Zak said. "Could we all please know," he asked Walter, "who the new owner of Calculator is going to be?"

No, no one could ask. Mavis, bewildered, did ask. Walter was rude to her, which no one liked. Walter realized that no one liked it, but said he couldn't help it, he was getting rid of Calculator, and since the horse was in his name only, not

Mavis's, she couldn't do anything about it. Mavis began to cry.

Donna went to her mother's defense and verbally attacked her father.

"You be quiet," he said angrily. "You've done enough harm."

Pierre put his arm round Donna's shoulders and told Walter not to talk to his daughter that way. He, Pierre, would borrow some money to pay his gambling debts, he said, and work, really work this time and save until it was paid off, and he would never let Donna take a penny from her father, and when he was out of debt he and Donna would get married and there was nothing Walter could do to stop them.

"Oh, Pierre," Donna wailed, and hid her face against his chest. Pierre, in snow-white shirtsleeves, put both arms round her, stroked her hair and looked very manly, handsome and protective. The audience approved of him with applause.

"Oh, goody," Cathy said from beside me. "Isn't he cute?"

"He sure is."

We were standing in the little lobby, watching from the shadows and, by a malign quirk of fate, all the faces I was most interested in were sitting with their backs to me. Filmer's neck, not far off, was rigid with tension, and Cumber Young, one table farther along, had got compulsively to his feet when Raoul had told Walter to kill himself, and had only slowly subsided, with Rose talking to him urgently. Mercer, just over midway along, sitting against the far right-hand side wall, had his head bowed, not watching the action. He couldn't help but hear, however. The actors were all courting laryngitis, making sure that those in the farthest corners weren't left out.

Mavis had a go at Walter, first angry, then pleading, then saying she might as well leave him, she obviously didn't count with him anymore. She prepared to go. Walter, stung beyond bearing, muttered something to her that stopped her dead.

"What?" she said.

Walter muttered again.

"He says he's being *blackmailed*," Mavis said in a high voice. "How can anyone blackmail someone into getting rid of a horse?"

Filmer, pinned against the left-hand wall by the Unwins in the aisle seats, sat as if with a rod up his backbone. Mercer turned his head to stare at Walter. Mercer had his back toward Filmer, and I wondered whether he'd sat that way round on purpose so as not to see his recent friend. He was sitting beside Sheridan and opposite Bambi. Xanthe sat opposite her brother, both in aisle seats. I could see both of the female faces, where I wanted to see the male. I would have done better, I supposed, to have watched from the far end, but on the other hand they might have seen me watching: watching them instead of the action.

Walter, under pressure, said loudly that yes, he was being blackmailed, and by the very nature of blackmail he couldn't say what about. He categorically refused to discuss it further. He had good and sufficient reasons and he was angry and upset enough about losing his horse without everyone attacking him.

And who was he losing it to? Zak asked. Because whoever's name turned up on the race-card at Vancouver as the owner, he or she would be the blackmailer.

Heads nodded. Walter said it wasn't so. The blackmailer had just said he must give the horse away.

"Who to?" Zak asked insistently. "Tell us. We'll soon know. We'll know at the races on Tuesday."

Walter, defeated, said, "I'm giving the horse to Giles."

General consternation followed. Mavis objected. Giles was a very nice, comforting fellow, but they hardly knew him, she said.

Raoul said bitterly that Walter should have given *him* the horse. He'd worked so hard . . .

Giles said that Walter had asked him, Giles, to have the

horse, and, of course, he'd said yes. After the race on Tuesday, he would decide Calculator's future.

Walter looked stony. Giles was being frightfully nice.

Donna suddenly detached herself from Pierre and said rather wildly, "No, Daddy, I won't let you do it. I understand what's happening . . . I won't let it happen."

Walter told her thunderously to shut up. Donna wouldn't be stopped. It was her fault that her father was being blackmailed and she wouldn't let him give his horse away.

"Be quiet," Walter ordered.

"I stole Mother's jewels," she said miserably to everyone. "I stole them to pay Pierre's debts. They said he would be beaten up if he didn't pay. Those jewels were going to be mine anyway, one day, they're in Mother's will . . . so I was only stealing from myself really . . . but then, he guessed . . ."

"Who guessed?" Zak demanded.

"Giles," she said. "He saw me coming out of Mother's room. I suppose I looked scared . . . maybe guilty. I had her jewels in a tote bag. I suppose it was afterward, when Mother came to say someone had stolen them, that he guessed. He made me give them to him. He said he'd have me arrested otherwise, and my parents wouldn't like that . . ."

"Stop him!" Zak yelled peremptorily as Giles made a dash for the lobby, and Raoul, a big fellow, intercepted him and twisted his arm up behind his back. Giles displayed pain.

Zak invited Walter to talk.

Walter, distressed, said that Giles had threatened to prove publicly that Donna had stolen the jewels if Walter wouldn't give him the horse. Even if Walter refused to press charges against his daughter, Giles had said, everyone would know she was a thief. Walter confessed that Giles had said, "What is one horse against your daughter's reputation?" Walter thought he'd had no choice.

Donna wept. Mavis wept. Half the audience wept.

Filmer was rigid. Also Mercer, Bambi and Sheridan; all unmoving in their seats.

"It wasn't sensible to love your daughter so much," Raoul said. "She stole the jewels. You shouldn't cover up for her. Look where it got you. Into the hands of a blackmailer, and losing the horse you love. And did you think it would stop there, with just one horse? You've got two more in my care, don't forget."

"Stop it," Mavis said, defending Walter now. "He's a wonderful man to give up his dearest possession to save his daughter."

"He's a fool," Raoul said.

During this bit, Zak came to the lobby as if to receive a message and went back into the center of the dining car opening an envelope and reading the contents.

He said the letter was from Ben, who had begged for money, did they remember? They remembered.

Ben, Zak said, had run away off the train because he was frightened, but he had left this letter to be opened after he'd gone. Zak read the letter portentously aloud.

"I know who killed Ricky. I know who threw him off the train. Ricky told me he knew who killed that lady, Angelica someone. Ricky saw the murderer with a lot of plastic rolled into a ball. He didn't know he was a murderer then, like. This man came up the train into the part where the grooms are and he was in the join part between two sleeping cars and he pushed the plastic out through one of the gaps, until it fell off the train, and then he saw Ricky looking at him. Ricky didn't think much of it until we were told about Angelica someone, and the plastic with her blood on it, and then he was afraid, and told me. And then he was thrown off the train. I knew who must have did it, but I wasn't saying. I didn't want to end up dead beside the railway tracks. But now I'm safe out of here I'll tell you, and it's that good-looking one they was calling Giles in Toronto station. I saw him there too, same as Ricky. It was him.' "

Zak stopped reading and Giles, struggling in Raoul's

grip, shouted that it was rubbish. Lies. All made up.

Raoul showed signs of breaking Giles's arm on account of him having killed Angelica, who was his wife, even if they had separated.

How could a groom like Ben make up anything like this? Zak said, waving the note. He said it was time someone searched Giles's room on the train for jewels, and for anything else incriminating.

"You've no right. You've no search warrant. And this man is breaking my arm."

"You murdered his wife, what do you expect?" Zak said, "and I don't need a search warrant. I'm chief of the railway detectives, don't forget. On trains, I investigate and search where I like." He marched off past me and went swaying down the corridor, pausing down at the end of the kitchen wall where he'd left a sports bag full of props, and soon came marching back. The other actors, meanwhile, had been emoting in character over the disclosure of Giles as murderer as well as blackmailer. Zak took the sports bag, it seemed to me by accident, to the table across from the Lorrimores. The people sitting at the table cleared the glasses and empty plates into a stack and Zak, dumping the bag on the pink cloth, unfastened a few zips.

To no one's surprise, he produced the jewels. Mavis was reunited with them, with joy slightly dampened by knowing who had stolen them. Reproachful looks, and so on.

Zak then discovered a folder of papers.

"A-hah!" he said.

Giles struggled, to no avail.

Zak said, "Here we have the motive for Angelica's murder. Here's a letter to Giles from Steven, Angelica's lover and business partner, complaining accusingly that he has been checking up, and Giles, in his capacity of blood-stock agent, has not bought the horses that he says he has, that Angelica and Steven have given him the money for. Steven is saying that unless Giles comes up with a very good explanation he is going to the police."

"Lies," Giles shouted.

"It's all here." Zak waved the letter, which everyone later inspected, along with Ben's note. They were accurately written: Zak's props were thorough. "Giles embezzled Angelica and Steve's money," he said, "and when they threatened him with disgrace, he killed them. Then he killed the groom who knew too much. Then he blackmailed Walter Bricknell, who was too fond of his daughter. This man Giles is beneath contempt. I will get the conductor of the train to arrange for him to be arrested and taken away in Revelstoke, where we stop in two hours."

He walked toward the lobby again.

Giles, finally breaking free of Raoul, snatched a gun that Zak was wearing in a holster on his hip and waved it about. Zak warned, "Put it down. This gun is loaded."

Giles shouted at Donna, "It's all your fault, you shouldn't have confessed. You spoiled it all. And I'll spoil you."

He pointed the gun at Donna. Pierre leaped in front of her to save her. Giles shot Pierre, who had, it transpired, chosen a romantic shoulder for the affected part. He clapped a hand on his snow-white shirt, which suddenly blossomed bright red. He fell artistically.

The audience truly gasped. Donna knelt frantically beside Pierre, having a grand dramatic time. Giles tried to escape and was subdued, none too gently, by Zak and Raoul. George Burley appeared on the scene, chuckling nonstop, waving a pair of stage handcuffs. As Zak later said, it was a riot.

17

Emil said there was enough champagne for everyone to have half a glass more, so he and I went around pouring while Oliver and Cathy cleared the hors d'oeuvre plates, straightened the cloths and began setting the places for the banquet.

I glanced very briefly at Filmer. He looked exceedingly pale, with sweat on his forehead. One hand, lying on the tablecloth, was tightly clenched. Beside him, the Redi-Hots were enthusing over Zak, who was standing beside their table agreeing that Pierre was a redeemable character who would make good. Zak gave me a smile and stepped to one side to let me fill the Redi-Hots' glasses.

Filmer said, in a harsh croaking voice, "Where did you get that story?"

As if accepting a compliment Zak answered, "Made it up."

"You must have got it from somewhere." He was positive, and angry. The Redi-Hots looked at him in surprise.

"I always make them up," Zak said lightly. "Why . . . didn't you enjoy it?"

"Champagne, sir?" I said to Filmer. I'd grown very bold, I thought.

Filmer didn't hear. Mrs. Redi-Hot passed me his glass,

which I replenished. She passed it back. He didn't notice.

"I thought it a great story," she said. "What a wicked revolting murderer. And he was so nice all along."

I stepped round Zak with a glimmer of eye contact in which I gave him my devout thanks for his discretion, and he accepted them with amusement.

At the next table Rose Young was protesting to Cumber that it had to have been a coincidence about committing suicide after getting rid of your best horse. Anyway, Ezra had sold his horse, she said, not given it away because he was being blackmailed.

"How do we know he wasn't?" Cumber demanded.

The Unwins were listening open-mouthed. I filled all their glasses quietly, unnoticed in their general preoccupation.

"Who now has Ezra's horses, that's what I want to know," Cumber said truculently. "And it'll be easy enough to find out." He spoke loudly: loudly enough, I thought, for Filmer to hear him, if he were listening.

Emil had beaten me to it with the Lorrimores, but they made a remarkable picture. Mercer's forearms rested on the table as he sat with his head bowed. Bambi, a glitter of tears in the frosty eyes, stretched out a hand, closed it over one of Mercer's fists and stroked his knuckles with comforting affection. Xanthe was saying anxiously, "What's the matter with everybody?" and Sheridan looked blank. Not supercilious, not arrogant, not even alarmed: a wiped blank slate.

There were a good many people in the aisle, not only the service crew but also the actors, who, still in character, were finishing off the drama in the ways they felt happy with: Walter and Mavis, for instance, agreeing that Pierre had saved Donna's life and couldn't be all bad, and maybe he would marry Donna, if he stopped gambling.

Threading his way through all this came the sleeping car attendant on his way to do the bunks in the dome car. He nodded to me with a smile as he passed, and I nodded back: and I thought that my main problem would probably be that the play had been all too successful, and that the people most upset by it wouldn't stay sitting down for dinner.

I wandered back to the kitchen where Angus's octopus act was reaching new heights and hoped especially that Filmer's physical reactions wouldn't get him restlessly to his feet and force him to leave.

He didn't move. The rigidity in his body very slowly relaxed. The impact of the play seemed to be lessening, and perhaps he really believed that Zak had made it all up.

I set the two tables nearest to the kitchen: automatically folded the napkins and arranged knives and forks. The sleeping car attendant came back eventually from the dome car, and I left my place settings unfinished and followed him.

"Are you sure?" he asked over his shoulder. "They seem pretty busy in the dining car."

"It's a good time," I assured him. "Fifteen minutes to dinner. How about if I start from this end, then I'll just stop and go back if I feel guilty."

"Right," he said. "Do you remember how to fold the chairs?"

He knocked on Filmer's door.

"The people are all along in the dining car, but knock first just in case," he said.

"OK."

We went into Filmer's room.

"Fold the chair while I'm here, so I can help if you need it."

"OK."

I folded, a shade slowly, Julius Apollo's armchair. The sleeping car attendant gave me a pat on the shoulder and left, saying he would start from the far end, as he usually did, and we might meet in the middle.

"And thanks a lot," he said.

I waved a hand. The thanks, did he but know it, were all mine. I left the door open and pulled Filmer's bed down into the night position, smoothing the bottom sheet, folding down a corner of top sheet, as I'd been shown.

I groped into Filmer's wardrobe space, gripped the black crocodile briefcase and rested it on the bed.

Zero-four-nine. One-five-one.

My fingers trembled with the compulsion for speed.

I aligned the little wheels, fumbling where I needed precision. Zero-four-nine . . . press the catch.

Click!

One-five-one. Press the catch. Click! The latches were open.

I laid the case flat on the bottom sheet, pushing the upper sheet back a little to accommodate it, and I lifted the lid. Heart thumping, breathing stopped.

The first thing inside was Filmer's passport. I looked at it briefly and then more closely, getting my suspended breath back in a jerky sort of silent laugh. The number of Filmer's passport was H049151. Hooray for the Brigadier.

I laid the passport on the bed, and looked through the other papers without removing them or changing their order. They were mainly a boring lot: all the bumf about the train trip, a few newspaper pages about the races, then a newspaper cutting from a Cambridge local paper about the building of a new library in one of the colleges, thanks to the generosity of Canadian philanthropist Mercer P. Lorrimore.

My God, I thought.

Beneath the clipping was a letter—a photocopy of a letter. I read it at breakneck speed, feeling danger creep up my spine, feeling my skin flood with heat.

It was short. Typewritten. There was no address at the top, no date, no salutation and no signature. It said:

As requested I examined the cadavers of the seven cats found pegged out, eviscerated and beheaded in the College gardens. I can find nothing significant except for wilful wickedness. These were not cult killings, in my opinion. The cats were killed over a period of perhaps three weeks, the last one yesterday. Each one, except the last, had been hidden under leaves, and had been attacked after death by insects and scavengers. They were all alive when they were pegged out, and during evisceration. Most, if not all, were alive at decapitation. I have disposed of the remains, as you asked.

I could see my hand trembling. I tipped up the next few sheets of paper, which were reports from stockbrokers, and then, at the very bottom, I came across a small yellow memo sticking to a foolscap-sized paper headed CONVEYANCE.

The memo said, "You will have to sign this, not Ivor Horfitz, but I think we can keep it quiet."

I looked a shade blankly at the legal words on the deed: "... all that parcel of land known as SF 90155 on the west side of ..." and heard the sleeping car attendant's voice coming nearer along the corridor.

"Tommy, where are you?"

I flicked the case shut and pushed it under the bed's top sheet. The passport was still in view. I shoved it under the pillow, walked out of the door hastily and closed it behind me.

"You've been ages in there," he said, but tolerantly. "Couldn't you undo the bed?"

"Managed it finally," I said, dry-mouthed.

"Right. Well, I didn't give you any chocolates." He handed me a box of big silver-wrapped bonbons. "Put one on each pillow."

"Yes," I said.

"Are you all right?" he asked curiously.

"Oh, yes. It was hot in the dining car."

"True." He went back toward his end of the car, unsuspicious. Heart still thumping, I returned to Filmer's room, retrieved his passport from under the pillow, replaced it in the briefcase, shut the locks, twirled the combination wheels, realized I hadn't noticed where they'd been set when I came in, hoped to hell that Filmer didn't set them deliberately, put the case back as I'd found it, straightened the bed and put the chocolate tidily where it belonged.

I went out of the room, closed the door and walked two paces toward the next door along.

"Hey, you," Filmer's voice said angrily from close behind me. "What were you doing in there?"

I turned. Looked innocent . . . felt stunned.

"Making your bed ready for the night, sir."

"Oh." He shrugged, accepting it.

I held the box of sweets toward him. "Would you like an extra chocolate, sir?"

"No I wouldn't," he said, and went abruptly into his bedroom.

I felt weak. I waited for him to come out exploding that I'd meddled with his belongings.

Nothing . . . nothing . . . happened.

I went into the room next door, folded the armchairs, lowered both beds, turned back the sheets, delivered the sweets. All automatic, all with a feeling of total unreality. I'd twice come too close to discovery. I had no great taste, I found, for the risks of a spy.

I was disturbed, in a way, by my pusillanimity. I supposed I'd never thought much about courage; had taken it for granted; physical courage, physical endurance, anyway. I'd been in hard places in the past, but these risks were different and more difficult, at least for me.

I did the third bedroom, by which time the sleeping car attendant, much faster, had almost finished the rest.

"Thanks a lot," he said cheerfully. "Appreciate it."

"Any time."

"Did you do your scene?" he asked.

I nodded. "It went fine."

Filmer came out of his room and called, "Hey, you."

The sleeping car attendant went toward him. "Yes, sir?"

Filmer spoke to him, his voice obliterated, as far as I was concerned, by rail noise, and went back into his room.

"He's not feeling well," the sleeping car attendant reported, going back toward his own roomette. "He asked for something to settle his stomach."

"Do you have things like that?"

"Antacids, sure. A few simple things."

I left him to his mission and went back to the dining car, where Emil greeted me with raised eyebrows and thrust into my hands a trayful of small plates, each bearing a square of pâté de foie gras with a thin slice of black truffle on top.

"We missed you. You're needed," Emil said. "The crackers for the pâté are on the tables."

"Right."

I went ahead with the delivery, going to the Redi-Hots' table first. I asked Mrs. Redi-Hot if Mr. Filmer would be coming back: should we put his pâté in his place?

She looked a little bewildered. "He didn't say if he was coming back. He went out in such a hurry he trampled on my feet."

"Leave the pâté," Mr. Redi-Hot said. "If he doesn't come back, I'll eat it."

With a smile I put some pâté in Filmer's place and went on to the Youngs' table, where Cumber had stopped talking about Ezra Gideon but looked dour and preoccupied. Rose received her pâté with a smile and made attempts not to let Cumber's moroseness spoil the occasion for the Unwins.

Cathy had taken pâté to the Lorrimores, who sat in glum silence except for Xanthe, who could be heard saying exasperatedly, "This is supposed to be a *party*, for God's sake."

For the rest of the passengers, that was true. The faces were bright, the smiles came easily, the euphoria of the whole journey bonded them in pleasure. It was the last night on the train and they were determined to make it a good one.

Nell was moving down the aisle handing out mementos: silver bracelets made of tiny gleaming railway carriages for the women, onyx paperweights set with miniature engines for the men. Charming gifts, received with delight. Xanthe clipped on her bracelet immediately and forgot to look sullen.

Emil and I collected the wrapping paper debris. "Miss Richmond might have waited until after dinner," Emil said.

We served and cleared the rest of the banquet: a salad of sliced yellow tomatoes and fresh basil, a scoop of champagne sorbet, rare roast rib of beef with julienned vegetables and finally apple snowballs appearing to float on raspberry puree. About six people, including Rose Young, asked how to make the apple snowballs, so I inquired of Angus.

He was looking languid and exhausted, but obliging. "Tell them it's sieved apple puree, sugar, whipped cream, whipped white of egg. Combine at the last minute. Very simple."

"Delicious," Rose said, when I relayed the information. "Do bring out the chef for us to congratulate him."

Emil brought out and introduced Angus to prolonged applause. Simone sulked determinedly in the kitchen. Rose Young said they should all thank the rest of the dining car crew who had worked so hard throughout. Everyone clapped: all most affecting.

Xanthe clapped, I noticed. I had great hopes for Xanthe.

I managed to step beside Nell's ear.

"Xanthe's longing to have a good time," I said. "Couldn't you rescue her?"

"What's the matter with the others?" she asked, frowning.

"Xanthe might tell you, if she knows."

Nell flashed me an acutely perceptive glance. "And you want me to tell you?"

"Yes, please, since you ask."

"One day you'll explain all this."

"One day soon."

I went back to the kitchen with the others to tackle the mountainous dishwashing and to eat anything left over, which wasn't much. Angus produced a bottle of scotch from a cupboard and drank from it deeply without troubling a glass. Apart from Simone, who had disappeared altogether, there was very good feeling in the kitchen. I wouldn't have missed it, I thought, for a fieldful of mushrooms.

When everything was scoured, polished and put away, we left Angus unbelievably beginning to make breads for breakfast. I stood in the lobby for a while, watching the dining car slowly clear as everyone drifted off to the dome car lounge for laughter and music. The Lorrimores had all gone, and so had Nell and the Unwins and the Youngs. Out of habit I began to collect, with Oliver, the used napkins and table-cloths, ready to put out clean ones for breakfast, and presently Nell came back and sat down wearily where I was working.

"For what it's worth," she said, "Xanthe doesn't know what has thrown her parents into such a tizzy. She says it can't have been something Mr. Filmer said in the lounge before cocktails because it sounded so silly."

"Did she tell you what he said?"

Nell nodded. "Xanthe said Mr. Filmer asked her father if he would let him have Voting Right, and her father said he wouldn't part with the horse for anything, and they were both smiling, Xanthe said. Then Mr. Filmer, still smiling, said, 'We'll have to have a little talk about cats.' And that was all. Mr. Filmer went into the dining car. Xanthe said she asked her father what Mr. Filmer meant, and he said, 'Don't bother me, darling.'" Nell shook her head in puzzlement. "So anyway, Xanthe is now having a good time in the dome car lounge and the rest of the family have gone off into their own car, and I'm damned tired, if you want to know."

"Go to bed, then."

"The actors are all along in the lounge having their photos taken," she said, dismissing my suggestion as frivolous. "They came up trumps tonight, didn't they?"

"Brilliant," I said.

"Someone was asking Zak who had tried to kidnap which horse at Toronto station."

"What did he say?" I asked, amused. It was the loosest of the loose ends.

"He said it had seemed a good idea at the time." She

laughed. "He said they'd had to change the script because the actor who was supposed to play the part of the kidnaper had broken his arm and couldn't appear. Everyone seemed to be satisfied. They're all very happy with the way it ended. People are kissing Donna and Mavis. Mavis is wearing the jewels!" She yawned and reflected. "Mr. Filmer didn't have any dinner, did he? Perhaps I'd better go and see if he's all right."

I dissuaded her. Antacids were taking care of it, I said. What one could give a man for a sick soul was another matter.

From his point of view, he had made his move a fraction too early, I thought. If he hadn't already made the threat, the play wouldn't have had such a cataclysmic effect either on him or on Mercer. Mercer might have been warned, as I'd intended, might have been made to think: but I couldn't have foreseen that it would happen the way it had, even though Filmer's smirk and Mercer's gloom had made me wonder. Just as well, perhaps, that I hadn't known about the cats when I invented the theft of the jewels. I might have been terribly tempted to hit even closer to home. Tortured horses, perhaps?

"What are you hatching now?" Nell demanded. "You've got that distant look."

"I haven't done a thing," I said.

"I'm not so sure." She stood up. She was wearing, in honor of the banquet, a boat-necked black lace blouse above the full black skirt, a pearl choker round her neck. Her fair hair was held back high in a comb, but not plaited, falling instead in informal curls. I thought with unnerving intensity that I didn't want to lose her, that for me it was no longer a game. I had known her for a week and a day. Reason said it wasn't long enough. Instinct said it was.

"Where are you staying in Vancouver?" I asked.

"At the Four Seasons Hotel, with all the passengers."

She gave me a small smile and went off toward the action. Oliver had finished clearing the cloths and was laying clean ones, to leave the place looking tidy, he said. I left him to finish and made my way up the train to talk to George Burley, passing Filmer's closed door on the way.

The sleeping car attendant was sitting in his roomette with the door open. I poked my head in and asked how the passenger was, who'd asked for the antacid.

"He went up the train a while ago, and came back. He didn't say anything, just walked past. He must be all right, I guess."

I nodded and went on, and came to George sitting at his table with endless forms.

"Come in," he invited, and I took my accustomed seat. "I showed that photo," he said. "Is that what you want to know about?"

"Yes."

"He's definitely on the train. Name of Johnson, according to the passenger list. He has a roomette right forward, and he stays in it most of the time. He eats in the forward dome car dining room, but only dinner, eh? He was in there just now when I went up to the engine, but he'd gone when I came back. A fast eater, they say. Never goes for breakfast or lunch. Never talks to anyone, eh?"

"I don't like it," I said.

George chuckled. "Wait till you hear the worst."

"What's the worst?"

"My assistant conductor—he's one of the sleeping car attendants up front—he says he's seen him before, eh?"

"Seen him where?"

George watched me for effect. "On the railways."

"On the—do you mean he's a *railwayman*?"

"He can't be sure. He says he looks like a baggage handler he once worked with on the Toronto to Montreal sector, long time ago. Fifteen years ago. Twenty. Says if it's him, he had a chip on his shoulder all the time, no one liked him. He could be violent. You didn't cross him. Might not be him, though. He's older. And he doesn't remember the name Johnson, though I suppose it's forgettable, it's common enough."

"Would a baggage handler," I said slowly, "know how to drain a fuel tank and uncouple the Lorrimores' car?"

George's eyes gleamed with pleasure. "The baggage handlers travel on the trains, eh? They're not fools. They take on small bits of freight at the stops and see the right stuff gets off. If you live around trains, you get to know how they work."

"Is there a baggage handler on this train?"

"You bet your life. He's not always in the baggage car, not when we're going along. He eats, eh? He's always there in the stations, unlocking the doors. This one's not the best we've got, mind. A bit old, a bit fat." He chuckled. "He said he'd never seen this man Johnson, but then he's always worked Vancouver to Banff, never Toronto to Montreal."

"Has the baggage handler or your assistant talked to Johnson?"

"My assistant conductor says the only person Johnson talks to is one of the owners who raps on Johnson's door when he goes along to see his horse. He went up there this evening not long ago, and they had some sort of row in the corridor outside my assistant's roomette."

"George! Did your assistant hear what it was about?"

"Important, is it?" George said, beaming.

"Could be, very."

"Well, he didn't." He shook his head regretfully. "He said he thought the owner told Johnson not to do something Johnson wanted to. They were shouting, he said, but he didn't really listen, eh? He wasn't interested. Anyway, the owner came back down here, he said, and he heard Johnson say 'I'll do what I frigging like,' very loudly, but he doesn't think the owner heard, as he'd gone by then."

"That's not much help," I said.

"It's easier to start a train going downhill than to stop it, eh?"

"Mm."

"It's the best I can do for you."

"Well," I said. "We do know he's on the train, and we know his name may or may not be Johnson, and we know he may or may not be a railwayman, and I know for certain he has a violent personality. It sounds as if he's still planning something and we don't know what. I suppose you are certain he can't get past the dragon-lady?"

"Nothing is certain."

"How about if you asked the baggage handler to sit in with her, with the horses."

He put his head to one side. "If you think she'd stand for it?"

"Tell her it's to keep the horses safe, which it is."

He chuckled. "Don't see why not." He looked at his watch. "Sicamous is coming up. I'll go up there outside, when we stop. Three or five minutes there. Then it'll be time to put the clocks forward an hour. Did your Miss Richmond remember to tell everyone?"

"Yes. They're all on Pacific time already, I think. Getting on for midnight."

We had stopped toward the end of dinner in a small place called Revelstoke for half an hour for all the cars to be refilled with water. At Kamloops, a far larger town, we would stop at two in the morning very briefly. Then it was North Bend at five-forty, then the last stretch to Vancouver, arriving at five past ten on Sunday morning, a week from the day we set off.

We slowed toward Sicamous while I was still with George.

"After here, though you won't see it," he said, "we follow the shoreline of Shuswap Lake. The train goes slowly."

"It hasn't exactly been whizzing along through the Rockies."

He nodded benignly. "We go at thirty, thirty-five miles an hour. Fast enough, eh? Uphill, downhill, round hairpin bends. There are more mountains ahead."

He swung down onto the ground when the train stopped

and crunched off forward to arrange things with the baggage handler.

It was snowing outside: big dry flakes settling on others that had already fallen, harbingers of deep winter. The trains almost always went through, George had said.

I thought I might as well see how the revelries were going, but it seemed that most people were feeling that the long evening, unlike the evening after the Winnipeg race, was dying. The lounge in the dome car was only half full. The observation deck was scarcely populated. The poker group, in shirtsleeves, were counting their money. The actors had vanished. Nell was walking toward me with Xanthe, whom she was seeing safely to bed in the upper bunk behind the felt curtains.

"Goodnight," Nell said softly.

"Sleep well," I replied.

"Goodnight," Xanthe said.

I smiled. "Goodnight."

I watched them go along the corridor beside the bar. Nell turned round, hesitated and waved. Xanthe turned also, and waved. I waved back.

Gentle was the word, I thought. Go gentle into this good night. No, no! It should be 'Do not go gentle into that good night.' Odd how poets' words stuck in one's head. Dylan Thomas, wasn't it? *Do not go gentle into that good night* . . . because that good night was death.

———

The train was slowly going to sleep.

There would be precious little peace, I thought, in the minds of the Lorrimores, father, mother and son. Little peace also in Filmer, who would know now from Johnson that the departure of Lenny Higgs had robbed him of the lever to be used against Daffodil; who would have doubts at the very least about Mercer's future reactions; who would know that Cumber Young would find out soon who had taken Ezra Gideon's horses; who would realize he was riding a flood tide of contempt. I wished him more than an upset stomach. I wished him remorse, which was the last thing he would feel.

I wandered back through the train past George's office, which was empty, and stretched out in my own room on the bed, still dressed, with the door open and the light on, meaning just to rest but stay awake: and not surprisingly I went straight to sleep.

I awoke to the sound of someone calling "George . . . George . . ." Woke with a start and looked at my watch. I hadn't slept long, not more than ten minutes, but in that time the train had stopped.

That message got me off the bed in a hurry. The train should have been moving; there was no stop scheduled for almost an hour. I went out into the passage and found an elderly man in a VIA gray suit like George's peering into the office. The elderly man looked at my uniform and said urgently, "Where's George?"

"I don't know," I said. "What's the matter?"

"We've got a hot box." He was deeply worried. "George must radio to the dispatcher to stop the Canadian."

Not again, I thought wildly. I went into George's office, following the VIA Rail man, who said he was the assistant conductor, George's deputy.

"Can't you use the radio?" I said.

"The conductor does it."

The assistant conductor was foremost a sleeping car attendant, I supposed. I thought I might see if I could raise someone myself, as George would have already tuned in the frequency, but when I pressed the transmit switch, nothing happened at all, not even a click, and then I could see why it wouldn't work—the radio was soaking wet.

There was an empty coffee cup beside it.

With intense alarm, I said to George's assistant, "What's a hot box?"

"A hot axle, of course," he said. "A journal box that holds the axle. It's under the horse car, and it's glowing dark

280

red. We can't go on until it cools down and we put more oil in."

"How long does that take?"

"Too long. They're putting snow on it." He began to understand about the radio. "It's wet . . ."

"It won't work," I said. Nor would the cellular telephone, not out in the mountains. "How do we stop the Canadian? There must be ways, from before radio."

"Yes, but—" He looked strained, the full enormity of the situation sinking in. "You'll have to go back along the track and plant fusees."

"Fusees?"

"Flares, of course. You're younger than me . . . you'll have to go . . . you'll be faster."

He opened a cupboard in George's office and pulled out three objects, each about a foot in length, with a sharp metal spike at one end, the rest being tubular with granulations on the tip. They looked like oversized matches, which was roughly what they were.

"You strike them on any rough or hard surface," he said. "Like a rock, or the rails. They burn bright red . . . they burn for twenty minutes. You stick the spike . . . throw it . . . into the wooden ties, in the middle of the track. The driver of the Canadian will stop at once when he sees it." His mind was going faster almost than his tongue. "You'll have to go half a mile, it'll take the Canadian that much to stop. Hurry, now, half a mile at least. And if the engineers are not in the cab . . ."

"What do you mean," I asked aghast, "if they're not in the cab?"

"They aren't always there. One of them regularly flushes out the boiler . . . the other could be in the bathroom . . . If they aren't there, if they haven't seen the flares and the train isn't stopping, you must light another fusee and throw it through the window into the cab. Then when they come back, they'll stop."

I stared at him. "That's impossible."

"They'll be there, they'll see the flares. Go now. Hurry. But that's what you do if you have to. Throw one through the window." He suddenly grabbed a fourth flare from the cupboard. "You'd better take another one, just in case."

"In case of what?" What else could there be?

"In case of bears," he said.

18

With a feeling of complete unreality I set off past the end of the train and along the single railway track in the direction of Toronto.

With one arm I clasped the four flares to my chest, in the other hand I carried George's bright-beamed flashlight, to show me the way.

Half a mile. How long was half a mile?

Hurry, George's assistant had said. Of all unnecessary instructions . . .

I half-walked, half-ran along the center of the track, trying to step on the flat wood of the ties, the sleepers, because the stones in between were rough and speed-inhibiting.

Bears . . . my God.

It was cold. It had stopped snowing. Some snow was sticking, but not enough to give me problems. I hadn't thought to put on a coat. It didn't matter, movement would keep me warm. Urgency and fierce anxiety would keep me warm.

I began to feel it wasn't totally impossible. After all, it must have been done often in the old days. Standard procedure still, one might say. The flares had been there, ready. All the same, it was fairly eerie running through the night with snow-dusted rocky tree-dotted hillsides climbing away on each side and the two rails shining silver into the distance in front.

I didn't see the danger in time, and it didn't growl; it wasn't a bear, it had two legs and it was human. He must have been hiding behind rocks or trees in the shadow thrown by my flashlight. I saw his movement in the very edge of my peripheral vision after I'd passed him. I sensed an upswept arm, a weapon, a blow coming.

There was barely a hundredth of a second for instinctive evasion. All I did as I ran was to lean forward a fraction so that the smash came across my shoulders, not on my head.

It felt as if I had cracked apart, but I hadn't. Feet, hands, muscles were all working. I staggered forward, dropped the flares and the flashlight, went down on one knee, knew another bang was traveling. Thought before action . . . I didn't have time. I turned toward him, not away. Turned inside and under the swinging arm, rising, butting upward with my head to find the aggressive chin, jerking my knee fiercely to contact between the braced legs, punching with clenched fist and the force of fury into the Adam's apple in his throat. One of the many useful things I'd learned on my travels was how to fight dirty, and never had I needed the knowledge more.

He grunted and wheezed with triple unexpected pain and dropped to his knees on the ground, and I wrenched the long piece of wood from his slackening hand and hit his own head with it, hoping I was doing it hard enough to knock him out, not hard enough to kill him. He fell quietly face down in the snow between the rails, and I rolled him over with my foot, and in the deflected beam of the flashlight, which lay unbroken a few paces away, saw the gaunt features of the man called Johnson.

He had got, I reckoned, a lot more than he was used to, and I felt intense satisfaction, which was no doubt reprehensible but couldn't be helped.

I bent down, lifted one of his wrists and hauled him unceremoniously over the rail and into the shadows away from the track. He was heavy. Also, the damage he'd done me, when it came to lugging unconscious persons about, was all too obvious. He might not have broken my back, which was what it had sounded like, but there were some badly squashed muscle fibers somewhere that weren't in first-class working order and were sending stabbing messages of protest.

I picked up the flashlight and looked for the flares, filled with an increased feeling of urgency of time running out. I found three of the flares, couldn't see the fourth, decided not to waste time, thought the bears would have to lump it.

Must be lightheaded, I thought. Got to get moving. I hadn't come anything like half a mile away from the train. I swung the beam back the way I'd come, but the train was out of sight round a corner that I hadn't noticed taking. For a desperate moment I couldn't remember which direction I'd come from: too utterly stupid if I ran the wrong way.

Think, for God's sake.

I swung the torch both ways along the track. Trees, rocks, silver parallel rails, all exactly similar.

Which way. *Think.*

I walked one way and it felt wrong. I turned and went back. That was right. It felt right. It was the wind on my face, I thought. I'd been running before into the wind.

The rails, the ties seemed to stretch to infinity. I was going uphill also, I thought. Another bend to the right lay ahead.

How long did half a mile take? I stole a glance at my watch, rolling my wrist round, which hurt somewhere high up, but with remote pain, not daunting. Couldn't believe the figures. Ten minutes only . . . or twelve . . . since I'd set off.

A mile in ten minutes was ordinarily easy . . . but not a mile of sleepers and stones.

Johnson had been waiting for me, I thought. Not for me personally, but for whoever would come running from the train with the flares.

Which meant he knew the radio wouldn't work.

I began actively to worry about George being missing.

Perhaps Johnson had fixed the hot box, to begin with.

Johnson had meant the trains to crash with himself safely away to the rear. Johnson was darned well not going to succeed.

With renewed purpose, with perhaps at last a feeling that all this was really happening and that I could indeed stop the Canadian, I pressed on along the track.

George's voice floated into my head, telling me about the row between Johnson and Filmer. Filmer told Johnson not to do something, Johnson said, "I'll do what I frigging like." Filmer could have told him not to try any more sabotage tricks on the train, realizing that trouble was anyway mounting up for him, trouble from which he might not be able to extricate himself if anything disastrous happened.

Johnson, once started, couldn't be stopped. "Easier to start a train running downhill than to stop it, eh?" Johnson with a chip on his shoulder from way back; the ex-railwayman, the violent frightener.

I had to have gone well over half a mile, I thought. Half a mile hadn't sounded far enough: the train itself was a quarter mile long. I stopped and looked at my watch. Worked it out. Found my tongue sticking to the roof of my mouth. The Canadian would come in a very few minutes. There was another curve just ahead. I mustn't leave it too late.

I ran faster, round the curve. There was another curve in a further hundred yards, but this would have to do. I put the flashlight down beside the track, rubbed the end of one of the flares sharply against one of the rails, and begged it, implored it, to ignite.

It lit with a huge red rush for which I was not prepared. Nearly dropped it. Rammed the spike into the wood of one of the ties.

The flare burned in a brilliant fiery scarlet that would have been visible for a mile, if only the track had been straight.

I picked up the flashlight and ran on round the next bend,

the red fire behind me washing all the snow with pink. Round that bend there was a much longer straight: I ran a good way, then stopped again and lit a second flare, jamming its point into the wood as before.

The Canadian had to be almost there. I'd lost count of the time. The Canadian would come with its bright headlights and see the flare and stop with plenty of margin in hand.

I saw pin-point lights in the distance. I hadn't known we were anywhere near habitation. Then I realized the lights were moving . . . coming . . . The Canadian seemed at first to be advancing slowly at first, and then faster and faster . . . and *it wasn't stopping* . . . There was no screeching of brakes urgently applied.

With a feeling of dreadful foreboding, I struck the third flare forcefully against the rail, almost broke it, felt it whoosh, stood waving it beside the track, beside the other flare stuck in the wood.

The Canadian came straight on. I couldn't bear it, couldn't *believe* it . . . It was almost impossible to throw the flare through the window . . . the window was too small, too high up, and moving at thirty-five miles an hour. I felt puny on the ground beside the huge roaring advance of the yellow bulk of the inexorable engine with its blinding lights and absence of brain.

It was there. Then or never. There were no faces looking out from the cab. I yelled in a frenzy, "Stop," and the sound blew away futilely on the bow wave of parting air.

I threw the flare. Threw it high, threw it too soon, missed the empty black window.

The flare flew forward of it and hit the outside of the windscreen, and fell onto the part of the engine sticking out in front; and then all sight of it was gone, the whole long heavy silver train rolling past me at a constant speed, making the ground tremble, extinguishing beneath it the second flare I'd planted in its path. It went on its mindless way, swept round the curve, and was gone.

I felt disintegrated and sick, failure flooding back in the

pain I'd disregarded. The trains would fold into each other, would concertina, would heap into killing chaos. In despair, I picked up the flashlight and began to jog the way the Canadian had gone. I would have to face what I hadn't been able to prevent . . . have to help even though I felt wretchedly guilty . . . couldn't bear the thought of the Canadian plowing into the Lorrimores' car. Someone would have warned the Lorrimores . . . oh, God, oh, God. Someone *must* have warned the Lorrimores . . . and everyone else. They would all be out of the train, away from the track . . . Nell . . . Zak . . . everybody.

I ran round the curve. Ahead, lying beside the track, still burning, was the flare I'd thrown. Fallen off the engine. The first flare that I'd planted a hundred yards ahead before the next curve had vanished altogether, swept away by the Canadian.

There was nothing. No noise, except the sighing wind. I wondered helplessly when I would hear the crash. I had no idea how far away the race train was; how far I'd run.

Growing cold and with leaden feet, I plodded past the fallen flare and along and round the next bend, and round the long curve following. I hadn't heard the screech of metal tearing into metal, though it reverberated in my head. They must have warned the Lorrimores, they *must*. I shivered among the freezing mountains from far more than frost.

There were two red lights on the rails far ahead. Not bright and burning like the flares, but small and insignificant, like reflectors. I wondered numbly what they were, and it wasn't until I'd gone about five more paces that I realized that they weren't reflectors, they were *lights*. Stationary lights. And I began running faster again, hardly daring to hope, but then seeing that they were indeed the rear lights of a train . . . a train . . . it could be only one train. There had been no night-tearing crash. The Canadian had stopped. I felt swamped with relief, near to tears, breathless. It had stopped . . . there was no collision . . . no tragedy . . . it had *stopped*.

I ran toward the lights, seeing the bulk of the train now in the flashlight's beam, unreasonably afraid that the engineers would set off again and accelerate away. I ran until I was panting, until I could touch the train. I ran alongside it, sprinting now, urgent to tell them not to go on.

There were several people on the ground up by the engine. They could see someone running toward them with a flashlight, and when I was fairly near to them, one of them shouted out authoritatively, "Get back on the train, there's no need for people to be out here."

I slowed to a walk, very out of breath. "I . . . er . . ." I called, "I came from the train in front." I gestured along the rails ahead, which were vacant as far as one could see in the headlights of the Canadian.

"What train?" one of them said, as I finally reached them.

"The race train." I tried to breathe. Air came in gasps. "Transcontinental . . . Mystery . . . Race Train."

There was a silence. One of them said, "It's supposed to be thirty-five minutes ahead of us."

"It had . . ." I said, dragging in oxygen, "a hot box."

It meant a great deal to them. It explained everything.

"Oh." They took note of my uniform. "It was you who lit the fusees?"

"Yes."

"How far ahead is the other train?"

"I don't know. Can't remember . . . how far I ran."

They consulted. One, from his uniform, was the conductor. Two, from their lack of it, were the engineers. There was another man there; perhaps the conductor's assistant. They decided—the conductor and the train driver himself—to go forward slowly. They said I'd better come with them in the cab.

Gratefully, lungs settling, I climbed up and stood watching as the engineer released the brakes, put on power and set the train going at no more than walking pace, headlights bright on the empty track ahead.

"Did you *throw* one of the fusees?" the engineer asked me.

"I didn't think you were going to stop." "It sounded prosaic, unemotional.

"We weren't in the cab," he said. "The one you threw hit the windscreen and I could see the glare all the way down inside the engine where I was checking a valve. Just as well you threw it. I came racing up here just in time to see the one on the track before we ran over it. Bit of luck, you know."

"Yes." Bit of luck. Deliverance from a lifetime's regret.

"Why didn't the conductor radio?" the conductor said crossly.

"It's out of order."

He tut-tutted a bit. We rolled forward slowly. There was a bend ahead to the right.

"I think we're near now," I said. "Not far."

"Right." The pace slowed further. The engineer inched carefully round the bend and it was as well he did, because when he braked at that point to halt, we finished with twenty yards between the front of the Canadian's yellow engine and the shining brass railing along the back platform of the Lorrimores' car.

"Well," the engineer said phlegmatically, "I wouldn't have wanted to come round the corner unawares to see *that*."

It wasn't until then that I remembered that Johnson was somewhere out on the track. I certainly hadn't spotted him lying unconscious or dead on the ground on the return journey, nor obviously had the Canadian's crew. I wondered briefly where he'd got to, but at that moment I didn't care. Everyone climbed down from the Canadian's cab, and the crew walked forward to join their opposite numbers ahead.

I went with them. The two groups greeted each other without fuss. The Race Train lot seemed to take it for granted that the Canadian would stop in time. They didn't discuss flares, but hot boxes.

The journal box that held the near side end of the rearmost of the six axles of the horse car had overheated, and it had overheated because, they surmised, the oil inside had somehow leaked away. That's what was usually wrong, when this happened. They hadn't yet opened it. It no longer glowed red, but was too hot to touch. They were applying fresh snow all the time. Another ten minutes, perhaps.

"Where's George Burley?" I asked.

The Race Train baggage handler said no one could find him, but two sleeping car attendants were still searching for him. He told the others that it was a good thing he'd happened to be traveling in the horse car. He had smelled the hot axle, he said. He'd smelled that smell once before. Terrible smell, he said. He'd gone straight forward to tell the engineer to stop at once. "Otherwise the axle would have broken and we could have had a derailment."

The others nodded. They all knew.

"Did you warn any of the passengers?" I asked.

"What? No, no, no need to wake them up."

"But the Canadian might not have stopped . . ."

"Of course it would, when it saw the flares."

Their faith amazed and frightened me. The conductor of the Canadian said that he would radio ahead to Kamloops and both trains would stop there again, where there were multiple tracks, not just the one. Kamloops, he thought, would be getting worried soon that the Race Train hadn't arrived, and he went off to inform them.

I walked back behind the horse car and boarded the race train, and almost immediately met George's assistant, who was walking forward.

"Where's George?" I said urgently.

He was worried. "I can't find him."

"There's one place he might be." And please let him be there, I thought. Please don't let him be lying miles back in some dreadful condition beside the track.

"Where?" he said.

"In one of the bedrooms. Look up the list. In Johnson's bedroom."

"Who?"

"Johnson."

Another sleeping car attendant happened to arrive at that point.

"I still can't find him," he said.

"Do you know where Johnson's room is?" I asked anxiously.

"Yes, nearly next to mine. Roomette, it is."

"Then let's look there."

"You can't go into a passenger's room in the middle of the night," he protested.

"If Johnson's there, we'll apologize."

"I can't think why you think George might be there," he grumbled, but he led the way back and pointed to a door. "That's his."

I opened it. George was lying on the bed, squirming in ropes, fighting against a gag. Very much alive.

Relieved beyond measure, I pulled off the gag, which was a wide band of adhesive plaster, firmly stuck on.

"Damn it, that hurt, eh?" George said. "What took you so long?"

———

George sat in his office, grimly drinking hot tea and refusing to lie down. He was concussed, one could see from his eyes, but he would not admit that the blow to his head that had knocked him out had had any effect. As soon as he was free of the ropes and had begun to understand about the hot box, he had insisted that he and the conductor from the Canadian have a talk together in the forward dome car of the Race Train, a meeting attended by various other crew members and myself.

The dispatcher in Kamloops, the Canadian's conductor reported, had said that as soon as the Race Train could set off again, it should proceed to Kamloops. The Canadian would follow ten minutes later. They would also alert a following freight train. The Race Train would remain at Kamloops for an hour. The Canadian would leave Kamloops first so that it fell as little behind its timetable as possible. After all the journal boxes of the Race Train had been checked for heat, it would go on its way to Vancouver. There wouldn't be any inquiry at Kamloops as it would be past three in the morning—Sunday morning—by then. The inquiry would take place at Vancouver.

Everyone nodded. George looked white, as if he wished he hadn't moved his head.

The Race Train's engineer came to say that the box had been finally opened, it had been dry and the oily waste had burned away, but all was now well, it was cool and filled again, it was not dripping out underneath, and the train could go on.

They wasted no time. The Canadian's crew left and the Race Train was soon on the move again as if nothing had happened. I went with George to his office and then fetched him the tea, and he groggily demanded I tell him from start to finish what was going on.

"You tell me first how you came to be knocked out," I said.

"I can't remember. I was walking up to see the engineers." He looked puzzled. "First thing I knew, I was lying there trussed up. I was there for ages. Couldn't understand it." He hadn't a chuckle left in him. "I was in Johnson's roomette, they said. Johnson did it, I suppose. Jumped me."

"Yes."

"Where is he now?"

"Heaven knows." I told George about Johnson's attacking me and how I'd left him, and how I hadn't seen him anywhere on the way back.

"Two possibilities," George said. "Three, I suppose. Either he buggered off somewhere or he's getting a ride on the Canadian right now."

I stared. Hadn't thought of that. "What's the third?" I asked.

A tired gleam crept into George's disoriented eyes "The mountain where we stopped," he said. "That was Squilax Mountain. Squilax is an Indian word for black bear."

I swallowed. "I didn't see any bears."

"Just as well."

I didn't somehow think Johnson had been eaten by a bear. I couldn't believe in it. I thought I must have been crazy, but I hadn't believed in bears all the time I'd been out there on black bear mountain.

"Know something?" George said. "The new rolling stock can't easily get hot boxes, the axles run in ball-bearings, eh, not oily waste. Only old cars like the horse car will always be vulnerable. Know what? You bet your life Johnson took most of the waste out of that box when we stopped in Revelstoke."

"Why do you say oily waste?" I asked.

"Rags. Rags in the oil. Makes a better cushion for the axle than plain oil. I've known one sabotaged before, mind. Only that time they didn't just take the rags out, they put iron filings in, eh? Derailed the train. Another railwayman with a grudge, that was. But hot boxes do happen by accident. They've got heat sensors with alarm systems beside the track in some places, because of that. How did that Johnson ever think he'd get away with it?"

"He doesn't know we have a photo of him."

George began to laugh and thought better of it. "You kill me, Tommy. But what was my assistant thinking of, sending you off with the fusees? It was his job, eh? He should have gone."

"He said I'd go faster."

"Well, yes, I suppose he was right. But you weren't really crew."

"He'd forgotten," I said. "But I thought he might have warned the Lorrimores and everyone else to get them out of danger."

George considered it. "I'm not going to say he should. I'm not going to say he shouldn't."

294

"Railwaymen stick together?"

"He's coming up to his pension. And no one was as much as jolted off their beds, eh?"

"Lucky."

"Trains always stop for flares," he said comfortably.

I left it. I supposed one couldn't lose a man his pension for not doing something that had proved unnecessary.

We ran presently into Kamloops where the axles were all checked, the radio was replaced, and everything else went according to plan. Once we were moving again George finally agreed to lie down in his clothes and try to sleep; and two doors along from him I tried the same.

Things always start hurting when one has time to think about them. The dull ache where Johnson's piece of wood had landed on the back of my left shoulder was intermittently sharply sore: all right when I was standing up, not so good lying down. A bore. It would be stiffer still, I thought, in the morning. A pest for serving breakfast.

I smiled to myself finally. In spite of Johnson's and Filmer's best efforts, the Great Transcontinental Mystery Race Train might yet limp without disaster to Vancouver.

Complacency, I should have remembered, was never a good idea.

19

It was discomfort as much as anything that had me on my feet again soon after six. Emil wouldn't have minded if I'd been late, as few of the passengers were early breakfasters, but I thought I'd do better in the dining car. I stripped off the waistcoat and shirt for a wash and a shave, and inspected in the mirror as best I could the fairly horrifying bruise already coloring a fair-sized area across my back. Better than on my head, I thought resignedly. Look on the bright side.

I put on a clean shirt and the spare clean waistcoat and decided that this was one VIA Rail operative who was not going to polish his shoes that morning, despite the wear and tear on them from the night's excursions. I brushed my hair instead. Tommy looked tidy enough, I thought, for his last appearance.

It wasn't yet light. I went forward through the sleeping train to the kitchen where Angus was not only awake but singing Scottish ballads at the top of his voice while filling the air with the fragrant yeasty smells of his baking. The dough, it seemed, had risen satisfactorily during the night.

Emil, Oliver, Cathy and I laid the tables and set out fresh flowers in the bud vases, and in time, with blue skies appearing outside, poured coffee and ferried sausages and bacon. The train stopped for a quarter of an hour in a place called North Bend, our last stop before Vancouver, and ran on down what the passengers were knowledgeably calling Fraser Canyon. Hell's Gate, they said with relish, lay ahead.

The track seemed to me to be clinging to the side of a cliff. Looking out of the window by the kitchen door, one could see right down to a torrent rushing between rocky walls, brownish tumbling water with foam-edged waves. The train, I was pleased to note, was negotiating this extraordinary feat of engineering at a suitably circumspect crawl. If it went too fast round these bends it would fly off into space.

I took a basket of bread down to the far end just as Mercer Lorrimore came through from the dome car. Although Cathy was down there also he turned from her to me and asked if I could possibly bring hot tea through to his own car.

"Certainly, sir. Any breads?"

He looked vaguely at the basket. "No. Just tea. For three of us." He nodded, turned and went away. Cathy raised her eyebrows and said with tolerance, "Chauvinist pig."

Emil shook his head a bit over the private order but made sure the tray I took looked right from his point of view, and I swayed through on the mission.

The lockable door in the Lorrimores' car was open. I knocked on it, however, and Mercer appeared in the far doorway to the saloon at the rear.

"Along here, please."

I went along there. Mercer, dressed in a suit and tie, gestured to me to put the tray on the coffee table. Bambi wasn't there. Sheridan sprawled in an armchair in jeans, trainers and a big white sweatshirt with the words MAKE WAVES on the front.

I found it difficult to look at Sheridan pleasantly. I could think of nothing but cats. He himself still wore the blank look of the evening before, as if he had opted out of thinking.

"We'll pour," Mercer said. "Come back in half an hour for the tray."

"Yes, sir."

I left them and returned to the dining car. The chill within Bambi, I thought, was because of the cats.

Nell and Xanthe had arrived during my absence.

"My goodness, you look grim," Nell exclaimed, then, remembering, said more formally, "Er, what's for breakfast?"

I got rid of the grimness and handed her the printed menu. Xanthe said she would have everything that was going.

"Has George told you that we're running late?" I asked Nell.

"No. His door was shut. Are we? How much?"

"About an hour and a half." I forestalled her question. "We had to stop in the night at Kamloops to get George's radio fixed, and then we had to wait there for the Canadian to go ahead of us."

"I'd better tell everyone, then. What time do we get to Vancouver?"

"About eleven-thirty, I think."

"Right. Thanks."

I almost said, "Be my guest," but not quite. Tommy wouldn't. Nell's eyes were smiling, all the same. Cathy chose that exact moment to go past me with a tray of breakfasts: or not exactly past, but rather against me where it seemed to hurt most.

"Sorry," she said contritely, going on her way.

"It's OK."

It was difficult always to pass in the swaying aisle without touching. Couldn't be helped.

Filmer came into the dining room and sat at the table nearest to the kitchen, normally the least favorite with the passengers. He looked as if he'd spent a bad night. "Here, you," he said abruptly at my approach, having apparently abandoned the mister-nice-guy image.

"Yes, sir?" I said.

"Coffee," he said.

"Yes, sir."

"Now."

"Yes, sir."

I gave Xanthe's order to Simone, who was stiffly laying a baking sheet of sausages in the oven in silent protest at life in general, and I took the coffee pot, on a tray, to Filmer.

"Why did we stop in the night?" he demanded.

"I believe it was to fix the radio, sir."

"We stopped twice," he said accusingly. "Why?"

"I don't know, sir. I expect the conductor could tell you."

I wondered what he'd do if I said, "Your man Johnson nearly succeeded in wrecking the train with you in it." It struck me then that perhaps his inquiry was actually anxiety: that he wanted to be told that nothing dangerous had happened. He did seem marginally relieved by my answer and I resisted the temptation of wiping out all that relief by telling him that the radio had been sabotaged, because the people at the next table were listening also. Spreading general gloom and fright was not in my brief. Selective gloom, selective fright . . . sure.

Others, it seemed, had noticed the long stops in the night, but no one seriously complained. No one minded letting the Canadian go on in front. The general good humor and the party atmosphere prevailed and excused everything. The train ride might be coming to an end, but meanwhile there was the spectacular gorge outside to be exclaimed over, the city of Vancouver to be looked forward to, the final race to promise a sunburst of a conclusion. The Great Transcontinental Race Train, they were saying, had been just that: Great.

After half an hour or so I went back to the Lorrimores' car to fetch the tray of tea cups. I knocked on the door, but as there was no answer I went anyway along to the saloon.

Mercer was standing there looking bewildered.

Looking haggard. Stricken with shock.

"Sir?" I said.

His eyes focused on me vaguely.

"My son," he said.

"Sir?"

Sheridan wasn't in the saloon. Mercer was alone.

"Stop the train," he said. "We must go back."

Oh, *God*, I thought.

"He went out . . . onto the platform . . . to look at the river . . ." Mercer could hardly speak. "When I looked up . . . he wasn't there."

The door to the platform was closed. I went past Mercer, opened the door and went out. There was no one on the platform, as he'd said.

There was wind in plenty. The polished brass top of the railings ran round at waist height, with both of the exit gates still firmly bolted.

Over the right-hand side, from time to time, there were places that offered a straight unimpeded hundred-foot drop to the fearsome frothing rocky river below. Death beckoned there. A quick death.

I went into the saloon and closed the door.

Mercer was swaying with more than the movement of the train.

"Sit down, sir," I said, taking his arm. "I'll tell the conductor. He'll know what to do."

"We must go back." He sat down with buckling legs. "He went out . . . and when I looked . . ."

"Will you be all right while I go to the conductor?"

He nodded dully. "Yes. Hurry."

I hurried, myself feeling much of Mercer's bewildered shock, if not his complicated grief. Half an hour earlier, Sheridan hadn't looked like someone about to jump off a cliff, but then I supposed that I'd never seen anyone else at that point, so how would I know. Perhaps the blank look, I thought, had been a sign, if anyone could have read it.

I hurried everywhere except through the dining car, so as not to be alarming, and when I reached George's room I found the door still shut. I knocked. No reply. I knocked again harder and called his name with urgency. *"George!"*

There was a grunt from inside. I opened the door without more ado and found him still lying on the bed in his clothes, waking from a deep sleep.

I closed his door behind me and sat on the edge of his bed, and told him we'd lost a passenger.

"Into Fraser Canyon," he repeated. He shunted himself up into a sitting position and put both hands to his head, wincing. "When?"

"About ten minutes ago, I should think."

He stretched out a hand to the radio, looking out of the window to get his bearings. "It's no use going back, you know. Not if he went into the water from this height. The river's bitter cold, and you can see how fast it is, and there's a whirlpool."

"His father will go, though."

"Of course."

The dispatcher he got through to this time was in Vancouver. He explained that Mercer Lorrimores's son—that was right, *the* Mercer Lorrimore—his twenty-year-old son had fallen from the rear of the Race Train into Fraser Canyon somewhere between Hell's Gate and a mile or two south of Yale. Mercer Lorrimore wanted the train stopped so that he could go back to find his son. He, George Burley, wanted instructions from Montreal. The dispatcher, sounding glazed, told him to hang on.

There was no chance now, I thought, of reaching Vancouver without a disaster. Sheridan was a disaster of major proportions, and the press would be at Vancouver station for all the wrong reasons.

"I think I'd better go back to Mercer," I said.

George nodded gingerly. "Tell him I'll come to talk to him when I get instructions from Montreal, eh?" He rubbed a hand over his chin. "He'll have to put up with stubble."

I returned to the dining car and found Nell still sitting

beside Xanthe. I said into Nell's ear, "Bring Xanthe into the private car."

She looked inquiringly into my face and saw nothing comforting, but she got Xanthe to move without alarming her. I led the way through the dome car and through the join into the rear car, knocking again on the unlocked door.

Mercer came out of his and Bambi's bedroom farther up the corridor looking gray and hollow-eyed, a face of unmistakable calamity.

"Daddy!" Xanthe said, pushing past me. "What's the matter?"

He folded his arms round her and hugged her, and took her with him toward the saloon. Neither Nell nor I heard the words he murmured to her, but we both heard her say sharply, "No! He couldn't!"

"Couldn't what?" Nell said to me quietly.

"Sheridan went off the back platform into the canyon."

"Do you mean . . ." she was horrified, ". . . that he's *dead*?"

"I would think so."

"Oh, *shit*," Nell said.

My feelings exactly, I thought.

We went on into the saloon. Mercer said almost mechanically, "Why don't we stop? We have to go back." He no longer sounded, I thought, as if he expected or even hoped to find Sheridan alive.

"Sir, the conductor is radioing for instructions," I said.

He nodded. He was a reasonable man in most circumstances. He had only to look out of the window to know that going back wouldn't help. He knew that it was practically impossible for anyone to fall off the platform by accident. He certainly believed, from his demeanor, that Sheridan had jumped.

Mercer sat on the sofa, his arm round Xanthe beside him, her head on his shoulder. Xanthe wasn't crying. She looked serious, but calm. The tragedy for Xanthe hadn't happened

302

within that half hour, it had been happening all her life. Her brother had been lost to her even when alive.

Nell said, "Shall we go, Mr. Lorrimore?" meaning herself and me. "Can I do anything for Mrs. Lorrimore?"

"No, no," he said. "Stay." He swallowed. "You'll have to know what's decided . . . what to tell everyone . . ." He shook his head helplessly. "We must make some decisions."

George arrived at that point and sat down in an armchair near Mercer, leaning forward with his forearms on his knees and saying how sorry he was, how very sorry.

"We have to go back," Mercer said.

"Yes, sir, but not the whole train, sir. Montreal says the train must go on to Vancouver as scheduled."

Mercer began to protest. George interrupted him. "Sir, Montreal says that they are already alerting all the authorities along the canyon to look out for your son. They say they will arrange transport for you to return, you and your family, as soon as we reach Vancouver. You can see," he glanced out of the window, "that the area is unpopulated, eh?, but there are often people working by the river. There is a road running along quite near the canyon, as well as another railway line on the other side. There's a small town over there called . . . er . . ." he coughed, "Hope. It's at the south end of the canyon, eh?, where the river broadens out and runs more slowly. We're almost at that point now, as you'll see. If you go to Hope, Montreal says, you will be in the area if there is any news."

"How do I get there?" Mercer said. "Is there a train back?"

George said, "There is, yes, but only one a day. It's the Supercontinental. It leaves Vancouver at four in the afternoon, passes through Hope at seven."

"That's useless," Mercer said. "How far is it by road?"

"About a hundred and fifty kilometers."

He reflected. "I'll get a helicopter," he said.

There was absolutely no point in being rich, I thought, if one didn't know how to use it.

DICK FRANCIS

The logistics of the return were making Mercer feel better, one could see. George told him that the train we were on would speed up considerably once we were clear of the canyon, and that we'd be in Vancouver in two hours and a half. They discussed how to engage a helicopter; Mercer already had a car meeting him at the station. Nell said Merry and Company would arrange everything, as they had indeed already arranged the car. No problem, if she could reach her office by telephone. George shook his head. He would relay the message by radio through Montreal. He brought out a notepad to write down Merry and Company's number and the instruction "Arrange helicopter, Nell will phone from Vancouver."

"I'll phone from the train," she said.

George stood up. "I'll get moving then, Mr. Lorrimore. We'll do everything possible." He looked big, awkward and unshaven, but Mercer had taken strength from him and was grateful. "My sympathy," George said, "to Mrs. Lorrimore."

The tray of empty tea cups still lay where I'd left it on the coffee table. I picked it up and asked if there was anything I could bring them, but Mercer shook his head.

"I'll come and find you," Xanthe said, "if they need anything." She sounded competent and grown up, years older than at breakfast. Nell gave her a swift sweet glance of appreciation, and she, George and I made our way back into the dome car, George hurrying off to his radio and Nell sighing heavily over what to say to the other passengers.

"It'll spoil the end of their trip," she said.

"Try them."

"You're cynical."

"Pretty often."

She shook her head as if I were a lost cause and went into the dining room with the bad news, which was predictably greeted with shock but no grief.

"Poor Xanthe," Rose Young exclaimed, and Mrs. Unwin said, "Poor Bambi." The sympathy stage lasted ten seconds.

The deliciously round-eyed "isn't it dreadful" stage went on all morning.

Julius Apollo Filmer was no longer in the dining room and I wished he had been as I would have liked to have seen his reactions. Chance would seem to have robbed him of his lever against Mercer; or would he reckon that Mercer would still sacrifice one horse to preserve the reputation of the dead? Filmer could read it wrong, I thought.

There was a cocktail party scheduled for that evening in the Four Seasons Hotel for Vancouver's racing bigwigs to meet the owners: would it still be held? several anxiously asked.

"Certainly," Nell answered robustly. "The party and the race will go on."

No one, not even I, was cynical enough to say, "Sheridan would have wished it."

———————

I helped clear away the breakfast and wash the dishes and pack everything into boxes for sending back to the caterers in Toronto, and when we'd finished I found that Nell had collected gratuities from the passengers to give to the waiters, and Emil, Cathy and Oliver had split it four ways. Emil put a bundle of notes into my hand, and he and the others were smiling.

"I can't take it," I said.

Emil said, "We know you aren't a waiter, and we know you aren't an actor, but you have worked for it. It's yours."

"And we know you've worked all morning although it's obvious you've hurt your arm," Cathy said. "I made it worse. I'm real sorry."

"And it would all have been very much harder work without you," Oliver said. "So we thought we'd like to give you a present."

"And that's it," Cathy added, pointing to the notes.

They waited expectantly, wanting my thanks.

"I . . . er, I don't know." I kissed Cathy suddenly; hugged her. "All right. I'll buy something to remember us by. To remember the journey. Thank you all very much."

They laughed, pleased. "It's been fun," Cathy said, and Emil added ironically, "But not every week."

I shook Emil's hand, and Oliver's. Kissed Cathy again. Shook hands with Angus. Was offered Simone's cheek for a peck. I looked round at their faces, wanting to hold on to the memory.

"See you again," I said, and they said, "Yes," and we all knew it was unlikely. I went away along the swaying corridor, taking Tommy to extinction and, as often in the past, not looking back. Too many regrets in looking back.

In the sleeping cars, everyone was packing and holding impromptu parties in each other's rooms, walking in and out of the open doors. Filmer's door was shut.

Nell was in her roomette, with the door open, packing.

"What's wrong with your arm?" she said, folding one of the straight skirts.

"Is it so obvious?"

"Most obvious when Cathy bumped into you with her tray. The shock went right through you."

"Yes, well, it's not serious."

"I'll get you a doctor."

"Don't be silly."

"I suppose," she said, "Mercer won't run his horse now on Tuesday. Such a shame. That *damned* Sheridan."

The biblical description, I thought, was accurate.

"Xanthe," Nell said, putting the skirt into her suitcase, "says you were kind to her at Lake Louise. Did you really say something about the corruption of self-importance? She said she learned a lot."

"She grew up this morning," I said.

"Yes, didn't she?"

"If we go to Hawaii," I said, "you can wear a sarong and a hibiscus behind your ear."

She paused in the packing. "They wouldn't really go," she said judiciously, "with a clipboard."

George came out of his office and told her the cellular telephone was now working, if she wanted to make her calls, and I went into my roomette and changed out of uniform into Tommy 's outdoor clothes, and packed everything away. The train journey might be finished, I was thinking, but my real job wasn't. There was much to be done. Filmer might be sick, but it was sick sharks that attacked swimmers, and there could still be a dorsal fin unseen below the surface.

Nell came out of George's office and along to my door.

"No helicopter needed," she said. "They've found Sheridan already."

"That was quick."

"Apparently he fell onto a fish ladder."

"You're kidding me."

"No, actually." She stifled a laugh, as improper to the occasion. "George says the ladders are a sort of staircase hundreds of meters long that are built in the river because the salmon can't swim upstream anymore to spawn against the strength of the water. The water flows much faster than it used to because a huge rock fall constricted it some years ago."

"I'll believe it," I said.

"Some men were working on the lower ladder," she said, "and Sheridan was swept down in the water."

"Dead?" I asked.

"Very."

"You'd better tell Mercer."

She made a reluctant face. "You do it."

"I can't. George could."

George agreed to go and hurried off so as to be back at his post when we reached the station.

"Did you know," I said to Nell, "that Emil, Cathy and Oliver wanted to share their tips with me?"

"Yes, they asked me if I thought it would be all right. I do hope," she said with sudden anxiety, "that you accepted? They said you'd been great. They wanted to thank you. They were so pleased with themselves."

"Yes," I said, relieved to be able to. "I accepted. I told them I'd buy something to remind me of them and the trip. And I will."

She relaxed. "I should have warned you. But then, I guess . . . no need." She smiled. "What are you really?"

"Happy," I said.

"Yuk."

"I try hard, but it keeps breaking out. My boss threatens to fire me for it."

"Who's your boss?"

"Brigadier Valentine Catto."

She blinked. "I never know when you're telling the truth."

Catto, I thought. Cats. Sobering.

"I have just," I said slowly, "been struck by a blinding idea."

"Yes, you rather look like it."

Time, I thought. Not enough of it.

"Come back," Nell said. "I've lost you."

"You don't happen to have a world air timetable with you, do you?"

"There are several in the office. What do you want?"

"A flight from London to Vancouver tomorrow."

She raised her eyebrows, went into George's office, consulted on the telephone and came out again.

"Air Canada leaves Heathrow three P.M., arrives Vancouver four-twenty-five."

"Consider yourself kissed."

"Are you still a waiter, then, in the eyes of the passengers?"

There were passengers all the time in the corridor.

"Mm," I said thoughtfully, "I think so. For another two days. To the end."

"All right."

George returned and reported that all three of the Lorrimores had received the news of Sheridan calmly and would go to the hotel as planned and make arrangements from there.

"Poor people," Nell said. "What a mess."

I asked George what he would be doing. Going back to Toronto, of course, possibly by train, as soon as the various VIA inquiries were completed, which would be tomorrow. Couldn't he stay for the race, I asked, and go back on the Tuesday evening? He wasn't sure. I took him into his office and convinced him, and he was chuckling again as the train slowed to a crawl and inched into the terminus at Vancouver.

The wheels stopped. Seven days almost to the hour since they'd set off the passengers climbed down from the traveling hotel and stood in little groups outside, still smiling and still talking. Zak and the other actors moved among them, shaking farewell hands. The actors had commitments back in Toronto and weren't staying for the race.

Zak saw me through the window and bounced up again into the sleeping car to say goodbye.

"Don't lose touch, now," he said. "Any time you want a job writing mysteries, let me know."

"OK."

"Bye, guy," he said.

"Bye."

He jumped off the train again and trailed away beneath his mop of curls toward the station buildings, with Donna, Pierre, Raoul, Mavis, Walter and Giles following like meteorites after a comet.

I waited for Filmer to pass. He walked on his own, looking heavy and intent. He was wearing an overcoat and carrying the briefcase and not bothering to be charming. There was a firmness of purpose in his step that I didn't much like, and when Nell took a pace forward to ask him something he answered her with a brief turn of his head but no break in stride.

When he'd gone, I jumped down beside Nell, who was

carefully checking other passengers off against a list on the clipboard as they passed. It was a list, I discovered by looking over her shoulder, of the people catching the special bus to check into the Four Seasons Hotel. Against Filmer's name, as against all the others, I was relieved to see a tick.

"That's everyone," Nell said finally. She looked toward the rear of the train. "Except the Lorrimores, of course. I'd better go and help them."

I stepped back on board to collect my gear and through the window watched the little solemn party pass by outside: Mercer, head up, looking sad, Bambi expressionless, Xanthe caring, Nell concerned.

Some way after them I walked forward through the train. It was quiet and empty, the racegoers having flooded away, the surly cook gone from the center diner, the dayniter no longer alive with singing, the doors of the empty bedrooms standing open, the Chinese cook vanished with his grin. I climbed down again and went on forward, past the horse car, where Leslie Brown was leaning out of the window, still a dragon.

"Bye," I said.

She looked at me, as if puzzled for a second, and then recognized me: Calgary and Lenny Higgs were three days back.

"Oh, yes . . . goodbye."

The train was due to shunt out backward, to take the horses and the grooms to a siding, from where they would go by road to Exhibition Park. Ms. Brown was going with them, it seemed.

"Good luck at the races," I said.

"I never bet."

"Well, have a good time."

She looked as if that were an unthinkable suggestion. I waved to her, the stalwart custodian, and went on past the baggage car where I collected my suitcase from the handler, and past the engine where the engineer was a shadowy figure high up beyond his impossibly small window, and went on into the station.

The Lorrimores had been interrupted by people with notebooks, cameras and deadlines. Mercer was being civil. Nell extricated the family and ushered them to their car, and herself climbed into the long bus with the owners. I hung back until they'd all gone, then traveled in a taxi, booked in at the Hyatt and telephoned to England.

The Brigadier wasn't at home in Newmarket. I could try his club in London, a voice said, giving me the familiar number, and I got connected to the bar of the Hobbs Sandwich where the Brigadier, I was relieved to hear, was at that moment receiving his first-of-the-evening well-watered scotch.

"Tor!" he said. "Where are you?"

"Vancouver." I could hear the clink of the glasses and the murmurings in the background. I pictured the dark oak walls with the gentlemen in the pictures with side-whiskers, big pads and little caps, and it all seemed far back in time, not just in distance.

"Um," I said. "Can I phone you again when you're alone? This is going to take some time. I mean, soon, really."

"Urgent?"

"Fairly."

"Hold on. I'll go upstairs to my bedroom and get them to transfer the call. Don't go away."

I waited through a few clicks until his voice came quietly on the line again without sound effects.

"Right. What's happened?"

I talked for what seemed a very long time. He punctuated my pauses with grunts to let me know he was still listening, and at the end he said, "You don't ask much, do you? Just for miracles."

"There's an Air Canada flight from Heathrow at three tomorrow afternoon," I said, "and they'll have all day and all Tuesday to find the information, because when it's only eleven in the morning in Vancouver on Tuesday, it'll be seven in the evening in England. And they could send it by Fax."

"Always supposing," he said dryly, "that there's a Fax machine in the Jockey Club in Exhibition Park."

"I'll check," I said. "If there isn't, I'll get one."

"What does Bill Baudelaire think of all this?" he asked.

"I haven't talked to him yet. I had to get your reaction first."

"What's your phone number?" he asked. "I'll think it over and ring you back in ten minutes."

"Thought before action?"

"You can't fault it, if there's time."

He thought for twice ten minutes, until I was itchy. When the bell rang, I took a deep breath and answered.

"We'll attempt it," he said, "as long as Bill Baudelaire agrees, of course. If we can't find the information in the time available, we may have to abort."

"All right."

"Apart from that," he said, "well done."

"Good staff work," I said.

He laughed. "Flattery will get you no promotion."

20

I was looking forward to talking to Mrs. Baudelaire. I dialed her number and Bill himself answered.

"Hello," I said, surprised. "It's Tor Kelsey. How's your mother?"

There was a long, awful pause.

"She's ill," I said with anxiety.

"She . . . er . . . she died . . . early this morning."

"Oh, no." She couldn't have, I thought. It couldn't be true. "I talked to her yesterday," I said.

"We knew . . . she knew . . . it would only be weeks. But yesterday evening there was a crisis."

I was silent. I felt her loss as if she'd been Aunt Viv restored to me and snatched away. I'd wanted so very much to meet her.

"Tor?" Bill's voice said.

I swallowed. "Your mother . . . was great."

He would hear the smothered tears in my voice, I thought. He would think me crazy.

"If it's of any use to you," he said, "she felt like that about you, too. You made her last week a good one. She wanted to live to find out what happened. One of the last things she said was, 'I don't want to go before the end of the story. I want to see that invisible young man.' She was slipping away . . . all the time."

> *Do not go gentle into that good night*
> *Old age should burn and rave at close of day;*
> *Rage, rage against the dying of the light.*

"Tor?" Bill said.

"I'm so very sorry," I said with more control. "So sorry."

"Thank you."

"I don't suppose . . ." I said, and paused, feeling helpless.

"You suppose wrong," he replied instantly. "I've been waiting here for you to phone. We would both fail her if we didn't go straight on. I've had hours to think this out. The last thing she would want would be for us to give up. So I'll start things off by telling you we've had a telex from Filmer announcing that he is the sole owner of Laurentide Ice, but we are going to inform him that the Ontario Racing Commission are rescinding his license to own horses. We're also telling him he won't be admitted to the president's lunch at Exhibition Park."

"I'd . . . er . . . like to do it differently," I said.

"How do you mean?"

I sighed deeply and talked to him also for a long time. He listened as the Brigadier had, with intermittent throat noises, and at the end he said simply, "I do wish she'd been alive to hear all this."

"Yes, so do I."

"Well," he paused. "I'll go along with it. The real problem is time."

"Mm."

"You'd better talk to Mercer Lorrimore yourself."

"But . . ."

"No buts. You're there. I can't get there until tomorrow late afternoon, not with all you want me to do here. Talk to Mercer without delay, you don't want him coming back to Toronto."

I said with reluctance, "All right." But I had known I would have to.

"Good. Use all the authority you need. Val and I will back you."

"Thank you . . . very much."

"See you tomorrow," he said.

I put the receiver down slowly. Death could be colossally unfair, one knew that, but rage, rage . . . I felt anger for her as much as grief. Do not go gentle into that good night . . . I thought it probable, if I remembered right, that the last word she'd said to me had been "Good night." Good night, dear, dear Mrs. Baudelaire. Go gentle. Go sweetly into that good night.

I sat for a while without energy, feeling the lack of sleep, feeling the nagging pain, feeling the despondency her death had opened the door to: feeling unequal to the next two days, even though I'd set them up myself.

With an effort after an age, I got through to the Four Seasons Hotel and asked for Mercer, but found myself talking to Nell.

"All the calls are being rerouted to me," she said. "Bambi is lying down. Mercer and Xanthe are on their way to Hope in the helicopter, which was reordered for him, so that he can identify Sheridan's body, which is being taken there by road."

"It all sounds so clinical."

"The authorities want to make sure it's Sheridan before they make any arrangements."

"When will Mercer and Xanthe be back, do you know?"

"About six, they expected."

"Um, the Jockey Club asked me to fix up a brief meeting. Do you think Mercer would agree to that?"

"He's being terrifically helpful to everyone. Almost too calm."

I thought things over. "Can you get hold of him in Hope?"

She hesitated. "Yes, I suppose so. I have the address and

the phone number of where he was going, but I think it's a police station or a mortuary."

"Could you . . . could you tell him that on their return to the hotel a car will be waiting to take him straight on to a brief meeting with the Jockey Club? Tell him the Jockey Club send their sincere condolences and ask for just a little of his time."

"I guess I could," she said doubtfully. "What about Xanthe?"

"Mercer alone," I said positively.

"Is it important?" she asked, and I could imagine her frowning.

"I think it's important for Mercer."

"All right." She made up her mind. "Xanthe can take the phone calls for her mother, then, because I have to go to this cocktail party." A thought struck her. "Aren't some of the Jockey Club coming to the party?"

"Mercer won't want to go. They want a quiet talk with him alone."

"OK then, I'll try to arrange it."

"Very many thanks," I said fervently, "I'll call back to check."

I called back at five o'clock. The helicopter was in the air on its way back, Nell said, and Mercer had agreed to being picked up at the hotel.

"You're brilliant."

"Tell the Jockey Club not to keep him long. He'll be tired. And he's identified Sheridan."

"I could kiss you," I said. "The way to a man's heart is through his travel agent."

She laughed. "Always supposing that's where one wants to go."

She put her receiver down with a delicate click. I did not want to lose her, I thought.

The car I sent for Mercer picked him up successfully and brought him to the Hyatt, the chauffeur telling him, as requested, the room to go straight up to. He rang the doorbell of the suite I'd engaged more or less in his honor, and I opened the door to let him in.

He came in about two paces and then stopped and peered with displeasure at my face.

"What is this?" he demanded with growing anger, preparing to depart.

I closed the door behind him.

"I work for the Jockey Club," I said. "The British Jockey Club. I am seconded here with the Canadian Jockey Club for the duration of the race train Celebration of Canadian Racing."

"But you're . . . you're . . ."

"My name is Tor Kelsey," I said. "It was judged better that I didn't go openly on the train as a sort of security agent for the Jockey Club, so I went as a waiter."

He looked me over. Looked at the rich young owner's good suit that I'd put on for the occasion. Looked at the expensive room.

"My God," he said weakly. He took a few paces forward. "Why am I here?"

"I work for Brigadier Valentine Catto in England," I said, "and Bill Baudelaire over here. They are the heads of the Jockey Club Security Services."

He nodded. He knew them.

"As they cannot be here, they have both given me their authority to speak to you on their behalf."

"Yes, but . . . what about?"

"Would you sit down? Would you like a drink?"

He looked at me with a certain dry humor. "Do you have any identification?"

"Yes." I fetched my passport. He opened it. Looked at my name, at my likeness, and at my occupation: investigator.

He handed it back. "Yes, I'll have a drink," he said, "as you're so good at serving them. Cognac if possible."

I opened the cupboard that the hotel had supplied at my request with wine, vodka, scotch and brandy, and poured the amount I knew he'd like, even adding the heretical ice. He took the glass with a twist of a smile and sat in one of the armchairs.

"No one guessed about you," he said. "No one came anywhere near it." He took a sip reflectively. "Why were you on the train?"

"I was sent because of one of the passengers. Because of Julius Filmer."

The ease that had been growing in him fled abruptly. He put the glass down on the table beside him and stared at me.

"Mr. Lorrimore," I said, sitting down opposite him, "I am sorry about your son. Truly sorry. All of the Jockey Club send their sympathy. I think though that I should tell you straightaway that Brigadier Catto, Bill Baudelaire and myself all know about the . . . er . . . incident . . . of the cats."

He looked deeply shocked. "You can't know!"

"I imagine that Julius Filmer knows also."

He made a hopeless gesture with one hand. "However did he find out?"

"The Brigadier is working on that in England."

"And how did *you* find out?"

"Not from anyone you swore to silence."

"Not from the college?"

"No."

He covered his face briefly with one hand.

"Julius Filmer may still suggest you give him Voting Right in exchange for his keeping quiet," I said.

He lowered the hand to his throat and closed his eyes. "I've thought of that," he said. He opened his eyes again. "Did you see the last scene of the mystery?"

"Yes," I said.

"I haven't known what to do since then."

"It's you who has to decide," I said. "But . . . can I tell you a few things?"

He gave a vague gesture of assent, and I talked to him, also, for quite a long time. He listened with total concentration, mostly watching my face. People who were repudiating in their minds every word one said didn't look at one's face but at the floor, or at a table, at anything else. I knew, by the end, that he would do what I was asking, and I was grateful because it wouldn't be easy for him.

When I'd finished, he said thoughtfully, "That mystery was no coincidence, was it? The father blackmailed because of his child's crime, the groom murdered because he knew too much, the man who would kill himself if he couldn't keep his racehorses. Did you write it yourself?"

"All that part, yes. Not from the beginning."

He smiled faintly. "You showed me what I was doing . . . was prepared to do. But beyond that . . . you showed Sheridan."

"I wondered," I said.

"Did you? Why?"

"He looked different afterward. He had changed."

Mercer said, "How could you see that?"

"It's my job."

He looked startled. "There isn't such a job."

"Yes," I said, "there is."

"Explain," he said.

"I watch for things that aren't what they were, and try to understand, and find out why."

"All the time?"

I nodded. "Yes."

He drank some brandy thoughtfully. "What change did you see in Sheridan?"

I hesitated. "I just thought that things had shifted in his mind. Like seeing something from a different perspective. A sort of revelation. I didn't know if it would last."

"It might not have done."

"No."

"He said," Mercer said, " 'Sorry, Dad.' "

It was my turn to stare.

"He said it before he went out onto the platform." Mercer swallowed with difficulty and eventually went on. "He had been so quiet. I couldn't sleep. I went out to the saloon about dawn, and he was sitting there. I asked him what was the matter, and he said, 'I fucked things up, didn't I?' We all knew he had. It wasn't anything new. But it was the first time he'd said so. I tried . . . I tried to comfort him, to say we would stand by him, no matter what. He knew about Filmer's threat, you know. Filmer said in front of all of us that he knew about the cats." He looked unseeingly over his glass. "It wasn't the only time it had happened. Sheridan killed two cats like that in our garden when he was fourteen. We got therapy for him. . . . They said it was the upheaval of adolescence." He paused. "One psychiatrist said Sheridan was psychopathic, he couldn't help what he did. But he could, really, most of the time. He could help being discourteous, but he thought being rich gave him the right. I told him it didn't."

"Why did you send him to Cambridge?" I asked.

"My father was there, and established a scholarship. They gave it to Sheridan as thanks—as a gift. He couldn't concentrate long enough to get into college otherwise. But then the master of the college said they couldn't keep him, scholarship or not, and I understood. Of course they couldn't. We thought he would be all right there. We so hoped he would."

They'd spent a lot of hope on Sheridan, I thought.

"I don't know if he meant to jump this morning when he went out on the platform," Mercer said. "I don't know if it was just an impulse. He gave way to impulses very easily. Unreasonable impulses . . . almost insane, sometimes."

"It was seductive, out there," I said. "Easy to jump."

Mercer looked at me gratefully. "Did you feel it?"

"Sort of."

"Sheridan's revelation lasted until this morning," he said.

"Yes," I said. "I saw . . . when I brought your tea."

"The waiter . . ." He shook his head slowly, still surprised.

"I'd be grateful," I said, "if you don't tell anyone else about the waiter."

"Why not?"

"Because most of my work depends on anonymity. My bosses don't want people like Filmer to know I exist."

He nodded slowly with comprehension. "I won't tell."

He stood up and shook my hand. "What do they pay you?" he asked.

I smiled. "Enough."

"I wish Sheridan had been able to have a job. He couldn't stick at anything." He sighed. "I'll believe that what he did this morning was for us. 'Sorry, Dad . . .' "

Mercer looked me in the eyes and made a simple statement, without defensiveness, without apology.

"I loved my son," he said.

On Monday morning, I went to Vancouver station to back up George Burley in the rail company's dual inquiry into the hot box and the suicide.

I was written down as T. Titmuss, Acting Crew, which amused me and seemed to cover several interpretations. George was stalwart and forthright, with the ironic chuckles subdued to merely a gleam. He was a railwayman of some prestige, I was glad to see, who was treated with respect if not quite deference, and his were the views they listened to.

He gave the railway investigators a photograph of Johnson and said that while he hadn't actually seen him pour liquid into the radio, he could say that it was in this man's roomette that he had awakened bound and gagged, and he could say that it was this man who had attacked Titmuss, when he, Titmuss, went back to plant the flares.

"Was that so?" they asked me. Could I identify him positively?

"Positively," I said.

They moved on to Sheridan's death. A sad business, they said. Apart from making a record of the time of the occurrence and the various radio messages, there was little to be done. The family had made no complaint to or about the railway company. Any other conclusions would have to be reached at the official inquest.

"That wasn't too bad, eh?" George said afterward.

"Would you come in uniform to the races?" I asked.

"If that's what you want."

"Yes, please." I gave him a card with directions and instructions and a pass cajoled from Nell to get him in through the gates.

"See you tomorrow, eh?"

I nodded. "At eleven o'clock."

We went our different ways, and with some reluctance but definite purpose I sought out a doctor recommended by the hotel and presented myself for inspection.

The doctor was thin, growing old and inclined to make jokes over his half-moon glasses.

"Ah," he said, when I'd removed my shirt. "Does it hurt when you cough?"

"It hurts when I do practically anything, as a matter of fact."

"We'd better have a wee X-ray then, don't you think?"

I agreed to the X-ray and waited around for ages until he reappeared with a large sheet of celluloid, which he clipped in front of a light.

"Well, now," he said, "the good news is that we don't have any broken ribs or chipped vertebrae."

"Fine." I was relieved and perhaps a bit surprised.

"What we do have is a fractured shoulder blade."

I stared at him. "I didn't think that was possible."

"Anything's possible," he said. "See that," he pointed, "that's a real granddaddy of a break. Goes right across, goes right through. The bottom part of your left scapula," he announced cheerfully, "is to all intents and purposes detached from the top."

"Um," I said blankly. "What do we do about it?"

He looked at me over the half-moons. "Rivets," he said,

"might be extreme, don't you think? Heavy strapping, immobility for two weeks, that'll do the trick."

"What about," I said, "if we do nothing at all? Will it mend?"

"Probably. Bones are remarkable. Young bones especially. You could try a sling. You'd be more comfortable though, if you let me strap your arm firmly skin to skin to your side and chest, under your shirt."

I shook my head and said I wanted to go on a sort of honeymoon to Hawaii.

"People who go on honeymoons with broken bones," he said with a straight face, "must be ready to giggle."

I giggled there and then. I asked him for a written medical report and the X-ray, and paid him for them, and bore away my evidence.

Stopping at a pharmacy on my way back to the hotel I bought an elbow-supporting sling made of wide black ribbon, which I tried on for effect in the shop, and which made things a good deal better. I was wearing it when I opened my door in the evening, first to the Brigadier on his arrival from Heathrow, and then to Bill Baudelaire, from Toronto.

Bill Baudelaire looked round the sitting room and commented to the Brigadier about the lavishness of my expense account.

"Expense account, my foot!" the Brigadier said, drinking my scotch. "He's paying for it himself."

Bill Baudelaire looked shocked. "You can't let him," he said.

"Didn't he tell you?" The Brigadier laughed. "He's as rich as Croesus."

"No, he didn't tell me."

"He never tells anybody. He's afraid of it."

Bill Baudelaire, with his carrotty hair and pitted skin, looked at me with acute curiosity.

"Why do you do this job?" he said.

The Brigadier gave me no time to answer. "What else

would he do to pass the time? Play backgammon? This game is better. Isn't that it, Tor?"

"This game is better," I agreed.

The Brigadier smiled. Although shorter than Bill Baudelaire, and older and leaner, and with fairer, thinning hair, he seemed to fill more of the room. I might be three inches taller than he, but I had the impression always of looking up to him, not down.

"To work, then," he suggested. "Strategy, tactics, plan of attack."

He had brought some papers from England, though some were still to come, and he spread them out on the coffee table so that all of us, leaning forward, could see them.

"It was a good guess of yours, Tor, that the report on the cats was a computer printout, because of its lack of headings. The master of the college had a call from Mercer Lorrimore at eight this morning . . . must have been midnight here . . . empowering him to tell us everything, as you'd asked. The master gave us the name of the veterinary pathology lab he'd employed and sent us a Fax of the letter he'd received from them. Is that the same as the one in Filmer's briefcase, Tor?"

He pushed a paper across and I glanced at it. "Identical, except for the headings."

"Good. The path lab confirmed they kept the letter stored in their computer but they don't know yet how anyone outside could get a printout. We're still trying. So are they. They don't like it happening."

"How about a list of their employees," I said, "including temporary secretaries or wizard hacker office boys?"

"Where do you get such language?" the Brigadier protested. He produced a sheet of names. "This was the best they could do."

I read the list. None of the names was familiar.

"Do you really need to know the connection?" Bill Baudelaire asked.

"It would be neater," I said.

The Brigadier nodded. "John Millington is working on it. We're talking to him by telephone before tomorrow's meeting. Now, the next thing," he turned to me. "That conveyance you saw in the briefcase. As you suggested, we checked the number SF 90155 with the Land Registry." He chuckled with all George Burley's enjoyment. "That alone would have been worth your trip."

He explained why. Bill Baudelaire said, "We've got him, then," with great satisfaction: and the joint commanders in chief began deciding in which order they would fire off their accumulated salvos.

———

Julius Apollo walked into a high-up private room in Exhibition Park racecourse on Tuesday morning to sign and receive, as he thought, certification that he was the sole owner of Laurentide Ice, which would run in his name that afternoon.

The room was the president of the racecourse's conference room, having a desk attended by three comfortable armchairs at one end, with a table surrounded by eight similar chairs at the other. The doorway from the passage was at midpoint between the groupings, so that one turned right to the desk, left to the conference table. A fawn carpet covered the floor, horse pictures covered the walls, soft yellow leather covered the armchairs: a cross between comfort and practicality, without windows but with interesting spotlighting from recesses in the ceiling.

When Filmer entered, both of the directors of Security were sitting behind the desk, with three senior members of the Vancouver Jockey Club and the British Columbia Racing Commission seated at the conference table. They were there to give weight to the proceedings and to bear witness afterward, but they had chosen to be there simply as observers, and they had agreed not to interrupt with questions. They would take notes, they said, and ask questions afterward, if necessary.

Three more people and I waited on the other side of a closed door that led from the conference table end of the room into a serving pantry, and from there out again into the passage.

When Filmer arrived I went along the passage and locked the door he had come in by, and put the key in the pocket of my gray raincoat, which I wore buttoned to the neck. Then I walked back along the passage and into the serving pantry where I stood quietly behind the others waiting there.

A microphone stood on the desk in front of the directors, with another on the conference table, both of them leading to a tape recorder. Out in the serving pantry, an amplifier quietly relayed everything that was said inside.

Bill Baudelaire's deep voice greeted Filmer, invited him to sit in the chair in front of the desk, and said, "You know Brigadier Catto, of course?"

As the two men had glared at each other times without number, yes, he knew him.

"And these other gentlemen are from the Jockey Club and Racing Commission here in Vancouver."

"What *is* this?" Filmer asked truculently. "All I want is some paperwork. A formality."

The Brigadier said, "We are taking this opportunity to make some preliminary inquiries into some racing matters, and it seemed best to do it now, as so many of the people involved are in Vancouver at this time."

"What are you talking about?" Filmer said.

"We should explain," the Brigadier said smoothly, "that we are recording what is said in this room this morning. This is not a formal trial or an official inquiry, but what is said here may be repeated at any trial or inquiry in the future. We would ask you to bear this in mind."

Filmer said strongly, "I object to this."

"At any future trial or Jockey Club inquiry," Bill Baudelaire said, "you may of course be accompanied by a legal representative. We will furnish you with a copy of the tape of this morning's preliminary proceedings, which you may care to give to your lawyer."

"You can't do this," Filmer said. "I'm not staying."

When he went to the door he had entered by, he found it locked.

"Let me out," Filmer said furiously. "You can't do this."

In the serving pantry Mercer Lorrimore took a deep breath, opened the door to the conference room, went through and closed it behind him.

"Good morning, Julius," he said.

"What are you doing here?" Filmer's voice was surprised but not overwhelmingly dismayed. "Tell them to give me my paper and be done with it."

"Sit down, Julius," Mercer said. He was speaking into the conference table microphone, his voice sounding much louder than Filmer's. "Sit down by the desk."

"The preliminary inquiry, Mr. Filmer," the Brigadier's voice said, "is principally into your actions before and during, and in conjunction with, the journey of the race train." There was a pause, presumably a wait for Filmer to settle. Then the Brigadier's voice again, "Mr. Lorrimore, may I ask you . . . ?"

Mercer cleared his throat. "My son, Sheridan," he said evenly, "who died two days ago, suffered intermittently from a mental instability that led him sometimes to do bizarre . . . and unpleasant . . . things."

There was a pause. No words from Filmer.

Mercer said, "To his great regret, there was an incident of that sort, back in May. Sheridan killed . . . some animals. The bodies were taken from where they were found by a veterinary pathologist, who then performed private autopsies on them." He paused again. The strain was clear in his voice, but he didn't falter. "You, Julius, indicated to my family on the train that you knew about this incident, and three of us . . . my wife, Bambi, my son, Sheridan, and myself . . . all understood during that evening that you would use Sheridan's regrettable act as leverage to get hold of my horse, Voting Right."

Filmer said furiously, "That damned play!"

"Yes," Mercer said. "It put things very clearly. After Sheridan died I gave permission to the master of my son's college, to the British Jockey Club Security Service, and to the veterinary pathologist himself, to find out how that piece of information came into your possession."

"We did find out," the Brigadier said, and repeated what a triumphant John Millington had relayed to us less than an hour ago. "It happened by chance, by accident. You, Mr. Filmer, owned a horse, trained in England at Newmarket, which died. You suspected poison of some sort and insisted on a post-mortem, making your trainer arrange to have some organs sent to the path lab. The lab wrote a letter to your trainer saying there was no foreign substance in the organs, and at your request they later sent a copy of the letter to you. One of their less bright computer operators had meanwhile loaded your letter onto a very private disk, which she shouldn't have used, and in some way chain-loaded it, so that you received not only a copy of your letter but copies of three other letters besides, letters that were private and confidential." The Brigadier paused. "We know this is so," he said, "because when one of our operators asked the lab to print out a copy for us of your own letter, the others came out attached to it, chain-loaded into the same secret document name."

The pathologist, Millington had said, was totally distraught and thinking of scrapping the lab's computer for a new one. "But it wasn't the computer," he said, "it was a nitwit girl, who apparently thought the poison inquiry on the horse was top secret also, and put it on the top secret disk. They can't sack her, she left weeks ago."

"Could the pathologist be prosecuted for the cover-up?" the Brigadier had asked.

"Doubtful," Millington had said, "now that Sheridan's dead."

Filmer's voice, slightly hoarse, came out of the loud-speaker into the pantry. "This is rubbish."

"You kept the letter," the Brigadier said. "It was dynamite, if you could find who it referred to. No doubt you kept all three of the letters, though the other two didn't concern criminal acts. Then you saw one day in your local paper that Mercer Lorrimore was putting up money for a new college library. And you would have had to ask only one question to find out that Mercer Lorrimore's son had left that college in a hurry during May. After that, you would have found that no one would say why. You became sure that the letter referred to Sheridan Lorrimore. You did nothing with your information until you heard that Mercer Lorrimore would be on the Transcontinental Race Train, and then you saw an opportunity of exploring the possibility of blackmailing Mr. Lorrimore into letting you have his horse, Voting Right."

"You can't prove any of this," Filmer said defiantly.

"We all believe," said Bill Baudelaire's voice, "that with you, Mr. Filmer, it is the urge to crush people and make them suffer that sets you going. We know you could afford to buy good horses. We know that for you simply owning horses isn't enough."

"Save me the sermon," Filmer said. "And if you can't put up, shut up."

"Very well," the Brigadier said. "We'll ask our next visitor to come in, please."

Daffodil Quentin, who was standing beside George in the pantry and had been listening with parted mouth and growing anger, opened the dividing door dramatically and slammed it shut behind her.

"You unspeakable toad," her voice said vehemently over the loudspeaker.

Attagirl, I thought.

She was wearing a scarlet dress with a wide shiny black belt and carrying a large shiny black handbag. Under the high curls and in a flaming rage, she attacked as an avenging angel in full spate.

"I will never give you or sell you my half of Laurentide Ice," she said forcefully, "and you can threaten and blackmail until you're blue in the face. You can frighten my stable lad until you think you're God Almighty, but you can't from now on frighten *me*—and I think you're contemptible and should be put in a zoo."

21

Bill Baudelaire, who had persuaded her to come with him to Vancouver, cleared his throat and sounded as if he were trying not to laugh.

"Mrs. Quentin," he said to the world at large, "is prepared to testify—"

"You bet I am," Daffodil interrupted.

". . . that you threatened to have her prosecuted for killing one of her own horses if she didn't give . . . *give* . . . you her remaining share of Laurentide Ice."

"You used me," Daffodil said furiously. "You bought your way onto the train and you were all charm and smarm and all you were aiming to do was ingratiate yourself with Mercer Lorrimore so you could sneer at him and cause him pain and take away his horse. You make me puke."

"I don't have to listen to this," Filmer said.

"Yes, you damned well do. It's time someone told you to your face what a slimy putrid blob of spit you are and gave you back some of the hatred you sow."

"Er," Bill Baudelaire said. "We have here a letter from Mrs. Quentin's insurance company, written yesterday, saying that they made exhaustive tests on her horse that died of colic and they are satisfied that they paid her claim correctly. We also have here an affidavit from the stable lad, Lenny

Higgs, to the effect that you learned about the colic and the specially numbered feeds for Laurentide Ice from him during one of your early visits to the horse car. He goes on to swear that he was later frightened into saying that Mrs. Quentin gave him some food to give to her horse who died of colic." He cleared his throat. "As you have heard, the insurance company are satisfied that whatever she gave her horse didn't cause its death. Lenny Higgs further testifies that the man who frightened him, by telling him he would be sent to prison where he would catch AIDS and die, that man is an ex–baggage handler once employed by VIA Rail, name of Alex Mitchell McLachlan."

"What?" For the first time there was fear in Filmer's voice, and I found it sweet.

"Lenny Higgs positively identifies him from his photograph." There was a pause while Bill Baudelaire handed it over. "This man traveled in the racegoers' part of the train under the name of Johnson. During yesterday, the photograph was shown widely to VIA employees in Toronto and Montreal, and he was several times identified as Alex McLachlan."

There was silence where Filmer might have spoken.

"You were observed to be speaking to McLachlan . . ."

"You bet you were," Daffodil interrupted. "You were talking to him, arguing with him, at Thunder Bay, and I didn't like the look of him. This is his picture. I identify it too. You used him to frighten Lenny. You told me Lenny would give evidence against me, and I didn't know you'd *frightened* the poor boy with such a terrible threat. You told me he hated me and would be glad to tell lies about me." The enormity of it almost choked her. "I don't know how you can live with yourself. I don't know how anyone can be so full of *sin*."

Her voice resonated with the full old meaning of the word: an offense against God. It was powerful, I thought, and it had silenced Filmer completely.

"It may come as an anticlimax," the Brigadier said after a

pause, "but we will now digress to another matter entirely. One that will be the subject of a full Stewards' inquiry at the Jockey Club, Portman Square, in the near future. I refer to the ownership of a parcel of land referred to in the Land Registry as SF 90155."

The Brigadier told me later that it was at that point that Filmer turned gray and began to sweat.

"This parcel of land," his military voice went on, "is known as West Hillside Stables, Newmarket. This was a stables owned by Ivor Horfitz and run by his paid private trainer in such a dishonest manner that Ivor Horfitz was barred from racing, and racing stables, for life. He was instructed to sell West Hillside Stables, as he couldn't set foot there, and it was presumed that he had. However, the new owner in his turn wants to sell and has found a buyer, but the buyer's lawyers' searches have been very thorough, and they have discovered that the stables were never Horfitz's to sell. They belonged, and they still do legally belong, to you, Mr. Filmer."

There was a faint sort of groan that might have come from Filmer.

"That being so, we will have to look into your relationship with Ivor Horfitz and with the illegal matters that were carried on for years at West Hillside Stables. We also have good reason to believe that Ivor Horfitz's son, Jason, knows you owned the stables and were concerned in its operation, and that Jason let that fact out to his friend, the stable lad Paul Shacklebury, who, as you will remember, was the subject of your trial for conspiracy to murder, which took place earlier this year."

There was a long, long silence.

Daffodil's voice said, murmuring, "I don't understand any of this, do you?"

Mercer, as quietly, answered: "They've found a way of warning him off for life."

"Oh, good, but it sounds so dull."

"Not to him," Mercer murmured.

"We'll now return," Bill Baudelaire's voice said more loudly, "to the matter of your attempt to wreck the train." He coughed. "Will you please come in, Mr. Burley."

I smiled at George, who had been listening to the Horfitz part in noncomprehension and the rest in horrified amazement.

"We're on," I said, removing my raincoat and laying it on a serving counter. "After you."

He and I, the last in the pantry, went through the door. He was wearing his gray uniform and carrying his conductor's cap. I was revealed in Tommy's gray trousers, gray-and-white shirt, deep yellow waistcoat and tidy striped tie. Polished, pressed, laundered, brushed: a credit to VIA Rail.

Julius Filmer saw the conductor and a waiter he'd hardly noticed in his preoccupation with his own affairs. The Brigadier and Bill Baudelaire saw the waiter for the first time, and there was an awakening and realization on each of their faces. Although I'd told them by now that I'd worked with the crew, they hadn't truly understood how perfect had been the bright camouflage.

"Oh, that's who you are!" exclaimed Daffodil, who was sitting now in one of the chairs round the conference table. "I couldn't place you, outside."

Mercer patted her hand, which lay on the table, and gave me the faintest of smiles over her head. The three Vancouver bigwigs took me at face value, knowing no different.

"Would you come forward, please?" Bill Baudelaire said.

George and I both advanced past the conference table until we were nearer the desk. The two directors were seated behind the desk, Filmer in the chair in front of it. Filmer's neck was rigid, his eyes were dark, and the sweat ran down his temples.

"The conductor, George Burley," Bill Baudelaire said, "yesterday gave VIA Rail an account of three acts of sabotage against the race train. Disaster was fortunately averted on all three occasions, but we believe that all these dangerous situations were the work of Alex McLachlan, who was acting on your instructions and was paid by you."

"No," Filmer said dully.

"Our inquiries are not yet complete," Bill Baudelaire said, "but we know that the VIA Rail offices in Montreal were visited three or four weeks ago by a man answering in general to your description who said he was researching for a thesis on the motivations of industrial sabotage. He asked for the names of any railroad saboteurs, so that he could interview them and see what made them tick. He was given a short list of people no longer to be employed on the railroads in any capacity."

Heads would roll, the VIA Rail executive had said. That list, although to be found in every railway station office in the country, should *never* have been given to an outsider.

"McLachlan's name is on that list," Bill Baudelaire observed.

Filmer said nothing. The realization of total disaster showed in every line of his body, in every twitch in his face.

"As we said," Bill Baudelaire went on, "McLachlan traveled on the train under the name of Johnson. During the first evening, at a place called Cartier, he uncoupled Mr. Lorrimore's private car and left it dead and dark on the track. The railroad investigators believe he waited in the vicinity to see the next train along, the regular transcontinental Canadian, come and crash into the Lorrimores' car. He had always been around to watch the consequences of his sabotage in the past: acts he had been sent to prison for committing. When the race train returned to pick up the Lorrimores' car, he simply reboarded and continued on the journey."

"He shouldn't have done it," Filmer said.

"We know that. We also know that in speech you continually mixed up Winnipeg with Vancouver. You instructed McLachlan to wreck the train before Winnipeg, when you meant before Vancouver."

Filmer looked dumbfounded.

"That's right," Daffodil said, sitting up straight, "Winnipeg and Vancouver. He got them mixed up all the time."

"In Banff," Bill Baudelaire said, "someone loosened the drain plug on the fuel tank for the boiler that provides steam heat for the train. If it hadn't been discovered, the train would have had to go through a freezing evening in the Rockies without heat for horses or passengers. Mr. Burley, would you tell us at firsthand about both of these occurrences, please?"

George gave his accounts of the uncoupling and the missing fuel with a railwayman's outrage quivering in his voice.

Filmer looked shrunken and sullen.

"During that last evening," Bill Baudelaire said, "you decided to cancel your instructions to McLachlan and you went forward to speak to him. You had a disagreement with him. You told him to do no more, but you had reckoned without McLachlan. He really is a perpetual saboteur. You misunderstood his mentality. You could start him off, but you couldn't stop him. You were responsible for putting him on the train to wreck it, and we will make that responsibility stick."

Filmer began weakly to protest, but Bill Baudelaire gave him no respite.

"Your man McLachlan," he said, "knocked out the conductor and left him tied up and gagged in the roomette he had been given in the name of Johnson. McLachlan then knocked out the radio by pouring liquid into it. These acts were necessary, as he saw it, because he had already, at a place called Revelstoke, removed oily waste from the journal box holding one of the axles under the horse car. One of two things could then happen: if the train crew failed to notice the axle getting red hot, the axle would break, cause damage, possibly derail the train. If it were discovered, the train would stop for the axle to be cooled. In either case the conductor would radio to the dispatcher in Vancouver, who would radio to the conductor of the regular train, the Canadian, coming along behind, to tell him to stop, so that there shouldn't be a collision. Is that clear?"

It was pellucid to everyone in the room.

"The train crew," he went on, "did discover the hot axle and the engineers stopped the train. No one could find the conductor, who was tied up in Johnson's roomette. No one could radio to Vancouver as the radio wouldn't work. The only recourse left to the crew was to send a man back along the line to light flares, to stop the Canadian in the old historic way." He paused briefly. "McLachlan, a railwayman, knew this would happen, so when the train stopped he went himself along the track, armed himself with a piece of wood and lay in wait for whoever came with the flares."

Filmer stared darkly, hearing it for the first time.

"McLachlan attacked the man with the flares, but by good fortune failed to knock him out. It was this man here who was sent with the flares." He nodded in my direction. "He succeeded in lighting the flares and stopping the Canadian." He paused and said to me, "Is that correct?"

"Yes, sir," I said. Word perfect, I thought.

He went on, "The Race Train engineers cooled the journal box with snow and refilled it with oil, and the train went on its way. The conductor was discovered in McLachlan's roomette. McLachlan did not reboard the train that time, and there will presently be a warrant issued for his arrest. You, Mr. Filmer, are answerable with McLachlan for what happened."

"I told him not to," Filmer's voice was a rising shout of protest. "I didn't want him to."

His lawyer would love that admission, I thought.

"McLachlan's assault was serious," Bill Baudelaire said calmly. He picked up my X-ray and the doctor's report and waved them in Filmer's direction. "McLachlan broke this crewman's shoulder blade. The crewman has positively identified McLachlan as the man who attacked him. The conductor has positively identified McLachlan as the passenger known to him as Johnson. The conductor has suffered concussion, and we have here another doctor's report on that."

No doubt a good defense lawyer might have seen gaps in

the story, but at that moment Filmer was beleaguered and confounded and hampered by the awareness of guilt. He was past thinking analytically, past asking how the crewman had escaped from McLachlan and been able to complete his mission, past wondering what was conjecture with the sabotage and what was provable fact.

The sight of Filmer reduced to sweating rubble was the purest revenge that any of us—Mercer, Daffodil, Val Catto, Bill Baudelaire, George Burley or I—could have envisaged, and we had it in full measure. Do unto others, I thought dryly, what they have done to your friends.

"We will proceed against you on all counts," the Brigadier said magisterially.

Control disintegrated in Filmer. He came up out of his chair fighting mad, driven to lashing out, to raging against his defeat, to punishing someone else for his troubles, even though it could achieve no purpose.

He made me his target. It couldn't have been a subconscious awareness that it was I who had been the real enemy all along: much the reverse, I suppose, in that he saw me as the least of the people there, the one he could best bash with most impunity.

I saw him coming a mile off. I also saw the alarm on the Brigadier's face and correctly interpreted it.

If I fought back as instinct dictated, if I did to Filmer the sort of damage I'd told the Brigadier I'd done to McLachlan, I would weaken our case.

Thought before action; if one had time.

Thought could be flash fast. I had time. *It would be an unexpected bonus for us if the damage were the other way round.*

He had iron-pumping muscle power. It would indeed be damage.

Oh, well . . .

I rolled my head a shade sideways and he punched me twice, quite hard, on the cheek and the jaw. I went back with a crash against the nearby wall, which wasn't all that good for the shoulder blade, and I slid the bottom of my spine down the wall until I was sitting on the floor, knees bent up, my head back against the paintwork.

Filmer was above me, lunging about and delivering another couple of stingingly heavy cuffs, and I thought, come on guys, it's high time for the arrival of the cavalry, and the cavalry—the Mounties—in the shape of George Burley and Bill Baudelaire obligingly grabbed Filmer's swinging arms and hauled him away.

I stayed where I was, feeling slightly pulped, watching the action.

The Brigadier pressed a button on the desk, which soon resulted in the arrival of two large racecourse security guards, one of whom, to Filmer's furious astonishment, placed a manacle upon the Julius Apollo wrist.

"You can't do this," he shouted.

The guard phlegmatically fastened the hanging half of the metal bracelet to his own thick wrist.

One of the Vancouver top-brass spoke for the first time, in an authoritative voice. "Take Mr. Filmer to the security office and detain him until I come down."

The guards said, "Yes, sir."

They moved like tanks. Filmer, humiliated to his socks, was tugged away between them as if of no account. One might almost have felt sorry for him . . . if one hadn't remembered Paul Shacklebury and Ezra Gideon, for whom he had had no pity.

Daffodil Quentin's eyes were stretched wide open. She came over and looked down at me with compassion.

"You poor boy," she said, horrified. "How perfectly *dreadful*."

"Mr. Burley," Bill Baudelaire said smoothly, "would you be so kind as to escort Mrs. Quentin for us? If you turn right in the passage you'll find some double doors ahead of you. Through there is the reception room where the passengers and the other owners from the train are gathering for cocktails and lunch. Would you take Mrs. Quentin there? We'll look after this crewman . . . get him some help . . . and we would be pleased if you could yourself stay for lunch."

George said to me, "Are you all right, Tommy?" and I said, "Yes, George," and he chuckled with kind relief and said it would be a pleasure, eh?, to stay for lunch.

He stood back to let Daffodil lead the way out of the far door, and when she reached there she paused and looked back.

"The poor boy," she said again. "Julius Filmer's a *beast*."

The Vancouver Jockey Club men rose and made courteous noises of sympathy in my direction; said they would hand Filmer on to the police with a report of the assault; said we would no doubt be needed to make statements later. They then followed Daffodil, as they were the hosts of the party.

When they'd gone, the Brigadier switched off the machine that had recorded every word.

"Poor boy, my foot," he said to me. "You chose to let him hit you. I saw you."

I smiled a little ruefully, acknowledging his perception.

"He couldn't!" Mercer protested, drawing nearer. "No one could just let himself be . . ."

"He could and he did." The Brigadier came round from behind the desk. "Quick thinking. Brilliant."

"But why?" Mercer said.

"To tie the slippery Mr. Filmer in tighter knots." The Brigadier stood in front of me, put a casual hand down to mine and pulled me to my feet.

"Did you truly?" Mercer said to me in disbelief.

"Mm." I nodded and straightened a bit, trying not to wince.

"Don't worry about him," the Brigadier said. "He used to ride bucking broncos, and God knows what else."

The three of them stood as in a triumvirate, looking at me in my uniform, as if I'd come from a different planet.

"I sent him on the train," the Brigadier said, "to stop Filmer doing whatever he was planning." He smiled briefly. "A sort of match . . . a two-horse race."

"It seems to have been neck and neck now and then," Mercer said.

The Brigadier considered it. "Maybe. But our runner had the edge."

––––––––––

Mercer Lorrimore and I watched the races from a smaller room next the large one where the reception was taking place. We were in the racecourse president's private room, to which he could retire with friends if he wanted to, and it was furnished accordingly in extreme comfort and soft turquoise and gold.

The president had been disappointed but understanding that Mercer felt he couldn't attend the lunch party so soon after his son's death, and had offered this room instead. Mercer had asked if I might join him, so he and I drank the president's champagne and looked down from his high window to the track far below, and talked about Filmer, mostly.

"I liked him, you know," Mercer said, wonderingly.

"He can be charming."

"Bill Baudelaire tried to warn me at Winnipeg," he said, "but I wouldn't listen. I really thought that his trial had been a travesty, and that he was innocent. He told me about it himself. He said he didn't bear the Jockey Club any malice."

I smiled. "Extreme malice," I said. "He threatened them to their faces that he would throw any available spanner into their international works. McLachlan was some spanner."

Mercer sat down in one of the huge armchairs. I stayed standing by the window.

"Why was Filmer prosecuted," he asked, "if there was such a poor case?"

"There was a cast-iron case," I said. "Filmer sent a particularly vicious frightener to intimidate all four prosecution witnesses, and the cast-iron became splinters. This time . . . this morning . . . we thought we'd stage a sort of preliminary trial, at which the witnesses couldn't have been reached, and have it all on record in case anyone retracted afterward."

He looked at me skeptically. "Did you think I could be intimidated? I assure you I can't. Not anymore."

After a pause I said, "You have Xanthe. Ezra Gideon had daughters and grandchildren. One of the witnesses in the Paul Shacklebury case backed away because of what she was told would happen to her sixteen-year-old daughter if she gave evidence."

"Dear God," he said, dismayed. "Surely he'll be sent to prison."

"He'll be warned off, anyhow, and that's what he wants least. He had Paul Shacklebury killed to prevent it. I think we will have got rid of him from racing. For the rest, we'll have to see what the Canadian police and VIA Rail can do, and hope they'll find McLachlan."

Let McLachlan not be eaten by a bear, I thought. (And he hadn't been: he was picked up for stealing tools from a railroad yard in Edmonton a week later, and subsequently convicted with Filmer of the serious ancient offense of attempted train-wrecking, chiefly on the evidence of a temporary crew member in his VIA Rail clothes. VIA put me on their personnel list retroactively, and shook my hand. Filmer was imprisoned despite his protest that he had not given specific instructions to McLachlan on any count and had tried to stop him before the end. It was proved that he had actively recruited a violent saboteur: any later possible change of mind was held to be irrelevant. Filmer never did find out that I wasn't a waiter, because it wasn't a question his lawyers ever thought to ask, and it went much against him with the jury that he'd violently attacked a defenseless rail employee without provocation in front of many witnesses even though he knew of the broken scapula. The Brigadier kept a straight face throughout. "It worked a treat," he said afterward. "Wasn't Daffodil Quentin a trouper, convincing them the poor boy had been brutally beaten for no reason except that he'd saved them all from being killed in their beds? Lovely stuff. It made nonsense of the change-of-heart defense. They couldn't wait to find Filmer guilty after that." McLachlan in his turn swore that I'd nearly murdered him, out on the track. I said he'd tripped and knocked himself out on the rails. McLachlan could produce no X-rays and wasn't believed, to his fury. "Broken bone or not, that waiter can fight like a goddamn tiger," he said. "No way could Filmer beat him up." Filmer, however, had done so. It had been seen, and was a fact.)

On the Tuesday of the Jockey Club Race Train Stakes at Exhibition Park, with the trial still months ahead, and the feel of Filmer's fists a reality, not a memory, the racecourse president came into his private room to see Mercer and me and to show us that if we drew the curtains along the right-hand side wall, we could see into the reception room.

"They can't see into here," he said. "It's one-way glass." He pulled strings and revealed the party. "I hear the meeting went well this morning except for the end." He looked at me questioningly. "Mr. Lorrimore and Bill Baudelaire asked that you be treated as a most honored guest . . . but shouldn't you be resting?"

"No point, sir," I said, "and I wouldn't miss the Great Race for anything."

Through the window one could fascinatingly see all the faces grown so familiar during the past ten days. The Unwins, the Redi-Hots, the Youngs . . .

"If I might ask you?" I said.

"Ask the world, according to Bill Baudelaire and Brigadier Catto."

I smiled. "Not the world. That young woman over there in the gray suit, with the fair hair in a plait and a worried expression."

"Nell Richmond," Mercer said.

"Would you mind if she came in here for a while?"

"Not in the least," the president said, and within minutes could be seen talking to her. He couldn't have told her who to expect in his room, though, because when she came in and saw me she was surprised and, I had to think, joyful.

"You're on your feet! Daffodil said the waiter was hurt badly." Her voice died away and she swallowed. "I was afraid . . ."

"That we wouldn't get to Hawaii?"

"Oh." It was a sound somewhere between a laugh and a sob. "I don't think I like you."

"Try harder."

"Well." She opened her handbag and began to look inside it, and glanced up and saw all the people next door. "How great," she said to Mercer. "You're both with us, even if you're not." She produced a folded piece of paper and gave it to me. "I have to go back to sort out the lunch places."

I didn't want her to go. I said, "Nell . . . ," and heard it sound too full of anxiety, too full of plain physical battering, but it was past calling back.

Her face changed. The games died away.

"Read that when I've gone," she said. "And I'll be there . . . through the glass."

She went out of the president's room without looking back and soon reappeared among the others. I unfolded the paper slowly, not wanting it to be bad news, and found it was a telex.

It said:

RICHMOND, FOUR SEASONS HOTEL,
VANCOUVER. CONFIRM YOUR TWO WEEKS
VACATION STARTING IMMEDIATELY. MERRY.
HAVE A GOOD TIME.

I closed my eyes.

"Is that despair?" Mercer said.

I opened my eyes. The telex still read the same way. I handed it to him, and he read it also.

"I daresay," he said ironically, "that Val Catto will match this."

"If he doesn't, I'll resign."

We spent the afternoon companionably and watched the

preliminary races with the interest of devotees. When it was time for the Jockey Club Race Train Stakes, Mercer decided that, Sheridan or not, he would go down to see Voting Right saddled, as he could go and return by express elevator to our eyrie to watch the race.

When he'd gone and the room next door had mostly emptied, I looked down on the flags and the banners and the streamers and balloons and the razzmatazz with which Exhibition Park had met the challenge of Assiniboia Downs and Woodbine and thought of all that had happened on the journey across Canada, and I wondered whether I would find flat-footing round British racecourses in the rain a relaxation or a bore, wondered if I would go on doing it; thought that time would show me the way, as it always had.

I thought of Mrs. Baudelaire, whom I would never meet, and wished she could have watched this next race; thought of Aunt Viv with gratitude.

Mercer came back looking happy: happier in a peaceful way, as if he had settled ghosts.

"Daffodil is amazing," he said. "She's down there holding court, kissing Laurentide Ice, laughing, on top of the world. There seems to be no difficulty in the horse running, even though half still presumably belongs to Filmer."

"It's in Daffodil's name in the race-card," I said.

"So it is. And the Youngs . . . Rose and Cumber . . . with Sparrowgrass, and the people with Redi-Hot. It's like a club, down there. They were pleased, they said, that I had come."

They genuinely would be, I thought. The party was incomplete without Mercer.

There was a large television set in the president's room, through which one could hear the bugles preceding the runners to the track and hear crowd noises and the commentary. Nothing like being down near the action, but better than silence. The race was being broadcast live throughout Canada and recorded for the rest of the world, and there was a long spiel going on about the Growing International Flavor of Canadian Racing, and how the Great Transcontinental

Mystery Race Train had awakened enormous interest everywhere and was altogether A Good Thing For Canada.

Mercer, who had been prepared to do a lot for Canadian racing, watched Voting Right lead the prerace parade, the horse on the screen appearing larger to us than the real one far down on the track.

"He's looking well," he told me. "I do hope . . ." He stopped. "I think he may be the best of all my horses. The best to come. But he may not be ready today. It's perhaps too soon. Sparrowgrass is favorite. It would be nice for the Youngs . . ."

We watched Sparrowgrass prance along in his turn.

"Cumber Young has found out it was Filmer who bought, or took, Ezra Gideon's horses. If Cumber had been up here this morning he'd have torn Filmer limb from limb."

"And been in trouble himself," I said.

"As Filmer is now?"

"Yes, roughly speaking."

"Rough is the word." He looked at me sideways, but made no further comment.

"Watch the horses," I said mildly. Not the lumps that were swelling.

With a wry twitch of the lips, he turned his attention back to Redi-Hot, who looked fit to scorch the dirt, and to Laurentide Ice, the color of his name.

Nine of the ten runners had traveled on the train. The tenth was a local Vancouver horse bought by the Unwins for the occasion. Not as good a prospect as Upper Gumtree, but the Unwins had wanted to take their part in the climax.

All of the owners and Nell, precious Nell, came to watch the race in the glassed-in part of the stands slanting down in front of the window of the president's room, so that it was over their excited heads that Mercer and I saw the horses loaded into the stalls and watched the flashing colors sprint out.

"All the way across Canada," Mercer said as if to himself, "for the next two minutes."

All the way across Canada, I thought, in worry and love and grief for his son.

Voting Right shot out of the gate and took a strong lead.

Mercer groaned quietly, "He's running away."

Laurentide Ice and Sparrowgrass, next, weren't in a hurry but kept a good pace going, their heads together, not an inch in it. Behind them came five or six in a bunch, with Redi-Hot last.

The sing-song commentary on the television read off the time of the first quarter-mile covered by Voting Right.

"Too fast," Mercer groaned.

At the half-mile, Voting Right was still in front, still going at high speed, ahead by a full twenty lengths.

"It's hopeless," Mercer said. "He'll blow up in the home stretch. He's never been ridden this way before."

"Didn't you discuss it with the jockey?"

"I just wished him luck. He knows the horse."

"Maybe the horse has been inspired by the train travel," I said flippantly.

"To come all this way. . ." Mercer said, taking no notice. "Oh, well, that's racing."

"He hasn't exactly blown up yet," I pointed out.

Voting Right was far in front, going down the backstretch a good deal faster than the race train had gone through the Rockies, and he didn't know he was going too fast, he simply kept on going.

The jockeys on Sparrowgrass, Laurentide Ice, Redi-Hot and the others left their move on the leader until they'd come round the last bend and spread across the track to give themselves a clear run home.

Then Laurentide Ice melted away as Mrs. Baudelaire said he would, and Redi-Hot produced a spurt, and Sparrowgrass with determination began to close at last on Voting Right.

"He's going to lose," Mercer said despairingly.

It looked like it. One couldn't say for certain, but his time was too fast.

Voting Right kept on going. Sparrowgrass raced hard to

the finish, but it was Voting Right, as Mrs. Baudelaire had predicted, Voting Right who had the edge, who went floating past the post in record time for the track; the best horse Mercer would ever own, the target kept safe from Filmer.

Sheridan lay in untroubled eternity, and who was to say that Mercer wasn't right, that in his impulsive way the son hadn't died to give his father this moment.

Mercer turned toward me, speechless, brimming to overflowing with inexpressible emotion, wanting to laugh, wanting to cry, like all owners at the fulfillment of a dreamed-of success. The sheen in his eyes was the same the world over: the love of the flying thoroughbred, the perfection of winning a great race.

He found his voice. Looked at me with awakening humor and a good deal of understanding.

"Thank you," he said.

About the Author

Dick Francis, a former champion steeplechase jockey who rode for the Queen Mother, is the author of many best-selling mysteries set in the world of horse racing. He divides his time between England and Florida.